TIME GODS

TIME GODS

By Wayne Boyd

Published in England and the USA
by Atma Communications, 2010

All rights reserved

Copyright © 2010 by Wayne Edward Boyd www.timegods.com

This book is copyright under the Berne Convention.

No part of this book may be stored on a retrieval system or transmitted in any form or by whatever means without the prior written consent of the publisher. This book may not be lent, resold, hired out or otherwise disposed of by way of trade in any form, binding or cover other than in which it is published, without the prior written consent of the publishers.

This novel is a work of fiction. All the people and places mentioned herein are either fictional or used in a fictional context.

Atma Communications

London, England

www.atma-communications.com

ISBN 978-0-9559112-1-7

British Library Cataloguing in Publication Data:

A catalogue record for this book is available from the British Library

Printed and bound by
Lightning Source, England and USA

Dedicated to the great yarn-spinners of my life, specifically:

My late Uncle Henry Boyd
who once convinced a school teacher that cabbages turn purple after it rains, and if you pick them right away they stay that way.

My late father, Francis (Frank) Boyd
who used to love showing kids that he could 'change' a one dollar bill to a five dollar bill with his 'Magic Roller', and who entertained us with stories in childhood of the 'McBoyds'.

The late Richard Dimbleby
One of the greatest figures in British broadcasting history, who, on April 1st 1957, narrated a BBC television spoof documentary describing how each strand of spaghetti grown on spaghetti trees is always the same length due to years of hard work by generations of growers.

Pyari Mohan dasa
who taught me how to pass one rubber band through another without letting go of the ends of either.

ACKNOWLEDGMENTS

This book took shape when my friend, Andre Petrov, introduced me to *The Master and Margarita*, by Mikhail Bulgakov and translated from Russian by Mirra Ginsburg (published by Grove Press). The novel presents an anti-Stalinist message in a complex allegory of good and evil which proved inspirational in the plot of my story.

While I was living in Canada, friends in Vancouver provided new ideas, criticisms and editing services; devotees at the Hare Krishna temple on Schermerhorn Street, Brooklyn, helped with historical accuracy; and in Ireland, Satsvarupa dasa Goswami permitted me to utilize sections of A.C. Bhaktivedanta Prabhupada's authorized biography, *Srila Prabhupada-lilamrta*. My brother, Jeffrey H. Boyd, a Psychiatrist, Minister and Author, provided constructive criticism and enthusiasm for the project.

However, without the help of Richard Cole, also known as Radha-Mohan dasa, this book would and could never have been completed. Working from the United Kingdom, Richard has read and re-read the manuscript dozens of times, always coming up with corrections, ideas, criticisms and encouragement.

Lastly, I owe tremendous gratitude to my wife, Charlotte Jean Boyd, for putting up with me while I pored over endless research and rewrites, and who, along with Richard Cole, checked spelling, punctuation, and consistency in the final edit before publication.

All of us hope you enjoy the story that follows.

Time Gods

PROLOGUE

Thursday, June 10, 2027

"Are we ready to dump the body?" Lobe asked.

Von Krod, a tall thin man with striking red hair, nodded as his chubby driver glanced at his Oyster-Perpetual Rolex watch. It was 11:03 PM.

Lobe pressed the automatic trunk release button and the two men emerged from the antique golden Rolls-Royce Phantom V parked at the back of the vacant lot. Stepping to the rear of the vehicle, they raised a heavy burlap sack tied to a cinder block and hoisted it over the guard rail. Dropping it into the East River in the Bronx they quickly returned to the Rolls and drove away.

Paul McPherson awoke and found himself in water, sinking rapidly. He struggled to free himself from the confines of the sack, but could not. Panic overwhelmed him as he settled on the muddy bottom. His automatic reflexes screamed for him to breathe. He could no longer hold his breath. In one final gulp he felt the water enter his lungs and he remembered nothing after that.

Wayne Boyd

Time Gods

PART ONE

One of Hawking's arguments in the conjecture is that we are not awash in thousands of time travelers from the future, and therefore time travel is impossible. This argument I find very dubious, and it reminds me very much of the argument that there cannot be intelligences elsewhere in space, because otherwise the Earth would be awash in aliens. I can think half a dozen ways in which we could not be awash in time travelers, and still time travel is possible.

Carl Sagan, American astronomer,
astrophysicist, and author

Wayne Boyd

CHAPTER 1

Brooklyn, New York. Monday, July 12, 1966

Schermerhorn Street and Nevins intersect a few blocks from Flatbush Avenue and Atlantic. Several shops, small apartments and offices occupied the surrounding buildings, including the law office of David Pierce, father of Mary, a young woman living across the East River in Manhattan. Below the law office and two doors along was a smoke shop owned by Gabriel Caprone, an Italian immigrant whose cousins were rumored to have ties to the mob.

Caprone stored a nine millimeter revolver under the counter, just to the right of his cash register. Not that it had done him much good the last time he was robbed. Perhaps one day it would save his life. It is the best he could do to make an honest living to support his young wife and two small children who lived upstairs.

This hot summer day, Caprone peered from behind the cash register and saw a peculiar customer enter his store. *A monk*, he assumed, dressed in flowing orange robes. The man had a fairly good muscular build in his shoulders and arms. He appeared to be in his mid-to-late twenties or early thirties, had a tuft of hair protruding from the back of his otherwise shaven head and looked confused. "Can I help you?" Caprone asked gruffly, yet politely.

"You got a holograph station?" the monk asked.

"A what?"

"For making a 3D phone call."

Time Gods

"There's a pay phone out on the street."

"Yeah, I saw it. Quaint. Uses coins."

"You need some coins, Mister?"

"How do you use coins in the phone?"

"You just drop a dime into the slot and make your call!"

"How do I get some change?"

"You buy sumthin' – you get change," Caprone insisted as professionally as he could muster. He had long ago learned the art of extracting blood from a stone.

Nodding, the monk glanced around, picked up a New York Times and plopped it more confidently on the counter than Gabriel had expected. He handed over a one dollar bill. Gabriel accepted the bill, opened the cash register, and returned ninety cents. This seemed to confuse the monk, who carefully counted the change twice. Finally, he looked up and asked, "Is this right?"

"Is what right?" Crapone asked.

"You gave me ninety cents."

"The paper cost a dime, and you gave me a dollar," Caprone explained, but the monk continued to appear disoriented. "You okay, Mister?" Caprone asked.

"I'm fine," the man in orange replied, "I don't understand why that door was locked."

"My door isn't locked, Mister."

"No, I mean just around the corner. 305 Schermerhorn Street. No one answers when I ring the bell. And those trees across the street. There should be a parking lot and building there."

Caprone sighed. "Mister, what's your name?"

"Paul McPherson," he answered. "Why?"

"Listen. Nobody *lives* at 305 Schermerhorn. That's the Odd Fellows Memorial."

The monk McPherson frowned dismissively, closed his wallet and a small business card fluttered to the floor.

Caprone cleared his throat and moved his eyes downward. "Dropped sumthin'."

McPherson looked down and saw a business card at his feet. He picked it up and read the note scribbled on the face: "Meet me at the south-west corner of Central Park, 6 PM."

"Isn't mine," he said.

"Fell from your wallet," Caprone insisted.

Paul McPherson glanced at it again then shrugged, crumpling the card. *It's nothing*, he thought. Turning to leave he dropped it in a wastebasket as he casually glanced at the date on top of the paper. "July 12, 1966."

He took two more steps toward the door and then stopped abruptly, looking at the date on the paper again. Slowly raising his eyes, he noted a wall calendar by the door. A photograph of a woman in a one-piece swimsuit was visible above the date: July 1966.

"What's the big idea?" he asked aloud, turning to face Caprone standing behind the cash register. "Is this some kind of prank?"

"S'matter?" Caprone replied incredulously.

"Did you sell me a sixty-one year old newspaper?"

"What the hell are you talking about?"

"I mean the date, both on the paper and the calendar."

"What about it?" asked Caprone, but McPherson simply pointed at the newspaper's front page, as if it were self evident. Caprone looked at him with a tilted head. "Mister, that's the correct date."

McPherson rolled his hazel colored eyes and shrugged. No wonder the paper was only ten cents. Practical joker. Tucking it under his arm, he stepped outside.

* * *

NSA/CSS Headquarters, October, 2075

"How many people have you and I killed over the years?" Special Agent Hilmore whispered as he picked up the large manila envelope from his chair and sat down beside his colleague. All the seats of the meeting room were now filled.

Caufield frowned and cleared his throat. He shook his head but said nothing.

"Okay. Lemme rephrase that. How many have we *removed – taken out – eliminated* for the sake of the secret government?"

"Don't know, don't care," Caufield resigned. "More than I can remember. What's with you today?"

Time Gods

"For Christ's sake, Caufield! Have you even looked at this thing?" They both glanced at the sealed envelopes on their laps.

"I've heard about it," Caufield calmly replied. "Sidney Dale talked about it last night."

Hilmore frowned and continued with a voice hinting at resignation. "Dale's a prick. This is about a monk. A goddamn friggin' monk." He cast a glance back at Prateep Tripathy who sat two rows behind, wearing sunglasses over his pockmarked face. Tripathy, who had a small bandage on his forehead nodded and twisted his lips into an unsettling smirk. *He* knew what a monk was, goddamn it, being from Orissa, India. It was Tripathy that let them get away on the bus up in the Himalayas. That costly mistake was why they were all gathered here today.

A door on the side of the room quietly opened and a stern-faced man wearing a fedora and a trench coat appeared. Removing his hat and coat, he placed them on a nearby chair and took his place behind the podium. Mounted on the wall behind him was the traditional round emblem with a bald eagle standing against a blue background. The eagle glared regally to the left as he stood proudly clutching a skeleton key in his claws, wearing a vest of stars and stripes.

At over six feet, the man had a square jaw and dark, probing eyes. His complexion was pale and expression firm. Adjusting his eyeglasses, he fastened the Bluetooth microphone to his ear. He tapped it gently and heard the boom from the speakers.

His eyes fell upon his chief hitmen, Special Agents Hilmore and Caufield, and then on Tripathy who filed yesterday's report. He noted Tripathy's wound on his forehead. An armed security guard stood at the doorway, flanked on either side by men dressed in black suits, white shirts and wearing dark glasses. One of them held a black briefcase with a Walther PPK semi-automatic pistol and silencer inside.

"Morning, everyone." His voice was deep and deliberate. "Guess most of you follow the news, so there's nothing much to say about the kidnapping. You already knew Professor Cali was working with us. Unfortunately, our reconnaissance agent, Mr. Tripathy here, almost had the matter in hand but they slipped away from him in India, and now it's up to the rest of us to get to them." He again glanced at Tripathy, who returned the glare through his mirrored sunglasses.

"As you know, Professor Cali was working on an important project, and to tell you the truth, it's the stolen goods that went missing with him that absolutely must be recovered. The Professor is expendable."

He raised his right arm, hand open, gesturing toward the manila envelopes on their laps as he paused to take a sip of water and clear his throat. "So if you have any question before we dismiss you to read the file, now's the time to ask."

A hand rose. He acknowledged a woman in the back.

"What about the drugs? Any of them missing as well?" she asked.

There had been concern in the press that some of the latest psychopathic drugs might have been stolen. These drugs, developed to control the threat of terrorism, proved to be most effective when combined with electroshock therapy and hypnotism to bring an enemy completely under one's control. They had first been reported in the Washington Post in a special exposé on government tactics to infiltrate terrorist cells around the world. The drugs were, however, still experimental in nature, and the exact dosage had yet to be determined.

"No," the man at the podium lied. "The drugs are safe. What we're concerned with is the missing prototype."

Hilmore perked up in his seat. *Prototype for what?*

The man at the podium looked to see if any other hands went up. They didn't yet know about Paul, Mary or the little man. They would learn about them in the report.

"Just remember: you must refrain from either confirming or denying any knowledge of what you read, and you should notify Q43 of any attempted inquiry. Is that clear? Remember: this is Code B. The President doesn't want this to affect his re-election campaign."

Hilmore glanced down at the manila package on his lap. *Damn.* He knew what Code B meant. Another assassination to protect another President. Since the collapse of the World

Time Gods

Trade Center towers 74 years ago, the National Security Agency and Central Security Service had become independent from congressional scrutiny. Only the President of the United States could review operations. Even that was on a need-to-know basis. Elected officials like the President were generally kept out of the loop. If the President was favorable to operations, then the NSA/CSS would support him. Otherwise a scandal would materialize to thwart further involvement.

Picking up his hat, the man at the podium concluded: "Very well. This meeting is adjourned until tomorrow, same time. You have twenty-four hours to familiarize yourself with the case. After that, we get to work."

With that, Sidney Dale settled his hat on his head and scooped up his trench coat.

Caufield rolled his eyes in disbelief as they rose from their chairs. "That's it?"

"Fine with me," Hilmore commented dryly. The audience stood and moved toward the outer secured area.

Emerging from the meeting room, they passed through the lobby and proceeded down the hallway toward the elevator. Hilmore and Caufield parted amicably with a handshake and Hilmore headed for his office.

Once alone, he dropped into a comfortable chair and examined the hefty packet carefully. Turning it over, Hilmore saw TDC's traditional wax seal with their triangular insignia on the back. Breaking the seal, he removed the report and read the cover page.

It was a quotation from the late Carl Sagan, an astronomer and Pulitzer Prize-winning author from the last century. "I can think half a dozen ways in which we could not be awash in time travelers, and still time travel is possible," the author wrote.

Hilmore flipped through the remaining pages and sighed. He didn't like killing religious people, but he knew he'd do what was necessary. It didn't help that Hilmore's nephew was a Hare Krishna.

* * *

Wayne Boyd

Fifth Avenue, New York. June 10, 2027

Paul McPherson stood scanning the towering mass of stone, metal and glass that soared from the sidewalk to the sky, 1453 feet above, and then again at the address scribbled on the crumpled paper in his hand. It was late afternoon. The sky was clear and the weather warm. A mild breeze cooled the sweat from the top of his shaven head.

When the light turned green, the hydrogen- and electric-powered vehicles pulled to a stop; the monk followed pedestrians across Fifth Avenue and walked a few yards down Thirty-third Street. Passing through the revolving doors, he entered the three-story high lobby of the Empire State Building and searched for an elevator. He did not get far.

Two men approached him from behind. One, a tall man with red hair, grabbed his left arm firmly. The other, a shorter, stocky man with gray hair, firmly gripped his right arm. "Gotcha. Come with us." They placed his hands behind his back and locked them in place with police-issue metal hand-restraints.

Ushered roughly inside an elevator, the monk found himself confronted by a very tall gentleman with gray skin, dressed in an expensive blue silk suit and black cape with gold trim. Hanging on his arms were two women – one an attractive blonde with an hour-glass figure, the other a round faced woman with red, spiked hair.

"Hello McPherson", greeted the caped man as the two captors also entered and the elevator doors closed behind them. One of the men punched a button on the wall, and the elevator began ascending.

"What's the meaning of this and how do you know my name?"

"Most people stay dead when they die," replied the caped man, "Stay dead this time."

"You're going to kill me?"

"Of course! Let's say your trip is canceled."

"What *trip*?"

Paul never heard the reply. By the time he regained consciousness, he was inside a body sack sinking to the bottom of the East River.

CHAPTER 2

Brooklyn, New York. June 10, 2027

"Very hot, man, no?" Joel asked rhetorically.

Joel Tobin was born in Jamaica and had migrated to New York six years before. Joel made his living selling watches and cheap jewelry from a table on the corner of Schermerhorn and Bond Streets. This afternoon he was trying to sell a GPS Timex to Jonathan Summerset, an African-American who had stopped by to check out his wares.

Summerset admired the view of the Freedom Tower, clearly visible over the top of the buildings on the other side of Brooklyn Bridge Boulevard. He looked back down and replied. "Yeah, real hot," wondering if Joel was referring to the weather or the watch. Summerset worked as a car-park attendant in the lot across the street from the Hare Krishna temple further down Schermerhorn. "How much?"

"That be a good watch, man. Sets its time from the global positioning satellites." Joel assured him with his thick Jamaican accent. "Only fifty-three units."

"There's no way it's worth that much."

"It's got Indiglo."

"All Timex watches have Indiglo. They've had Indiglo since the twentieth century. This watch doesn't even have 3D time."

"This watch is worth more than seventy-five

Time Gods

international units. Fifty-three is a good price."

Filling the air was a cacophony of sounds: hydrogen-powered cars and trucks rumbling by, some of them with horns honking angrily; ghetto blasters blaring heavy metal, punk, and rap; people talking, laughing and shouting, and feet drumming on the sidewalk.

Joel was distracted by a beautiful golden Rolls-Royce Phantom V which pulled to the curb. You didn't often see a gas-powered Rolls-Royce on Schermerhorn Street. Even the hubcaps were gold and the treads on the white wall tires deep and clean. The dark, tinted windows concealed the occupants. A popular Atlantic City Casino logo was painted on the car door and it had New Jersey license plates.

The chauffeur, if indeed you could call him that, stepped from the vehicle. He was a smooth-looking man with the sophisticated manners of the privileged business class. His face was slightly chubby, robust and cunning. His hair was gray, complexion ruddy and eyes sharp and calculating. He wore an expensive, exquisitely tailored charcoal-gray suit with a subdued blue tie and matching handkerchief protruding from his jacket pocket. An Oyster-Perpetual Rolex watch crafted in 18 karat gold decorated his wrist, shaming any timepiece Joel had to sell. The man had an air of authority and seductiveness about him, charismatic yet dangerous. As his glance passed over Joel and Jonathan Summerset, both of them felt strangely affected.

"Who *is that guy?*" Summerset half-whispered.

"Never seen him before," Joel replied.

Then, a thin man with a stern, swarthy-looking face and pointed chin emerged from the passenger side and onto the sidewalk. His hair was unnaturally red. His nose was as curved and sharp as a scimitar, and he moved in a trained, predatory manner that anyone could recognize as dangerous. In contrast to the driver, he wore a red suede jacket, red pinstriped pants, and black, metal tipped shoes with white tops. "Sick and tired of doing this over and over again," he said as he flung the door shut so violently that the whole vehicle rocked.

As if anger were a switch that could be turned on and off with the flick of a finger, he politely opened the rear door of the car. Joel and Jonathan understood this man's angry behavior was unpredictable and dangerous.

A strikingly beautiful woman with an hour-glass figure emerged from the rear seat. She wore a tight red dress, that accentuated her full breasts, shapely hips and thin waist and which was both low-cut and short, highlighting her long graceful legs and bright red high heels. Her long, shiny blonde hair cascaded in loose curls down her bare back. Her oval face was extraordinarily enchanting, her nose perfectly shaped, and thick long eyelashes decorated with mascara framed her large, restless blue eyes. Her moist lips, bright red with lipstick, and perfectly manicured fingernails painted to match, glittered in the sun. Several diamond rings adorned her fingers, though none adorned the fourth finger of her left hand. A priceless golden necklace set with large diamonds dangled enticingly around her neck. A subtle scent of jasmine mixed with roses pervaded the air in her vicinity and her complexion was soft and white. The woman had an aura of innocent sensuality about her that captured the mind, yet one also sensed she was experienced in the world of pleasure.

"Mother of Jesus," Joel whispered, seeing the incredibly beautiful woman. She cast a quick sidelong glance at him and he felt immediately aroused.

"Watch out for her," Summerset cautioned. "Is she gorgeous or what?"

For hundreds of feet around, people stopped whatever they were doing to watch her. Across the street a deliveryman for UPS, who was unloading boxes from his hydrogen powered truck, simply froze. Several of the boxes tumbled to the ground as he stared, slack-jawed.

In effect, the woman brought the entire area to a standstill.

As she stood by the side of the thin man with red hair, the driver came around to join them. All three carefully watched the far sidewalk further down the block.

Soon they spotted a Hare Krishna monk who, in his saffron robes, could easily be seen within the crowd as he approached.

"That's him," the man with red hair snorted.

As they watched, the Hare Krishna devotee passed by. His robes swung freely in the breeze. He wore simple rubber

Time Gods

flip-flops on his feet. A tuft of hair flowed from the back of his shaven head. His right hand was inserted into the opening of a small cloth bag, with his index finger protruding from a smaller opening on the other side. Within the bag he rolled a set of *japa* meditation beads, similar to a rosary, which he held with his thumb and middle finger. He could be heard murmuring a *mantra* softly as he walked along. He quietly disappeared down the stairs of the Hoyt-Schermerhorn subway station.

"I'd *still* like to get that guy in bed," said the woman.

The man with red hair shot her an annoyed glare, and then turned back toward the subway. "Let's follow him and do it right this time."

* * *

Dorchester Apartment Building, Manhattan. July 11, 1966

Wendy and Mary were sitting on the side of the bed, passing a joint back and forth while Mary's black and white television played *Another World* on NBC. Mary liked the show because it focused on exotic melodrama between families of different classes and philosophies. Even abortion, usually taboo on television, was frequently discussed.

The apartment walls were plastered with posters, from wall to ceiling - some psychedelic, some of teddy bears, some of baseball heroes.

"I can't believe you actually broke up with Peter," Wendy sighed. "You two seemed happy together."

"Should've done it weeks ago."

"I mean, I think he's hot," Wendy Murphy admitted as she exhaled the smoke. Wendy was an attractive short haired blonde who lived two floors above in the same building. She wore a pale yellow blouse and jeans. The two women had known each other since their days at NYU when both had studied sociology. Now, whenever Wendy could escape, she rock climbed in the Tetons.

Mary Pierce nodded in agreement, her shiny brunette hair cascading half way down her back. She wore a red sleeveless t-shirt and a knee length skirt. "You know, he can be one of the most charming and flattering guys around." She passed the smoldering joint back to Wendy. "But if I even looked at another guy he would go nuts. He was constantly accusing me of cheating on him. A regular psychopath."

"You guys played guitar and sang well together," Wendy pointed out. "People were actually *paying* you to come and sing in bars!"

"He's too paranoid to make a good boyfriend for anyone. Besides, I don't like the Vietnam War anymore than you, but let's be honest. As long as Peter's a draft dodger he'll never be able to make an honest living."

"That's the problem with having a rich father," Wendy offered. "You don't need to work and you don't need a boyfriend or husband to support you. You're spoiled."

"My dad's not rich," Mary insisted. "But he makes enough to support me until I find something I want to do with my life."

"Lucky you."

"I'm not the one who inherited a quarter of a million bucks when your grandfather died."

"Guess we're both lucky," Wendy conceded.

"And rock climbing is your sport! You once told me you could probably climb a skyscraper."

"Thought about it. Never tried."

There was a loud, insistent knock on the door. Both girls were startled.

"You expecting someone?" Wendy asked, suddenly nervous.

"No," Mary replied. "Put that thing out."

"Cops?" Wendy asked as she snuffed out the marijuana and quickly picked up the aerosol fragrance. The room reeked of pot smoke. This is just what they didn't want to happen: a drug bust.

Mary quietly crept to the door and peered through the peephole.

"Who is it?"

"Bell Telephone."

"What do you want?"

She saw a man in brown coveralls standing in the

Time Gods

hallway. He wore a utility belt holding wire cutters, a hammer, screwdrivers, a small role of coiled wire and other tools.

"Ma'am, we have a man testing lines inside a manhole on Washington Square West. You might be able to see the workers if you look out your window. We're updating the lines and we need to check your signal strength."

The man looked legitimate enough. "You got any credentials?"

The man held up an ID card that clearly indicated he was working for the telephone company.

"He's not a cop, Wendy." Mary unbolted the door and opened it, allowing a cloud of marijuana smoke to drift into the hallway.

The man stepped inside. "Whew! You girls doing a little smoking?"

"Why? You want some?" Mary asked.

"Don't smoke weed myself, Ma'am, but my son does. Where is your telephone?"

She pointed.

The man went over and picked up the receiver while Mary and Wendy watched. He clicked the button on top a few times, then flipped the phone over and using a screwdriver from his utility belt, removed the metal plate on the bottom. He attached some wires hooked to a hand-held meter. "Woah!"

"What?"

"Ma'am. Worse than I thought. These old tenement buildings, you know. In this part of Manhattan all of the lines run underground and the insulation on the cables under the street are starting to crack. They haven't been updated in years."

"What does that mean for me?"

"Nothing, Ma'am. I'll just place this small device in here like this, attach it here, like that. There. All done." He replaced the bottom of the phone and screwed in the plate.

"What will that do?"

"Simple signal booster. Your phone was one of the worst I've seen in weeks. Sorry to bother you."

CHAPTER 3

Harlem Hospital Center on 135th and Lenox, New York

Paul McPherson reached up to feel his forehead and noticed the bandage wrapped around his head. He also noted the stubble of new hair on the top of his head through gaps in the bandage.

There was a second bed a few feet away and an old television on the table in the corner playing some kind of strange black and white soap opera, but the sound had been muted. Sunlight poured through the window. Usually these hospitals had holograph projection phones. He looked to find one.

He couldn't remember how he came to be here. All he could remember was entering the Empire State Building, being forcibly restrained and shoved into an elevator. There had been some people there, and one of them had struck him on the back of the head.

He closed his eyes and rested for awhile. He didn't know for how long. His throat was sore.

A deep, masculine voice broke the silence. "Want to tell us your name?"

Paul opened his eyes. The bright lights of the room silhouetted the doctor hovering over him. With a stethoscope around his neck, the doctor was a self-assured looking African-American with a plump, dark face. Wearing a white gown, with a pen and folded papers protruding from his chest pocket, he held a clipboard under his arm.

"Excuse me?" the monk inquired hoarsely.

"The nurse told me you were awake and talking with her awhile ago. You've been unconscious for two days. Can you tell us your name?"

He rubbed his eyes. "Paul McPherson. I think."

"You think? You're not sure?"

"No, no. It's Paul McPherson."

"I'm Doctor Jones," explained the physician. "How do you feel?"

"My head hurts."

"Understandable," offered the doctor. "Mind if I ask you some questions?"

"Be my guest."

"How old are you?"

"Twenty-six." The doctor scribbled something on his clipboard.

"Born in New York City?"

"New Rochelle," corrected Paul.

"Mother? Father? Family?"

"Yes, both parents still live there. I have a younger sister."

"Her name?"

"Josette. That's about it for family. I'm not married."

"Do you know the name of your mother and father?"

"Yes," Paul replied. "Of course. Paula and Joseph McPherson."

"Who was the first President of the United States?"

"What?"

"Who was..."

"What kind of question is that?" Paul interrupted, irritated.

The doctor frowned and apologized. "I need to know whether you're bleeding internally, inside the cranial cavity. If you are, it's going to compress your brain and cause a lot of serious neurological problems. To rule that out, we need to determine your mental status, and that's done by a series of tests, starting with some simple questions."

Paul nodded, and his head hurt. "Why don't you just do a DP scan?"

"A what?"

Wayne Boyd

"You know. One of the Dimensional Probe scanners. The hand held?"

"I have no idea what you're talking about."

"Well then, have you at least done a CT scan? While I was unconscious?"

"Now let's just get back to who was the first..."

"George Washington," Paul replied.

The doctor smiled politely. "Alright, let me ask about your education."

"New York Institute of Technology in Yonkers. I have a degree in interactive holograph imaging and computer programming."

"Holograph what?"

"Holograph Imaging. You know. Like your cell phone's projector."

"Sounds pretty sophisticated. Does that have to do with computers?"

"Well, of course it does," Paul said.

The doctor nodded and noted Paul's general physique. "You look in fairly good shape, if you don't mind my saying so."

"I work out," McPherson explained. "Used to be into baseball and wrestling. These days I'm into martial arts."

"And you're some kind of religious person?"

"A monk of sorts," Paul offered.

"I see," the doctor mumbled. Contradictory for a monk to be athletic, he thought. Then again, everyone needed to enjoy good health. Sounded like he was some kind of computer genius as well. He leaned forward and shone an ophthalmoscope in Paul's eyes, noting the dilation of his pupils.

"So am I seriously hurt? Will I be alright?"

The doctor cleared his throat and raised his eyebrows, but didn't reply immediately. "So far things look pretty good. The nurse says your blood pressure is back to normal."

Behind the Doctor, Paul noticed a very short man with an old, withered face standing at the doorway. He was dressed in a suit and tie, peering into the room. He had an average-size trunk, short arms and legs, slightly enlarged head, prominent forehead and large nose. Oddly, a pair of

Time Gods

binoculars dangled around his neck. He had a receding hairline above long lobed ears that protruded prominently from his head. He retreated and disappeared down the hallway. Paul also noticed other people passing by in the hallway. Visiting hours, no doubt.

Doctor Jones leaned over. "Look straight ahead, at the TV in front of you."

"It's a black and white CRT. Where did you guys find one of those?"

"Well, I think color TV throughout the hospital is a few years off, but it's coming."

Paul laughed, but was also confused by the reply. "How did I get here?"

"Don't know," the doctor replied. He moved to the other side of the bed, pointing his light. "Someone informed ER you were lying on the pavement outside the ambulance entrance. How many fingers do you see?" He held his hand in front of Paul's face and started flashing his fingers – first two, then three, then one.

"Two. Three. One. So you mean I was just lying outside on the pavement?"

"Luckily for you," confirmed the doctor before putting his hand down and turning off the light. "Head injury and water in your lungs."

"How soon can I get out of here?"

"Two days is a long time to be unconscious. We need to monitor you for a few more days. Any nausea?"

"Not at the moment," replied Paul.

Doctor Jones smiled and left the room, and the tech came in and took his vital signs. Soon he was alone again and rested his head gently on the soft pillow. He closed his eyes.

Hardly a minute later, the little man with the withered face reappeared at the doorway. He stood not more than three feet high. Approaching the table near Paul's bedside, he climbed up on a chair and slid open the drawer. Removing the wallet he found there, he took a blank, business sized card from his own pocket, scribbled something with a pen, and then examined what he had written. "Meet me at the south-west corner of Central Park, 6 PM." He inserted it in the folds of McPherson's wallet.

Then, without taking anything, carefully placed the wallet where he found it. The drawer squeaked as he closed it with a slight thud.

Opening his eyes and seeing the little man inches away, Paul jerked his head and his headache returned. "Hey," he exclaimed. "What are you doing? Who are you?"

The man looked concerned and with his short arm held his finger to his mouth. "Shhh," he hushed, climbing down the chair and turning to leave. "My card's in your wallet." Quickly wobbling out of the room, he was gone.

Strange man. No privacy in a hospital. Paul drifted back to sleep and dreamed happy visions. It would be his last happy dream in a long time.

Time Gods

CHAPTER 4

July 12, 1966

Mary did notice there was a problem with her phone, but it started after the repairman had left, not before. Now, every time she made a call, she heard clicking noises. Once she even heard a faint yet discernible beep when she was talking to her mother, but her mother had said she thought it was something on her end.

Wendy suggested she call the phone company and get it checked out again, but Mary put it off. She just didn't like having strange people parade around her little apartment.

This morning she was talking with Wendy on the phone when there was a loud scratching noise and then a pop.

"Was that on your end or mine?" Wendy asked.

"You heard it too?"

"Loud and clear."

Perhaps more peculiar was that Mary had received an unsolicited gift, delivered straight to her door this morning. It was a bottle of Jefferson's Reserve Bourbon from Bardstown, Kentucky, the heart of the bourbon capital of the world, wrapped in a decorative box. An enclosed brochure said that it had matured since 1940 and had a rich bouquet, golden color and mellow flavor.

From an unknown admirer named Professor Cali? Who the heck was he? Mary tried to recall the name. An associate professor? She just couldn't place it. She moved the bottle up into the kitchen cabinet, next to the coffee container. It remained there, unopened. One day, perhaps during a special occasion, she would bring it out. She would not drink it alone, and she didn't like to mix alcohol with LSD or pot.

She looked at her calendar and then her watch. Mary told her father she would come and see him that afternoon. Riding to Brooklyn on the subway wasn't her favorite trip, but the A Train was the most efficient mode of travel between the boroughs. She dressed informally for the hot weather in jeans and a light-colored cotton blouse tied around her midriff with a knot.

* * *

Meanwhile, elsewhere in the country, a telephone call was being placed from a secret military facility about ninety miles north of Las Vegas. General Brian Morgan III spoke over a secure, scrambled line with Senator Jonathan Perry, who was calling from an eighteen-story resort, the tallest in the Bahamas. The Senator had been on vacation, enjoying the pine-sheltered beach and colossal pool when he made his call from his private suite.

"We've been having problems with some of the locals around here at Groom Lake," the General explained. "People are suspicious it's a bit more than a dried lake bed in the desert."

"Well it's obviously more than a dried lake bed."

"You know what I mean. Damn UFO people."

"Stonewall with disinformation," the Senator ordered. "Our standard procedure. Pretty soon people will tune it out of their minds."

"Yes, of course. Just like we did with the Roswell incident, Senator. Certainly easier than what you politicians are going through in Washington with the anti-Vietnam War protests. How do you like the Bahamas?"

"Beautiful," the Senator said, looking from his balcony at the aqua colored cove stretching out before him. The pure, white sandy beach was shimmering as the waves washed over it. He shook his head and sighed silently, then returned his gaze toward the strange woman with orange-

Time Gods

spiked hair who sat opposite him on the bed. "General, I was wondering if you could do a little favor for me."

"Favor?" the General asked. "Does this concern the upcoming signing of proposed MUPDA and LTTA agreements in Milam Valley?"

"Not exactly, General."

"Sir, you are the one in charge. How can I help?"

"I don't want Washington to hear about this," the Senator explained as he looked down at the photos the woman with orange-spiked hair had handed him a few minutes before. He cleared his throat nervously and his cheeks blushed red. If anyone were to find out about this, his political career would be dangerously in peril, and his wife would probably divorce him. "General, I need you to send some men to guard a newly classified area in New York City."

"Where at, Senator?"

"Astoria, Queens," the Senator replied, flipping through the enlarged prints that the General could not see. "Deep underground. Secret facility." How could this woman have acquired these photographs? What had seemed like a chance encounter with a seductive blonde woman named Connie two nights before had proved to be disastrous. "Just north of the Queensborough Bridge."

"Didn't know such a facility existed, Senator."

"It's top secret. More valuable than Fort Knox."

"In Queens, New York?"

"Underground," the Senator repeated. "Enough wealth to win in Vietnam hands down."

"Certainly, Sir," the General confirmed. "I'll dispatch a detail there right away."

"The entire area must be sealed off," Senator Perry insisted. "No unauthorized personnel should be allowed in or out. I'll send you a list of who is authorized, as well as the exact location. Oh, and General, I've been asked to tell you that this should be a standing order, regardless of what may happen in the future. This is directly involved with the meeting in India."

"Yes, Senator."

"Brian, you can tell the President I've seen what the Professor can do and it's genuine. I suggest that the United

States spearhead this whole event. We want to be seen leading the free world, not dragging our feet."

After a few parting words, the Senator put down the receiver and then looked up at the orange-haired woman with the checkered jacket. "It's done," he said.

"Thank you, Senator Perry," Ms. Dee said politely. "We'll keep the negatives just in case, but rest assured, as long as you keep your end of the bargain, so will we."

"Look, I don't know who you people are," the Senator said, "but if my wife were to ever find out..."

"She won't," Ms. Dee interrupted, "as long as the gold is protected by General Morgan and the President attends the meeting in Milam Valley. We'll also reward you, Senator, as promised. You'll get your share. All your ambitions will be fulfilled and your re-election will be fully financed."

CHAPTER 5

Nevins Street, Brooklyn, New York

"We're sorry. The number you have dialed is out of service."

Paul held the pay phone away from his ear in disbelief. He hung up. Now what should he do? He put the change he had received from Gabriel Caprone back in his pocket and stepped across Nevins Street. He passed a 1955 Oldsmobile parked at the curb. An old car. The rotary phone. The date on the newspaper.

Something was seriously wrong. He realized it almost immediately after stepping out of the hospital, but his head hurt so much at the time he didn't dwell on it. Now it was like he was living on some kind of period movie set.

It seemed like just the other day when he had set out from the temple. The Temple President, Shakuntala dasi, had given him thirty dollars in paper money for purchasing a part for the temple air conditioner. Since paper currency wasn't commonly in use in 2027, people were trying to find vendors that would help get rid of it.

Karaja, a heavyset German devotee who worked the front desk, told Paul about a message he'd received from someone called Professor Cali. The message had read, "Travel arrangements canceled – say goodbye." Even more peculiar, however, was that he'd received a similar message the day before, left by a little person, a man people still called a midget. "You're going on a trip. Make arrangements to be away for awhile." He had no idea what it meant, or who the mysterious people were that had left the messages, so McPherson had ignored them. The twenty-first century may have seen the completion of the Freedom Tower, but New York was still New York, and many strange people roamed the streets.

He returned to the temple entrance on Schermerhorn Street. Rapping on the glass door repeatedly he hoped this bad dream would melt away. But the louder he knocked, the more deserted the temple seemed.

Walking across the street, newspaper still tucked under his arm, he looked up at the top of the temple building. In bold, crisp letters, spreading the width of 305 Schermerhorn Street were the words, "Odd Fellows Memorial." Nothing about Hare Krishna.

What about the homeless man Paul had seen leaving the temple that day? Karaja had laughed, saying the man called himself "Madness." Paul spied him leaving just as he arrived at the front desk. "Asked if the devotees had heard about a place called 'Milam Valley,'" Karaja explained. "He also asked if you lived here and if you were going on a journey."

Now Paul really *was* on some kind of journey. A journey through time, it seemed. All of these memories from just before his accident seemed improbable. The cars around him were from the nineteen fifties. No hybrid, hydrogen- or electric-powered vehicles anywhere. These were pure gasoline vehicles. The date on the newspaper seemed to indicate he was somewhere in the previous century. He glanced down at the New York Times in his hand. "July 12, 1966," clearly written at the top of the page. There was no mistaking the date. Such strange headlines, too.

> *McNamara Orders Air Munitions Cut. Peking Restricts Foreigners' Trips. Talks Bog Down in Airline Tie-up; Both Sides Firm. Practical Nurses in Stoppage Here. City Warned by Bankers on its Estimates of Funds. Jobs for Teen-Agers Up Sharply in June, Except for Negroes.*

Time Gods

A black and white front-page photo depicted crowds of African-Americans in Chicago. The caption read "AT CIVIL RIGHTS RALLY IN CHICAGO: Crowd gathers at Soldier Field during rally addressed by Floyd B. McKissick, CORE head, and the Rev. Dr. Martin Luther King Jr."

A man carrying a briefcase, dressed in a suit and tie passed by. Paul stopped him. "Excuse me, sir. Can you tell me the date?"

"It's July twelfth," the man replied.

"What year?"

"What do you mean what year? Sixty-six. Why?"

"Twenty sixty-six?"

The man raised his eyebrows in surprise, looked serious, then perplexed, and finally started to chuckle. He raised his hand and pointed at Paul. "Hey. That's pretty funny! Pretty funny! You gotta love New York!" He turned and walked off, shaking his head. "Gotta love these New Yorkers!"

Glancing up and down the street, Paul saw a black Cadillac with dark tinted windows parked at the curb. Approaching the vehicle, he examined the license plate. The date on the tab was 1966.

A cold sweat appeared on his forehead as he began to question his sanity. If it was really 1966 it meant Paul had traveled backward in time 61 years. That was impossible.

Frantically, he looked down the street in the other direction. All the cars were old, yet looked new. He saw a blue 1963 Ford, a green Volkswagen bug, and a shiny red Chevy which must have been a 1962 or 1963 model, just like the one's he'd seen in pictures on the Internet. Next to it was a 1955 Dodge Nash with odd rounded curves and small windows, and another car beyond that and another car – all of them twentieth century fifties and early sixties. All of them powered by gasoline only.

Another person walked by. Paul tried to stop him. "Excuse me, sir." He ignored Paul.

A young lady walked by.

"Excuse me, ma'am," he said, with some urgency in his voice.

She stopped. She was an attractive young woman, about five feet four in her early twenties. Informally dressed for the hot weather, she wore jeans and a light-colored cotton blouse tied with a knot, exposing her navel. She had sincere, green eyes, fair complexion, a pretty nose, and long, dark shimmering brown hair cascading halfway down her back.

"Yes?" she asked.

"Ummm..." he stammered. He wasn't at all sure what to say.

"Well? What is it?" she inquired diffidently, glancing briefly at his odd clothing.

"Can you tell me what's today's date?"

"July twelfth," she quickly replied.

"What year?"

"Nineteen sixty-six."

"I see," Paul said. There was a look of disbelief in his eyes.

She looked him over carefully. He seemed confused.

"How on earth can that be?" he asked rhetorically.

She was not bothered by his hairless head or the stubble on his face. It was his pleading eyes that troubled her. Being dressed in peculiar robes, not unlike orange colored bed sheets, gave him an exotic Eastern appearance, which intrigued her. Many of her friends talked about making pilgrimages to places like India. That was a place where you could find spiritual enlightenment. Yet there was a disturbing element about him. He looked disoriented which made her feel ill at ease. Making an attempt to excuse herself, she decided not to waste her time. "Well, if that's all, I must get going."

It wasn't that she didn't care to help him, but what could she do? The city was full of people who needed some kind of help. It wasn't her problem. Politely stepping around him, she tried to continue on her way.

Paul saw she was leaving. "No! Wait," he insisted, thinking quickly. "I need some directions."

She stopped to look at him again. There was something about his eyes, something about him. Vacillating between conflicting impulses, she started to move off again, and then hesitating, at last capitulated, remaining a moment longer. "Where do you want to go?"

"To the Hare Krishna Temple."

"Where's that?" she asked.

Time Gods

"305 Schermerhorn Street."

"This is Schermerhorn Street," she said. After a moment of contemplation, she pointed at the building across the street. "That's probably the building over there."

"Yes, that's the place," Paul mumbled, looking at the building and shaking his head. He cast a brief glance back at the trees in the wooded area and then again at the building.

"Something very peculiar has happened to me," he admitted, "but it's difficult to explain."

"What's wrong?"

"Well, you see those trees there?" nodding his head at the wooded area behind them.

She looked. "Yes?"

"Well, I seem to remember a parking lot there. You know?"

The young lady noticed a tear in the corner of his eye and she felt sympathy for him. She stood helplessly, perplexed. "Look," she said after a moment. "I'm familiar with this area. I walk down this street all the time. There's never been a parking lot as long as I can remember. Are you sure you're not confused with another street?"

He lowered his head, rubbing his forehead with his hand. "No, this is the right street," he hesitatingly replied.

She smiled pleasantly trying to encourage him. "Are you like those guys in the park?" she asked.

"Yeah. The park. What park?"

"Tompkins Square Park in Manhattan. I've seen people that look like you there. They give out free food and sing with tambourines and stuff."

"Oh yes!" Paul said, looking up hopefully. He saw the kindness in her eyes. "That sounds like it. That's the Food for Life program! The Hare Krishnas distribute free, vegetarian food to needy people...but..."

"But what?" she asked.

"Did you say this is nineteen sixty-six?"

"Of course," she replied.

They fell into silence for a few seconds. She thought about leaving again but felt compelled to wait longer. Then she decided to say something. "What's your name?"

"Paul McPherson."

Wayne Boyd

A nice name, she thought, but she didn't want to tell him that. Obviously a descendant from Irish immigrants.

"What's yours?" he asked, looking into her kind eyes.

"Mary," she replied, studying his concerned, brown eyes. She noted the pupils. They were normal, not dilated, as she would have expected had he taken drugs. He sure was confused about what year this was, though.

"Glad to meet you, Mary," he said, and then, somewhat flushed, hung his head down.

"Nice to meet you too, Paul," she said pleasantly.

He looked up, puzzled for a moment. Dejected still, he could see she was trying to help. "You live around here?" he thought to ask.

"Not exactly," she replied. "Manhattan. My father is an attorney here in Brooklyn. Nevins Street in fact, just around the corner. I was just on my way to see him."

"I see," he said. "I was in an accident."

"An accident?" she inquired.

"Hit over the back of my head. See?"

He turned around and showed her the back of his head. Seeing the lump, she winced compassionately. "Ouch. Must have hurt. How did it happen?" She placed her hands on his head gently, and tilted it slightly forward to get a better look. Her hands were cool and soft. He smelled perfume.

Then McPherson noticed three men on the other side of the street. One was a fair-skinned man with a brimmed hat, spectacles and light-colored shirt and tie. A trench coat was draped over his arm. The other two were dressed in black, wearing dark sunglasses. They stood looking at Paul deliberately.

"I was attacked," he continued, careful not to call Mary's attention to the men. There was no doubt about it. They were definitely watching him. It made him feel uneasy.

"Were you robbed?" she asked, releasing his head gently and letting her hand linger briefly on his broad shoulder. Unusual for a monk to be so muscular, she thought.

He turned to face her and again their eyes met. For a fleeting moment they felt some stirrings between them. It was Paul who felt the awkwardness of the moment and blushed slightly. He looked down. "No. That's the curious part. I don't know what they were after." He looked away, as

Time Gods

if seeing the men he was describing. "I had thirty dollars in cash when they attacked me, and when I woke up in the hospital I still had thirty dollars."

"How many people attacked you?"

"There were five of them. One had gray complexion, an expensive suit and a cape. A cape, can you imagine? Two other men put me in cuffs and shoved me in an elevator in the Empire State Building. Then there were these two women."

"Sounds like a strange group. Were they Mafia?"

"Don't know. Never saw them before."

"That's awful," she said – still intent until his eyes once again met hers. She was quite sure now that this was a providential encounter. Only half an hour ago she had been terribly bored, but here was someone interesting. He seemed like he was in genuine distress and perhaps she really could help. She found him polite, well-spoken, and though dressed like a monk from India, muscular and handsome.

"They not only clubbed me on the back of the head, but apparently tried to drown me," Paul explained, "I was in the hospital for six days and was released a few hours ago."

Bellevue?" she asked. Bellevue hospital hosted a microsurgery center, a regional center for brain and spinal cord injuries and comprehensive pediatric services. The psychiatric services, however, were the most renowned, and it was to this the young lady inferred.

"No. Not Bellevue. I was in Harlem Hospital Center on 135th and Lenox. I know what you're thinking. I'm not a psychiatric patient. This is the way people from my religion dress."

"Sounds like a professional hit job," she suggested. "Do you know anybody who would want to kill you?"

"I don't know. But, you see..."

"See what?"

"It's the date. You know?"

"What about the date?"

He swallowed nervously and then began to speak cautiously. "When I went into the hospital, it was the twenty-first century. As fantastic as it may seem, I have somehow traveled backward in time." He pointed at some buildings down the street, in the direction of Manhattan. "Where I'm from there's a really tall building over in that direction called the Freedom Tower. It replaced the World Trade Center towers after the terrorist attack on September eleventh, 2001. I was born that day. September eleventh, 2001, the moment the first tower collapsed, they say. You could once see those towers right from where we're standing, and the Freedom Tower was right there."

"I don't see anything."

"That's what I'm saying."

"Look. I don't know what you're talking about. I read they're just starting to build the World Trade Center towers this year. They've been planned for years, and when they finish them they're supposed to be even taller than the Empire State Building. They'll be the tallest buildings in the world."

"Until they build the Sears Tower in Chicago."

"What?"

"Never mind," Paul mumbled. "There'll be a lot of taller buildings in the future, like the Burj Khalifa in Dubai."

By now Mary's afternoon had been permanently altered. Her impulse to walk away had completely vanished, weird as the state of affairs were. Clearly this strangely dressed guy needed help. There was obviously no such thing as time travel. That was silly science fiction. This guy had taken some kind of drugs, probably. He actually *believed* he was from the future, but he was not dangerous, and she liked him anyway.

"I see," Mary said cautiously. "Well, you know it's highly improbable that you've somehow traveled through time. You've had a bad accident, and from the sound of it you may not be out of danger."

Paul nodded. She continued: "In any case, what do you want to do now?"

"I have no idea," he replied with resignation. He knew she didn't believe him.

"You see," she said, "I was just on my way to see my Dad, but it's not important."

"No," Paul objected. "Please. Don't let my problems interfere with your plans."

"There's no interference, Paul. May I call you Paul?" He

nodded. "Life is full of surprises. If I can't accept this as one of them, then I'd be pretty dense. Why don't you and I go somewhere? You can change into some proper clothes, drink some coffee and come down from your trip. Maybe we can figure out all this time travel stuff while we're at it."

"I'm not sure what I should do," he stammered, somewhat taken back by her generous offer. "I'm not on any kind of 'trip', you know. I'm really from the future."

"Sure you are." Taking a chance, she took his hand in hers, and looked deeply into his eyes. "C'mon," she said softly, but insistently. "Let's go talk for a while."

She started to pull him gently toward the subway. He did not resist. As they moved away, he took a last glance across the street, searching for the mysterious man with the brimmed hat and two others who had been watching them, but they were no longer there.

CHAPTER 6

"Methodological competence and critical awareness," Mary described her studies at New York University. In other words, geopolitical alternatives to the Vietnam War. "My father's not pressuring me to work until I find the right career," she admitted, "so I have the luxury of living on my own and being presently unemployed. I need to find a job that doesn't go against my ideals. What about you?"

Mary seemed particularly interested to learn Paul had dovetailed his athletic propensities by taking up martial arts, especially Taekwondo, which he did for the security of his monastery or temple or whatever he called it.

As they approached their stop on the F train, she wanted to know how he had become involved in whatever it was that he was involved in, which she quickly learned was called Krishna Consciousness. He explained how he had grown increasingly dissatisfied with materialistic society and saw no point in just working for mundane existence like everyone else. He had met the devotees of Krishna selling books. Impressed with the philosophy and lifestyle taught by someone named Srila Prabhupada, McPherson later moved into the temple and busied himself working simultaneously on their computers and martial arts training.

She suspected he was running away from life under the guise of joining some kind of religious sect.

The two ambled through Washington Square Park talking amicably, finally wandering beneath the great

Time Gods

marble arch at the north end.

"This arch was designed in the eighteen hundreds," Mary told Paul. "It's over 75 feet high."

"Is that a fact?" Paul was surprised. "You know, I lived in New York in the twenty-first century and never knew that."

"See? I know some stuff," Mary laughed. "Rumor has it they found human remains, a coffin and an old gravestone when they were digging the foundation."

"Wait. You're kidding, right?"

Mary shook her head. "For real. The architect said it stood as a gateway for times past and future."

"Figures," Paul mumbled. "Now here I am from the future walking underneath it."

Finally they arrived outside a brownstone apartment building named "Dorchester" on MacDougal Street and Mary entered the front door. Paul followed cautiously behind. He simply had no other place to go.

Inside they ascended a narrow staircase. She stopped on the landing of the third floor and proceeded a short distance to her door. It was hot, humid and unbearably stuffy. A naked yellow light from a low-wattage bulb hung from a wire in the ceiling. Jimmy Hendrix blared from another apartment. Taking some keys from her jean pocket, she inserted them, one after another, in a series of locks. They avoided a small pile of trash outside her door as they went inside.

Mary lived in an efficiency apartment. She had a full-size bed, an old sofa with its back against two windows and a kitchen area with a stove and refrigerator. A round table with four chairs separated the kitchen from the living area. A door led to what Paul assumed was the bathroom. The closet door was ajar and he saw clothes hanging on hooks and boxes on the floor. A folk guitar rested in the corner of the room.

"Here's my pad. Like it?" Mary asked.

"Yeah. You sure like posters," he said, amazed at the menagerie of wall and ceiling decor. Then noting the guitar, he added cautiously, "You play music?"

"Sometimes. My ex-boyfriend and I used to play in Greenwich Village for the bohemian crowd. Do you want to change out of those clothes into something more

Wayne Boyd

comfortable?"

Paul suddenly felt awkward. He was bound by his vows not to sleep with a woman until marriage, at which time his orange robes were to be exchanged for white ones.

"Ah... well... No, it's okay."

Mary was startled. "Did I say something wrong?"

"No," he tried to reassure her, looking nervous. "You didn't say anything wrong. It's just that..."

Mary was incredulous. "What's wrong? There's some men's clothes in the closet. Do you want to walk around all the time in those weird-looking robes?"

Paul shook his head no.

"There's the bathroom. You can change in there," she pointed.

As Mary went into the kitchen area, Paul rummaged through the closet feeling like an idiot. He found a baseball cap on the shelf. It would hide that shaved head if he needed to. He picked it up and selected a man's pair of jeans and a light-blue t-shirt which hung next to Mary's clothes. He slipped into the bathroom and locked the door.

After pulling on the jeans he stuffed the baseball cap in his back pocket and examined his head injury in the mirror. When he re-emerged, he found Mary sitting at the table munching potato chips. "Where do I put these?" he asked, holding his bundled orange robes.

"In the hamper right there. Want a drink? I've got some bourbon."

"No thanks," Paul said, realizing she had no idea about his religious principles. "What do you have to eat around here?"

"Not too much. You can check the refrigerator. I'm a vegetarian, so you probably won't find much you like."

"What did you say?"

"Yeah, don't eat meat. Hope that's not a problem with you."

"No," Paul said happily. "That's no problem at all. I'm a vegetarian, too. In fact, the leader of my religion was a vegetarian and all of his followers are as well."

"Well, that's groovy," Mary replied sincerely. At least they had one thing in common. "But don't expect me to follow your religion. I do it 'cause I believe in harmony and peace."

Time Gods

"That's amazing," Paul said as he pulled open the refrigerator. It was empty except for a couple of potatoes, a carrot and some celery sticks. "What do you eat? There's not much in here."

"I need to go shopping," Mary said.

"Yeah, you do." He pulled out a celery stick and picked up a jar of peanut butter on her counter.

Devout Hare Krishnas offer their food to God before eating. The philosophy is that all food should be offered to Krishna with special prayers before every meal. Paul knew such behavior would seem peculiar to Mary, so he just dipped the celery into the peanut butter and whispered the name "Vishnu" three times. "Do you mind if I use your phone?" he asked, crunching down the end of the celery stick.

"No, go right ahead. No double dipping the celery. Put the peanut butter on a plate if you're going to do that. Plates are above the stove."

Paul reached up and grabbed a plate, and then found a spoon in a drawer. He scooped himself a generous portion of the peanut butter onto the plate and then headed for the phone. "Got a phone book?"

"Who you going to call? Thought you didn't know anyone from this century."

"Well, my parents haven't been born yet, but my father's parents should be living in New Rochelle somewhere."

"If you say so. The phone book is in the drawer by the bed."

Inside the draw Paul discovered roach paper, a small plastic bag of what he assumed to be marijuana, and some sugar cubes. Lifting the book and bringing it back to the telephone, he began flipping through the pages. Quickly finding what he thought was the correct number, he lifted the black rotary phone and dialed.

A familiar voice answered. "Hello?"

"Hello, Grandma? This is Paul."

"Hello? Who is this? May I help you?" Sure sounded like his grandmother.

Thinking for a moment, he asked, "Hello, is this Mrs. Helen McPherson?"

"Yes, it is. With whom am I speaking, please?"

Wayne Boyd

"Grandma! It's me! Paul!"

"I'm sorry," came the voice on the other end. "You must have the wrong number."

Paul was stunned. After a brief pause, he gathered his thoughts.

"I'm sorry. Perhaps I do have the wrong number. I'm looking for Helen, husband to Henry McPherson."

"My husband is Henry. Who are you? What do you want?" There was a definite tone of suspicion in her voice.

"How old are you?" he inquired.

"None of your business unless you tell me who you are."

"My name's Paul. I believe we're related. I'm just trying to see if I have the right number. Do you mind telling me how old you are?"

There was a brief pause, and then a reply. "I'm twenty five. I can't be your grandmother since I don't even have children."

Paul was dumbfounded. Even his own grandmother didn't know him. With nothing more to say, he simply hung up the phone.

*   *   *

Helen McPherson heard a click and the line went dead, but she did not hang up immediately. She heard a scratching sound and a faint electronic beep. A further pause, and more scratching sounds. When the sounds stopped she nervously replaced the receiver. It almost sounded like someone had traced that call to her phone.

She was a plain woman, slightly plump, with shoulder-length blonde-brown hair. Her curved nose was set on a soft, heart-shaped face with full cheeks. This afternoon she wore a simple flower-print dress down to her knees, and matching blouse.

"Who was that?" asked Henry, glancing at his watch. It was 4:47 PM.

Henry was a bright, up-and-coming young man, reclining in his brother's easy chair reading the newspaper. He was average build; about five feet nine inches tall, and had medium-length black hair slightly over the top of his ears. His nose was straight, eyes brown, and forehead wide

Time Gods

on a beardless face. Dressed in a blue shirt and loosened tie, he relaxed in black, stocking feet protruding from creased pants whose wrinkles betrayed the end of his work day.

The couple had been married for just over two years. He worked as a pharmacist from 7 AM until 3 PM, five days a week, freeing him to spend late afternoons and early evenings at home with his wife. So far he had avoided Vietnam with a high draft number. His bachelor brother had not been so fortunate and was now overseas. They stayed in his place. Helen was unemployed, but had worked at the checkout for A&P a few months previously.

"A prank call," she explained. "I think."

"A man?"

"Yes, claiming to be our grandson."

"Grandson! Good Lord, I guess kids think all adults are really old!"

"Such a strange call," she pondered.

"Nothing to worry about," he laughed. "Kids like to do prank calls sometimes. I used to make prank calls when I was a kid. Might be one of those bullies down the block. Does it bother you?"

"Not really," replied Helen. "Except that he knew both of us by name."

"There, I told you," Henry justified. "Someone who knows us. Nothing to be worried about. Obviously anyone who knows us knows we don't have kids, what to speak of grandkids."

"Yes," she agreed. "Very strange."

Helen and Henry McPherson put it out of their minds.

They did not know the call had been traced and now someone evil was looking up their address.

CHAPTER 7

"What was *that* all about?" Mary asked.

"That was my grandmother."

"From the way you were talking, it seemed she didn't recognize you."

"No, she didn't. How could she?"

"What do you mean?"

"Well, I was born in 2001, so I haven't been born yet. Even my parents haven't been born yet."

"Do you hear what you're saying?"

"Of course I do," Paul replied.

"Then are you *listening* to what you're saying? You sound crazy."

"I'm not crazy, but what's happening to me sure seems crazy."

Sitting in her chair, Mary leaned on the table as Paul stood nearby. "Look," she said. "You had a nasty bump to your head. Or maybe you're on LSD or something. I don't know what's wrong with you. Will you please cut the crap?"

"I know it *sounds* ridiculous. But somehow, it's true! I'm not supposed to be here at all. This is some kind of cosmic mistake."

"Cosmic mistake or your mistake," Mary declared.

Then Paul had a disturbing thought. "Unless..."

"Unless what?"

"Unless I'm dead. Maybe I died when those guys hit me."

"You don't look dead to me. I could be wrong, though."

"I have an idea. You said you've seen people like me in

Time Gods

Tompkins Square Park. That's not too far from here. Let's go there."

"It's rush hour. I'm not going on the subway now."

"We don't need to take the train. We can walk. It's not that far. It'll take us maybe a half hour."

"I'm not going anywhere tonight," she stated firmly. "New York is no place to walk around at night."

For a short while both of them were silent as she studied him. At length, she spoke again. "Look, where are you going to stay tonight? Here?"

Paul's hesitancy returned. "No I can't stay with a woman."

She rolled her eyes toward the ceiling and threw up her hands. "I see. This is great. Look, I don't know what this is all about, but you seem like a nice enough guy. I've got a couch. You can sleep there. I'm offering you a crash pad for a day or two until you sort out your life. If you've got some problem about staying with a woman, then I think you're pretty strange. And I already think you're strange, by the way."

With holograph projection devices, Krishna philosophy and martial arts, Paul was brilliant. With women, he was an utter clod. He had proven that many times before in his life. In fact, it had been one of the factors that had contributed to him choosing to be a monk in the first place, though he kept that a secret from everyone except himself. A broken relationship – embarrassment – hide from the world. "Okay," he agreed. "I'll stay. Thank you. Honestly, I don't have anywhere else to go."

After a few moments Paul held his arm out to her. "Pinch me."

"What?"

"Go ahead, pinch me."

She liked that idea. Reaching over, she pinched Paul hard on the arm.

"Ouch!"

"Sorry!" Mary apologized, smilingly. "You asked me to do it!"

Paul drew his arm back. "I don't think I'm dead."

"Most observant my dear Watson."

"But how did I get here?" He asked rhetorically. "How is

all of this possible?"

Mary decided to change the topic. This time travel nonsense was going nowhere fast. "So are you going to walk over to Tompkins Square Park tonight?"

Paul thought about it. "The park can wait until tomorrow."

*   *   *

Area 51, Nevada. July 12, 1966

General Brian F. Morgan III sat in a cushioned maroon-leather chair, puffing on his Ashton Aged Maduro Cigar, handmade in the Dominican. Though the room was air conditioned, he stroked his gray, bushy mustache as sweat beaded on his lip underneath. He gazed out his window at the early evening pink, desert sky over the Nellis Bombing and Gunnery Range in Southern Nevada. The Range was approximately three million acres in size, or about four thousand seven hundred square miles – almost as big as the state of Connecticut and larger than Lebanon. Within this restricted range was a dry lake bed named Groom Lake, popularly known as Area 51, which encompassed sixty square miles. The General's office was located in the center of Area 51, near an airstrip.

The General stood slowly and walked to the plate glass window to take in the beautiful sunset. Behind him sat Major Jenkins, an intense, cleanly shaven Afro-American man with a pockmarked face.

The General thought about the MUPDA and LTTA agreement – where the meeting at Milam Valley was scheduled at the end of the month. The President and his cabinet would be there. Britain would probably go. All of those other countries as well. General Morgan would be there, too, along with the real men in power, the men beyond the politicians. Some remote resort. A place where they would learn the secrets of the future - technology revealed. Microchips, miniaturization, cellular and stealth technology, global positioning, flying cars powered by hydrogen fuel-cells - all of this and more had been promised

Time Gods

to those that would attend. It was to be the ultimate advantage over the Communists. What to speak of the LTTA! Senator Perry had assured him it was all genuine, and the Professor planned similar demonstrations for other world leaders in the days to follow.

"Major, I've received word that we're to send a dispatch immediately to New York," the General sighed. "Senator Perry says the President himself has requested we provide government protection in advance of the meeting in India."

"When, Sir?" asked the Major.

"Effective immediately," the General replied. "I want you to go personally."

"Does this have anything to do with the aliens?" the Major asked, nodding toward the setting sun over Area 51.

General Morgan turned from the window, pink sky behind him, and faced the Major. "You know about the so-called Leprechaun incident?"

"Leprechaun aliens, Sir?"

"Yeah, but not Leprechauns and not from outer space. Apparently they're some kind of bounty hunters from the future. President Johnson wants us to do autopsies, but right now his main concern is this Milam Valley thing. Ending the Cold War once and for all. For the time being, it even takes priority over your work here at Groom Lake."

"I understand, Sir," the Major assured him.

"There's gold there."

"Where, Sir?"

"In Queens. A great deal of gold. More than Fort Knox. Underground. A secret facility."

"Never heard of it, Sir."

"Neither had I," General Morgan admitted. "Not until yesterday. Never know what those bastards in Washington are up to. Apparently this is the Professor's private stash, brought here from who knows where."

"Our mission, Sir?"

"Protect the gold. Don't allow anyone to go in or out unless they're on a special list."

"Sounds highly irregular, Sir."

General Morgan nodded. "The whole goddamn thing is irregular, but since this Professor came along, we've got to ascertain where we stand in the world."

CHAPTER 8

Dorchester Apartment Building, Manhattan. 1966

We're not "these bodies." We are eternal, spiritual beings, parts and parcels of Krishna, or God. Out of forgetfulness we're identifying with our body, and thus feel threatened by old age, disease and death. Kind of like having amnesia. Through the process of chanting a special *mantra* we can remember who we are and become eternally happy again. We can live the life we forgot.

Mary had never heard anything like it. If only Paul had a book, she would have gladly read more. But alas, he kept saying that the Hare Krishna books were "in the future."

Paul baked potatoes in the oven and offered them to Krishna. That was their evening dinner. They added a little butter, salt and pepper, and it tasted great.

At 7:00 PM they turned the TV to channel 2 and watched *The CBS Evening News* with Walter Cronkite. The first half of the thirty-minute newscast was devoted to the war in Vietnam. Watching real-life scenes from the war depressed both of them. In the second half of the broadcast, Mr. Cronkite mentioned the new police commissioner that had been appointed by the Mayor of New York because of his outstanding record of human services. The new commissioner's name was Richard O'Rorke. He vowed to tackle corruption in the City. They showed him standing close to a woman with orange, spiked hair on the steps of

Time Gods

City Hall, whom the reporter said was "Mrs. Dee" and who had ties to politicians in Washington. There was also mention about some upcoming summit in India to be attended by most of the leaders of the free world.

They tuned to ABC on channel 7 and watched *Combat*, a World War II drama series. The show was just completing its fourth year in a five-year run, which was longer than the American participation in World War II itself. *The Man from U.N.C.L.E.*, a cult craze among teenagers, aired on NBC's channel 4, and still later ABC aired *The Fugitive*, apparently all summer re-runs.

Commercials included Miss Clairol Hair Coloring. "Does she or doesn't she?" the advertisement asked. "Only her hairdresser knows for sure." Coca-Cola ran an ad, "Things go better with Coke." Sea and Ski sang a tune about their suntan lotion producing a "show-off tan" and boasted their new "Boywatcher" and "Thunderbird" polarized wrap-around sunglasses with "racing driver" styling. Cheerios ran a cartoon ad touting all the goodness of "pow-pow-power oats."

These black and white shows with their incessant commercials both bored and intrigued Paul at the same time, but by eleven he'd had enough and felt drowsy. It didn't take him long to fall soundly asleep on the couch. He hoped to awake and find this had all been a dream.

It was Mary who turned off the light. In the dim light coming from the window she studied him as he slept and smiled to herself. She quietly slipped the flip-flops from his feet and draped a sheet over him.

She undressed and slipped into a nightgown before climbing into her bed and drifting soundly to sleep.

*   *   *

Paris, France. 1966

Meanwhile, the sun had already risen in Europe. The first President of the Fifth Republic, now serving his second seven-year term, opened the shudders of his window and breathed in the pleasant morning air. The sun was crimson color, looming large above the horizon, obscured somewhat by smog from the traffic below.

Ah, how things had changed since the early days. Back in 1940, a court martial had sentenced him to death for treason, and he had fled to London. Now he was a hero, and his country a permanent member of the United Nations Security Council. However, he had his reservations about NATO. He had recently withdrawn his forces, disregarding the wishes of the rest of Europe. Indeed, the General was an independent man, with strong opinions of his own. He had visited the USSR only last month, and had recently established diplomatic relations with the Peoples Republic of China.

The offer to obtain financial and military secrets of "futuristic technology" definitely intrigued him. If the U.S. President and British Prime Minister were going, he would too.

His phone rang, and the former general turned with surprise. *So early in the morning?* It could only be the Professor, he thought. No one else was authorized to call at that time of day.

"De Gaulle," he answered. And then he listened before again speaking. "*Oui, bien sur. Nous y allons. Je ne voudrais pas que l'Angleterre et l'Amérique nous doublent.* Yes, of course. We are going. It is in our national interest. I wouldn't want them to get ahead of us."

"The last day of July" the caller replied, in French. "For diplomatic reasons, it's very important that you go personally. The leaders of your military must also be there. You will not be sorry, General."

"Oui," the General replied. "We are all going. Do not worry, Professor."

He ended the call, and then looked out again at the rising sun. "Milam Valley," he whispered to himself. What was it about the whole arrangement that caused him alarm? Was it the MUPDA and LTTA agreement? He distrusted the whole arrangement almost as much as he distrusted the Americans.

*   *   *

Time Gods

Back in New York, the Professor hung up and thought about the President of France. "Everything is going as planned," he said to Connie. "Except for McPherson. Time to find out what he's up to."

CHAPTER 9

Manhattan, New York. July 13, 1966. 12:25 AM

The City that never sleeps did quiet down in the early hours after midnight. Late at night, in residential areas you could always hear the occasional drunkard on the street. Sometimes you could hear street arguments, perhaps even a fistfight. Then there were the sirens. Police and ambulance sirens were fairly frequent even late at night.

The pedestrian traffic became lighter into the early morning hours, except for the prostitutes and drug dealers. Still, late night was usually the best time to sleep.

It was after midnight and despite the calmness, Paul wasn't sleeping well on Mary's couch. Perhaps he should have taken an aspirin before resting, because his head was starting to hurt again. His injury bothered him even in his dreams.

The song "Jumping Jack Flash" by the Rolling Stones entered his head and went round and round over and over.

> *I was drowned, I was washed up and left for dead.*
> *I fell down to my feet and I saw they bled.*
> *I frowned at the crumbs of a crust of bread.*
> *Yeah, yeah, yeah.*
> *I was crowned with a spike right thru my head.*

Time Gods

But it's all right now, in fact, it's a gas!
But it's all right, I'm Jumpin' Jack Flash,
It's a Gas! Gas! Gas!

He saw himself jumping like a frog through time and space, finally landing on the corner of Fifth Avenue and Thirty-Third Street, looking up at the towering Empire State Building. Elevator doors slid shut behind him, and he turned around to find himself in a small room face to face with a derelict.

"Madness," he said. "People call me Madness."

Paul looked around. He was inside an ascending elevator. Everything was hazy. A bell rang and the elevator doors slid open. Paul faced a man in an expensive, blue silk suit, wearing a cape trimmed in gold, laughing.

"Who are you?" McPherson asked, suddenly realizing he was now standing in a great cavernous hall with a throne in the middle.

The man produced a metal pipe and raised it above his head. Paul concluded the man was going to strike him, so he turned to flee. Vanishing behind him, the man rematerialized directly in front of McPherson.

Paul jumped back.

The man clasped the metal pipe in one hand, cupped with the other hand. As he continued to laugh dauntingly, the unsettling echo filled Paul's ears.

Paul turned to run and the man disappeared and reappeared directly in front of him yet again. This man seemed to be everywhere. There was no escape.

The stranger took the pipe and raised it high in the air. Bringing it down with great force, it struck Paul on the head. As he crumpled to the floor in a pool of his own blood, he heard two women laughing.

"Dump Jumping Jack in the river!" said a lady with spiked orange hair. "Let him drown! Lifetime after lifetime!"

"No more interference from you!" added a blonde woman.

As his head started to spin, everything went dark. Next, he found he was inside a burlap sack. He struggled to get out, but the end was tied. He felt someone lifting him and then he felt himself falling. There was a splash and the sack filled with water. He gasped desperately and then again everything went dark.

Finally, Paul heard a man's voice. "We've got work to do. You can't die yet." He vaguely had the notion that he was no longer under water.

The voice faded. The sound of a passing automobile drew his attention.

Paul abruptly sat up. Sweat was pouring down his face. The lights of a passing car reflected from across the street momentarily lit up the window. The room was dark and he found that he was on a couch. Nearby was a bed, and someone was sleeping there. That was Mary. Paul wiped the perspiration from his face with the bottom of his t-shirt. *A dream. I was having a dream*, he thought.

He slowly got up and headed for the kitchen area. In the dark, he accidentally kicked the leg of one of the chairs. "Ouch," he said aloud, but not too loudly. Mary stirred in her bed, but didn't awaken. Limping to the sink, he took a glass from the cupboard and poured himself some water. After drinking he noticed the back of his head still hurt.

Moving in the dark room, he made his way quietly over to the window, wanting to peek outside. He wasn't sure why. He felt restless. Casually lifting the curtain with his right hand, he peered down at MacDougal Street.

Stunned, the hairs on his arms stood on end and he shuddered. There, outside the window, on the sidewalk below, stood the man with the gray complexion, wearing the same black cape, *looking straight up at Paul*. The man from the Empire State Building. The caped man from the future.

A thousand thoughts rushed through Paul's head all at once. *Who is he? Where did he come from? I was attacked in the Empire State Building in 2027. Its 1966 now. Sixty-one years! How can he be here too?*

Numb, McPherson staggered from the window, nearly falling over. His head was reeling.

There was no time to lose. He *had* to confront the man on the street, face to face. Quickly turning, he ran toward the apartment door, stumbling over a chair. He fell loudly to the floor with a thud.

Mary was startled awake and sat up. "What was that!" she called out. Fumbling for the light near her side, she clicked it on. The light momentarily blinded both of them.

Time Gods

They looked at each other with mutual surprise. Paul was on the floor in the kitchen.

"What happened?" she asked, trying to comprehend why he was lying on the floor.

Paul didn't reply. He was too much in a panic to be concerned with what she might be thinking. He had to get downstairs before that man on the street went away. The man held the secret to Paul's time travel. That man himself was a time traveler. Scrambling from the floor, he darted toward the door. It was locked. He clawed at the bolts and flung open the door wildly, running swiftly into the hallway.

Mary jumped up and ran after him. "Paul! Where are you going?" Why was he running out on her in the middle of the night?

McPherson didn't reply. Running barefoot to the stairs, he quickly scrambled down to the ground level, almost stumbling. When he reached the bottom of the stairs he crashed through the door and burst onto MacDougal Street.

In the dim streetlight he came face to face with a beautiful blonde woman. "Hello," she said seductively.

The night air closed around him. It was cooler and more pleasant than it had been during the day. The slight breeze somehow seemed erotically appealing.

Paul looked up and down the street. The man with the cape was gone. It took too long to get down here, he guessed.

"My name is Convoitise," the woman whispered seductively, "but my friends call me Connie." Paul looked at her and observed that she wore a mink wrap over her tight fitting, short red dress. Her waist was thin, hips broad and she had beautiful long legs. Diamond rings decorated her fingers. She stood a few feet away and slowly began to walk toward him, hips swaying. He tried prying his eyes away from her, yet her very aura attracted attention to her lustful advances. There was something mystical and terribly sensuous about her. He looked away. He hadn't expected to run into a prostitute, but they were probably fairly active in this neighborhood at night.

Then something else attracted his attention. Spinning around, Paul saw an astounding car careening out of an alley and racing away in the opposite direction. Never before in his lifetime had Paul McPherson seen a golden Rolls-Royce. He suspected the man in the cape was in that extraordinary vehicle, otherwise why was it speeding away?

Sensing an aroma of jasmine, Paul realized that the woman was at his side. She threw her arms around his neck and forced a strong, warm kiss directly on his lips, pressing her body against his as she tightly held him in her surprisingly powerful grip. She slipped her tongue between his lips entwining his with hers. The French kiss. Invasive. Erotic. Sexual.

Shocked, Paul struggled to push her away and, having done so, wiped his mouth with the back of his hand. "Hey!" he exclaimed. "What do you think you're doing?" He tried not to admit that he had accepted her kiss, and had indeed played with her tongue has she had with his.

The woman backed away a few feet, and smiled seductively. "You're sexy for a mortal who's managed to return from the dead," she said. "Who saved you? Was it Odus again?"

Her question grabbed Paul's attention. What did she know about Paul's accident? "Odus? Who's Odus?"

She smiled enticingly. "Oh, I see," she whispered. "Time layers. A regular Jumping Jack Flash. We jump here, and you jump there!"

Even before her last words, however, her body seemed to become distorted. Paul blinked and stared with disbelief as the woman transmogrified before his eyes. She appeared to grow taller, and her shapely figure became contorted. Her breasts absorbed and vanish into her chest. Alas, within moments the woman had become a hideous being in woman's clothing. The face was now disfigured with huge moles and warts. The being had red teeth and brutally hairy legs. Seeing the grotesque figure, McPherson gasped at the inexplicable transformation. In the next moment, the lady-turned-demon slowly dematerialized as a mist might blow away in the wind, and within a few seconds had completely vanished like a quark into a parallel universe.

Paul McPherson was dumbfounded. Were his eyes beguiling him? Mary's voice interrupted the silence. She had come down to the street, dressed in her nightgown. A sweater pulled over her shoulders, she saw McPherson

Time Gods

standing alone. "Paul?" she asked. "Are you alright?"

"Did you see that guy out your window?" he queried without looking at her. His gaze still fixed up the street.

"What guy?"

"A man with a cape. Didn't you see him?"

"No," she replied. "Did you have a nightmare?"

Paul looked down at the back of his hand, which he had used to wipe away the kiss of the vanishing prostitute-demon. Red lipstick smeared on his hand - hard evidence that she had been a reality. He showed the back of his hand to Mary and asked, "Do you see that?"

"Lipstick," she said. "Isn't it?"

"Lipstick."

"Where did you get that from? There's no one here!"

"Someone was here, but they both vanished."

"What do you mean they vanished?"

"I don't have an explanation, Mary. The only thing I'm sure about is that others have followed me to the past. I saw two of them tonight."

"You sure you didn't have a bad dream?"

"The lipstick on my hand is real. It didn't come from a dream."

"That's pretty scary if people have been following you," said Mary, ignoring the reference to time travel. "How do you think they found out you were staying with me?"

"I don't know," Paul replied, confused. "None of this makes any sense."

Being the daughter of a lawyer had, in the past, drawn Mary to fantasize over mystery crime novels, a favorite of hers before she had entered college. Here was a real life mystery, but she admitted to herself that she had never met anyone as intriguing as Paul. Maybe he was just crazy, but somehow she didn't think so. She just didn't have all the pieces to the puzzle yet.

Mary took Paul by the hand. "C'mon. Let's go back to sleep. It's late."

They turned and went hand-in-hand back indoors.

*   *   *

A very short man appeared around the corner, near the

park. He watched Paul and Mary through binoculars as they disappeared inside the building.

He was the same little person from the hospital.

CHAPTER 10

Queens, New York. July 13, 1966. 6:00 AM

An unmarked, black UH-1E helicopter, lowered itself onto the roof of a small, cube building in an empty lot in Queens, New York, as the propellers beat the air roughly. Two men dressed in black suits, wearing dark glasses, hopped out into the sunlight, ducking from the wind produced by spinning rotors. This was the Bell Huey chopper, originally designed for the U.S. Marines for assault support with salt-water corrosion protection and extra avionics. Two machine guns were mounted on the front.

The men who stepped from the chopper looked nondescript, yet ominous and menacing as they surveyed the scene. Both had black shoes, black string ties, and white shirts. One had blonde hair, the other, who was wearing a black baseball hat, was bald. They looked to be about thirty or forty, skin pale, high cheekbones and chiseled facial features. Both tall and thin. One carried a black briefcase, which he never put down. A third man in black remained behind the controls of the helicopter. Not far behind them flowed the East River, and beyond that midtown Manhattan. The Empire State Building pricked the skyline on the other side of Roosevelt Island. There was no Freedom Tower and no World Trade Center here in 1966 New York. The Roosevelt Island Bridge was not far away. The helicopter slowly powered down and the spinning rotors gradually came to a full stop.

The building upon which they had landed was constructed with cinder blocks and the roof only about 12 feet high, easily within talking distance to men on the ground. A ladder extended from the heliport to the parking lot below. The men from the helicopter stepped to the edge of the roof and saw U.S. Army troops scouting the perimeter fence and the main gate leading to the street.

An Army truck with five men carrying gas powered M14 assault rifles with 20 round magazines pulled up outside the main gate. An Afro-American military officer with an intense, cleanly shaved, pockmarked face stepped from the passenger seat of the truck into the blazing hot summer sun while the soldiers poured out the back. He showed his ID to the sentries, got back into the truck, and drove into the lot. They came to a stop near the cube building, the top of their truck nearly even where the men on the roof remained standing.

It was the hottest summer on record for New York, but it didn't bother this officer. He had grown accustomed to heat while working in Korea and the Nevada desert.

After directing his men to unload their supplies, the officer approached the cube building as the rotors of the helicopter gradually came to a halt.

"Major Alfred Jenkins," he called up to the men in black standing on the roof. He saluted them. "At your service by special order of General Morgan, Area 51, Nevada."

"Mean Al" had joined the army after finishing college. He had seen combat in Korea where he excelled in leadership under fire. It was there that he had first been introduced to General Morgan, who took the young aspiring officer under his wing and arranged to have him reassigned to the coveted Area 51 facility north of Las Vegas. The soldiers on the base admired him for his dedication, yet feared him because of his short temper. You didn't want to get on the wrong side of Major Jenkins.

His temporary reassignment to New York was a chance for the Major to oversee an important field assignment and for the General to get rid of him.

The men on top of the cube building, standing by the helicopter, nodded, their eyes concealed behind dark

Time Gods

glasses. One of them spoke into a microphone wired to his lapel. "The Army has arrived, Sir. Major Jenkins is here." He held his hand to his ear, listening for a response in his earpiece, and after a moment turned to look down at Major Jenkins. "He wants to see you immediately."

The Major saluted, and approached the only door in the cube building. He went inside, entered the elevator, and began his long descent underground.

*   *   *

The Bahamas. July 13, 1966. Morning

Senator Jonathan Perry packed his suitcase and prepared to return to Washington to consult with the Joint Chiefs of Staff about troop movements in North Vietnam. The glistening ocean sparkled in the cove outside his window. On either side of the beach, tall pine trees surrounded the hotel and framed the white sand and ocean.

The Senator paused a moment and breathed in the refreshing salt air wafting through his open balcony. How he would miss this island.

A map of a mountainous region was pinned to the wall behind him. Across the top of it were the words, "Milam Valley – the Ultimate Advantage." It was a scam. The Senator knew that. They were blackmailers and crooks. He would tell the President if he got a chance. He removed the map from the wall and rolled it up.

He briefly, and with a moment of guilt, glanced at the blackened ashes in his wastebasket, satisfied that at least for now, his passionate meeting with the blonde had been kept a secret. His marriage and political career were safe, and the Senator was significantly wealthier. He worried about the negatives but felt confident that Ms. Dee would keep her word until he could arrange the CIA to eliminate her. Only then would he request the President to cancel the meeting in India.

Blackmail was one thing, but treason was another. Senator Perry was a patriot, and he would not allow the President of the United States to fool-heartedly rush into a

Wayne Boyd

dubious meeting on a scale never before seen. Perry knew the President was depending on his final approval, and now the meeting would go ahead unless he let the cat out of the bag. That was exactly what he intended to do.

He looked up, surprised, when there was a sharp knock. The porter, he thought, and opened the door. Standing just outside his room was a tall man with unnaturally red hair and an angry, chiseled face. He held a needle and a syringe hidden behind his back. "Senator Perry?" he asked.

"Yes?"

"Sir, your usefulness has just expired."

* * *

Manhattan, New York. July 13, 1966. 7:55 AM

Someone opened a fire hydrant not far from Mary Pierce's apartment building, and young children could be heard gleefully jumping in and out of the cooling spray. When the fire department sent men to turn it off, local residents hurled stones at them and used abusive language. Opening hydrants and defending the children from the fire department had become a fad all over New York. Sometimes it was discussed on television.

It was nearly eight in the morning when McPherson climbed from the sofa, much later than he usually rose. Mary found a razor, which she lent to Paul to clean up three days' worth of stubble on his face. He nicked himself shaving and used some tissue paper to stop the bleeding. *I wouldn't bleed if I was dreaming or dead,* he realized as he dabbed himself. *But if I* am *suffering from paranoid schizophrenia, how would I know what is real and what isn't real, especially since no one else believes me.*

Then he turned on the hot water and hopped in the shower. The water smarted a little when it hit the back of his head. It was more than enough to convince him he was experiencing reality.

After getting dressed, he pulled his wallet from his rear pocket. His Social Security card had been damaged by the water but his drivers license was alright. He could use it to

Time Gods

prove he was from the future. The money from the Temple President, Shakuntala dasi, was still there, albeit crinkled. He removed the now dried bills and straightened them out and found ninety cents change in his pocket as well.

When he emerged from the bathroom Mary was sitting at the table with a guitar leaning against the chair, talking on the telephone with one hand. Her other hand was wrapped around a cup of hot coffee.

"No, my dad didn't mind," Mary said to Wendy on the other end of the line. "I just called him to say I met someone on the way. I'll come by your place the day after tomorrow. Okay? I'm a bit busy with this guy for now." There was a pause as she listened to Wendy's reply. "Okay. Bye."

"Friend of yours?" Paul asked.

"My best friend. Lives upstairs. Rock climber."

"A rock climber here in New York?"

"Yeah. She once climbed Yosemite with ropes, harnesses and carabiners. Went to a rock climbing school after we left college."

"Sounds like she's a serious climber."

"She knows her stuff," Mary agreed.

"You tell her I was crazy and I think I'm a time traveler?"

"I told her I was crazy about you."

"You didn't."

"You're right. I didn't. Sleep okay?"

"What do you think? I got up in the middle of the night, tripped in the kitchen, and ran out on the street to chase two ghosts from my future."

"Sounds about right."

"You think I'm crazy?"

"I think you're different, not crazy," she reassured him.

"You saw the lipstick on my hand."

"That proves nothing."

"It proves something to me," Paul insisted.

"Like what?"

"Like I wasn't dreaming. It was all real."

After eating a bowl of cereal, Paul told her he had to go "chant his rounds." He asked her if she wanted to come along with him to Tompkins Square Park. She agreed.

Along the journey, Paul had his little cloth bag with him, which he kept on his right hand.

Wayne Boyd

"What's in the bag?" Mary inquired.

He took out his *japa* beads and showed them to her. "They're small wooden beads, from India. There's one hundred eight of them on a string, and on each bead, we chant the Hare Krishna *mantra*. When you go all the way around, that's called one round. I chant sixteen rounds a day. Chanting produces a spiritual sound vibration that purifies the mind. When the mind is purified, you can gradually come to realize that we're not our bodies, but eternal servants of God, Krishna."

"Hypnotism!"

"It's not hypnotism. It's meditation."

"Where did you learn all that from?" she asked.

"The temple," he replied.

After a pause, she noted, "The temple. From the future."

"The twenty first century," he explained as he stopped and looked at her. The two of them stood right in the middle of the sidewalk. People had to walk around them.

"You still don't believe me, do you?"

"Do you believe it yourself?" she asked. She wanted to believe. She wanted to accept everything about him, but it was just too fantastic.

Paul was undaunted. He had *irrefutable* proof. "Here, let me show you something." He reached into his pocket and produced his wallet. Then he removed a crinkled dollar bill and handed it to her. "Take a look at this."

"What do you want me to look at? It's a dollar."

"Look closely. What's the date on it?" he persisted.

Mary looked at the bill carefully. Her eyebrows raised in surprise. "2015."

"Yes," Paul said. "In 2027 people rarely use paper money. They don't print it anymore and it's gradually going out of circulation."

"This is a counterfeit bill!" she proclaimed.

"Does it look counterfeit to you?"

"Well, that's the whole point of counterfeit money, isn't it? You're not supposed to be able to tell."

Paul looked at her. "Does it *look* real to you?"

"Oh yes!" Mary noted. "It looks like a real bill."

"Well, if it's such a good counterfeit," Paul pointed out, "then why would someone print a date like that on it? Why

Time Gods

wouldn't they print a date like 1963? Counterfeiters don't want to get caught. Take a good look at that bill, Mary. It's real."

She examined the note for a few seconds and handed the bill back to Paul. "This is very peculiar," she admitted.

"Tell me about it. Keep the dollar if you want," Paul told her. "Take it to a bank and ask them to look at it."

Mary stuffed the bill in her jean pocket. The bill with a date from the future was interesting.

Whether he was crazy or really from the future didn't matter. She had no compunction about her desire to sleep with him, though she kept it to herself for the time being. She was certainly no virgin and he wouldn't be her first man. If only he would loosen up and relax with her.

As they walked, they passed a newspaper stand. Paul stopped and glanced over the headlines of the New York Times:

> *Robertson, Smith Apparent Losers in Virginia Race. Talks Broken Off by Airline Union. Retired Pentagon Officer Is Seized as Spy for Soviet. Hanoi Alarms U.S. On Fate of Fliers. $17-Billion Voted for Defense Items.*

"They sure are spending a lot of money on Vietnam," Paul noted.

"Tell me about it," agreed Mary. "We should make love, not war." She poked him. "Hint hint."

Paul wondered if her hint was sexual in nature or perhaps it was some odd comment about his present situation. If it were the latter it didn't seem to make sense. If it were the former, well, women didn't just openly hint about that sort of thing to a celibate monk, did they? Why would she be interested in him anyway? She probably thought he was a paranoid schizophrenic. Even if she was attracted to him on a physical level, maybe he didn't want to know about it. Maybe he shouldn't know about that – if he wanted to remain a celibate monk that is. Best thing was to ignore her comment and see where it took him.

"I can tell you about the future. I can tell you who will be the President of the United States in what year, I can tell you about the end of the Vietnam War. I can even tell you about future wars, like the Gulf War. Did you know, for example, that in the future there won't be a USSR?"

"Say that again?"

"That grab your attention?" Paul observed. "You guys are all worried about the Soviets bombing you, and for that reason you've got this Cold War going on. That's what the Vietnam War is all about. However, the Soviet Union itself is going to break up."

"Oh, right. Sure!" Mary said sarcastically. "I suppose over the Vietnam War, right? Why does this sound like I'm hearing predictions from some old lady with a crystal ball? Breakup of the Soviet Union?

"Not over the Vietnam War, but that's just the way it's headed."

They talked on. Paul told Mary all sorts of things that he probably should have avoided. After all, he could be altering the future of history by revealing too much, and he'd have to be careful about that.

Mary listened, but didn't believe or understand all she heard. Whatever he was, he was definitely a good storyteller. Then he showed her his driver license from 2027.

"That's a weird looking driver license," Mary said.

"What's weird about it?"

"I mean, look it. Looks like some sort of circuit board on the back."

"That *is* a circuit board on the back," Paul explained. "We use it to start cars and buy stuff."

"That's a pretty sucky concept."

Finally they came around a corner, a few blocks from the park. As they approached, they saw hundreds of young people lying all over the grass. They were dressed in loose fitting clothes of bright colors, and most of the men also had long hair, many with beards. Some were smoking pot, others beating bongo drums, others staring at the sky. Some couples were passionately kissing on the grass while kids ran around unattended. One young woman sat topless on the grass, surrounded by young men. Crowds of people were scattered everywhere, and a few old people sat on benches by the walkway. The weather was hot and the day

Time Gods

was still young. A dog barked and chased a Frisbee thrown by a bearded man with no shirt.

Tompkins Square Park was a large square, about the size of a small city block, encircled by apartment buildings. A network of walkways weaved between small mounds of earth covered with grass and tall trees. A young man looked up from his spot on the grass to see the two of them walking by. "Hey, Mary!" he called out.

"Oh, Hello," Mary replied in a deadpan voice.

"Peace, man!" he said, making a V sign with his fingers.

Mary returned the hand gesture and smiled patronizingly. "Jerk," she said softly so only Paul could hear. The last person in the world she had wanted to see this morning was her paranoid ex-boyfriend.

Wayne Boyd

CHAPTER 11

Tompkins Square Park, Manhattan, New York, 1966

Peter Wilson took careful note that the man walking with Mary Pierce appeared to be wearing his clothes. "Bitch," he said to his friend as he passed him his joint. "Now the broad's passing my clothes out to her new boyfriend. I shouldn't have to take that."

"Yeah?" Pete's long-haired friend said as he exhaled a puff of marijuana. "What are you gonna do about it?"

Peter Wilson thought a moment. What *was* he going to do? Just roll over and play dead? Hell, no. She would pay. She and her friends. Especially that other dumb bitch, Wendy. Those two, Wendy and Mary, were like two peas in a pod. Smart asses, so *they* thought. Pete knew better. He was smarter than both of them together, and he would prove it.

"I have an idea," Pete replied thoughtfully. "Remember that hundred bucks I owe you?"

"Sure," his friend answered. "Where you gonna get it from?"

"Like I said. You wait. A couple of days, max. I'll have a hundred bucks in my hand with your name on it."

"I'll believe it when I see it. Thought you and Mary split up."

"I still know how to milk the cow," Peter Wilson intimated. "Hurt a friend, and the other friend is hurt too.

Time Gods

Can you imagine what Mary would feel like if I nailed her girlfriend?"

"You mean have sex with her best friend?"

"Exactly. I'll get money from her, too."

*   *   *

Paul and Mary were now walking into the park. "Who was that guy, the one you called a jerk?"

"Just my ex-boyfriend," Mary replied. "You're wearing the clothes he left behind when we split up. His name is Peter. Used to be a baseball player. Plays the guitar. Draft dodger. Professional jerk."

"Professional jerk?"

She laughed. "A long story, an abusive relationship."

"I used to play baseball, too," McPherson offered. "One of my favorite sports."

"No kidding? Apparently, Pete was good at that, and he's a good singer, too. Unfortunately, he's got a mean temper. I hope you're not like that."

"Only when I'm upset," he chuckled. She did not seem amused.

"Like I said: make love, not war. I mean, I think you're a nice guy. I wouldn't want you to turn out to be like him. He used to be paranoid of any guy he'd see me talking with."

"Like me?"

"Like you. Except now I have nothing holding me back. I can be with whomever I want to be."

"He still comes over to your place?"

"Sometimes," Mary explained, "but we're not together anymore. No way. The only reason he comes over these days is to sell weed to my friend and trip out on LSD."

Paul saw someone had stretched a large banner across the grass, and they were painting the last few letters on it. "Stop the war in Vietnam," it said in large, dripping, red letters resembling blood.

"You didn't get drafted?" Mary asked, seeing the sign as well.

"Drafted? You mean in the army?"

"Yes. You know, Vietnam? Peter dodged the draft, so he's kind of like wanted by the authorities. He keeps a low profile."

"I see," Paul said. "No. I wasn't drafted. The Vietnam War ended long before I was born. In my time period it's an all volunteer military."

The presence of many young people made the park alluring for aspiring religious leaders. A preacher for a local church was passing out pamphlets. A Jehovah Witness couple were sitting with a woman on the grass, talking with her. It made sense that a fledgling religion like the Hare Krishnas would come here and preach, too.

However, soon the hopes that had brought McPherson to the park began to fade. There was no sign of any Hare Krishnas. After a few minutes, the two of them sat down on a park bench and watched the pigeons.

"Sure you saw some people dressed like me here before?"

"Yeah," Mary confirmed. "Less than a week ago. But they didn't have shaved heads like yours. Most had long hair."

"Can you describe exactly what you saw?"

"Well, I was sitting over there, smoking some weed with my friends." She pointed at a grassy strip. "Then I saw there was a big group of people in a circle by that tree. They were singing and dancing. And there was this really old looking man sitting down in the middle of the crowd on some big Persian carpet. He had a shaved head."

"Did you get a good look at the old man?"

"Not really. I wasn't joining in or anything. I was just watching. He looked Indian. Not American Indian. I mean like from India. They had a really nice sound. Smooth. Sounded Eastern. The old man was beating on some old bongo drum and people stood around with their hands up in the air, singing a repetitive chant."

"How was the elderly man dressed?"

"Like you were dressed, yesterday," Mary replied. "In robes. And someone was passing out free food. My friend Wendy brought me some. Delicious stuff."

"*Prasadam*," McPherson suggested.

"Huh?"

"Vegetarian food, offered to Krishna," he explained. "They call it Prasadam."

"Yeah. It was vegetarian. I asked. I won't eat it unless it's vegetarian. Except eggs. I like eggs."

Time Gods

"So they *are* here," McPherson exclaimed.

"Where? I don't see anybody."

"No, I mean in the City. Maybe they're not in the park today, but they're here in New York."

Just then Paul and Mary looked up and saw Pete sauntering over towards them. "Oh oh," Mary gasped.

Paul swallowed hard.

*   *   *

Empire State Building. 1966

"Madness" settled himself into the hand tied, maroon leather recliner and glanced confidently around the lavish office. It was a comfortable seat, he noted, with brass nail head trim built over a solid oak frame. He resisted the temptation to push back and rest for awhile. Business was business, after all.

Madness was doing his job quite well. A spell here, an incantation there, a little magic power and poof. Making one insignificant monk question his own sanity was just part of his every day work. It's why they called him Madness. Though he worked for Kali, he was useful whenever the government needed to cover up a UFO, New Jersey Devil, Sasquatch, Boo Hag, and similar sightings. For the paranormal experience, he was *the* expert in disinformation. Of course, he went by other names and dress when dealing with the authorities, but the job was always the same. Make people believe what was real to be not real and what was not real to be real. Pretty much it worked everywhere. It worked in religion. It worked in science. It worked in the press. And now he sought to make it work in Paul McPherson.

The furnishings of the room revealed a predilection for elegance and comfort. The leather armchairs all had soft seats and backs made by Russian and French cabinetmakers. The walls were decorated with inlaid panels from seventeenth-century South Germany hand carved from maple and pear. An eighteenth century grandfather clock, with its movement, weights and ivory pendulum built into a

Wayne Boyd

Black Walnut and Cherry case, ticked softly in the corner to his left. The hardwood floor was decorated with an exquisite Persian Rug.

Across from Madness, on the other side of the massive, solid mahogany desk, sat a somewhat plump man with gray hair wearing an 18 karat Oyster-Perpetual Rolex watch. The broad window behind him, through which one could glimpse the top of the Chrysler Building and midtown Manhattan, was framed with thick, gold trim drapes.

The man behind the desk glanced at his watch, frowned deeply and then looked up at the so-called derelict that sat comfortably in the leather recliner. He was tired of doing the math, even though the figures were so incredible. His casinos in Atlantic City back in the twenty-first century were doing well, and they had brought the proceeds back with them. All was going so well it was maddening. "You've spoken with the man from TDC?" His voice was deep and deliberate.

Madness focused his mind. "Of course. We wouldn't have the prototype technology without him, and he promises to obey our commands – at least until the gathering at Milam Valley."

Raising his eyebrows, the chubby man behind the mahogany desk leaned forward. "Of that I'm sure. He knows better than that. Blood in, blood out. He knows the rules. A double agent is a double agent. Don't trust him, but don't let him have his way. He's our man, and our man exclusively." Pushing himself away from the desk, he stood and turned toward the spectacular view from his eighty-fifth floor window of the Empire State Building. "You know what to do if he tries to cop out." It was a rhetorical question.

Lobe turned around and looked at Madness. "What is the current situation with McPherson and the other two?"

"McPherson is questioning reality and is quite harmless. Just to be sure, our agent is watching both he and the girl. We don't know where the third one is at this juncture."

"Damn layer jumper," Lobe cursed as he sat back down behind his mahogany desk. "We can't let Odus get behind us on the continuum again. He can hurt us if he gets even one day behind us."

"He could change everything," Madness agreed.

Time Gods

"As he's already proven." Nothing scared Mr. Lobe more than the threat of non-existence. It bothered him to the core. He slowly raised his arm and stroked his chin with his hand thoughtfully. Layer jumping, changing events of the past and future, were complicated issues even for Greed Personified. All of that parallel universe branching stuff they talked about in physics. He had never liked physics. For him it was all about money. "On the other hand..."

"You like my idea, then?"

"The kidnapping idea *does* have merits," Lobe agreed. "Tell me, does our inside guy know about the rest of us?"

"Only about the King. He knows I answer to him."

"Keep it that way. He thinks he's clever. Double agent. I don't trust him anymore than he trusts us."

"Kidnapping it is, then. Any change to the general plan?"

"By the book, as they say. Ambulance and all, in case there are witnesses."

CHAPTER 12

Tompkins Square Park. 1966

"Drop dead," Mary Pierce snapped.

"Now, now," Pete replied as he came to a halt a few feet away. "You really do need to watch that temper of yours."

"Me? Temper?" Mary was outraged. "You have some nerve to talk about temper!"

"Hey, hey!" Pete chimed in. "Am I the one overreacting, or what? Who's the boyfriend this time? Someone I know?"

Paul stood up and stuck out his right hand. "Paul McPherson," he announced firmly. "By the way, I'm not her *boyfriend*."

Pete accepted the handshake and noted Paul's muscular build. Was he military, maybe? Head was recently shaved and the handshake was firm. "Nice to meet you McPherson," he said, looking him over curiously. "Pete Wilson. In the army?"

Paul shook his head. Good news for Wilson. Being a draft dodger had its disadvantages.

Mary interrupted. "Look, will you just go away, please? Paul and I were just sitting here peacefully talking."

"No need to get so jumpy, Mary," Wilson said, and then turning back to Paul, added: "Better watch out for *her* temper!"

Mary stood up in anger. "You!" She pointed at the other end of the park.

Time Gods

Pete Wilson ignored her and turned to Paul again. "Nice shirt and pants, there, McPherson. Where'd you get them?"

"Mary loaned them to me," Paul replied, embarrassed.

"Been spending the night together, have you? That bitch will sleep with anyone, you know."

"Pete, we are *not* sleeping together, but it's my life now. What I do with my life is none of your business!" Mary seethed angrily. "Now will you please leave us alone?"

"Look," McPherson tried to say calmly. "I don't know anything about this. I'm just a friend, and Mary loaned me these clothes. I really had no idea they were yours."

"Why would you need clothes while you were over at her apartment?" Wilson sneered sarcastically.

"That's none of your business," McPherson insisted, facing Wilson squarely. "I think the young lady wants you to leave and you should do what she wants. Now." He was calm and assertive.

Pete Wilson looked him over carefully and then smiled and took a step backward. "Okay," he said. "I was just trying to have a little friendly conversation."

McPherson inched up to Wilson, looking him in the eye, and for the first time, Wilson felt intimidated. McPherson looked like he could take care of business. "I've heard just about as much as I care to hear from you today. The lady told you to leave. Now I expect you to do what she says."

Swallowing some of his own medicine, Pete Wilson cowered. "Fine," he said, backing away slowly, feeling unnerved. "Have it your way."

Anyway, it didn't matter. Pete had a devious plan. He turned and walked away, smiling to himself. He was going to get his hundred dollars and have some fun at the same time.

Mary sat on the park bench, flustered. Paul sat next to her and watched Wilson walk away. She had angry tears in her eyes. "I'm so sorry. I didn't mean to drag you into the problems with my ex-boyfriend."

"No need to apologize. I understand. The guy is a stalker. Besides, I'm not afraid of him. I'm trained to take care of myself."

Mary placed her head on his shoulder as she wiped a tear from her eye. Paul was a different kind of person. He had respect for her and had defended her rights. She appreciated that, especially now.

Looking down at the top of Mary's head as she rested lightly on his shoulder, Paul noticed streaks of light blonde in her dark hair. She was pretty and smelled fresh, like a rose. Instinctively, he started to put his arm around her to console her, but then hesitated.

"So what do you want to do now?" she asked, breaking the spell. She lifted her head and looked deeply into his brown eyes. She was close – very close.

McPherson awkwardly placed his hovering arm over the back of the bench and cleared his throat. "Well I guess we'd better get out of here and head over to Second Avenue."

"What do you want to go to Second Avenue for?"

"Well, that's where the Hare Krishna Movement began," he explained, still feeling the piercing of Cupid's arrow. "Twenty-Six Second Avenue. Don't know exactly when it started, but if the devotees were here in the park, it's already going on." He stood up. "Let's go. We'll go down to Houston and head into the Bowery."

* * *

26 Second Avenue, New York. 1966

A simple storefront. Just to the right, a Mobil Gas Station. Gas was thirty cents a gallon.

Most people didn't even know it existed. Certainly, the taxi and truck drivers that zoomed along the one-way street, honking their horns incessantly, paid no attention.

The sign said "Matchless Gifts." The painting in the window was oil. Religious. A saint and some other people from hundreds of years ago. Lord Chaitanya. To the Hare Krishnas he was the most recent incarnation of Krishna who appeared in West Bengal in the fifteenth century.

A small piece of paper was taped in the window.

LECTURES IN BHAGAVAD-GITA
A.C. BHAKTIVEDANTA SWAMI

Time Gods

MONDAY, WEDNESDAY, AND FRIDAY
7:00 TO 9:00 P.M.

Immediately to the left was a coin laundry. One door served as the entrance to both storefronts.

How would he explain his nearly shaved head and tuft of hair when devotees hadn't started shaving their heads yet? He pulled Pete's baseball cap from his trouser pocket and fitted it neatly on his head, covering his pig-tail at the back, known as a *sikha*. With Mary at his side, he walked to the door. His hand hovered nervously above the handle.

"Well?" Mary asked. "What are you waiting for?"

Suddenly the door opened by itself. Paul found himself face to face with a large-bodied man with long, dark hair, a profuse beard, and black-framed eyeglasses. He appeared to be in his mid to late twenties. "Hare Krishna," the man beamed, smiling. "Welcome to the Swami's place! Won't you come in?"

They passed through an inner door into a hallway leading to a flight of stairs. The hallway also led to a courtyard that Paul managed to glimpse briefly. On their right was a door. They walked over and the man opened it.

"Swamiji's the talk of the Lower East Side," the man explained. "Please leave your shoes in the hallway here. We're not supposed to wear them inside."

"You want me to take off my shoes?" Mary asked. Paul already had slipped his flip-flops off to the side for that was second nature to him.

"Yes," the man replied. "If you don't mind. It's one of Swamiji's rules."

Paul and Mary passed barefoot through the door into a larger room. It was quite barren - no pictures, no furniture, no carpets. There wasn't even a single chair. There were only a few plain straw mats on the floor. A single bulb hung from the ceiling into the center of the room.

"This is the temple room," the man proudly announced. "That's Swami's mat over there. He lectures three times a week."

"We saw the sign. Not much here in the way of furniture," Mary observed.

"Nice" Paul said, looking around. He turned to his new guide. "Say, what's your name?"

"Howard."

"As in Howard *Wheeler*?" He knew that name well. According to Srila Prabhupada's biography, Howard Wheeler was one of Srila Prabhupada's early disciples. He later became Hayagriva dasa, the name given to him by Srila Prabhupada at the time of his initiation. To receive a spiritual name from a guru at the time of initiation was part of the Indian custom.

Howard was surprised. "Yes, that's right. Have we met?"

"I read your book." It was then that Paul realized his mistake, but it was difficult to take it back. Howard wrote a book after Prabhupada's death, years in the future. "I mean ah... well... I think I've seen you around town somewhere."

Howard eyed Paul cautiously. "I've never written a book."

"Oh, I'm sure you will in the future," Paul said. "In fact, I'd be willing to bet you'll call it *The Hare Krishna Explosion*."

"Not a bad title for a book. You got a name?"

"Paul. And this is my friend, Mary."

"Nice to meet you both," Howard said. He looked straight at Paul. "He's up in his room. I can take you there if you like."

"Who is?"

"Swamiji is."

"Oh," Mary interrupted. "I'm sure he must be busy. We wouldn't want to disturb him."

"No, it's no problem," Howard replied. "He likes to have people visit. I'll take you."

Turning and walking to the door, Howard led the couple back to their shoes. Soon they walked down the hallway, past the stairs, and through a doorway at the back into a small courtyard outside, surrounded by tenement buildings. The sun shone brightly.

At the back of the courtyard they climbed stairs to the second floor and knocked. After a brief moment, the door opened. A young man stared back. His head, like Paul's, was shaved. The man eyed McPherson up and down, and then looked at Mary.

"These are some nice people that would like to visit

Time Gods

Swamiji," Howard announced.

"Hmmm," the other man pondered. "Hold on a second." Turning towards the inside, he said, "Swamiji, there's a couple of young people out here that want to come in and see you. Is it alright?"

Mary heard a distinctively deep voice with a heavy Bengali accent reply, "Oh yes. Let them come."

The man turned back to the three of them and said, "Swamiji says you can come in."

"Thanks, Keith," Howard said as they filed past him into the room.

This must be Kirtanananda, Paul realized, one of Srila Prabhupada's earliest disciples. Although Keith was not yet initiated, soon he and Howard would become one of the earliest disciples.

In the beginning, Srila Prabhupada was known simply as "Swamiji" and had started his movement all alone. He'd migrating penniless to America from India at the age of seventy. It was only after months of personal hardship and struggle that he managed to establish the International Society for Krishna Consciousness in July of 1966 at the location they were now visiting.

Yet, Paul knew in the years to come, Srila Prabhupada would inspire the construction of large and impressive cultural hubs around the world as well as back in India. With the help of his followers, he would establish centers in London, New York, Los Angeles, Hong Kong, Sidney, Durban, and many other locations.

Srila Prabhupada's most significant contribution, however, would be his books. Highly respected for their authority, depth and clarity, they would soon be used as standard textbooks in numerous college courses. His writings would be translated into over seventy languages. Through these books millions of people around the world would learn about Krishna Consciousness, just as Paul had done.

As Mukunda Goswami would later write in his forward to Srila Prabhupada's yet unpublished *Science of Self Realization*: "Srila Prabhupada wasn't just another oriental scholar, *guru*, mystic, yoga teacher, or meditation instructor. He was the embodiment of a whole culture. He was first and foremost someone who truly cared, who completely sacrificed his own comfort to work for the good of others. He had no private life, but lived only for others. He taught spiritual science, philosophy, common sense, the arts, languages, the Vedic way of life – hygiene, nutrition, medicine, etiquette, family living, farming, social organization, schooling, economics – and many more things to many people. To me he was a master, a father, and my most dear friend."

So it was with all of this knowledge of the future that Paul entered Srila Prabhupada's apartment behind the courtyard at Twenty-Six Second Avenue.

The future was about to be changed forever.

Time Gods

PART TWO

He built a house in which the whole world could live.

Bhavananda dasa

CHAPTER 13

Paul and Mary discovered Swamiji sitting humbly on the floor behind a small suitcase that he was using for his desk. He was seventy – younger than McPherson had seen in photographs – and sat cross-legged in an erect, stately posture. His head was shaved and his face was the image of a saint who had spent most of his life absorbed in study. He wore reddish horn-rimmed glasses, which he removed as they came in the room, setting them down on the suitcase-desk.

They both felt reassuring warmth and compassion emanating from him. He had a twinkle in his bright and alert eyes. Srila Prabhupada was seeing *them*, the souls within, not the exterior veneer that most people viewed. Here was a man who had the ability to see your mind and help you grow spiritually. Here was a true *guru*.

The room's simple decor and Swamiji's humble appearance were, perhaps, the most astonishing and heart rendering of experiences. Tears welled in McPherson's eyes and he prostrated himself flat on the floor, arms extended outward.

Howard, Keith and Mary stood nearby, mouths agape. What was Paul doing? They had never seen anyone prostrate before Swamiji before. Srila Prabhupada, however, smiled and nodded his head approvingly.

When Paul picked himself up, Srila Prabhupada looked deeply at him. There was a moment of silence.

"Srila Prabhupada!" Then he stopped to correct himself. "I mean Swamiji," Paul continued. "I can understand that tens of thousands of people in the future will be chanting the names of Krishna because of you!" He had to stop when his voice became choked with emotion.

Swamiji nodded his head from side to side. He studied Paul carefully before speaking in a personal way, slow and deliberate. "Yes that is our real mission – to deliver the world by preaching Krishna's message to others. But an even higher realization, is to save oneself."

Paul and Mary nodded.

"Swamiji, this is Paul and Mary," Howard interjected, breaking the moment of silence.

Swamiji looked up at her and smiled disarmingly. He was both mysterious and friendly, she thought. A trustworthy man.

"You've read my books?"

"No. Sorry. Haven't had the chance."

"Keith, give them some books before they leave."

"My friend Paul tells me you're a vegetarian," Mary said. "I am also a vegetarian."

"How did she know about the vegetarian thing?" Howard whispered to Keith. "I haven't told them yet."

"I have no idea," Keith whispered in reply. "Where did they come from?"

"I don't know. They showed up at the door. Must have come back from India or something."

Swamiji cast an annoyed glance at the two whispering off on the side. "You are making noise," he complained. Embarrassed, Howard and Keith stopped.

Swamiji went on to explain to Mary that a Krishna Conscious person saw all beings were part and parcel of the Lord. That was why devotees were automatically vegetarian. They saw all creatures, even the animals, as their brothers and sisters.

How this preternatural meeting was able to take place was a mystery. Here was Paul from the future face to face with the founder of the Hare Krishna religion from the past. Yet, in the unfolding of this inexplicable event, Paul saw there was reason to hope. Swamiji was himself a spiritual seer – a man in touch with God and who understood the fabric of time and space. He would understand what was going on with Paul. He would be able to help Paul.

Unfortunately, Paul's question sounded confusing. "How does time travel work, exactly? How can I be here with you now? How can I return to my future?"

Swamiji replied without hesitation. The soul was eternal, he said, whereas all material things were temporary. Time passes by but the soul never changes. Paul's future could be reached by taking the necessary steps in the present.

The main thing Paul took away from the conversation was time only applied to the external, material body. Paul's problems otherwise paled into insignificance.

At length Paul and Mary thanked Swamiji for his time and Paul offered words of praise.

"Thank you very much. Please come again," Swamiji told them.

"Thank *you* very much," Paul returned.

"Yes," Swamiji added. "Take some *prasadam*."

Srila Prabhupada directed Keith to give the two guests some sweets and Keith quickly produced a jar of spongy, sticky brown colored balls in some kind of syrup.

When Mary bit into the delectable treat, her mouth exploded with incredible flavor. It was unmistakably the most delicious thing she had ever tasted.

*   *   *

Wendy Murphy's Apartment. 1966

Wendy looked around her room with fascination. Of particular interest was the floor – gentle waves, rising and falling. In motion. Had she a fishing pole, she might cast a line and see what she could catch. She couldn't walk without holding on to the wall, and she couldn't hold on to the wall because it seemed to bend.

The colors were astounding, too. They always seemed astounding. How they sparkled on the window! The room was vibrant!

Pete Wilson was there. Just arrived from Tompkins Square Park, he had said. She didn't feel guilty about that. If Mary wasn't going to date him anymore, she didn't see any reason why she couldn't. He was definitely good looking in her eyes and fun in bed. She just could not conceive yet how much of a scoundrel he really was.

There were four of them. Wendy counted them. Pete Wilson, John Hewitt, Kate Trissel and herself. But who was who was difficult to say at that point.

It was odd, because her mind was perfectly clear. In fact, she was thinking with more clarity than she had ever thought before. Reality was not escaping her. She knew, for example, about Kate's heroine addiction. Kate had stolen money from Mary once before, she remembered. Wendy was careful to keep an eye on her. But which eye? She seemed to have many.

She spun her head around, looking at the ceiling, and she collapsed backward into Kate's lap.

Lysergic acid diethylamide, or "acid" for short, later became one of several psychedelic drugs that were placed under the U.S. Controlled Substances Act in 1970, but here in 1966 it was still open territory. First synthesized in 1938, LSD had been used as a circulatory and respiratory stimulant. By the sixties, some psychiatric and medical professionals began using it themselves and sharing it with friends and associates. It usually came in the form of small paper squares or, on occasion, in tablets. Mary kept it in the form of sugar cubes in her drawer by the bed. Wendy kept sugar cubes in her pocket.

The ceiling was moving now. Dripping colors. How odd. Wendy had never seen the ceiling dripping colors before. "I think I'm tripping now. Call me when we land back on Planet Earth."

She didn't know that in her hallucinogenic stupor she was about to be robbed.

CHAPTER 14

Second Avenue, New York. 1966

Cars and trucks rumbled south along the one-way street. It was well over 90 degrees Fahrenheit and humid. A plump woman with orange hair sticking straight up, wearing a checkered jacket and a man with bright red hair wearing a black duster stood across the street.

"You sure that's the place?"

"That's always the place," the man with the red hair replied. "Each time we kill him he comes back from the future to this location."

"The whole problem is because of Odus," the woman said.

"Why don't we just go in there and kill everyone in the storefront?"

"You know the rules," admonished the woman. "Can't touch the religious people directly. Got to work through others."

"We already have plans to put agents in there."

"Right now we just need to concentrate on Mary," she said. "Lobe told us to go forward with the plan."

"You mean the brunette?"

She nodded, then turned to him abruptly. "You were supposed to take care of this. McPherson is supposed to be dead."

"I know. We did it, too. Stuffed him in a body sack tied to

a cinder block and dumped him in the East River. No one can get out of that."

"Doesn't look so dead to me."

"Someone is interfering. Odus, I suspect."

"Someone pulled him out of the body sack. Should have tried that lethal injection you gave the Senator in the Bahamas. Odus can't bring someone back from the dead."

"Anyone can bring someone back from the dead if they go back in time before they died and save them."

"Therein is the problem," she said.

"This McPherson is taking too much of our time. We have far more important things to deal with than *him*."

"We cannot ignore the prophesy. He was born on the exact moment."

"You don't believe in all that astrology stuff, do you?"

"How can you know what you know and not believe in astrology, too?"

"Look. I admit we had no idea the extent of the problems he could cause. He could disrupt our plans in Milam Valley. What should we do?"

"You know what to do," she said. "Take him to the King, then throw him in the vats."

*   *   *

Inside, Howard Wheeler invited Paul and Mary to stay for lunch at one o'clock. Since that was more than an hour away, they spent time downstairs chatting with someone named Roy, a devotee who was living under Swamiji's care.

After a few minutes, a mild-mannered gentleman entered the storefront. He was in his thirties, shabbily dressed, bearded and intellectual in appearance. "Hello, Wally," said Roy. "This is Paul and Mary."

They shook hands. "What do you do?" Wally asked them.

"I live near Washington Square," Mary said. "Antiwar protester. Musician. hippie, I guess."

"As were many of us," Wally smiled, then turned toward Paul.

"I'm a... well lately I'm kind of a traveler of sorts," McPherson offered. "I explore history, sort of."

"Oh, that's great! You're a historian!"

"More like a *futurian*," Mary added.

"A what?"

"Yes, I'm a bit of an expert on knowing about the future from things that happened in the past."

"*Futurian.* Sounds fascinating," Wally said. "Never heard that term before."

Paul knew about Wally from Srila Prabhupada's biography. "For example, bet you're into Alan Watts and Hermann Hesse," he declared.

"Wow," Wally said. "Are you psychic, or what?"

"No," Paul said with a knowing smile. "I just had a hunch."

"Well, you're pretty sharp. That was amazing. You have me figured out precisely. Say, is that person across the street connected with you?"

"No, we came alone," Mary replied.

"What person?"

"The guy across the street."

The conversation shifted to other topics. Soon another young man entered the storefront.

"Hare Krishna everyone!" he announced.

"Hare Krishna, Michael," Howard replied. "Paul, Mary, this is Michael."

Paul immediately recognized Michael Grant, later to become Mukunda Goswami. "Does anyone know who that man is across the street? He's just staring at the storefront as if he wants to come in."

Paul was concerned. "What does he look like?"

"Oh, I don't know," Michael said. "Really bright-red hair. Tall. Mean face. Looks upset."

Paul quickly jumped up and ran to the window. Looking across the street he saw the man. Swallowing nervously, he gasped. "Mary, that's one of the guys!"

"What guys?" she asked, coming over to the window to look. "You mean the man that you saw last night?"

"No, one of the other guys that put me in handcuffs and shoved me in the elevator. I'm sure of it. My God! How did *he* get here?" Paul nervously turned to face the others in the storefront. "Everyone sees that guy over there, right?"

They looked out the window. Michael answered. "Yeah. Big tall guy with red hair. Why?"

By now, Mary felt the anxiety Paul was experiencing. "You said you wanted to talk with that man last night," she said, trying to reassure him. "Why don't you speak with this guy? Invite him in. That'll throw him off balance."

* * *

Philosophical concepts boggled Von Krod as he brushed a curl of red hair from his forehead, surveying the storefront. He'd heard all the bullshit when he was assisting 'the Professor' back in Princeton in the year 2075. Changing the past creates alternate futures, which in turn spawns unscheduled earthquakes along existing fault lines. That's what caused the 1737, 1783, 1884, and 1985 New York City tremors, and why Princeton University scientists later installed a time travel limiting circuit, LTTA, preventing reverse time travel further than a hundred and fifty years. Lord knows what would happen if they ever attempted time travel in Los Angeles.

To hell with earthquakes, however. Von Krod knew he would rejoice hearing Paul McPherson scream when his skin melted in the vats of molten gold. No more body sacks. No more tossing in the East River. This time he would ensure McPherson was so dead that even Odus wouldn't be able to save him.

Paul stepped from the storefront and looked straight across the street in his direction. The man dropped his cigarette and crushed it with his foot. He looked toward Paul and grinned. Their eyes met and fixed. There was recognition. Both of them were aware they had traveled through time. Only one of them knew how.

Second Avenue was a one-way, 5-lane road with an additional lane for bicycles. It was impossible to cross at this time of day except at an intersection. The nearest crosswalk was only fifty feet south, past the gas station. As Paul walked to the intersection, he watched Von Krod carefully.

Von Krod, understood McPherson's intention, casually turned and began to walk north, away from Paul. The bait had been dangled and he would now lure McPherson away from the crowded streets.

The light changed and the traffic ground to a halt. A red 1963 Ford Thunderbird Hardtop, waiting on East First, rambled across Second Avenue, but offered no obstruction. Paul bolted to the other side of the street, turned right and jogged north.

Von Krod also started running. Looking back to make sure Paul was following, he crashed into a pedestrian wearing a long trench coat, brimmed hat and thick, black, glasses, sending the brimmed hat flying off to the sidewalk.

"Excuse me," apologized the man in the trench coat. Von Krod angrily pushed him out of the way and continued to run up Second Avenue.

Reaching over and calmly collecting his hat off the sidewalk, the pedestrian dusted the brim. He smiled to himself as he watched the red-haired man run north. Then he looked toward McPherson, who was catching up from the south.

Scooting around the man with the hat, Paul continued chasing for a few seconds until the strap on his right shoe snapped loose, sending the cheap flip-flop spinning into the air, finally landing in the gutter.

With one foot bare, Paul was forced to stop and watch helplessly as the red-haired man rounded the corner to the left at the intersection of East Second Street and Second Avenue, and lose himself in the sea of pedestrians and traffic that was New York City.

McPherson collected his broken flip-flop from the gutter. *I'll need a new pair*, he noted. They were cheap. No problem.

Turning around to look south, he noted the man with the brimmed hat and trench coat was entering the arched doorway of Urge's Produce. He'd seen that trench coat before, but could not remember when.

Paul walked barefoot back to the Temple, broken shoe in hand.

CHAPTER 15

Wednesday, July 13, 1966. 7:00 PM

A few minutes before seven in the evening a dozen people gathered in the storefront of 26 Second Avenue, including Paul and Mary. It was hot. The back windows and front door of the storefront were wide open. Young men dressed in denims and sport shirts with broad, dull stripes were sitting on the floor. A pile of sneakers was at the front door.

When the side door opened and Swamiji walked in, Mary immediately noticed he wasn't wearing a shirt and the saffron cloth that draped his torso exposed parts of his bare chest and arms. The elderly guru's complexion was smooth and golden brown. His head was shaved and his ears had long lobes.

Tilting his head back, he stepped out of his white shoes, and sat down on his thin mat. Facing his congregation, he indicated they could all be seated, but there were no seats – only the floor. Mary sat down on the floor next to Paul, not far from the front. Bearded Howard sat just behind them. Roy sat just in front. Keith, Michael and Carl were also there, along with others from the local hippie scene. Being a bit of a hippie herself, Mary felt comfortable in their company.

Swamiji passed several pairs of brass cymbals to Roy who passed them out to the congregation. He handed a pair to Mary who looked at them before passing them on to Paul.

Swamiji then briefly demonstrated the rhythm – *one, two, three*. Then he began playing, making a startling, ringing sound with the hand cymbals as he sang a repetitive mantra. "*Hare Krishna, Hare Krishna, Krishna Krishna, Hare Hare, Hare Rama, Hare Rama, Rama Rama, Hare Hare.*" After singing once through, Swamiji expected the audience to respond. "Chant," he instructed. Mary saw that Paul already seemed to know what to do and gradually the others caught on, too. After a few minutes, most were singing together. Mary clapped her hands but remained silent.

She saw the audience easily adapted to the singing. Many were just like her and had at one time or other launched on a psychedelic journey in search of the horizons of expanded consciousness through chemical stimulation. Whatever distant states of consciousness they had or had not reached, these young explorers always seemed to return to the real world unfulfilled. Now, at last, they gathered together here, exploring new depths while singing the Hare Krishna *mantra*.

After some time, Swamiji stopped and put away his hand symbols. Although the chanting had swept away the material world, the Lower East Side rushed in again. Children outside began to chatter and laugh. Cars and trucks on the busy street made their rumbling heard again. Mary was startled to hear an angry voice from a nearby apartment demanding quiet.

Half an hour had elapsed.

Children were on summer vacation, and they stayed out on the street until well past dark. A big dog was barking nearby and the traffic created constant noise pollution. Yet, despite the confusion of children, traffic and dogs, Swamiji insisted that the door should remain open so that others may come in.

When Swamiji began to lecture, some of the group felt impatient and rudely rose upon hearing the first words, put on their shoes at the front door, and left.

Amidst shrieking children outside, Mary overheard a man shouting from his window in the distance: "Get outta here! Get outta here!"

"Ask them not to make noise," Swamiji said, looking

around the room.

Mary saw no one responded to Swamiji's request until Paul jumped to his feet to look out the window.

On the sidewalk Paul saw a man was coming to chase the children away. "A man is chasing the children away now," he explained, pleased to have the opportunity to render direct service to Srila Prabhupada, who had passed away long before Paul's birth.

Paul sat down again and Mary had to move a little to make room for him. Howard shifted a little back to make more room too. Mary's knees hurt and she struggled to pull her skirt lower.

Swamiji continued his lecture. He used the noise of the traffic to give an example. "When a car briefly comes into our vision on Second Avenue," he said, "we certainly don't think that it had no existence before we saw it. Nor does it cease to exist once it has passed from view." Swamiji used this example to explain that when Krishna, who Swamiji said was God, goes from this planet to another, it doesn't mean he no longer exists. Krishna has only left our sight. Krishna and his incarnations constantly appear and disappear on innumerable planets throughout the innumerable universes of the material creation. Around the time of King Pariksit, five thousand years, ago he walked on planet earth.

Mary wondered how anyone could know what happened five thousand years ago.

The traffic continued to rumble incessantly, competing with every word the Swami uttered. Mary strained to hear. "So it doesn't matter what a person was doing before, what sinful activities. A person may not be perfect at first, but if he's engaged in service, then he will be purified."

Just at that moment, a Bowery derelict entered the storefront, whistling and shouting. The audience remained seated, not knowing what to make of it. "How are ya?" he drunkenly called out to Srila Prabhupada. "I'll be right back. I brought another thing."

The audience was startled. Everyone turned around to glare at the drunkard.

"Don't disturb," Srila Prabhupada said. "Sit down. We're talking seriously."

"I'll put it up there," the drunken man said, pointing at a shelf. "In a church? All right. I'll be right back."

The man was white-haired, with a short, grizzly beard and patched clothing. His odor reeked through the temple. Mary waved her hand in front of her face to blow away the smell, while Paul held his nose. But as quickly as he appeared, he disappeared out the door and was gone.

Srila Prabhupada chuckled softly and returned immediately to his lecture, but after five minutes the old derelict returned. "How are ya?" He was carrying something. He maneuvered his way through the group, straight to the back of the storefront, where Swamiji was sitting. He opened the toilet room door, put down two rolls of bathroom tissue and then closed the door. Then he turned to the sink, sat some paper towels on top of it and put two more rolls of bathroom tissue paper and some more paper towels under the sink. Then he stood straight and turned toward Srila Prabhupada and the audience.

"What is this?" Srila Prabhupada asked the man.

But the man was silent now and looked at the audience. When his eyes fell upon Paul his face lit up. "Hey! I know you!"

Mary turned to look at Paul, who had a puzzled expression.

"In Queens," the drunkard continued. "Saved your life earlier today from the men with the guns and helicopter! Glad to see you got out alright." The man then smiled, looked up at Swamiji and waved, and began to move toward the front door while Paul wondered why the man seemed to have mistaken him for someone else.

Srila Prabhupada began to laugh, thanking his visitor. "Thank you," Srila Prabhupada said. "Thank you very much." Then the man exited the door and was gone. "Just see," Swamiji told his audience. "It's a natural tendency to give some service. That man was not in order, but he thought that, 'Here is something. Let me give some service.' It comes automatically. This is natural."

Mary looked at Paul in total amazement. This was *really* far out. First the chanting with the brass cymbals, the Swami looking like Buddha and now this stuff with the bum. Mary could not believe that the Swami stayed cool throughout the whole episode. Really cool, just sitting on the floor unafraid of anything, talking philosophy about the soul.

After almost an hour, the dog was still barking and the kids were still squealing. Swamiji answered some questions and then started another *kirtan* – more music.

At the end, a young man brought Swamiji an apple, a small wooden bowl, and a knife. As most of the audience sat still and watched, Swamiji cut the apple in half, then in fourths, then in eighths, until there were many pieces. He took one himself and asked one of the boys to pass around the bowl.

Mary munched silently on her little piece of apple. After a short time, Swamiji stood up, slipped into his shoes, and exited through the side door. Paul McPherson was the only one in the room who bowed his head to the Swami. That was something they hadn't learned yet. When he sat up, he found people looking at him curiously.

As people drifted from the storefront, Paul realized again his predicament. These people were fortunate because some of them would become leaders of the Hare Krishna religion in the future, but if McPherson were to tell anyone about who he was and where he came from, they'd never believe him. Paul McPherson was a homeless man from the future. Mary had been kind but he dared not impose on her further. Yet, the prospect of sleeping on the streets frightened him.

Mary, on the other hand, worried Paul might leave her, and she'd grown to like him a lot. Why couldn't he just stay with her? These were the sixties, after all. No one would raise an eyebrow if she was sleeping with a man in her apartment here in Manhattan. It certainly hadn't been the first time. So as the last stragglers left the storefront, she spoke to him quietly. "Where are you going to stay tonight?"

Paul looked at her, but didn't know how to respond. He had two options and both scared him. Sleep in the park or sleep in an apartment with an attractive woman while he tried to keep his vow of celibacy.

"Stay at my place as long as you like," she said softly with a touch of compassion. There was something in her eyes he could not quite identify. A pleading, a yearning of desire, a glimmer of affection. He dared not ask. He dared not acknowledge his own feeling of attraction to her. He swallowed nervously and nodded with a guilty conscience. There was no other option. This was his destiny.

They left the storefront side by side, discussing the events at the storefront.

"Odd thing that drunkard said about seeing you in Queens," Mary observed.

"Yeah," Paul agreed. "Don't know what he was talking about. Never seen him before."

CHAPTER 16

Paul had managed to temporarily patch his flip flops, but they wouldn't last long. On Lafeyette Street they entered a late night store that sold BRS sneakers. Two years later the company would change its name to Nike.

Walking on West 4th Street in his new sneakers purchased by Mary, Paul had a disturbing series of thoughts. Perhaps the more things he acquired, either through Mary or through others, the more he interfered with future events. Perhaps the very sneakers he wore meant he was cementing his presence in the past and altering the future beyond recognition. Maybe even wearing the sneakers she had bought would act like a hook and prevent his being able to travel to the future. Perhaps this suggested his relationship with Mary was wrong. Terribly wrong.

What would happen, for example, if he were to break his vows tonight? Suppose they slept together and she became pregnant? A baby born of parents from two different time lines might somehow crack the very fabric of the universal order. A baby like that could not exist in either world.

Maybe he should have opted to sleep on the street.

"You sure are quiet tonight," Mary said after awhile.

"Huh? Oh. Sorry. I was just thinking. Didn't mean to be such a bad conversationalist."

Once home at the Dorchester Apartment Building, Mary expressed her excitement over the evening's events. "I'd like to write a song about Swamiji," she said. "Didn't you say you play the guitar?"

"I used to play pretty well."

"Practice makes perfect. We could make a living doing that, you know."

"I'm not interested in making a living."

"Everybody's got to make a living. We can't live off my father's money for ever, you know."

Paul looked at her cautiously. "We?"

"Well, you know. If we were just to stay here, together. You and me. We'd need to make a living somehow!"

"Look, I'm just a crazy monk trying to get back to the future. As far as you're concerned, I'm totally nuts, thinking I'm a time traveler."

"You had a dollar bill from the future. I have it in my pocket."

"So you're saying you believe me?"

"I'm saying we could play some music. Right now we could write a song about the old Swami in the storefront."

"I'm not feeling very musically inclined right now."

Shaking her head, Mary grabbed the guitar leaning in the corner and handed it to Paul.

"I don't know any good songs," he admitted. "I haven't played for almost *three years.*"

She folded her arms over her chest and frowned before nodding at the guitar again. "Play."

He sat down heavily by the kitchen table. What could he possibly play that would not be peculiar to this pretty young lady? He thought about history. Who was around this century making music that Paul was familiar with? Were the Beatles or Grateful Dead playing songs during this time period? Yes, he thought. Of course they were.

It took him a minute to pick up the tune he was searching for – one originally recorded during the Beggars Banquet in 1968, but kept off the album and later released as a single, so he knew that Mary would be unfamiliar with it. It was the song he had dreamed about last night, still in his head tonight.

> *I was born in a cross-fire hurricane*
> *And I howled at my ma in the driving rain,*
> *But it's all right now, in fact, it's a gas!*

*But it's all right. I'm Jumpin' Jack Flash,
It's a Gas! Gas! Gas!*

Paul played fairly well, though at times he sang notably off key. Singing wasn't his strong point. Regardless, Mary was impressed and his efforts made her smile. She applauded at the conclusion and he wondered if it was because she liked it, or she was glad the torture was over.

"Did you write that yourself?"

"No," Paul said. "That's Jumping Jack Flash by Mick Jagger."

"Really? The Rolling Stones? I never heard that one before."

"That's because the song will come out a couple of years from now."

Mary could see where the conversation was going. "And I suppose the Rolling Stones will still be together in your future?"

"I'm from sixty-one years in the future. Mick Jagger died years ago, just like Michael Jackson."

"Little Michael from the Jackson 5?"

"He grew up but died young. Jagger lived much longer. But the Rolling Stones will exist for decades in your future. It's the Beatles that will split up."

Mary had been standing, but now she dropped into a chair. "The Beatles split up? When? Are you sure?"

"Yes. And later John Lennon will be assassinated."

"What?"

A loud knocking on the door interrupted them. Paul and Mary glanced at one another. "Are you expecting someone?"

"No," she replied.

She walked to the door and looked through the peephole. "There's a man outside," she whispered.

"What does he look like?"

"White guy. Got on some kind of trench coat."

"Red hair?"

"No," she reassured him. "Dark. Under a brimmed hat."

Mary unbolted the door and opened it. A pleasant-looking gentleman wearing glasses stood outside. He politely removed his hat when he began to speak. He appeared to be in his late forties.

"Excuse me, Miss," he said, in a quiet yet authoritative way. "I'm looking for a gentleman who goes by the name of Paul McPherson."

CHAPTER 17

"I'm Paul McPherson. Have we met somewhere before? You look vaguely familiar."

The man's broad forehead glistened with light beads of sweat in the humid evening air. His aquiline nose supported a pair of thick, black plastic glasses that were crowned by his dark, bushy eyebrows. His eyes were blue. He had a pale complexion, with a gentle but firm countenance. A small aqua colored triangular logo was pinned to the lapel of the trench coat as it dangled from his arm.

"I don't believe we've met in person," the man replied evasively.

Mary stepped aside and made a gesture with her hand, welcoming the stranger. The man nodded politely and stepped inside. She closed and bolted the door before turning her attention back to her guest. "And who might you be?" she inquired.

He turned toward Mary. "Special Agent Sidney E. Dale." He opened and flashed an FBI ID briefly before stuffing it away in his upper shirt pocket. He looked over at Mary rather civilly. "And you must be?"

"Mary Pierce," she replied.

"Glad to meet you," Dale said politely. He extended his hand, but she did not shake it.

"What can we do for you?" she asked, arms folded.

He awkwardly lowered his hand and nodded toward Paul.

"Well step right in and have a seat." She gestured toward

the table.

"Thank you," he said politely.

Mary took his coat and hat and placed them in the closet while Dale settled himself into a chair at the kitchen table.

"Can I get you some coffee?" she asked when she returned.

Dale looked thoughtful. "Actually, I wouldn't mind something a bit stronger if it's not too much trouble."

"How about bourbon? Got some of that."

"Perfect," Mr. Dale replied. "Neat. On the rocks."

"Drinking on duty?" Paul sneered.

Mary headed for the kitchen cabinets while Special Agent Dale looked deeply at McPherson. "I'm not on official duty," he said. "Think of this more as a social visit. I have three simple questions that I'd like to ask and then I'll be on my way."

Dale sat quietly for a moment, studying Paul's hazel colored eyes. Paul returned the stare. Soon, Mary showed up at the table with a glass and ice, a cork screw and the unopened bottle of bourbon that she had received from someone named Professor Cali. She placed them on the table and proceeded to work on removing the cork.

"Well, go ahead," Paul said.

"Mr. McPherson, have you, by any chance, found or are you in possession of a small hand-held device? It's about 2 inches by 4 inches, and perhaps a half inch thick, with buttons, of course, and a small aerial, micro-dish antenna. Very dangerous device."

"What's a micro-dish antenna?"

"A small parabolic antenna."

The cork popped and Dale politely took the bottle from Mary's hand. "Allow me," he smiled at her. Mr. Dale poured his own drink over the ice in the glass while observing Paul and Mary.

"No, I'm sorry Mr. Dale," Paul apologized. "I have no idea about any device like that."

There was a moment of silence as Dale sipped his drink. Paul took the opportunity to ask a question of his own. "So how did you come to know my name?"

"The shopkeeper in Brooklyn on Nevins Street," Dale explained. "I believe you were recently in Brooklyn."

"Yes, that's right," Paul nodded. "I went to Brooklyn after I discharged from the hospital. I bought a newspaper on Nevins Street."

Dale pulled a dollar bill out of his shirt pocket and slid it forward on the table. "Which brings us to my second of three questions. Is this the dollar you used to purchase that newspaper?"

Paul looked puzzled. "How would I know?"

"Perhaps you'd like to look at it more closely."

"Let me see that," Mary said, snatching up the dollar. She looked at the lower right corner carefully. "Printed in the year 2015," she exclaimed. She handed the bill to Paul.

"Old fashioned paper money," Paul mumbled as he looked it over. "They don't even print the stuff anymore."

"Mr. McPherson, you *are* aware that this dollar bill has a date from the future, are you not?"

"Depends on your perspective," Paul quipped.

He plucked the bill from Paul's hands and stuffed it in his shirt pocket. "The bill is counterfeit," Dale said sternly. "For all intents and purposes it's genuine except for the date. Where did you get it?"

"Shakuntala," Paul explained, "my Temple President. To purchase parts for the air conditioner. She was trying to get rid of the bills because where I'm from its hard to get people to take paper money anymore. We use credit."

Dale leaned in to the table. "Anyone who looks at this dollar carefully will notice the date."

"I never thought about it," Paul admitted.

Agent Dale sat back and let his arm dangle over the back of the chair. "Alright. So we've covered the electronic device you say you haven't seen, and the counterfeit money you say you received from someone else. Now let me ask the third question. Have you seen any little people? You know, what people commonly call midgets."

Paul frowned. He recalled that a little man *had* entered his hospital room, but that had been nearly a week ago. "No, don't believe I've seen a little person recently. Do you think a little person had something to do with this counterfeit money?"

Agent Dale nodded his head slowly, keeping his eyes pinned on Paul. Paul shifted nervously. After a long pause

Dale rubbed his chin with the index finger and thumb of his right hand and smiled. "Well, alright then. No electronic device, counterfeit money which I'm sure you didn't make yourself, and no sign of any little people. I guess that about sums up my three questions."

"Will that be all, Agent Dale?" Mary inquired.

"Yes, I think so," Dale agreed as he downed the rest of his drink and pushed himself away from the table. He stood up when Mary returned quickly with his hat and coat.

"Those were odd questions you asked," Paul said. "Except about the money. I can understand that one."

"It's an odd world," Dale added, looking at Paul. "We follow all sorts of leads. Let me give you my card in case anything else comes up or if you happen to find any more of that 'funny money'. Alright?"

Dale reached into an upper pocket of his trench coat looking for a card. Meanwhile Paul managed to get a closer view of the peculiar aqua colored, triangular insignia attached to Dale's lapel. It had the letters "TDC" superimposed on it.

Dale produced a small business card and handed it over.

"Thanks," Paul said in a deadpan tone.

Dale discretely touched his belt buckle. There was a quiet clicking sound. A high resolution digital photograph had been secretly recorded. Later he would put it in the computer for processing by facial recognition software, technology not available in 1966. "Yes," Dale said. "Well, sorry to have taken up so much of your time. Good evening."

Sidney E. Dale moved toward Mary's door. Unlatching the bolts, he pried the door open and waved before stepping into the hallway.

When the door shut, Mary looked at Paul. "Amazing!" she said. "Where did you get those bills?"

"Told you already," he insisted. "From the future. What I wonder about is that electronic device and the little people he was asking about."

Mary strained to hear noises outside her door. "Shush! I hear someone talking," she said.

Paul listened. "Yes – in the hallway. Someone is out there."

"I'll take a look." She approached the peephole and peered through the eyepiece. After a few seconds the blood rushed from her face and she backed away. "Oh my God!" she exclaimed.

"What's the matter? What did you see?"

Mary looked confused. She swallowed deliberately and took a deep breath. "I saw *you*," she said. "Outside, talking to that FBI guy in the hallway."

"That's ridiculous. Let me see."

Paul looked through the peephole and saw Dale and someone dressed in black with a baseball cap turning to go down the stairway.

"I see Mr. Dale with someone," Paul said. "I admit that he looks like me. But it's not me." He turned to face Mary. "How could it be? I'm here!"

"You don't have a twin brother, do you?"

"No, of course not," Paul assured her.

Mary glared at him. She *knew* what she had seen. "Did you see his face? It was *your* face!"

CHAPTER 18

Wendy Murphy's Apartment. July 14, 1966. 7:22 AM

Wendy came out of the bathroom wearing only a towel wrapped around her head. She pulled on some panties and wiggled into jeans, noticing a lump in her pocket. "Well, whadaya know," she murmured to herself. The LSD laced sugar cubes were still where she'd left them. Glancing through the open bedroom door, she saw Pete still sprawled out, naked and asleep.

Now that her LSD trip was over she discovered a hundred dollars missing from her drawer. She'd been robbed and knew who did it.

* * *

Washington Square Park. July 14, 1966. 7:30 AM

Paul sat quietly enjoying the early morning sun, externally chanting on his beads as pigeons cooed around him, but internally thinking about Mary.

What a predicament. A man from 2027 falling in love with a woman from 1966. If he continued to live here in the past, the time would come when he would see his father born two years from now and himself born in 2001. Then there would be two of him, an older self and a younger self. Would the world blow up? What if he stayed here, got Mary pregnant, and a child was born? His offspring would be born thirty-five years before his own birth! This was all pretty confusing, he figured. Time travel wasn't supposed to be this complicated.

Paul wandered over to a newsstand on the street corner and looked at the headlines on the New York Times.

> *Patients Shifted as Strikes Loom at Five*
> *Hospitals. Airlines Parleys under Way Again;*
> *Progress noted. U.S. Foils Czech Bugging Plot.*
> *FBI Had Sanction in Eavesdropping. Senator*
> *Perry Dies of Heart Attack in Bahamas.*

It was already a hot, humid day. Paul wiped his forehead and decided to head over to Twenty-Six Second Avenue without Mary. He needed answers. Time travel was his problem, not hers.

Along the way two youths burst into laughter when they saw his nearly shaved head and pig tail at the back. Paul didn't care. None of these people had a clue what he was going through.

Fifty feet behind, a very short man struggled to keep the pace. The little person had to know where Paul was going.

After a long walk through the Lower East Side, Paul eventually came to Twenty-Six Second Avenue. Fitting the baseball cap over his head, he entered the storefront.

Several devotees, including Roy and Keith, were talking to each other inside. Paul told them he would like to see Swamiji again.

"Sure," Keith said. "Come with us."

* * *

The little person stopped on the other side of Second Avenue. He removed a small electronic device from his pocket and adjusted the micro dish antenna. Tucking it back under his belt, he passed through the arched doorway of Urge's Produce and hid inside.

* * *

Inside Swamiji's room, Prabhupada was talking to a couple of young musicians about philosophy. Paul discreetly sat behind them and listened.

"What about other processes?" one young man asked Srila Prabhupada. "Everyone says his or her way is the best. Do you say that as well?"

"No," he replied. "There are different processes, but at the present moment people are very, very fallen. This is called the age of Kali. People in this age are most fallen." Srila Prabhupada shook his head compassionately. "The so-called material advancement is not the solution because God is eternal, we are eternal, and in the material condition we are changing our body. On account of our ignorance we are thinking 'I am this body', but I am not this body. I am that spark, spirit, part and parcel of God."

Srila Prabhupada, or Swamiji as they knew him, said the present day and age was called the age of Kali, or the age of quarrel and hypocrisy. "You know about Kali? He was banned by the Emperor Pariksit." The only way to counter the influence of the age of Kali was to give up illicit sex life, intoxication, meat-eating and gambling and to chant Hare Krishna. That would make everything pure and drive out the influence of Kali. "That is the only remedy," he told them.

Paul asked about the existence of parallel universes. Swamiji said there were innumerable parallel universes. Krishna and His associates continually appeared in every universe.

"Not many people can understand that," Paul observed.

Prabhupada agreed with him. "This cannot be understood while one is still in the conditioned state."

Srila Prabhupada, Paul and the others spoke on deep philosophical issues for about twenty minutes. Being with Srila Prabhupada was a timeless experience for Paul and nothing else seemed to matter while listening to him carefully.

He didn't know about the spies waiting for him outside the storefront.

* * *

Wayne Boyd

Ujjaini Express Train, Northern India, 1966

The Prime Minister of India wore a silk sari this early evening. She brushed the gray in her otherwise dark hair with her finger. She was the most powerful political figure in Southwestern Asia and the leader of the largest democracy in the world.

Though the day had been long, soon she would be back in New Delhi making preparations for the upcoming summit at the end of the month. She glanced at her watch. It was 6:45 PM and the sun was still shining.

Indira looked out at the lush farmlands passing her train window. A man walked barefoot in the field behind an oxen pulling a simple plowshare. Impoverished women had spread a cloth on the ground, piled kernel wheat upon it, and were beating the wheat with sticks. A road passed by, barriers down for Indira Gandhi's train, a few cars and trucks waiting to cross. A dead buffalo lay on the ground as vultures stood looking at the carcass. There were few trees. The land was mostly flat, farmland extending to the horizon.

Economic growth in India was inhibited because protectionist policies after World War II disallowed significant foreign investment. These policies, unfortunately, were the main cause of poverty, as the population was exploding far faster than the economy, which in turn fueled bitterness within the CPI, or Communist Party of India.

Indira knew this, and she played the hands of both the USSR and the Americans. Now she hoped she would get the upper hand in this first of many surprise political moves.

The sky was blue, but it had flooded in New Delhi earlier that day. Monsoon season was not entirely over. Because of the rain storms everything was green and wild flowers grew along the train tracks.

"So we've seen the tunnel entrance in Tharali. Looks very well done, and preparations are in place. Have they all agreed to come?" she inquired in perfect English.

"Some of the leaders are still not committed," an Indian man in a gray, silk suit and tie replied.

"It's extraordinary what he's done in the mountains.

Does that train take a long time to get through to the valley?"

"It's a high speed ride, Indira. Very modern. A wide body train, fully equipped. A pity we couldn't ride into the valley until all the arrangements are complete."

"It's no matter," Indira said. "Security will be very tight if the American President attends. I hear de Gaulle is also planning to attend."

"The last hold out, I'm afraid. France is not definite."

"He will come. I know him."

The woman looked away again toward the setting sun and noticed the dark clouds forming on the horizon. It would be night soon, she realized.

It had been a long, hard day, but she had to see it for herself – such an extraordinary tunnel in the mountains, north of Rishikesh. Now Professor Cali would reveal all to everyone who attended. She hoped Pakistan would stay away. She did not like Pakistan. One day she would wage war with Pakistan, she thought.

Sitting near were several top ministers in her government. She looked toward them, and they nodded and smiled. Shallow smiles. Did she trust any of them?

"This will be a stunning move to give international recognition to both the Indian government and yourself," one of her aides added.

A slight smile crossed her lips as she thought of her fortune. She had been elected India's first female Prime Minister only last January. She had the perfect last name: Gandhi. There was no blood relation to Mahatma Gandhi. No sir. But having the name Gandhi certainly helped her win the election among India's ignorant masses and fractured political structure. The Indian Congress was split in two factions, the socialists led by Gandhi, and the conservatives led by Morarji Desai. These fractures bothered her, and to unite the country she had decided on a bold move. India would host an international summit at Professor Cali's secure headquarters in Milam Valley.

She was prone to bold and independent moves. Furthermore, she knew that hosting so many international guests would either make or break her strong ruling of the country. It satisfied her hunger for power and recognition and would give national pride to her country's people.

Everything North of Rishikesh appeared ready. But it would not be without cost. Already there were stirrings of discontent in Parliament. She'd been accused of wanting to rule by decree, and indeed she knew she would if she had the chance.

"I want that our country be recognized for hosting this summit. After all, the world leaders must pass through India to get to Milam Valley. Our country will be seen as the crown jewel of the world."

CHAPTER 19

Mary Pierce's Apartment. July 14, 1966. 8:22 AM

At the same moment in a different time zone, Mary was talking on the phone with Wendy two floors above.

"Meditation he calls it. Got wooden beads he chants on."

"Rosary," Wendy suggested.

"Kinda like that. He didn't talk much this morning. I figured he needed space. You know how guys are."

"Yeah," Wendy chuckled over the phone. "They gotta crawl into their cave sometimes."

"He's troubled by something. Might be about all this time travel stuff."

"Sounds like he's a bit off his rocker, if you ask me."

"I dunno, Wendy. He's got money."

"Well, nice to know a rich kid."

"No, I don't mean money as in rich. I mean funny money," Mary explained.

"What do you mean?"

"Money from the future."

"What?"

"I mean he's got money with dates from the future, and a drivers license with a date of birth that says 2001."

"For real?"

"For real. I mean, he's like 26 years old, so this license is supposed to be from 2027 or something. He said in the future people can't even start their cars without using their license. It's kinda' like an ignition key."

"That's creepy. What does it look like?"

"Like a small circuit board with writing and a picture on one side. Think about it, Wendy. Do you think that in 2027 the driver license is going to look the same as it does now?"

"Well, I guess not."

Mary had a disturbing thought. She remembered the FBI agent said he was looking for a small electronic device. Could he be referring to Paul's driver license? Possibly, she thought.

Nearby, Mary's breakfast cereal was warming on the stove. The morning sun beamed brightly through the window.

"This weird guy from the FBI came over here last night saying Paul passed a dollar bill with a date from the future."

"So are they looking to arrest him?"

"Oh no, it didn't seem like it. Come down here and I'll tell you about it."

"I will in a little while," Wendy said. "I still have your ex-boyfriend lying naked in my bed."

"So you two had sex?"

"I don't remember," Wendy admitted. "Woke up and there we were, both as naked as the day we were born and a wet wash cloth between my legs."

"Oh, Wendy. You shouldn't have. You might get pregnant."

"I don't think so. I'm on the pill. Since you two split up I figured we'd get laced together and see what happens."

"Yeah, well you can have him as far as I'm concerned," Mary said. "Take him mountain climbing with you if you want."

"Don't be silly, Mary. He's not the type. Know what else?"

"What?"

"Kate Trissel stole a hundred bucks. She was here tripping with us."

"Wouldn't be the first time," Mary reminded her.

"Hard drugs, I figure," Wendy continued. "Steals even from her friends."

"Are you sure it wasn't Peter?"

"If Pete had stolen the money, he wouldn't be here the next morning, would he?"

"You don't know Pete like I do," Mary said.
"No way, Mary. Kate stole the money, not Pete."
"If you say so."
"I know so, girl. Say, I'm like half dressed. Haven't even put on a bra. I'll come down in a couple of minutes."
"Okay," Mary agreed. "See you soon."
"Bye."

* * *

Wendy hung up the phone and folded her arms, peering into the bedroom as Pete sat naked on the side of the bed, scratching his scrotum. "I'm gonna go downstairs to Mary's apartment."

"Dressed like that?"

"No, I'm going to put on a blouse, silly. You gonna stay?"

"Nah. Gotta leave," Pete replied, smiling to himself.

Wendy nodded. "Okay. We'll do it again sometime?" She hoped he'd say no.

"Maybe."

Peter hadn't used a condom. He hoped she'd get pregnant. That would really screw up her life. He'd just say, "Sorry, bitch. Your problem for being friends with Mary," and then he'd tell her to get lost. Besides, he had her hundred bucks in his jeans by the bedside. That's what he'd come for in the first place.

* * *

Downstairs, Mary popped some bread in the toaster and thought about Swamiji. She liked that so many young people her age were flocking to him – further confirmation that he was what they called "hip."

She unplugged her coffee maker just as the toaster popped. Her lacto-vegetarian breakfast was ready.

There was a knock on the door.

"Damn, girl. That was fast." She went over to the door and looked out the peephole, but was surprised. A man in a suit and tie stood outside, not Wendy. A silk suit, she guessed. Round face, calculating eyes. Had thinning gray hair. Didn't look dangerous.

"Who is it?" she called out.

"Avi Lobe."

"What do you want?"

"Ma'am. I was sent over by your father, Mr. Pierce."

"Oh yeah? What for?"

"To give you this." He held up a small box in front of the peephole.

What was with all these people leaving gifts for her at her door? "What's that?"

"It's from your father, Ma'am. Mr. Pierce told me to deliver it to you personally."

She threw the bolts and swung the door open.

Lobe grabbed Mary by the arm and she panicked, trying to strike him with the other hand. He grabbed her other wrist and pushed her inside the apartment. A woman with orange, spiked hair darted up the stairs and forced her way in behind them. She held a syringe in her hand. She jammed the needle directly into Mary's neck and she instantly fell limp in Mr. Lobe's arms

"Is she dead?"

"It's not the same chemical Von Krod used on Senator Perry, if that's what you want to know," Ms. Dee said, brushing a lock of orange hair. "Close the door. See if you can find that device."

Mr. Lobe placed Mary's unconscious body on the floor and began to tear into everything he could find. He pulled off the bed sheet, tore up the mattress with a big knife, found marijuana in her drawer, looked in her kitchen cabinets, smashed her lamp and looked inside the ceramic base, and pulled all of the clothes and boxes out of her closet. He ripped into each box with a knife.

"Nothing."

"McPherson might have it, then," Ms. Dee declared.

"Or maybe they don't have it all."

"Then how is he traveling through time? Either way, it doesn't matter. As long as it's not here, we don't need to worry." She looked out the window. "Our ambulance is here."

They heard people coming up the stairs. Lobe opened the door. Men dressed in white entered the apartment, and

Time Gods

without comment, lowered a stretcher next to Mary.

A man with a stethoscope and blood pressure cuff checked her vital signs while a second man unfastened large black straps fixed to the aluminum stretcher frame.

They hoisted Mary onto the stretcher and strapped her in. A third man in white came up the stairs and in through the open door. He had a cylindrical tank hooked to a tube and mask. He quickly fastened the mask over Mary's nose and mouth.

Lobe turned to Ms. Dee. "Durukti, what about McPherson's grandparents?"

"They're next. Kill the grandparents and McPherson will exist no more."

When the medics were satisfied Mary was properly strapped into the stretcher and sedated, they lifted her up and began to carry her from the room into the hallway.

At the same moment, Wendy came down the stairs. "Oh my God!" she blurted. "What happened?"

Noticing Wendy, Lobe turned to the medics and said, "No witnesses."

Before Wendy could react, another man in white emerged from Mary's apartment grabbed her and injected her with a needle.

That would be Wendy's last memory until she woke up shackled inside a cage, ready to be used like a rat in an experiment.

CHAPTER 20

26 Second Avenue. July 14, 1966. 10:05 AM

Paul sat in the storefront tasting *prasadam*, so-called spiritual food offered to Krishna. Someone said Swamiji himself had cooked it. It was indeed delicious.

Despite the pleasantries, he felt perturbed. Perhaps he should take his chances with Mary rather than with the devotees. Living on the street was untenable, and he didn't want to change the future of the Hare Krishna religion.

Mary was the only person with whom he dared discuss time travel. He missed her and discovered he harbored deep emotional attachment for her. So what if it was wrong for him to fall in love with a woman from the past? This was not the past anymore. This was now. Forget about the past and future. As Baba Ram Das had said, be here, now.

Paul had an overwhelming urge to phone Mary and let her know he was coming back to be with her for good. It was useless to think about 2027. He was here now, and couldn't get back to the future. He'd have to find one of those old fashioned telephones to tell her. There was no such thing as cell phones or holograph stations for 3D calls in 1966.

Politely excusing himself, Paul stepped into the sizzling sunlight and locked eyes with the man with red hair, standing on the other side of Second Avenue as he had yesterday.

Paul decided to walk north, and the man followed on the other side of the street. Now, Paul thought, he had the man following him rather than the other way around. That was better. After walking north a few blocks, Paul ducked into a jewelry store and a bell on the door jingled.

The blast of cool air welcomed him from the sweltering heat outside. He saw glass cases displaying gold, silver and diamonds.

"May I help you?" asked the storekeeper. He had a small mustache, thin face, and brown complexion. He wore a white shirt and tie.

Ijaz Akbar had migrated with his family to America from Pakistan, and had managed to purchase the jewelry store a couple of years ago. Business was marginal since he wasn't in the jewelry district.

"I've got a problem," explained Paul. "You see, there's some guy following me across the street."

Ijaz peered out the window and noticed the man with red hair on the other side of Second Avenue. He spoke with a strong Pakistani accent. "You are talking about that man over there?"

"Yeah," confirmed Paul.

"Yes, he is looking very angry man," Ijaz noted.

"My thoughts as well," agreed Paul. "I was wondering if I could use your phone to call this number." He showed the man a card.

> *Sidney E. Dale*
> *Special Agent*
> *Federal Bureau of Investigation*

A New York Telephone number was listed.

"Certainly. Over here." Ijaz led Paul down the counter near the cash register. He reached down, produced a telephone and placed it before Paul.

Paul dialed the number on the card. "TDC," announced a man's voice on the line.

"I'd like to speak to Special Agent Sidney E. Dale, please."

There was a brief pause. "What's this in connection with?"

Paul was confused. "Is this the Federal Bureau of Investigation?"

"Oh, I see. Hold on a second."

That's odd, Paul thought.

Another voice. "Hello?"

"Hello," Paul said. "I'd like to speak to Special Agent Dale from the FBI, please."

A long pause. "Paul? Paul, is that you?"

"Yes. Is this Mr. Dale?"

"Yes," came the response. "What's up?"

"There's someone following me. I think he might be one of the counterfeiters."

"Where are you?"

"I'm in a jewelry store on Second Avenue, a few blocks north of the Mobil Gas Station. What should I do?"

"You could be in extreme danger. We'll send an agent over straight away. Don't go anywhere."

"I'm in a jewelry store. I can't just stay here."

"Don't attract undue attention. What's the address?"

Paul asked Ijee, and then repeated the address to Agent Dale.

"Just act normally. Take care, Mr. McPherson," Dale said.

"Sure. Okay. Thanks. Bye."

Paul hung up the phone and asked, "Do you mind if I make another call?"

"Go right ahead," the jeweler reassured.

Paul dialed Mary's number. He thought he would feel comfort in hearing her voice.

Unfortunately, there was no answer.

Paul thanked Ijaz and stepped outside. He didn't feel comfortable milling around a small jewelry store without purchasing something. He had to leave.

He walked north and the man across the street followed. Passing a small alleyway on his right, he turned his back on Second Avenue and headed between buildings. Garbage cans and boxes were piled along the left side of the alley. Paul turned left at a T-junction without looking back, and immediately hid around the corner. He waited silently.

He strained his ears, but heard no footsteps echoing in the narrow alley. A minute and a half ticked by, then two.

Still no sign of the man. Five minutes passed, then ten. Paul didn't move.

After awhile his ears began to play tricks on him and he did hear a sound. The sound of grinding glass, as a foot might make stepping on a broken bottle. Then more silence. Another tink. A bottle cap sliding, perhaps. A cat meowed.

*　　*　　*

At the jewelry store the small bell jingled, announcing a customer.

"May I help you?" Ijaz asked. He looked up to see a tall man dressed in black, wearing dark, reflective wraparound sunglasses completely concealing his eyes. He carried a black briefcase at his left side.

"Was there someone in your shop a little while ago with a shaved head?" He produced the 8x10 photograph taken by Special Agent Sidney E. Dale from his belt buckle.

"Yes, indeed," the shop owner replied. "He was in here a few minutes ago. Said he was being followed."

"What did he want from you?"

"The telephone," Ijaz explained. "He made two calls."

"Two calls? To whom?"

"Well, the FBI. Other one I don't know."

"Why did you help him?"

"Why not? Who are you?"

The man in black didn't answer. Placing his briefcase on the counter, he popped it open and removed a Walther PPK semi-automatic pistol and long silencer. He calmly began to screw the silencer onto the barrel of the gun.

The term silencer, of course, was a misnomer. Very few effectively stopped all the sound of a gun firing. It merely quieted the sound of the gun and rendered it unrecognizable as gunfire. That's why the devices were more commonly referred to as suppressors. The cylinder of the suppressor was wider than the barrel of the pistol. The large hollow interior contained numerous baffles to divide the inside of the cylinder into multiple smaller chambers.

Ijaz became alarmed. "Mister, are you going to rob me? Here, take everything in my cash register."

The man did not desire anything from the store. Instead,

he aimed the barrel of his pistol directly at Ijaz and squeezed the trigger. A hammer in the back of the gun fell, striking the firing pin, which in turn struck the primer in the back of the bullet's cartridge. This ignited the gunpowder behind the bullet and produced rapidly expanding gases, propelling the bullet out of the gun. Spiral grooves in the gun barrel caused the projectile to spin gyroscopically to stabilize accuracy. The chambers in the silencer allowed the hot gases to expand, putting less pressure on the bullet and letting it travel more slowly. Since the bullet traveled at lower speeds upon leaving the end of the silencer and the gas was not expanding as rapidly, the weapon made a slight pop noise rather than a loud bang.

Ijaz crashed backward against the wall behind the cash register, blood oozing from his forehead as he slid down to the floor, dead.

CHAPTER 21

Another scuttling noise. A mouse rounded the corner. Fifteen minutes had passed.

Paul pushed himself away from the brick building and rounded the corner in the alley, and as soon as he came out from hiding he came face to face with the man with red hair.

The man snarled, whipped a knife from his pocket, and with the other hand covered Paul's mouth, violently pushing him back against the alley wall. He raised the knife to Paul's throat.

"You make one sound, and I swear I'll slit your throat!" the man warned.

Paul looked at the man's angry eyes and nodded. The man lowered his hand from Paul's mouth, but kept the knife close.

"What are you doing here?" the man demanded.

"What am *I* doing here? What do you mean?"

"Shut up!" the man demanded, again pushing Paul hard against the wall. "Answer my question! You're supposed to be dead."

"I am?"

"You workin' for Odus again?"

"Working for *who*?"

"Yeah. Working for who alright. Mister Who. As long as you cooperate with us, no one dies. You understand?"

"I think he's telling the truth," said a female voice. Paul didn't dare move his head with a knife to his neck, so he rolled his eyes to the side and saw her. She wore the same low cut, one-piece dress, and fur wrap over her shoulders as she had two nights ago.

"I like him," the woman said softly, licking her lips seductively. She touched the man on the shoulder. "Don't hurt him, Von Krod. He's not the one we're after."

"The hell he's not."

"It's the midget we have to worry about."

Paul looked at her. "Who *are* you?"

"I am a product of your desire," she answered with a smile.

The red haired man pressed his other hand hard against Paul's chest, pressing him firmly against the wall. "But how did you get here after we dumped you in the river?"

"Oh you know the answer to that, Von Krod," the woman said. "Time layers, parallel universes. All that crap. Odus must be at it again. Like rerecording the end of a magnetic recording tape."

"What do you want with me?" Paul demanded.

"We're fellow travelers. Cooperate and you and the two girls will live," the man sneered.

"What girls?" Paul asked.

The woman stepped around Von Krod and placed her hand on Paul's cheek. Her skin was soft, and warm. "Remember me? Convoitise," she whispered seductively. "Call me Connie."

He remembered alright. Outside Mary's apartment. She'd turned into a hideous man-like creature with warts before vanishing into thin air. No one could forget that.

She smiled coyly, placing her hand on Paul's crotch. "Give me half an hour with him, and he'll be ours."

Von Krod withdrew the knife and after Connie stepped back, abruptly slugged Paul hard in the stomach. McPherson buckled over, winded. Von Krod grabbed his arm like a vice grip. "Come with us. We're going for a little ride."

He began to drag the time traveling monk from the alley. Connie casually followed behind, curling her blonde hair in her fingers.

Paul saw a shiny gold Rolls-Royce had pulled up at the head of the alley. It had New Jersey Plates and the logo of a popular Atlantic City casino on the side. Had he known, it might seem peculiar since no casino operated in Atlantic City until after 1977. These people were time travelers. Even their Rolls-Royce was from the future. White wall tires. Dark, limousine tint on the side and back windows. If there were occupants, they were concealed from view.

Von Krod opened the back door and stuffed Paul into the back seat. Convoitise climbed into the front passenger seat. A robust woman with spiked orange hair sat behind the wheel. Von Krod slid in next to Paul.

Paul grabbed the door handle on his side of the vehicle, but it was locked and he could not see how to unlock it.

The man squeezed his arm powerfully. Paul would have to wait until he had a better opportunity before using his martial arts skills. Too confined in the car.

He spent a moment to absorb his surroundings. He was inside a luxurious automobile. The seats had leather upholstery. This enormously impressive vehicle was a Rolls-Royce Phantom V with a powerful Silver Cloud III engine. Paul awed at the dashboard instruments and gauges, set in whorled wood, not plastic. He could not even imagine that all the exposed, interior metallic surfaces, such as door handles and apparently inoperable lock, were twenty-karat gold. The rest of the body was caste in eighteen karat gold to give solidity to the frame. Very little steel had been used in the construction of this vehicle. Lining the seat backs, facing the rear seat, was a complete bar with every kind of liquor imaginable, including a bottle of Jefferson's Reserve Bourbon from Bardstown, Kentucky – the same brand in Mary's apartment.

The two women turned around and faced the red-haired man in the back. "Does anyone know about this?" the driver asked him.

"His girlfriend, Dale and a shopkeeper," Von Krod replied. "It's being dealt with."

"Good," she said. Then, looking at Paul, she asked, "Comfortable?"

"Hardly. What do you want with me?"

"My brother is the one you seek," the orange haired driver said, glancing at Paul in the rear-view mirror.

"This guy?" Paul said nodding towards the man with his

hand on his arm.

She laughed again. "No. That's Vex Von Krod."

Von Krod nodded silently at the introduction, face stern. "What's *your* name?"

"I'm Durukti," she replied. "Popularly known as Ms. Dee."

"I want to get out of the car, now."

No one said a word. Durukti turned to drive and the automobile pulled from the curb. Paul noted there wasn't a squeak or rattle anywhere and the engine was inaudible.

As Durukti drove, Convoitise put her arm around her and began to kiss her on the ear as Paul looked on, bemused.

Unexpectedly, she glanced back at Paul as if she had read his mind.

"What... who... what *are* you?"

"I am the lust you feel inside," Convoitise said.

They continued southwest on Second Avenue, passing Swamiji's "Matchless Gifts" storefront, continuing to Chrystie Street where they turned left on Delancey. Paul fell silent when he realized he wasn't being blindfolded. Either these people wanted him to know where they were going or they intended to kill him when they got there. He hoped it was the former, not the latter. Conversation was over for now.

After crossing the Williamsburg Bridge they drove onto Northern Boulevard and traveled about 2 miles before turning right on 40th Road. They were now north of the Queensborough Bridge, Paul guessed, somewhere in Astoria, Queens.

Durukti made some sharp left and right turns through an old neighborhood and then Paul noticed they passed through what could only be described as a checkpoint booth manned by the U.S. Military. After that they drove into a secured compound encircled by abandoned industrial buildings with boarded windows and passed four U.S. Army trucks headed in the opposite direction. Finally they came to an empty lot enclosed by a high chain-linked fence with coiled razor wire along the top. A man dressed in army fatigues stood sentry at the entrance, and upon seeing the golden Rolls, saluted, allowing them to pass. Several other armed military personnel milled around the area. These guys were supposed to be the good guys. Why were they keeping Paul captive and what was going to happen next?

As the Rolls-Royce drew to a full stop, Paul could see the edge of the East River through his darkly tinted window. Manhattan towered over the other side of Roosevelt Island.

"You are military people?"

The plump, graying Casino owner, Mr. Lobe, stood waiting for them. He opened the rear door and Paul immediately recognized him from the Empire State Building incident. Von Krod shoved Paul out of the car.

Durukti climbed out and spoke to billionaire Lobe. "Is everything prepared?"

"Yes. Everyone is waiting," he nodded.

In the center of the gravel covered lot encircled by a tall chain linked fence, stood a lone, cube-shaped cinder block building. The structure was perhaps twenty feet square and about as high. There were no windows, and one metal door. An unmarked black helicopter with 30 millimeter automatic machine guns mounted under the front sat perched on the roof, rotors still. Two men, dressed in ordinary, off-the-rack black suits with white shirts, wearing dark sunglasses, stood nearby, silently watching as the group approached. They had ID badges pinned to their lapels. Behind these men was a black 1965 Cadillac guarded by military sentries: Lobe's present day car. The Rolls, on the other hand, had been brought from the future.

With Lobe in the lead, they pushed Paul toward the cube building. Paul shuffled along as Von Krod angrily prodded him from behind. He could have, he realized, attempted escape but there were guns here. A lot of guns, and Paul didn't want to take the risk. They were escorting him somewhere and he wanted to know where. The fact that U.S. military personnel were present suggested to him that his time travel debacle had been orchestrated with direct involvement from high levels in the government.

The men in black stepped aside without comment as the group reached the cube shaped cinder block building and opened the metal door. Inside it was dark. Someone flipped a switch and the small room became flooded with light.

Lobe, in his silk suit and thinning, gray hair, drew a gate

closed blocking the door. To the right of the door was a panel with buttons. Convoitise pushed one of them and then draped her arm over Paul's shoulder. Paul backed a few inches against the wall, but she did not remove her hand.

"Get away from me," he ordered. He placed his hand on her wrist. "Every time I meet you people," Paul said, "it's in an elevator, and it's never good."

"There is one difference between then and now," Connie said. "The last time we met on an elevator it was going up. This one is going down. In either case, the result for you will be the same. Your trip is canceled."

The room lurched and Paul could feel they were rapidly descending. Minutes went by and the elevator appeared to descend thousands of feet. Finally it slowed and came to a halt. Paul forgot to breathe as he straightened himself, feeling the pressure on his ear drums. The green-suited Mr. Lobe pulled back the gate, and the doors slid open.

They were in a tunnel carved out of granite. Along the walls, on either side, were mounted ornate electric light fittings. The air felt cool, damp and musty. A small utility closet branched off to their left, just beyond the elevator doors. The stone walls were rough, not smooth, and studded with diamonds and rubies. The finest quality polished inlaid red granite decorated the floor. Mounted on the wall of the tunnel on the right was a one foot round, wooden plaque, painted black. In the center of the plaque was the image of a deep blue pyramid. In the center of the pyramid was a small black circle with an orange halo. Upon the circle was the image of an evil, naked eye.

Durukti was first to proceed from the elevator, closely followed by Convoitise, and behind her, Lobe and Von Krod with Paul.

As the group of five made their way down the tunnel, Paul noticed again the utility closet off to the side, door open. There would be no escape running into that closet.

The tunnel stretched far ahead into the distance, and Paul felt claustrophobic as he conceptualized millions of tons of earth, stone and water that lay above them. It was difficult to know how deep underground they were, but judging on the speed and time the elevator took to descend, coupled with the pressure on his ear drums, he concluded they were several thousand feet down, well below the river bottom. No building foundation or subway train ever ventured this far. They were no longer in New York. They were deep in the Earth's crust.

Trudging forward with no definable end of the tunnel in sight, they occasionally passed right angle junctions of other tunnels, although they proceeded always straight. Clearly they were in a vast underground network of secret caverns. At one point they passed a tunnel on the right with a sign that read, in plain English, "Elevator to Subway Access: 7 AM to 7:10 AM and 7 PM to 7:10 PM only." Some distance down that cavern was a sealed vault door blocking the exit. A room that looked like a lab of some sort branched off to the side. Obviously, no subway came down this deep, but indications were there must be a way up to the subway train via that route.

The group marched Paul forward.

They walked about three miles. Paul heard haunting laughter echoing down the tunnel. The sounds grew louder, and ahead he could see an opening on the left. Much to his surprise, a large Friesian cow came running out of the opening. The route now partially blocked by the terrified animal, the group hesitated. A rope was tied around the cow's neck which trailed on the floor behind her. The bovine shook her head and let out a long pitiable cry as tears streamed down her face. Paul had never seen a cow cry before.

A man wearing a white, bloodstained apron, carrying a large machete and stun gun, appeared from the opening and caught the end of the rope. He had a bandage wrapped around his forehead, as if he had a recent head injury. "Get in here!" he shouted at the animal in a raspy voice, and the cow again cried in terror. With difficulty, the man dragged the animal back into the side room.

The passage now clear, the group pressed forward, and as they passed the opening, Paul caught a glimpse inside. It was an immense space with a cement floor covered with disemboweled animal organs and bloody intestines. On the far side of the large cavernous room, just beyond a low fence, he saw restaurants serving grilled beef and many people sitting at tables eating. The man in the white, bloodstained apron stood near the opening to the tunnel. He held a stun-gun to the cow's forehead, gave the animal a powerful jolt of electricity, and then forcefully brought down a machete onto the back of the cow's neck. Her helpless body collapsed headless on the ground with a thud while jets of blood spurted on the floor. Other beheaded carcasses hung from hooks in a huge, open meat freezer nearby. The man clipped the stun gun on his belt, placed the machete on a stainless steel table, and reached down for the cow's head.

Paul felt absolutely nauseous. *My God*, he thought. *What kind of hellish place is this?*

After walking past that slaughterhouse area he began to hear a cacophony of electronic sounds which got louder and louder. The sounds came from another opening ahead on the right. As they approached, Paul saw a huge casino extending outward into the sides of the cave. Through large, glass exit doors leading further into the bedrock, sprawled several other casinos. People were gambling, talking, laughing, and drinking. Gold coins clattered loudly, electronic music played, and slot machines chimed.

Seeing these civilians, Paul frantically called out to them. "Help! Someone! These people have kidnapped me!"

Several people near the door looked up, shrugged, and then returned their attention to their games of roulette and poker. One woman pointed at him and laughed.

Von Krod poked Paul from behind, but seemed otherwise unconcerned about his outcry. These people were all accomplices and Paul could expect no help from any of them. Within a moment, the casino too had passed behind them. Piano music could then be heard up ahead. Paul saw two more openings on the sides of the tunnel. The first, on the left, and another, further ahead, on the right.

Passing the first opening, he noted a large, lavishly decorated cavernous area, with indirect colored lighting carefully placed behind stalactites and stalagmites. Hundreds of round, wooden tables and chairs sat upon highly polished stone floors and wet bars, ascetically perched among natural cylinders of calcium carbonate deposits projecting upward from the floor. People sat at these tables or at the bars consuming alcoholic beverages. A man playing the piano created a festive mood, while people stood around pool tables watching various matches. A giant salt water aquarium with exotic fish lined an entire wall behind one of the many bars. Several women dressed in revealing clothes wandered from table to table, occasionally sitting on laps of either men or women. These ladies, thick with makeup, were clearly intoxicated, some embracing and kissing, others engaged in informal conversation when not serving drinks at the tables. Other than the strong stench of alcohol and cigarette smoke, Paul detected a sweet smell in the air, hinting of marijuana or something stronger.

When that room passed from view and the sound of the piano began to fade, they passed the last opening on the right, which expanded into several rooms. These rooms were covered with mirrors and divided into various sections. In one area there was a store selling pornographic videos, vibrators, dildos and other sex toys, and nearby were several opulently decorated rooms that expanded deep within the bedrock. Dozens of moaning, naked people of both genders openly engaged in explicit sexual acts of every imaginable description. He was witnessing a public orgy.

"The pleasure rooms are my favorite," Convoitise proclaimed to Paul as she lustfully nodded in the direction of the rooms. "Maybe you and I can come back here later and get to know each other better. Ask and you shall receive."

Fat chance, Paul thought, his lips curling with distaste.

Now he heard a new sound straight ahead, steam hissing he thought, and Paul saw they had reached the end of the tunnel.

Before them loomed a large, heavy, vault door, guarded by two armed men carrying Thompson submachine guns. Also known as the Tommy Gun, these weapons were commonly used during the American Prohibition era because of their compact design, large .45 ACP cartridge, and rapid automatic fire. The guards were dressed in green and wore black helmets, unlike any uniform Paul had seen before.

One of the men turned to the vault door, and spun a large circular wheel mounted in its center. He then pushed and the heavy door opened slowly inward.

"Any news on yesterday's security breach?" Durukti asked the guard.

"Yes, Ma'am," he replied. "The intruder struck the butcher on the head with a whiskey bottle and stole his stun gun. You might have seen the butcher had a head bandage when you walked by. The intruder then went up to the surface via the main elevator. We chased him with the helicopter, but the man escaped."

"Do not let this happen again," Durukuti warned him, looking sternly into the guard's eyes before stepping through the vault with the others. The guard nervously nodded in obedience and swallowed the lump in his throat. One of his co-worker had been thrown in the vats only last week, and he didn't want to meet the same fate.

Once inside the vault door, the guards closed and sealed the massive door from the outside.

There was a fire extinguisher and fire alarm on the stone wall nearby. The glass cover on the fire alarm was broken and taped with duct tape, obviously no longer operational. Yet there was no sign of anything charred. Whatever had been set on fire, Paul guessed, had long ago been extinguished.

Here the confines of the underground space expanded to reveal an immense room larger than a commercial jet hanger. The area was perhaps fifty or sixty feet wide and two hundred feet in length, stretching out before them. The walls, floor, and ceiling of this incredible underground cavern were hollowed out of bedrock forming an expansive cavity under the earth from which grew stalactites and stalagmites. An iron walkway with grating painted blood red stretched out over the entire length of the space, bridging high over monstrous stone cauldrons of what seemed to be vats of molten steel or iron emitting smoke and heat. Slim railings lining the sides of the walkway provided little sense of security to Paul as the group headed out over the walkway bridge. Huge pipes and tubes spewing steam and gases crisscrossed far above and below. Their feet clanged harshly on the grating, and as Paul peered down, he estimated they were about sixty or seventy feet above the floor and another thirty feet to the stonework above them. If one were to fall from here he might find himself impaled on a stalagmite projecting upward from the cave floor or worse, scalded in a giant vat of molten metal.

After proceeding a dozen feet along the walkway, they stopped at a gate in the railing directly above a vat of glowing, hot, fuming liquid far below.

The air was sulfurous, and black smoke rose from the vats. Wandering on the floor space between the stalagmites and vats of hot liquid metal, were the workers – men and women with blackened cheeks and foreheads, wearing steel tipped boots, leather gloves and brown coveralls, laughing and shouting at each other.

"Why have we stopped?" Paul asked with a lump in his throat.

"To show you what your fate will be," Darukti explained. "You will be thrown into the vats from here, but for now our orders are to keep you alive."

"What's in those vats?"

"Gold," Mr. Lobe informed him. "Molten gold."

"Molten gold? There's... there's *so much of it*!"

Convoitise laughed. "You think these hundreds of cauldrons are anything more than a mere sampling of our wealth? Our leader controls the world economy from down here."

"You have more gold than Fort Knox," McPherson estimated. "Is it for real?"

"Pure molten gold," Lobe assured him. "You can trust us on that. Incidentally, we also control Fort Knox."

"Just who *are* you people?"

"We'll get around to that soon enough," Lobe snapped.

Von Krod forced an unsettling grin. Paul found him the most frightful of all. He spoke with a hiss. "It's fun when we throw people in the vats. A long fall. A brief scream of total terror. A flash of flames and then the surface of the gold turns red for a few moments until it blends completely with the liquid."

"The impurities of the dead are vaporized," Durukti added. "But not every one of our visitors dies in this way. We also need live subjects for our experiments. The meeting is at the end of this month, and still they haven't got it right."

She turned, and the group followed behind as they proceeded further along the footbridge. When they arrived at the far end of the vast cavern, they filed onto a two-foot wide stone ledge along the outer, far edge of the cavern. There was no railing here, and as they skirted along single file, Paul stumbled on the uneven surface. "Don't fall off," snickered Von Krod callously.

Finally, they arrived at a wide area on the ledge where there was a colossal, ornate, solid gold door. Mounted upon that great golden door was another of the round, wooden plaques, painted black. It too had a deep blue pyramid with a small black circle painted upon it, and in the center of the circle was another evil eye.

Lobe pushed the great door and slowly it creaked open.

"This is where my brother stays," explained Durukti. "Welcome to our headquarters." She gestured for everyone to enter.

As Paul cautiously stepped through the doorway, he sensed something vile was about to happen. To a point, his adventure into the past had been wonderful. After all, he had miraculously met Srila Prabhupada and many of his early followers. His discussions with the old religious leader had been enlightening. Further, he had fallen in love with a very special woman. Now, however, his escapade had taken a decidedly dark turn. Kidnapped by demonic freaks, he found himself in the recesses of the earth's crust in a frightfully dreadful milieu. His optimism had given way to trepidation. Nothing good could come from any of this.

CHAPTER 22

Underground Lab. July 14, 1966

Wendy saw the metal bars and blinked. She blinked again.

Her head ached. Her side was stiff. She found herself lying on a rock floor.

For a long time she stared at the bars and tried to think where the hell she was. Then she remembered.

They had injected her with something outside Mary's apartment. Now where was she? She tried to sit up but realized her hands were cuffed behind and her feet tightly shackled together with chains. She couldn't move.

She was in a cage of some sort. Beyond the bars was a well lit room. In the room's center she saw a dozen tables that looked like beds. Each had straps and electrodes. Various wires hung down from above. Confused and helpless, her heart quickened as her eyes darted back and forth restlessly. She struggled again to sit up. This time she succeeded.

"You're awake," noted a female voice.

She turned her head. To her right was an overweight woman in her thirties with dark, ruffled hair and smudge marks on her face. Her handcuffs behind her back were looped through the shackles around her ankles, forcing her legs to be bent at the knees. The woman was laying on her side, looking at Wendy intently.

"They're going to take our minds away," she said. "I watched them do it to him." She nodded with her head. Wendy noticed a man sitting on the other side of her. He was not chained, but stared blankly into space.

"Hello?" Wendy said to him. He did not even blink his eyes.

"They took his mind," the dark haired woman explained. "I saw them do it. They're going to do the same to you and me. We're going to become one of them."

Wendy turned her head and looked at the woman. "Become one of whom?" she asked.

"One of *them*. Look at him. He's had only one treatment. When they're finished with him, he'll have no mind of his own. He'll be like a puppet. I'll be next. I'm so afraid!"

"Where are we?" Wendy asked. How did I get here? How did you get here? For God's sake, tell me what's going on!"

"They tried to take my daughter," the woman said, tears streaming down her dirty cheek. "I tried to stop them, but they took me as well."

"Who did?" Wendy wanted to know.

"The men in white," she replied. "They came with an ambulance, but they were not from any hospital. They work for *him*."

"I don't understand what you're talking about," Wendy complained. "Where is this place? Where are we?"

"We're in hell," the woman answered, voice trembling and full of fear.

A graying man dressed in a white technician overcoat entered the room from a doorway at the far end. Seeing Wendy and the woman talking, he spoke. "Ah. Miss Murphy, I believe. Glad to see you finally came around. We need you to be fully awake for the procedure, you know."

"Just who the fuck are you and how do you know my name?"

"Chief lab tech," he replied dismissively.

"Where's my friend, Mary? What have you done with her?"

The lab tech smiled. "Oh, her. I believe they took her to see the King himself. Lucky girl."

"What fucking King?"

The lab tech chuckled absurdly. "The King, my dear

lady. There is only one."

A second lab technician, much younger, entered through the doorway at the far end of the room.

"Ah. Excellent. Alright Jennifer. You next."

"Leave me alone you assholes," the woman next to Wendy warned them. "You won't take my mind without a fight."

"Take your mind?" the chief tech chuckled as they approached the cage. "We have no intention of taking your mind. This is for your own good. We will *wash* your mind. After the first treatment you won't feel a thing."

They unlocked the cage door.

The chief tech instructed his assistant to remove the man with the blank stare. They said they were going to put him in the 'Quiet Room.'

"We've got to calculate the most effective chemical combination, that's all," he said to his assistant. "Catatonic won't do at all. This man is fit only for the vats."

*   *   *

King Kali's Underground Throne Room. 1966

A vast circular hall, palatial in size, opulent beyond description, sprawled out before Paul's eyes. Large black and gold marble tiles decorated the floor, drawing the eye to the perfect circle of red, inlaid tile in the floor at the hall's center. Illuminating the cavern were a dozen enormous gold and crystal chandeliers descending from the shadows of the high stone ceiling. Lining the walls were ornate onyx pillars, studded with diamonds and rubies, each holding sconces emitting gentle, soft light.

Most remarkably, neatly set throughout the room like so many pieces of furniture, were dozens of meter high stacks of shiny gold bullion "Good Delivery bars", each weighing 400 Troy Ounces, or 12.44 kilograms, eleven inches in length and 99.5% pure, having been originally cast by a small group of metal refiners accredited by the professional bullion dealing communities in London, New York and Zurich. These gold bullion bars were very large and impossible for a private individual to own even one, what to speak of the thousands stacked in meter high stacks throughout this room.

Nude statues surrounded the hall. Oil paintings of snow peaked mountains and what appeared to be flying automobiles decorated the deep, maroon wallpaper on the smooth walls.

Set on a raised platform some distance from the center of the hall was a large ornate throne. It too was golden, upholstered in beautiful red velvet, looking soft enough to sink into. The throne itself, including its arms and footrest, was inlaid with elaborately formed birds, flowers and other figures, and decorated with fabulous jewels - rubies, pearls, emeralds and sapphires. Six marble steps led up to this incredible sitting place, yet it presently faced away from the hall's entrance and was mounted to on a turntable device at its base.

Placed near the red marble circle at the center of the hall and facing the steps up to the throne's turntable were three ornately carved teakwood chairs, and upon each chair sat a hostage, bound and gagged, their backs toward the entrance. Paul could see that there was one man and two women tied to those chairs.

Two buglers standing on either side of the golden doorway, wearing one-piece red suits, sounded their trumpets, making a horrible, cacophonous blare of disharmony.

Mr. Lobe looked up toward the back of the throne and cleared his throat nervously. "My Lord," he said loudly. "We've brought him on your behest."

As Paul looked towards the throne atop the raised platform, it slowly began to turn.

Gradually, as the throne rotated to face them, Paul could see that a man sat proudly upon it. He was dressed as an emperor, replete with gold crown and royal dress. As the rotation of the extraordinarily opulent sitting place slowly brought him into full view, Paul saw the king was a handsome man with fine, distinct facial features, yet oddly, a gray complexion to his familiar face.

The King had a spatula-shaped chin and well-formed nose. His deeply penetrating icy blue eyes seeming to stare right into Paul's very soul. He wore a cloth-of-gold shirt with silky satin pants, his waist girdled with a golden, bejeweled belt. Draped over his shoulders was a blue velvet cape, which was lined with golden embroidered lace patterned to highlight the diamonds scattered throughout the material. He looked confident, opulent and regal, yet decidedly evil. On his head rested a beautifully crafted gold helmet bedecked with diamonds, rubies, emeralds and sapphires, lined at the base with pearls. He relaxed one hand on the throne's armrest, while the other rested comfortably on his thigh.

The man chuckled. Paul had the unnerving sensation that he had read his mind, and he shuddered at the prospect.

McPherson recognized the King – the same man who had been in the silk suit and black cape on the elevator in the Empire State Building – the one who had also been staring at him outside of Mary's apartment. Now they were together at last. Finally he would get some answers. At least he hoped so. Even if they planned to kill him, surely they would honor a dying man's request to understand what had happened to him and why.

Paul spoke indifferently and with sufficient volume as to be heard clearly. "Who the hell are you?"

The King bellowed a hearty laugh and as he did, the others turned toward Paul, joining the laughter. While this was going on there was movement in the room, behind the throne. Paul distinctly observed a man run out from the far side of the platform and scoot halfway across the room before crouching behind a stack of gold bullion. Catching Paul's glance, Durukti turned to look, but she saw nothing. Someone was there, concealing himself, and only Paul had seen him.

"Search him," the King ordered. "Make sure he doesn't have that particle beam gun."

Durukti signaled and Mr. Lobe stepped forward and conducted a pat search.

That's when Paul saw the movement again. The man hiding behind the pile of gold stood and quickly crept to the side of the hall, disappearing through a small, open doorway.

"Someone else is here?" the King boomed, observing the movement of Paul's eyes. He glanced around the cavernous room, but saw no one.

"Look," said Paul. "Who are you people and what do you want?"

The King sneered. "Well, that depends on your perspective." He sat back and relaxed into the back of his upholstered throne for a few moments before leaning forward again. "Wouldn't you like to meet my other guests?" With a gesture of his hand, he motioned Paul to approach the three hostages tied to the chairs.

Cautiously stepping forward, he came closer to see the faces of three bound hostages. When he looked at them he was shocked.

Time Gods

PART THREE

Today, we know that time travel need not be confined to myths, science fiction, Hollywood movies, or even speculation by theoretical physicists. Time travel is possible. For example, an object traveling at high speeds ages more slowly than a stationary object. This means that if you were to travel into outer space and return, moving close to light speed, you could travel thousands of years into the Earth's future.

Clifford Pickover,
IBM researcher and science writer

CHAPTER 23

Underground Laboratory. July 14, 1966

The woman next to Wendy who had said her name was Jennifer, screamed. Tears streamed down her dirty face as she struggled to back away from the two technicians, but it was no use. Her hands and feet were securely cuffed and she could only wriggle in protest. The lab techs lifted her off the floor and carried her out of the cage into the brightly-lit room. They placed her on a birthing bed and unlocked her handcuffs. When she tried to strike them, they held her hands and strapped her limbs to the bed.

"You won't make me a *Kali-Chela!*" she screamed. "I won't let you."

One of the technicians inserted a ball bag in her mouth, snapping two leather straps in the back of her neck to hold it in place, and then walked over to refill his cup from the coffee maker on the counter behind him. He returned with a second cup and handed it to his partner.

"Relax," the chief tech said to her. "In a few minutes you won't remember any of this. Ignorance is bliss." They began cutting off her clothing with scissors, and when at last she was naked, they began attaching electrodes to her head, limbs and extremities.

"What's a *Kali-Chela?*" Wendy asked, watching through the metal bars from her little cell.

"I'm told it's from the ancient Sanskrit language. Chela means 'student,' or sometimes 'child'" the chief tech replied

Time Gods

without looking up at her. "Got to figure out the right combination of chemicals, is all."

He then nodded at the other technician, who searched for a vein to stick a needle into.

"What's the dosage this time?" the assistant asked over the constrained woman's gurney.

The chief technician looked up and then at his clipboard. "This batch contains 5% lithium, 7% fluoxetine, 1.3% carbamazepine, 4% propranolol, 2.7% buspirone, 5.5% methotrimeprazine, a hint of amitriptyline and the rest is one provided by Kali."

"Undiluted?"

"Except as above. As instructed," the chief lab tech replied.

"Sheesh. This stuff could kill her."

Wendy realized she and the other prisoners were nothing more than guinea pigs for some experimental drugs that didn't seem to work as planned, and that when they were done with Jenifer they would be coming after her. She had to do something, but what?

As she watched through the bars of her cage, the technicians turned on electric circuits and flooded Jennifer's writhing body with current.

Two hours later, Jennifer was returned to the cage, still naked, but without restraints. Though her eyes were open, she was listless and stared blankly, and the technicians were already talking about modifying the dosage for the next trial subject. Wendy understood only too well who that was, and suddenly felt sick. There was *no way* they were going to subject *her* to *that*. The woman that had first greeted her when she woke up in this horrible place was now nothing more than a vegetable.

"I have to go to the bathroom," she stated to the technicians before they closed the cage door.

The men hesitated. Wendy bravely seized on the opportunity with a vengeance. "You don't want me to piss on you when you have me on your table, do you?"

The tech assistant chuckled, but the chief lab tech did not. He considered the situation carefully. He looked toward his assistant and nodded silently. The assistant moved forward with the key and unshackled Wendy's hands and feet. Then he backed away from her cautiously.

"Very well," he told her. "But don't think about escaping. There's no other exit from the toilet. We have no windows down here. If you act violently we will have to use whatever force is required to gain your compliance. Do we understand each other?"

Wendy nodded. Use of force, she knew, would not be necessary. She slowly climbed to her feet, rubbing her sore wrists. "God, do you have to make those things so tight? Which way to the bathroom?"

"Over there," the chief technician indicated with a nod of his head. Wendy climbed out of the cage and stood up, sticking her hands in her pockets as she walked, feeling the lumps that were still there. She stopped at the coffee machine.

"Can I have a cup of coffee?" she asked, grabbing the coffee maker with both hands.

"Put it down," the chief tech ordered.

Wendy stomped her foot on the ground and frowned. "Just one cup?"

"Do you have to use the bathroom or not?"

Wendy shrugged and entered the bathroom door. She'd already done what she had intended.

* * *

Underground Throne Room. July 14, 1966

It was no longer just about Paul. These people had leverage and it looked like they planned to use it. The horror of the situation was just beginning to sink in.

Tied to the first chair was Mary Pierce. In the other two chairs were a young man and a slightly pudgy woman who looked familiar, but Paul couldn't quite place them. All three had gags in their mouths.

"I think you'll recognize one of the two ladies," the King laughed.

Squirming in the chair, hair disheveled, Mary tried to speak behind her gag. Her eyes told of terror and indignation, but also something else – anger at Paul, perhaps? Why would she be angry at *him*?

The King continued: "The other two you know very well, but you may not recognize them. This woman is your future grandmother, and the man next to her is... well, you can guess. Of course, they don't know you, since even your parents haven't been born yet."

Paul was stunned. His future paternal grandparents! They seemed young, about the same age as himself!

Memories of his grandparents flooded his mind: learning how to ride a bicycle; fishing at Lake George; hiking the Appalachian Trail; rebuilding the car engine in the garage... and his loving grandmother, taking care of him when his mother was working, overdressing him as a child in winter, always a hot meal or apple pie ready, keeping peace between Paul and his sister.

How young they looked now in 1966! This phenomenal circumstance was both beautiful and terrifying.

Mary tried to kick Paul angrily, but her feet, tied securely to the front legs of the chair, could not reach him. Paul's memories evaporated and the dangerous circumstance which he, Mary, and his future grandparents were now in became his only focus.

Paul could not understand why Mary was so angry with him. He was obviously just as much a prisoner as she was at this point. He wasn't tied up, like she was, but he had no further freedom than she. What could possibly be the source of her anger?

"I ask again. Who are you all, and why have you brought us here?" Paul bravely demanded.

The King laughed once more, joined by his trusty servants. After settling, the King leered down from his high seat. "I thought you were more intelligent than that. Why don't you use your intuition?"

Paul turned and eyed the four standing at his side. "I know your servants' by name only," Paul said. "Lobe, Von Krod, Durukti and Connie."

The King laughed. "Do you know the meaning of their names?"

"No," Paul said. "I don't." He turned back to face the man on the throne. "All I know is you'd better release us right now or you'll be arrested by the FBI! They're keeping tabs on me!"

The King bellowed another hearty laugh. "FBI, he says!"

"This is nuts! You're all crazy," Paul boldly declared.

"Crazy? Humans are crazy. Greed and madness overtake them. In the international arena, lust, greed, and anger rule. Banks and multi-national businesses control the world governments, which are ultimately controlled by the gold supply, and I control the gold. Look around, Paul McPherson. Do you not know who I am?"

"No I don't know who you are," Paul answered defiantly.

"The man on the throne roared in glee. "This is how I've been blessed to live. I live wherever there's cow killing, gambling, sex only for pleasure, intoxication and the hoarding of gold. You've seen my gold. I own thousands of vats of molten gold, and stacks of gold bullion in caverns like this all over the world. Soon, indeed on the last day of this month, all the governments of the world will come under my direct control.

"Look at Mr. Lobe standing behind you. '*Lobha*' in Sanskrit means *Greed*. His first name is Avarice, but sometimes goes by the name 'Avi.' This wealthy Casino owner from the future is the veritable *personification* of greed. Always invoking unlimited opulence, he divines greed deep within the heart of humanity, entrapping them in their own insatiable desires."

Suddenly there were two distinct, electronic chirps. They came from the small room on the side where Paul had seen that other man hide himself. Who was he? The King briefly glanced in that direction and then continued. But he was immediately interrupted by a loud buzzing sound, which stopped as quickly as it began. He looked again toward the small room, but then continued.

"Now look at this tall man with his unnaturally red hair: Vex Von Krod. *Krodha* is another Sanskrit word which means *anger*. He is Anger Personified. He's my father and we are both thousands of years old. Von Krod divines anger both in himself and in the hearts of men all over the world. He married his own sister, *Himsa*, or Envy Personified.

"Now our beautiful blonde friend, over there, is Convoitise, or Connie for short. *La convoitise* is French for *Lust*. Indeed, this woman is *Lust Personified*. By her influence the entire world is ensnared. She's only a woman when she wants to be. Otherwise, she's a hideous monster.

"Finally we come to their leader, who happens to be both my wife and my sister, Ms. Dee. We call her Durukti, which in Sanskrit means 'Irreligion.' People everywhere have lost interest in that mythical being they call God. Durukti paves the road for Lust, Anger and Greed to do their business and directs them to destroy the morals of society. With the help of these family members and friends I'll soon rule the entire world."

"And who might you be?"

"What difference does a name make? Some call me Lucifer and imagine I have horns and a tail. Buddhists know me as Mara. The followers of the Vedas of ancient India know me by my original name, Kali. The CIA and intelligentsia know me as Professor Cali. It is I who am behind the *Kali-yuga*, this age of quarrel and hypocrisy which began five thousand years ago and will continue for another glorious four hundred twenty-seven thousand years. Yes, Paul McPherson. This is *my* age for a very long time to come!"

Paul remembered Srila Prabhupada had mentioned the Age of Kali to him in their last discussion.

"You see," Kali continued, "thousands of years ago, the great King of the Aryans, Pariksit, found me beating a cow and a bull. Back in those days, in his kingdom, cruelty to man and beast was nonexistent. Threatening me with death as a punishment for harming innocent creatures, I was tactful enough to throw myself at his feet. Since he was a member of a prestigious and noble family, he was forced by his own code of ethics to spare my life.

"He granted me shelter in his kingdom, sending me into the Himalayas and isolating me. But I built my own tunnel to escape and thus I have lived happily on Earth ever since. I have seen many civilizations come and go, and I personally guided their leaders. The Egyptians, Minoans, Romans, Greeks, Persians, Arabs, Slavs, Chinese, Spaniards, Portuguese, Germans, French, British, Americans, and now the Global World Economy – the big multi-national corporations – including the oil companies of course. I am he that throws himself across God's plan. The monkey wrench in the works, as it were, the fallen angel."

"'A liar and the father of all liars,'" Paul added.

"An educated man in more than one religion, I see," Kali observed. "From John 8:44. Now I've got the very fabric of God's creation in my hand – time itself."

"So what you're saying is that you're manipulating past and present events for some presumably evil purpose of your own."

"Precisely. My primary tool, of course, is to manipulate the system of central banking to control governments. Remember that recession of 2009-2012?"

"You mean in the future. That recession is in the future."

"Come now Paul. It's in your past. It's in my past. All of the gold in this room isn't from this time period. It's from the future! The government bailout? The takeover of banking? Do you think that was all accomplished without my involvement? I have an iron grip on the world economy, deliberately causing inflation and depressions at will. My operatives only think they work for the New World Order – men and women in high positions in government and industry. With the help of time travel technology, I will soon secure control of the twenty-first century, including the European Union, United Nations, World Bank, International Monetary Fund and the proposed North American Union."

"Big plans," Paul said.

"Very big plans," Kali agreed. "Unfortunately, just recently your stupid religious movement became a disturbance. Those books translated by your leader told the *actual* history of Emperor Parikshit, and that had to be stopped. I couldn't risk my anonymity becoming compromised. And then along came the year 2075."

"What happened then?" Paul asked.

"A physicist at Princeton University named Oswin Köhler discovered particles that move backward or forward in time, demonstrating that intuitive notions of causality were flawed. Because tachyons travel faster than light, Köhler hypothesized that a field generated by tachyon particles aimed at physical objects would send them forward or backward in time. Köhler only needed financial support to test his theory, which of course Lobe and I provided."

"In other words, you built a time machine."

Time Gods

"Princeton Lab Technicians did the work, but Köhler was worried about paradoxes and had a limiter field installed in the space-time dilator called an LTTA. I later had my technicians remove that limiter for my own purposes, but what I am selling is the time machine with the LTTA installed."

"Why were you interested in time travel in the first place?"

"Time travel is the ultimate weapon! Change the future by changing the past. I can now stop all religion and remove all references to my past. Especially I don't want the history of Emperor Pariksit known. That's why I need to take over the world."

"Okay. So you're a megalomaniac with a time machine."

Kali did not seem offended. Instead, he nodded in approval. "You know, Paul, there's a prophesy that you will save the world."

"Really? Could be useful right about now."

Kali laughed again. "The room we're in is thousands of feet directly under the 16 acre site where the World Trade Center construction began earlier in 1966. You were born the day the twin towers collapsed. The long tunnel you came through brought you from Queens to Manhattan. This is the largest confluence of leylines in the world. By bringing you here I hope to astrologically neutralize the prophesy."

"What do you want from me?"

"All I ask from you is cooperation, and then we'll gladly set your lady friend and grandparents free. And you – I will send you back to the twenty-first century where you belong. Just kill Odus and have nothing more to do with that stupid Hare Krishna movement. We'll amply reward you with whatever riches, women or fame you desire. Name your price and it's yours; an offer no one could refuse. Any questions?"

"Who's Odus?"

CHAPTER 24

Area 51, Nevada

General Morgan chewed on the end of his Ashton cigar and then lit up as he leaned back in his chair. His deep set eyes were transfixed at the picture of the glacier covered mountains labeled "Milam Valley" facing him on his desk.

"Yes," he said gravely. "Sad about Major Jenkins. How did it happen?"

"An accident, from what we understand, General. I wasn't given the details."

Befitting, the General thought as he looked up at the Lieutenant sitting across from him. "And the men?"

"We haven't told them," Lieutenant Longbine explained. "The area, of course, is still secured."

"Good."

The General puffed on his cigar while he thought about the situation carefully. Major Jenkins deserved it, he knew. He had started to become too nosy. Longbine, on the other hand, was not in the loop and the General intended to keep it that way. The Milam Valley conference was strictly on a need to know basis, and Longbine didn't need to know, plain and simple.

"Very well, Lieutenant Longbine" the General said at length. "See to it that the Queens facilities remain secure."

After Longbine excused himself the General pressed his Intercom button. "Miss Blythe?"

Time Gods

"Yes General?" came her reply.
"Get me the President."
"Yes, General."
Within minutes she had the two great leaders on her switchboard.

*   *   *

The White House

"Hello, General," the President said cheerfully into the telephone as he paced from the white marble mantel toward the window in the Oval Office. "How are things in Nevada these days?" The President looked out his window at the beautiful Rose Garden and closely cut green lawn. Casually he sat back on the corner of his desk. Only a year and a half ago he had won the Presidency with 61 percent of the vote, capturing the widest popular margin in American history – more than fifteen million votes.

"Mr. President, to be honest, it's not Area 51 that I'm worried about."

"I understand General Morgan. Never mind that. Just keep the media distracted. What's on your mind?"

"It's this Milam Valley thing, Lyndon. You're still planning to go?"

"Hell yes," the President replied. "Senator Perry gave his okay, did he not?"

"Yes, Sir," the General admitted. "But..."

"Well, I'll be damned if the good Senator's last wish be denied. By the time a man scratches his ass, clears his throat, and tells me how smart he is, we've already wasted fifteen minutes. This Professor Cali is powerful, Brian. Real powerful. I never trust a man unless I've got his pecker in my pocket, and I admit that I don't have the Professor's pecker. From what I hear of Senator Perry's assurance, he can really do what he says, Brian. Important stuff. We're definitely going to Milam Valley."

"People are dying," the General complained. "The Senator died under suspicious circumstances, now one of my men."

"So I was informed. I'm sorry about those unfortunate

incidents, but frankly, we did not choose to be the guardians of the gate. There's no one else. We've talked long enough in this country about equal rights. It's time now to write the next chapter."

CHAPTER 25

Underground Throne Room

Vex Von Krod handed Paul a folder.

"Go ahead," Kali said. "Open it."

Inside Paul found a photo of the dwarf he had briefly seen at the hospital.

"You know this guy?" Kali asked.

"I saw him once," Paul replied. "Don't know who he is."

"I thought so. Kill him. It doesn't matter how you do it, just kill him."

"And if I refuse?"

"If you do not cooperate, something unfortunate will befall your friends here and you will be *erased*. Do I need to explain? If your grandparents die you'll never be born. We in the time travel world call that a Granny Paradox."

Paul was mortified. His eyes met with his grandfather-to-be, who looked angry as hell. "I don't even know how to find this little man."

"He will find you," Kali assured him.

Paul threw up his hands in resignation. "There was no way. You might as well kill all of us now. If you think I'm going to go around murdering people for you, you've got a big surprise coming."

Kali was undeterred, and studied Paul carefully. When he finally spoke again, it was slow and deliberate. "You know, Paul, I'm sure you don't need us to describe how painful it would be for Mary to have her fingernails pulled out. You wouldn't wish that on anyone, would you?"

Paul turned and cast a terrified glance at Mary bound in the chair, struggling. Paul caught her eyes, and he sensed her overwhelming fear. *How could he allow this bastard to torture her?*

"Can you please explain to me how the hell you found all of us?" Paul demanded.

Kali smiled and nodded. "We installed a simple device on Mary's phone that traced all calls made from her telephone. You called your grandparents from Mary's phone, remember?"

"But how did you know to bug Mary's phone in the first place?"

"This is not the first time we've met. The last time Von Krod and Lobe hit you on the head in 2027, stuffed you in a burlap sack, and dropped you in the East River. Unfortunately, Odus keeps bringing you back. This time I thought I'd try something different and have you kill him."

"So you bugged her phone and that's how you found my grandparents?"

"Exactly, and if you don't cooperate we will torture Mary and kill them all."

"Doesn't sound very appealing."

"So you agree to my proposal?"

"No, I most certainly do not."

"Then we shall have some entertainment. Von Krod, let's show Paul what it's like to remove Mary's fingernails, one by one, and then cut out her tongue and gouge her eyes. It'll be an interesting diversion. Oh, and remove her gag so we can hear the screams"

Von Krod pulled Mary's gag from her mouth.

"You bastard!" Mary shouted, spitting towards Kali.

He laughed. "Oh, aren't you being obstreperous today! Good! Within a few moments, you'll be begging for mercy and only Paul McPherson will be able to help." Then he nodded at Von Krod, whose short, red hair seemed brighter and more menacing than ever.

Mary was both angry and fearful. She glared at Paul. "Look at you! You had time to change your clothes?"

Paul looked down at his clothes and then again at Mary.

He was wearing the same clothes as when he left the apartment that morning. "What do you mean?"

"You know what I mean," she hissed. "First you come in here dressed in rags and remove my gag, then you put the gag back in my mouth. Whose side are you on, anyway?"

"Mary," objected Paul. "I don't know what you're talking about! I've just arrived here. I wasn't the one who put that gag in your mouth."

"The hell you weren't," she insisted. "You stuffed this gag in my mouth just before everyone came in here."

Paul was dumbfounded. "No, Mary. It must be some kind of trick."

Both were certain. Both were correct.

One of the two buglers stepped forward and handed Von Krod a pair of pliers. When the servant stepped back, Von Krod moved behind Mary's chair. "You want her hands behind her or in front when I pull out her nails?"

Kali considered momentarily. "Tie her hands to the arms of the chair in the front so we can watch."

Von Krod then pulled out a knife and slit the ropes binding Mary's hands.

Her arms freed, Mary rubbed her sore, red wrists. "Paul," Mary said with a tear in her eye. "What are they going to do?"

Paul looked at her, but could not reply.

Kali shouted gleefully from his high seat. "Why don't you answer? Why don't you tell her that she won't require nail polish anymore? Why don't you tell her how she's going to suffer immeasurable pain because you're such a cruel and heartless fool and plan to watch her suffer and do nothing?"

"Shut up!" Paul shouted back. "If you lay so much as a finger on her, I'll kill you!"

"You? Kill me?" He roared with laughter once again. "You humans have no power to harm me. You already tried to kill me before, and failed!"

"What the hell are you talking about?" Paul complained.

Kali smiled. Stupid kid. But Paul *had* tried to stop him before, and the king wasn't about to let it happen again. "Get on with it, Von Krod. We're wasting time. If the boy doesn't cooperate, we'll torture them right in front of him, one by one."

155

Mary's waist and legs were still securely tied. With great content, Von Krod grabbed her by the hands to tie her arms to the chair in front.

"Let go of her!" Paul demanded. Furious, he rushed forward and grabbed Von Krod by the shoulders, tugging him away from Mary with all his might.

CHAPTER 26

Lower Manhattan, New York. July 14, 1966

"Cooper Nine code four," the dispatcher crackled on the radio.

NYPD Detective Janet Cooper, from Precinct 9, reached for her radio, held it to her face, and punched the button. "Nine, code four. Whadaya got?"

It was hot. Too damn hot to have to deal with this shit. Another New York day in Manhattan South, another goddamn murder. This one right around the corner from the precinct house. Didn't people have any respect anymore?

"I'm showing an identity on the deceased. Ijaz Akbar. DOB oh four oh seven of twenty-nine. Shows as Asian male, five foot six, one-eighty, black hair, brown eyes. Over."

"Sounds about right, over."

"Out of Pakistan," the dispatcher continued. "Emigrated five years ago with his family. Completely legal. Has wife and two kids. Over."

"Ten-four. Copy. Confirm that." She clipped the radio back on her belt. "Shit," she said, turning to uniformed Officer Moreno. "Guy was only in his forties. Has the deceased man's wife been informed?"

"Yes, Ma'am. We have informed her. She hasn't arrived yet, but she's on the way."

"Witnesses?"

"Not a witness. Man who discovered the crime scene. Over there." Officer Moreno pointed his finger. "Just a customer who entered the store after it happened."

"Where's my partner?"

"Ortega is inside the crime scene, Ma'am."

Cooper walked up to the man standing outside the jewelry store and looked him in the eye. "Excuse me, sir. You were the one who reported the murder?"

The man was all tears. His curly, black hair hung in strands and the whites of his green eyes were red. He glanced up, nodded, and then quickly looked away. A uniformed cop stood near him. "It was horrible," he said. "Horrible." He covered his mouth with jittery hands and closed his bloodshot eyes briefly.

"Alright, sir. Just tell me what happened." Detective Cooper commanded confidence, standing firmly, back straight, feet spread wide. As the distressed man began to speak, she scanned her surroundings cautiously, but kept her hand off her pistol. She saw nothing out of the ordinary. No person in the crowd stood out. Murderer was probably long gone.

"I just wandered into the store," the man explained. "I was going to buy a bracelet for my wife..." He stopped. "I saw the blood on the counter. And then..."

"Where was the body?"

"Behind the counter. Blood everywhere."

"Did you touch anything? Move anything?"

"No, Ma'am. I didn't touch anything at all!"

Meanwhile, Police Officer Moreno worked diligently, cordoning the sidewalk. A black Cadillac pulled up and he tried to stop it, but Police Commissioner Richard "Dicky" O'Rorke, with 5 gold stars on his shield, got out from the back seat. Moreno thought this was highly unusual. Why would the Commissioner of NYPD show up at a murder scene involving a jewelry store?

"What the hell is *he* doing here?" Moreno asked a fellow uniformed officer. "This is a simple homicide-robbery. Happens all the time."

More squad cars showed up on the scene, and these did not have "9 pct" painted in blue letters. They were from the neighboring 5th, 6th and 7th precincts of Manhattan South.

The newly arrived squad cars blocked the entrance of the street on either end of the block and brought traffic on Second Avenue to a halt. One of the cops jumped from behind his wheel and started redirecting traffic to turn on 6th Street.

A tall man wearing a trench coat and brimmed hat approached Moreno and flashed an FBI wallet identification. "Special Agent Sidney E. Dale."

"What can I do for you, Special Agent Dale?"

"Why all the cops? Isn't this a simple homicide investigation?"

"That's what I thought," Moreno said. "Check it out. The Police Commissioner himself just arrived along with all those squad cars from neighboring precincts. What's your interest?"

"Looking for the detective in charge," Mr. Dale replied.

"That would be Detective Janet Cooper. She's that black lady talking to the man over there."

"Two people killed?"

"Two?" Moreno was surprised. "Agent Dale, there was only one as far as I know. The shopkeeper."

Meanwhile, Police Commissioner O'Rorke gathered a couple of officers around him. "I don't want any reporters. Any show up here, you tell them nothing, and you don't let them past that line. Understood?" He pointed. "Who's that?"

"FBI," one of the officers replied, looking at the federal agent who was approaching Detective Cooper.

"This is a local crime. FBI has no jurisdiction here," O'Rorke told the officers. "I'll talk to him."

Commissioner O'Rorke hurried to intercept Agent Dale. "Can I help you?"

"Hello, Dicky."

"Sidney."

"Got everything under control, here?"

The Commissioner looked around before replying. "Under wraps."

"Then I guess no need for us Feds to get involved, eh?"

"I'll handle it, Sidney. Gotta run. My detective just finished her interview with the witness over there."

O'Rorke walked around Sidney Dale and approached the plainclothes female detective.

"Detective Cooper, what's it look like?"

"Hello, Commissioner. Pleasant surprise. What's with all the fire power?" Cooper asked. "You've got cops here from all of the surrounding precincts."

"Need to know basis, Detective. What's your report?"

"Robbery-Homicide," Cooper explained. "Jewelry store owner. Somebody just walked in and plugged him in the head."

"How much was taken?"

"Can't say for sure. Nothing obvious."

"So robbery is out of the question?"

"Too early to say," Cooper replied. "My partner, Detective Ortega, is investigating inside the store now."

"How are you and Lance getting on?"

"My husband and I divorced two months ago, Sir."

"Sorry to hear that. You doing okay?"

"I'm doing fine, Commissioner. Never better."

"Good. Glad to hear it. That man over there responsible for this?" O'Rorke asked, nodding toward the distressed man, knowing damn well he had nothing to do with it.

"No sir," Cooper replied. "He discovered the body. We have no suspects, no motive."

"Make it a suicide," O'Rorke demanded.

Cooper blinked, and looked the Commissioner in the eye. "Excuse me, Sir?"

"I said, make it a suicide. Understand? He shot himself. He had family problems. Plain and simple. I don't want a homicide on this one. You understand, Cooper?"

"I don't know if I can do that, sir," Cooper objected.

"This is a suicide. Got it? Or else I'll have your ass."

"How are you going to explain the bullet wound to the center of the guy's forehead?"

"Leave that to me. I know the coroner. This was a suicide. Wrap it up, get the body bagged, and we'll get all these cops out of here."

Detective Cooper nodded hesitantly and O'Rorke walked back to his car. He opened the back door and got in, then picked up the radio microphone fixed to the back of the driver seat. "You there?"

"I'm still here," the reply crackled.

"Cooper will cooperate. I've got her ass." O'Rorke was

referring to the other night when he caught Cooper doing a little bookkeeping business on the side. He could have her ejected from the force for that, and Cooper knew it.

"Good," the voice on the radio replied. "Make sure it's kept under control."

Across the street, a man with a black suit, white shirt and tie, holding a briefcase containing a Walther PPK with a silencer, adjusted his dark, wraparound sunglasses. He turned off his walkie talkie, clipped it on his belt and walked away from the crime scene. An unmarked, black Bell Huey helicopter was waiting for him on the roof of the skyscraper a few blocks down the street.

CHAPTER 27

Underground Throne Room

Von Krod let go of Mary's wrists, clenched his fists and spun around swinging his right arm, wind rushing over his knuckles. But he did not connect with the head of Paul McPherson as he expected. The monk had ducked.

As the fist passed over his head, Paul slugged the man low in the stomach, first with his right fist, then his left, then again his right and left, but this man's muscles were iron and he realized he was wasting his time.

Von Krod locked the fingers of both hands tightly together, raised his arms and then swung his full might downward toward the monk's back, but McPherson dove to the side, slid on the floor, and again there was no contact.

Kali laughed uproariously. "Never mind him, Von Krod!"

Von Krod turned back to Mary who flailed her untied arms at him. He grabbed one of her wrists, whipped out a length of rope from his pocket, and jammed her forearm onto the chair.

Paul charged Von Krod from behind, and when he was two yards out he let his feet leave the ground. His body tilted backward and the heals of his feet connected with the back of Von Krod's knees, buckling him forward. The man toppled over Mary's chair, and Paul landed upright with one foot on either side of the assailant's head. As his foot started to lift, Von Krod grabbed the ankle and brought

Time Gods

Paul tumbling downward.

Standing up, he dragged Paul across the floor, face down. Paul tried unsuccessfully to free himself by kicking.

Clearing Mary's chair, Von Krod spun him in a full circle and sent him sailing into the air and into a stack of the good delivery bars, tearing his t-shirt and flesh. The stack did not topple, however. Each shiny bullion bar weighed 12.44 kilograms, or over 27 pounds. It was the same as throwing him into a solid rock face.

Enjoying the performance, Kali laughed from his throne and clapped his hands. Lobe, Connie and Durukti also looked on with sadistic pleasure while McPherson rolled over onto his hands and knees and then tried to stand. "Let him have some fun before he dies," Durukti told the others.

Von Krod howled frightfully and charged forward.

Meanwhile, Mary's hands were no longer tied, but she was still tied to the chair around the waist, and her feet to the chair legs. She frantically attempted to reach the knots behind her back.

Adrenaline surging through his veins, Paul's fingers closed around a gold bar at the top of the stack and he tried to lift it. Heavy, and 11 inches in length, the bar was difficult to raise, so he grabbed it with both hands, peeling it off the top of the pile.

The golden missile hit Von Krod hard and impacted with a crunching noise. His upper torso spun backward, his feet flew upward, and his back crashed into the tile floor, gold bar landing solidly at his side.

Paul ran toward Mary, but fell over when Von Krod grabbed his foot again. This time Von Krod's fingers wrapped around his ankle and squeezed hard as he stood up. With one hand he tossed McPherson through the air and onto the floor, sliding backward into another pile of gold bullion.

Von Krod looked down and coughed. A trickle of blood dripped from his mouth, then in the next moment he was healed. Hissing and grinding his teeth, he picked up the gold bar at his feet and hurled it with great speed using only one hand.

Frequent practice of Taekwondo had piqued Paul's reactive time, equipping him with combative skills. Rolling sideways on the floor, he watched as the gold bar hurled past end over end, brushing his shirt and missing his chest by a fraction of an inch.

The heavy missile buried itself low and deep into the stack of bullion. There was a loud crash and golden bricks flew into the air, upward and backward. Paul continued to roll sideways. The bars were too heavy to bounce. When they hit the floor, they stayed where they were.

Paul felt dizzy. In the side of his eye there was movement as Von Krod came at him again, but he could not escape. He tried to duck and turn sideways, but the powerful man's hand grabbed him by the neck, picked him up and lifted his feet off the ground.

Choking, Paul tried to kick and punch, but his arms were not long enough and his kicking ineffectual. He watched the man clench his other fist and he turned his head. The powerful blow came to the side of his face, sending Paul into an arcing trajectory through the air.

His hands reached out but there was nothing to grab. His feet swung wildly, but there was no ground to grip. When he finally landed, he slid backwards across the smooth surface, through a small opening in the wall, and across a small room, his back striking the far wall.

There was a man in this space, back to Paul, punching buttons on a panel. The man turned and raised his finger to his mouth, hushing, and Paul remembered he had seen this person hiding behind the stacks of gold before running into this room. He had kept the intruder a secret, and now he was looking at him face to face.

The man was dressed in identical clothing that Paul was wearing. The side of his face was bleeding. There was also blood on his torn shirt. Paul looked down, and saw his own shirt had been torn the same way.

When he looked up he saw the man had turned his back to him and was again punching buttons on the panel. He spoke to him with his back turned.

"Get out, now. Face Von Krod."

Paul slid to his hands and knees. "Who are you?"

"I'm your best friend in the whole world," the man said, and the voice sounded familiar. "Get out now!"

Best friend? Sending him back out into the hands of that

monster? But Mary and his grandparents were out there. If he didn't keep trying, they would torture them. He couldn't allow that to happen.

Paul looked toward the throne where Kali sat and saw Von Krod fast approaching. He raised himself up on his toes and charged out of the room, diving his head into Von Krod's stomach, pushing him backwards and toppling them both over.

When they landed, Paul was on top, and the man with red hair wrapped his arms around him and began to squeeze. His grip was powerful, and Paul thought his ribs might crack. He could not breath. He wanted to strike Von Krod, but his arms were pinned underneath his. He tried to jab him with his knees, but the grip was too powerful and he didn't have enough room. Finally, he did the only thing that came to his mind. He drove his forehead hard into Von Krod's snout.

The hold loosened and blood spurted from Von Krod's nose. Paul pushed himself off and stood up, but Von Krod gripped his legs with both arms and again began to squeeze. Paul clenched his fists and struck the man again and again on the back, but the man did not release his grip.

Still holding Paul by his legs, just above his knees, Von Krod stood up and lifted Paul's feet off the ground. He flipped him backwards and smashed the monk onto his back.

Paul groaned but adrenaline empowered him. He stood up and tried to run forward, but powerful and large hands seized his neck and Von Krod began to strangle him. As Von Krod's grip grew tighter around his neck, Paul understood he had from three to seven seconds to either free himself or lose consciousness. He drew both arms between Von Krod's arms and reached for the ceiling. In training, that worked. Today it did not.

Paul brought his arms back down to his side, and raised his right arm sideways above his head and straight up - pinching Von Krod's left fingers between Paul's neck and his upraised shoulder. Paul then turned sideways.

Von Krod was unable to keep his grip on Paul's neck and was forced to let go. As Paul continued to twist on his feet to a right angle, he grabbed Von Krod's still groping left hand

and jammed his right arm out and backwards, catching him on the side of the face with his clenched fist. Paul then forced his right foot backwards just below Von Krod's knee, scraping the attacker's shin and stomping hard on his foot. With a normal person, more than seven pounds pressure would fracture the Cuneiform and Metatarsal bones in the top of the foot, but Von Krod's foot felt like a piece of steel.

A voice shouted from the small room: "Yes!"

Von Krod turned toward the opening, forgetting Paul McPherson for the moment. A high-voltage, self-regenerative resonant blue lightning-like spark shot from the room, and then another and another. As the bands of blue electrical energy streaked from the room, making a tumultuous snapping sound, the ground quaked violently, cracking the marble floor. Glass shards from overhanging chandeliers fell, shattering on the floor. An entire stack of gold collapsed and scattered bullion everywhere.

Von Krod punched Paul's stomach, who buckled over, gasping for air. As Paul fell to the ground, Von Krod walked into the small side room. The shooting streaks of electricity ceased. He looked around, puzzled. The room was empty. No one was operating the controls. Had their been a short circuit? Was that possible?

If Paul wanted to stay alive and rescue his girlfriend and future grandparents, all tied to chairs behind him, he'd have to act decisively. Yet his muscles were so drained that he could move only with difficulty. Was this the way he was meant to die?

Von Krod had his back to him, standing in that small room. Paul saw a chance to attack again if he could only muster the strength. Perhaps Von Krod was talking with the man in there. He didn't know. He didn't care. All that mattered was that he was in there, back turned. Paul gasped for air and stood up.

Von Krod turned around. Paul charged. He gripped Paul by his shoulders, lifting him off the ground with a grin, and threw him against an onyx pillar on the outer wall of Kali's cavernous room. Nearby, a marble statue fell over and shattered.

Von Krod moved in for the final blow. He lifted his foot back, ready to give Paul a lethal kick to his stomach.

"That's enough!" boomed Kali from the throne. Paul never thought he'd be relieved to hear Kali's voice. Kali had been enjoying the show, but now it was time to get on with business. They had made their point. "Play time is over. Let's get back to the girl."

However, Von Krod couldn't control his anger. He didn't kick, but leaned over, lifting Paul by the scruff of his neck. Hurling him backward, he sent him reeling headfirst into the small room again.

Paul saw the room was now vacant. That was odd. There seemed to be only one way in or out of the room. Where had that man punching the buttons disappeared to?

It didn't matter. There were many things happening he didn't understand.

His head reeled. He tried to stand, but his feet slipped out from under him. He breathed in deeply. When he stood up again he became dizzy, falling sideways. He put his hand out to break his fall and his palm landed on a large black button on the wall. There was a bright flash. Ribbons of blue energy shot out from the upper corners of the room. Paul lost consciousness as electrical sparks danced all around him.

* * *

Vex Von Krod rushed into the room as the sparks subsided, but found the room vacant. Paul McPherson had dematerialized.

"Fool!" blared Kali, standing up from his throne.

CHAPTER 28

Bharatvarsha (India), 2,980 B.C.

Mahashay Manu rested comfortably between satin sheets, dreaming he was walking barefoot through a rice patty, mud oozing pleasantly between his toes, smelling sweet flowering jasmine trees in the soft breeze.

He was startled from slumber by a loud knock on the heavy teakwood door. He sat up abruptly.

The room was not entirely dark. A tall, brass ghee lamp flickered orange light in the corner of the plush bed chamber. Had someone knocked, or was he dreaming?

The knock came again.

"Yes, yes," he said in his native Sanskrit tongue. "Just a moment."

He was alone in bed. It was not the custom for a man to sleep with his wife unless they were trying to have children. The women of the palace slept in separate chambers.

Mahashay slipped the covers off and stepped onto the polished white marble floor, covering himself with a robe draped near the bedside.

The knocking came a third time, more insistent.

He crossed the spacious room and opened the large, ornately carved wooden door. The hallway outside his door glowed with flickering light from pitch torches. A lone guard stood facing him, wearing the traditional royal uniform.

The man spoke gruffly, though Mahashay knew him to

be a considerate man. "His Majesty wishes to meet with the Council of *Brahmins* immediately."

"At this hour? Is he unwell?"

"Not as far as I know, Your Holiness."

"Then what is wrong?"

"I do not know, venerable sir. Ever since returning from his journey, His Majesty has seemed troubled. Tonight he could not sleep."

Mahashay furled his brow. It was not unusual for His Majesty to consult with Mahashay and the Council of *Brahmins*, but why the urgency and at this hour? Were things not well in the kingdom? Were the citizens unhappy in some way? Was there some threat of war with an opposing king? Surely that could not be. The Emperor had conquered and made peace with all of the neighboring kingdoms. People were happy under his rule.

As a *Brahmin,* Mahashay was a spiritual leader of society, socially higher than even the king, who belonged to the *kshatriya*, or warrior class. Customarily, the king would consult the Council of *Brahmins* whenever there were difficult decisions to make. He trusted their spiritual guidance. Something serious must have happened. A crises of sorts.

"I will be with you in a few moments," Mahashay said, still half asleep.

After washing his face and mouth in a bowl near the lamp, Mahashay straightened his white hair and beard. He attired himself in silk robes, hung his wooden *japa* beads around his neck and left with the guard.

The two moved briskly into the warm night. Stars filled the black sky and a partial moon lit the stone pathway through the King's court. Mahashay glanced up at the moon and realized, astrologically, waxing moons were favorable, waning moons not. This was not a good time for important decisions.

The Brahmin Chamber, adjunct to the public hall where King Pariksit had his bedazzled throne, was a lavishly decorated structure with massive supporting fluted columns, intricately carved from stone.

The guard excused himself and Mahashay climbed the steps, passing through the arched entryway. Inside, the floor was made of highly polished black and white marble tiles, and the high-ceiling was inlaid with intricate patterns. Beautiful stone pillars embedded with rubies and sapphires lined the walls. In the center of the hall Mahashay saw the other eight members of the Council waiting, standing near ornate rosewood chairs around a huge walnut table.

The King had not yet arrived, and so they remained standing as Mahashay entered. Folding their hands in the traditional gesture of prayer, he greeted them, as they similarly greeted him. He moved forward and embraced each of them firmly.

Then Mahashay asked, "Is something wrong?"

"The Emperor is troubled," replied Guru Acharya, a senior member of the Council of *Brahmins*. "He was unable to sleep and called for us."

"His health is failing?" asked Mahashay, still trying to fathom the depth of the concern.

"Not that I am aware," Guru Acharya replied. "Something metaphysical disturbs him, I'm afraid."

Guru Acharya was an ascetic who had renounced family life for spiritual pursuit. While the others wore white or multi-colored silk garments, he wore orange robes, the dress of a renunciate. Though a year younger than Mahashay Manu, Guru Acharya was senior through renunciation. Both of them were regarded highly by the Emperor, as were all the members of the Council.

These nine holy men were known as *sama-darsi*, wise advisors. They taught the King to devote himself to God and to the welfare of his citizens. It was custom for the Emperor to seek guidance from them on important issues, including spiritual and practical affairs. The King, being a pious man, would accept their guidance when formulating decisions.

As for the Emperor himself, he was a popular king who ruled his subjects with kindness and consideration. His citizens were happy with his rule and considered the King their father. Similarly, the King regarded his citizens as his own flesh and blood and would gladly lay down his life for their protection.

The country was at peace. There had not been a war since his own father had been unfairly slain in the great battle at Kurukshetra, north of Hastinapura. Yet, not all was well in the kingdom.

Astrological advisers foretold of increasing danger due to paranormal influence. The King, too, sensed the danger, but was not able to get more information from his astrologers. He spoke frequently about being vigilant to guard the kingdom, although no other kingdom threatened them. Mahashay had even wondered about the King's sanity.

After a short time, the great Emperor arrived at the Council of *Brahmins*, and walked alone into their midst, leaving his entourage of guards waiting outside.

Mahashay regarded him carefully. He was young for a king, raised by his grandfather and grand-uncles, themselves all sons of the great King Pandu.

According to legend, in the last days of the Great War, a King named Ashvatam used some kind of metaphysical *mantra* in an attempt to kill King Pariksit while he was still within his mother's womb. Lord Krishna saved the unborn baby from death and then disfigured King Ashvatam's face, leaving him with a dented forehead. Dishonored in this way, Krishna banished Ashvatam to live thousands of years in the Himalayas without dying. Even in modern times people say there is a connection between the Abominable Snowman and the disfigured Ashvatam.

Having been saved from Ashvatam by Lord Krishna before birth, King Pariksit grew up always seeking God in all things, and that is why his mother named him Pariksit, "one who seeks."

Earlier tonight King Pariksit adorned himself in simple, royal attire. He dispensed with crown and jewelry, wearing only a bejeweled shawl and silk pants. As he entered the Council Hall, he saw his Brahmin advisors were already present. Humbly bowing before them, he came forward and touched their feet beginning with Mahashay Manu and Guru Acharya.

The King then motioned for all to be seated and he himself sat at the head of the assembly. He then spoke, using pleasing words filled with gravity, deploying the finest of Sanskrit grammar. His voice was deep and his words were slow and deliberate.

"My dear *Brahmins*. Please forgive me for summoning you so late at night. I am deeply perturbed, and seek advice on a matter of utmost urgency.

"You may recall that only last week I returned from a journey throughout the kingdom on your behest to discover what ails our countrymen. Our astrologers have predicted this would be a dark and foreboding time, and so I was given the task by your holy selves to set out on a chariot to discovering what dissatisfaction, if any, exists with our people.

"Oh *Brahmins*, I am happy to report that everywhere people greeted me with honor and respect. Yet I could sense that, as the astrologers predicted, not all was well. There was something in the air, an atmosphere of inauspiciousness, the source of which I could not trace out. Equipped with bow and arrow, I rode my chariot into the mountains in search for answers.

"What I discovered was unthinkable and unconscionable! Neither I, nor my ancestors before me, have ever before witnessed such an atrocity!"

"Pray tell!" gasped Guru Acharya, as the members of the Council of *Brahmins* sat erect. "What did you see, dear King?"

The great Emperor looked downtrodden. His eyes filled with tears as he shook his head dejectedly. Looking up at the members of the Council with great concern, he continued his narration.

"There was a man – a most peculiar man, if I dare call him a man. He was dressed like a king, yet he was beating a cow and a bull with a club. Oh *Brahmins*, how could such a thing take place in my kingdom? The cow is our holy mother, who provides milk for us to drink. The bull is our father, for he tills the field and provides us with fresh fruits and vegetables by which we sustain ourselves. To think that anyone could harm such defenseless creatures was inconceivable to me.

"Seated on my gold-embossed chariot, I addressed that vile man with a voice sounding like thunder. 'Who are you who tortures the poor bull? You appear to be strong and yet you dare kill, within my protection, those who are helpless. By dress you pose as a king, but I see you are nothing but a rogue! Now, for the first time in a kingdom well protected by the descendants of the Kuru dynasty, I see defenseless creatures grieving with tears in their eyes.'

"I then said to him: 'As you are beating the innocent you are a culprit and must be killed!' Immediately I drew my sword and towered over that cowardly person. Alas, I should have killed him then and there, but that monstrous man fell at my feet with his hands folded. He said, 'O King, spare me from your sharpened sword! I am Kali, empowered by Lord Vishnu to wreak havoc on the earth in order to fulfill the desires of the conditioned souls rotting in material existence. Please do not kill me!'

"What was I do? You all know my code of honor. A surrendered soul or a fleeing enemy cannot be killed. Seeing that devil clasping my feet, I hesitated. I ask of you, dear *Brahmins*, was I mistaken not to take his life?"

The Brahmins all shook their heads in response. "You acted correctly, my King," Mahashay ventured. "According to moral code you may not slay a surrendered soul."

King Pariksit continued. "How cunning this was. A cowardly man deserving death was saved by his own scheming. His falling on my feet made him impossible for me to kill, and I am certain he knew this! This was the will of Providence!"

"What happened next?" asked Guru Acharya.

"I said to that trembling person, 'Rise up, cowardly man! Since you have surrendered yourself with folded hands you need not fear for your life. But you cannot remain in my kingdom. You do not deserve to remain here.'

"Kali then said, 'O chief protector of religiosity, your kingdom is everywhere! Grant me a residence where I can live permanently protected within the limits of your rein.'

"'Very well,' I replied, drawing on the power of my own piety. 'You may live wherever you find gambling, intoxication, illicit sex, and the slaughter of animals.'

"However, that man replied, 'Thank you, Your Majesty! But alas! As long as you are the Emperor, such places do not exist! Therefore, I beg you to also find me a practical place I may reside!'

"What was I to do? My code of ethics bound me to make a determination where this low life could live under my own protection!"

The Emperor paused. His eyes became filled with

concern. The members of the Council of *Brahmins* could understand how troubled he appeared to be. Mahashay leaned forward and placed his question before the Emperor. "Did you agree to that proposal, dear King?"

The Emperor looked up and his eyes glanced into the eyes of each and every Council member. At length he replied with a hesitant nod. "Indeed. I granted King Kali permission to reside where there is the hoarding of gold."

"Was he satisfied with that?" asked Mahashaya.

"We shall see," replied the Emperor. "We shall see. If he cannot be contained, we will have to banish him to the mountains. I know of a valley in the Himalayas. There he can be imprisoned by towering peaks.

CHAPTER 29

Underground Lab, New York, 1966

She had dropped the LSD-laced sugar cubes from her pocket into the coffee maker before she went to the bathroom, and now Wendy Murphy was back in her cage. The technicians had taken several cups of coffee since then and were now thoroughly tripping on acid.

The effects of LSD are somewhat unpredictable. The outcome depends on amount taken, personality, mood, expectations and surroundings. That Wendy had slipped them four times the amount she normally ingested only contributed to the unpredictability of the outcome. Under normal circumstances a user can detect the first effects of the drug within a half hour; these technicians were tripping after only fifteen.

One technician was lying on his back, staring at the ceiling. The other tech was staring at Wendy, entertaining the hallucination that she was a famous movie actress. Neither man had any idea why they were tripping, or even that they were hallucinating at all. Their state of consciousness was so far into outer space, it was amazing that they did not float away.

The first effects that Wendy observed were their impaired motor skills and dilated pupils. She assumed they also experienced numbness, rapid reflexes and an increase in their blood pressure and heart rate. Now that the technicians were beyond the initial symptoms, Wendy knew they must also be experiencing distorted perceptions of time, distance, gravity and the space between one's self and one's environment – feeling oneness with the universe.

The problem was that they drank their coffee after locking Wendy back in shackles inside the secured cage. Now she was hogtied with handcuffs and shackles in a room monitored by crazed technicians.

Her friend, the other woman in the cage with her, was now effectively a vegetable. Wendy realized she could do nothing to help her at the moment. She had to save herself first.

"I feel hot," Wendy said.

The man in the white coat staring at her did not blink. She smiled, he smiled.

"I need to take off my clothes. Can you help me?"

She smiled again, he smiled back again.

"Can you please unlock my hands and feet so I can take off my clothes? If you do, I promise I'll make it worth your while." She pursed her lips and blew a kiss at him.

The man blinked. "You'd do that for me?"

"Let's just say I'm no virgin. Don't you want to see what I can do without clothes on?"

The man nodded and fumbled for keys in his pocket.

"The keys are on the gurney," Wendy told him. "You put them there awhile ago."

He nodded, then reached for the keys and came toward the cage door.

A few minutes later, Wendy walked out of the lab wearing one of the white jackets. She had already cleaned herself up as best she could in the bathroom. The two technicians were safely handcuffed to the bars of the cage, too tripped out on hallucinogens to know what was happening or why.

Closing the door behind her, she found herself in an underground tunnel. To her right she saw the intersection of more tunnels. The floor was highly polished granite. The rough-cut walls studded with gems. Electric fixtures along the walls provided adequate lighting.

The next step was to rescue her friend Mary. The technicians had told her earlier that Mary was being held captive by "the King." She assumed he was some kind of rock star.

A man in a suit and tie walked by. "Excuse me," she said. "I'm lost. Which way to the King?"

"The King, are you serious?"

"Why, don't I look serious?"

"Well, judging by your white coat, you obviously work here. So you should already know."

"Know what?"

"Nobody sees the King."

"Why, is he like the Wizard of Oz?"

The man chuckled. "Well, never thought of it like that. I guess. Nowhere, no how, does anyone get to see the King."

"Then how do you know there is a King?"

"I don't! All I know is the powers that be talk about him. He apparently owns this whole underground joint. I just come here to gamble."

"How do you get here to gamble?"

"There's a secret passage from the subway that leads to an elevator which descends down here. You have to be on a special list to ride the elevator. They check everyone's ID."

"So if there was a King, where might one find him?"

"I'm headed in that general direction," the man said. "Follow me. Security is tight where you want to go. Hope you got the credentials."

"Will I need a guitar?"

"Guitar? Listen, lady. For a worker down here, you should know this is no King of Rock and Roll we're dealing with. This is more like a King of Saudi Arabia or something."

The two strolled through the long tunnel carved in stone and earth. Along the way, Wendy ran her fingers through her blonde hair and tried to untangle the knots as best she could.

CHAPTER 30

Underground Throne Room

His eyelids fluttered open. He strained his ears, yet all was quiet.

The floor was cold and hard. Paul McPherson's body ached from his bruises, his shirt was torn and blood stained. Slowly sitting up, he looked around. The room was empty. He heard only silence.

He had passed out. He knew that now. But for how long?

Then he heard faint sounds, muffled grunts and groans in the distance. Von Krod was about to charge in and finish him off.

When no one came into the opening of the small room, he peered out into Kali's grand hall. He saw the throne. Mary and his two grandparents were still tied to the chairs, struggling. Mary's hands looked like they were tied behind her back again. All three of them were gagged.

Strangely, the rest of Kali's hall was quiet and the throne was deserted. A full minute passed, and still no one came to confront Paul.

As he waited, he tried to understand what he had learned from his abductors. Kali had said he wanted Paul to murder a little person with an odd name. *But why him?* With people like Von Krod around Kali didn't need Paul to do his work. It made no sense to require Paul to kill someone.

Another minute passed, and still, no one entered the small room.

Paul quietly stepped into the large chamber and looked around. He noticed the pile of gold bars that had been scattered in the fight with Anger Personified was neatly stacked. The marble statue that had fallen and broken was no longer broken. Had it been replaced with a new, identical statue?

As he stepped forward, Mary, Helen and Henry turned their heads and saw him. Elated, but unable to speak, they could scarcely contain themselves.

Carefully examining his surroundings once more, Paul felt confident that King Kali and the kidnappers were gone, but he did not understand why they had gone. It was probably some kind of trick, he realized, but he would take the bait anyway. He had to do what he could to free his grandparents and Mary.

He reached Mary's chair first. Her arms were tied behind her back, as they were before. He removed the gag from her mouth.

"Paul!" she exclaimed. "What happened to you?"

"You still mad at me?"

"What do you mean, mad at you?" she repeated. "Look at you. You look awful. What did they do to you? How did you find me?"

"You sure have a way of confusing me, Mary. One minute you're angry at me for I don't know what reason, and now you're happy. What do you mean what happened to me?"

"Oh, never mind! Quick, untie me," she insisted.

"Do you mind if I remove the gag from my grandparents first?"

"Your grandparents?" She looked over at the other two tied beside her. "Are you nuts?"

"Mary, they're my future grandparents," explained Paul. "Didn't you understand anything Kali said?"

"Who is Kali?"

Suddenly there were voices outside the golden door of the hall. Paul's heart pounded. "They're coming back," he gasped. His hands hovered over his grandmother's gag, but it was too late. Moving quickly back to Mary, he looked pitifully at her. "Forgive me!" he pleaded, and replaced the gag back over her mouth.

Mary was furious, and protested, of course, but could no longer say anything. She couldn't believe Paul put the gag back in her mouth.

"You have to be just as you were. Sorry! Don't say anything. Don't let them know I'm still here. I'll come back as soon as they're gone."

He decided the small room was a safer place to hide than behind a pile of gold. However, first he would have to cross the cavernous hall. There wasn't enough time. They were already coming in.

The large, golden door opened slowly, and in walked two doorkeepers, holding over-sized bugles. They carefully surveyed the large hall. Besides the three hostages, they saw no one. One of them pushed the huge door closed again, and they took their positions on either side. "We have to be on call all the time. It's not fair," said one of the men. "There are so many people down here having fun, and all we get to do is stand guard."

"Never mind. It pays well," said the other. "Where else would you get paid in land and property for a few month's work?"

"Yeah, but I would give anything to see the sun once in awhile."

Paul concealed himself behind the platform that supported Kali's throne. Cautiously, he peered at the guards. He had expected something more dramatic to occur, such as the return of Kali and his cronies. Yet, the doorkeepers were also Kali's men, and possibly every bit as dangerous.

Soon there were more sounds outside. The doorkeepers prepared themselves to blow their bugles.

"That must be him!" Nervously, they both stood at attention.

Paul realized that the others were returning, but why they left so suddenly was still a mystery. The great, golden door swung slowly open and in stepped Kali himself. Powerful and regal, he looked carefully around the cavernous room, noting the three hostages tied to their chairs. Nearing his throne, he approached the three hostages. "Hello," he said. "I hope you're all comfortable and enjoying yourselves. I suppose you are wondering why we brought you here today. We will let you know shortly."

Kali then turned and climbed the stairs to his throne. Once situated, he pressed a button on his armrest and the large throne slowly pivoted on its turntable until he faced away from the golden door. Now he was directly above Paul, who crouched hidden below.

Around that time Paul felt the urge to pee. He had not previously noticed the pressure in his bladder, which felt full. But there was nowhere he could go here. The sense of urgency to urinate cannot be properly appreciated until one needs to go but cannot.

While trying to get his mind off his bladder, he felt a sudden tickling in the nerve endings in his nose. Unfortunately, sneezes were an automatic reflex that couldn't be stopped once commenced. No matter what, therefore, he must not let a sneeze begin.

His eyes began to water and he still felt his bladder was full.

* * *

London, England. 1966

Behind a black door with a lion's head knocker, screwed to a door with a letterbox inscribed "First Lord of the Treasury," the Prime Minister, Harold Wilson, spoke to the President of the United States over a secure line. "A week is a long time in politics," he said. "What to speak of two."

"Ya'll know it's the end of the month," the President said with his characteristic Texas drawl. "Mark it on your calendar. You've got to be there, Harold. Your MI6 people as well."

"Yes, my advisors find your position is reasonable."

This was diplomacy. One had to be diplomatic, especially when speaking to the great Texan on the phone. He wasn't sure the meeting was a good idea or not, but the United Kingdom was committed.

Harold's childhood had been humble. His father was a

chemist and his mother a teacher. He first made a name for himself by careful planning in the political sphere. Only three years ago he managed to become Leader of the Opposition. The following year he led the Labour Party to a general election which catapulted him into the role of Prime Minister. Now he had direct access to the Queen, and she supported the idea that the Brits should spearhead the future of the free world by attending the meeting in the Himalayas.

Convincing the Conservative Party to go for President Johnson's cowboy scheme would not be difficult. It was his own Labour Party that he worried about. This wasn't his idea of savvy politics.

"Really, Mr. President. Even if I go personally, you can't expect the head of the British Secret Intelligence Service to attend as well!"

"It's not an option, Harold. Also your military leaders have to be there. You don't want history to forget you."

President Johnson hit the nail on the head. Harold didn't want history to forget him. After all, the Prime Minister lived on historical land. Once a marshy bog, the area was first settled by the Romans who drained the water away two thousand years ago. Later, King Edward the Confessor changed the name of the island to Westminster, upon which 10 Downing Street was now situated. Harold Wilson hoped he too would leave his mark on Westminster by being the first Prime Minister to bring flying automobiles and time travel to England.

The President furled his brow and spoke confidentially, yet firmly. "I can see you're a thinking man, because you don't agree on everything. I always said that if two men agree on everything, you may be sure that only one of them is doing the thinking. But you don't want to be left behind, do you Harold? It's important that Britain is on board."

Politics. The Prime Minister knew it well. What did he expect when speaking to LBJ? Of course he would try to pressure him. Getting other leaders of the free world to attend would help the Americans justify the risk.

Yet there was also truth in what the President had said. "He who rejects change is the architect of decay," the Prime Minister had himself once said. "The only human institution which rejects progress is the cemetery."

"Alright, Mr. President," he finally agreed. "Britain is on board."

"You know damn well it will end the Cold War," the President explained. "Remember, without signing the MUPDA, the United States will not agree with LTTA either, and I have secured Professor Cali's word on that. It may be, it just may be, that life as we know it is more unique than many have thought. Just imagine."

The Prime Minister tried to envision the whole proposal. The Himalayas for a conference with Professor Cali? If it would give his country the technology the professor was promising, it would definitely be worth the journey. Above all, it would keep the yanks happy.

"One more thing, Harold," Lyndon added.

"What's that, ol' boy?"

"Do you believe in the theory that the Professor has about people getting shorter?"

"Shorter, Sir?"

"Like Leprechauns. Those little people who dress in green with funny hats."

"I know what a Leprechaun is, Mr. President. What is the Professor saying?"

"He says people in the future get smaller and the CIA has given me a weird report from Area 51 that seems to confirm it. We captured these weird Leprechaun people when they popped out of some kind of space-time hole or something. Alternate universes and all that crap."

Harold nodded his head. "At this point, Lyndon, I would believe anything Professor Cali says."

CHAPTER 31

Kali's Underground Kingdom, New York. 1966

Once again, the giant golden door slowly creaked open, and in walked five people. Concealed carefully at the bottom of the platform, Paul peered out and saw Connie, Durukti and Lobe. Behind them Von Krod pushed in a prisoner. Paul couldn't see him clearly because the others were crowded around.

The two men standing on either side of the doorway sounded their bugles. The chubby man, Lobe, looked up toward the throne and cleared his throat nervously. "My Lord," he said loudly. "We've brought him on your behest."

The throne atop the platform revolved around, and as it gradually came to full front, the rotation gently stopped, and Kali chuckled to himself.

Someone in the room asked, "Who the hell are you?"

Paul was dumbfounded upon hearing the familiar voice – that was his *own* voice.

"Search him," the King ordered. "Make sure he doesn't have that particle beam gun." Paul looked up, but was certain he could not be seen hiding under the throne. Peeking carefully, he looked at the face of the prisoner that Von Krod and company had brought before the King.

It was Paul's own face. Paul McPherson was looking at Paul McPherson.

Promnesia, the antonym of amnesia, was an experience

of feeling sure one has witnessed or experienced a new situation previously, popularly known as Déjà vu. The etymology of Déjà vu was French, and meant "already seen." Psychoanalysts attributed this phenomena to fantasy. Psychiatrists suggested it was caused by the brain mixing up present and past. Parapsychologists thought it might be due to past-life experiences. Paul attributed it to time travel – about twenty minutes into the past it seemed.

He remembered the man in the small room awhile ago. That had also been Paul. Somehow the boundaries of past and future were becoming blurred, and Paul was running into Paul. He wasn't sure how that could happen, but it had something to do with that room over there. Maybe that button he accidentally pushed was connected to Kali's time machine. Maybe that would explain why Von Krod hadn't come back in the room to beat on him. Paul had accidentally escaped twenty minutes into the past and was now looking at himself!

From his hiding place, he peered across the huge room. Beyond several stacks of gold bullion he saw the opening to the small room. He knew now that he had to return there. He pulled his new sneakers off his feet and prepared to run back to the room in silence.

Kali laughed loudly, and as he did, the others also laughed.

Since everyone had turned away, Paul saw his opportunity. He quickly scurried across the room and crouched down behind a pile of gold bullion. He was halfway there. Unfortunately, he did not go entirely unnoticed. His other self at the door had spotted him, and as soon as that happened, Kali spun around on his throne.

Paul tucked himself tightly against the pile of gold. He waited, and finally heard Kali let out a hearty laugh yet again.

That was his queue. Peeking from around the edge of the gold, Paul saw Lobe step forward and frisk his other self. He had time for a final dash back to the safety of the small room. He quickly ran from behind the pile of gold, sneakers in hand, and straight into the little room.

Ducking around the corner so he could not be seen, he looked around and saw the room was still vacant. He tried to catch his breath as quietly as possible, heart racing.

The conversation in the big room continued exactly as it had twenty minutes before, and Paul realized he didn't have a lot of time. He quietly slipped his sneakers back on and examined the small room. Large, ceramic coils in the four corners of the ceiling pointed towards the center of the floor. There was a panel with a complex LED display, a keypad with numbers and symbols, and a big black button.

"Wouldn't you like to meet my other guests?"

Kali was introducing his other self to the hostages now.

Meanwhile, Paul examined the digital readout on the panel. If only he could figure out how to operate this thing he could go further into the past and rescue Mary and his grandparents before they were kidnapped. That was a plan!

Methodically, he punched buttons and watched the digital display. Time and time again, he was frustrated as the word "Error" appeared on the screen. It was vastly complex, and working blindly the odds were stacked firmly against him.

The sequence of events in the larger hall continued to play out as before, but he ignored what was happening there. This was important now. Gradually, he noticed a pattern to the panel's layout. By following various sequences, he was able to get it to respond by displaying helpful messages. One of those messages gave an explanation of how to get help, and when he pushed more buttons, he found himself looking at a lengthy multi-page help screen.

Kali's voice echoed freely into the little room from the larger adjoining cavern. He heard him say, "You've seen my gold. I own thousands of vats of molten gold, and stacks of gold bullion in caverns like this all over the world."

After reading the help screen, he keyed in new sequences, and the panel chirped twice. *It chirped! That's positive,* Paul thought, *but also dangerous. Someone might hear it.*

As he worked, he kept referring to the help screen. The process was complicated. Once he pushed the wrong button and it complained with a long buzzing sound. This frightened Paul, and he stopped to check if the others had heard, but they did not react.

Paul pushed another series of buttons, but the readout displayed the message: "*Error – division by zero.*" He was trying to enter a minus number so that he could go backward in time, but the control panel wasn't cooperating. There were a few details that didn't seem to be properly explained.

Outside Kali was ordering Von Krod to remove Mary's fingernails, "and then cut out her tongue and gouge her eyes. It'll be an interesting diversion. Oh, and remove the gag so we can hear her screams."

Next he assumed Mary's gag had been removed, because he overheard her shout. "You bastard!"

Paul heard Kali laughing. "*Error – division by zero.*" Again the readout displayed that most unhelpful message.

Kali gave a speech about how Mary would soon be begging for mercy, and then he heard Mary say to his other self, "Look at you! You had time to change your clothes?"

Then he heard himself reply, "What do you mean?"

"You know what I mean. First you come in here dressed in rags and remove my gag, then you put the gag back in my mouth. Whose side are you on, anyway?"

"Mary," Paul could hear himself saying. "I don't know what you're talking about! I've just arrived here. I wasn't the one who put that gag in your mouth."

"The hell you weren't," she insisted. "You stuffed this gag in my mouth just before everyone came in here."

Paul understood now that Mary was confused. She was mad at the wrong person. He was the one who put her gag back in her mouth, not that Paul that she was talking to from twenty minutes ago.

Shaking his head, Paul went back to work punching buttons. *One day I'll explain it all to her,* he thought. First, however, he had to go back in time and stop this whole thing from happening in the first place. At that thought he stopped punching buttons and scratched his head. If he stopped this from happening in the first place, he realized, he'd never have the chance to explain all this to her because none of this will have ever happened in the first place!

Paul cleared the panel and reset the display. He was gradually becoming familiar with the method of input. He continued working frantically, and as he did he heard shouting and rustling noises. He decided to peek, and when he did, he saw his other self wrestling with Von Krod in the large hall. The fight had begun.

He returned to the panel and reset it yet again. Calling up the help screen, it occurred to him that he might have missed a few important preliminary steps. He pushed a few more buttons and a new screen explained those steps.

Before long, he was pushing the buttons and the panel was receiving them without displaying error messages. Meanwhile, as the fight proceeded, he overheard his other self being badly beaten. Paul could almost feel the pain being inflicted upon himself all over again. Sooner than expected, he heard something heavy slide into the room, and for a moment he thought Von Krod had discovered him in the room!

He spun around and locked eyes with himself, Paul McPherson from twenty minutes ago. This time things were reversed. He was the one punching buttons on the panel and his other self was lying on the floor.

His other self looked confused. It was important that he not divulge Paul's plan! Paul raised his finger to his mouth, hushing himself!

Paul from twenty minutes ago looked at Paul standing up by the panel and then looked down and examined his shirt.

This must be confusing, Paul thought. It had been to him awhile ago, so it was probably true for the other Paul, too. Unfortunately, the other guy had would have to get back into the fight and Paul would have to finish punching buttons on the panel.

He turned his back and started punching buttons again, and with his back turned to the other Paul, said, "Get out, now. Face Von Krod."

"Who are you?"

"I'm your best friend in the whole world," Paul from the present said to his other self from the past. "Get out now!"

Paul's counterpart, although confused, acknowledged the request. Bewildered, he charged out of the small room and back into the hands of Von Krod.

Suddenly the display on the panel said something completely unexpected. He blinked and re-read the display.

The message said, "Ready."

Could that be it? Maybe he had made a mistake! Maybe the machine was ready for something unwanted!

Paul's hand hovered over the big black button. He had pushed it before. Almost electrocuted himself, as he recalled. Dare he push it again? He knew what would happen. All those electrical sparks would shoot out from the ceramic coils in the ceiling and jolt him. Maybe kill him.

Once as a child, Paul's parents had taken him to visit a farm in New Hampshire. The farmer had placed an electric fence around his field to keep his animals contained. Paul remembered touching it and getting a big electrical jolt that knocked him off his feet. Punching this button, he realized, would be like touching that electric fence.

The problem was what would happen if he didn't push the button. Out there in that room was Mary along with Helen and Henry McPherson, his future grandparents. Their lives were in jeopardy, and as far as he could see, this was the only way to save them. He had access to Kali's time machine. He had to use it!

He slammed the button with his hand. "Yes!" he shouted.

The four coils in the corners of the room flashed and within a fraction of a second, Paul was enveloped in blue ribbons of energy. There was another flash of light, and then the whole machine lost power before anything else happened.

Oh no!

It had failed! Short circuit, or mis-programmed. Either way, it failed! Now Paul was in some serious hot water.

CHAPTER 32

Underground Tunnel

As Wendy Murphy walked down the tunnel in the lab coat she'd taken from the intoxicated technician, she occasionally passed other personnel who nodded at her but kept walking.

After awhile she came across a horrific slaughter house which branched off to the side of the tunnel. In that room she saw a man in a blood stained apron slaughtering cows using a stun gun and a machete. Wendy enjoyed hamburgers and steak, but that place had the stench of rotting meat and had blood and guts all over the floor. It made her sick to her stomach.

She next passed a casino branching off the tunnel, and noted hundreds of men and women at slot machines, as well as card, crap and roulette tables. Most of these clients were well dressed. Some were happy, some distressed. Scantily clad ladies carrying free drinks wandered among the crowds, some stopping to talk or laugh with customers.

Bewildered, Wendy entered.

As she wandered among the many slot machines, she saw that she was in a massive casino. She stopped by an elderly woman playing a penny slot machine.

"Excuse me. May I ask you a question?"

The woman never let her eye leave the screen of the slot machine, but she did manage a reply. "All the way to the back. You'll see a sign."

"What's all the way to the back?"

"The Ladies Room. But don't smoke in there. The smoke detectors set off an alarm if you smoke there."

"I'm not looking for the ladies room," Wendy said politely.

"Then how can I help you, young lady?"

"Just wanted to ask you some questions."

"Well, you can smoke anywhere you want down here except in the restrooms. Smoking cigarettes, marijuana or crack cocaine is encouraged."

"Thanks for the info," Wendy said, "but it's not what I wanted to know. Mind if I ask where are you from?"

"Jamaica," she said.

"As in Queens?"

"That's right," the lady replied.

"How did you get down here?"

"Oh, you gotta have the connections. But you know that, because..." she stopped and looked up at Wendy. "Oh. You work here. You have your connections already."

"Does everyone down here work here?"

"Of course not. Do I look like a worker?"

"I didn't know all of this was legal in New York."

"New York? The way I heard it is this King from Saudi Arabia or someplace named Kali made a deal to buy all of the mineral and land use rights 2 miles below the City. Technically, none of this belongs to New York or even the United States."

"So you're saying this is outside of New York jurisdiction?"

"Lady, the Mayor and Governor come down here all the time!"

Just then Wendy saw a security guard walk by carrying a Thompson submachine gun.

"What about those security guards?" Wendy asked the lady. "Who do they work for?"

"I think all of the security people work for King Kali," the woman said. "And so do the buglers."

"Buglers?"

"You know. Those musician guys with the big trumpet things. The ones we see going in and out of the vault door."

"I was looking for that vault door," Wendy said. "We just

finished our lab tests. Gotta make a report."

"Just keep heading down the tunnel a ways. You'll run right into it. Can't go no further. But watch out."

"For what?"

The woman looked up from her slot machine again. "Those pleasure rooms they call them. It's just a legal whorehouse. I wouldn't go near the place, but you gotta walk right by it to get to the vault door. Just go back out to the tunnel and turn right. First you'll see the lounge on your left. Great place to have a drink. Beyond you'll see the pleasure rooms on the right. The vault door is past all of that."

Wendy thanked the woman profusely and made her way back to the tunnel. Following directions, she strolled along the highly polished granite floor until she came to the lounge on her left.

This was a lavishly decorated cavern, replete with stalactites and stalagmites. Where the floor was level, it was paved with highly polished stones. People sat at hundreds of tables or at the bars consuming alcoholic beverages. A musician played the piano. A giant salt water aquarium with exotic fish lined an entire wall behind one of the many bars. An official in a one-piece red suit, wearing a caboose style hat, sat having a drink. Leaning against him was a large trumpet. She'd heard about those guys.

Passing this cavern, Wendy continued down the tunnel until she came upon the so-called pleasure rooms on her right.

Not far beyond that she saw the giant circular vault door which sealed off the end of the tunnel from further passage. Two armed guards carrying machine guns and walkie talkies stood at attention.

Wendy went back to the lounge.

*   *   *

Paul entered Kali's vast hall.

The throne stood vacant upon the large platform. The three chairs were gone. The hostages were nowhere to be seen. Everyone else was gone, too.

He headed for the golden door and pulled it open. Once

on the other side, he came out onto the walkway carved into the stone wall, high in the huge underground cavern. He was above the giant underground factory with the cauldrons of seething, molten gold. He edged his way along the ledge until he came to the iron bridge with the blood red grated walkway. No one was up here on this level, and he started across the metallic bridge.

Workers with brown uniforms appeared among the cauldrons far below, and Paul crouched upon seeing them. He was, perhaps, sixty or seventy feet above the floor. Though walking on the grating made some noise, there were other noises in this cavern, too. Steam pipes, bubbling liquid, people talking. It was a noisy place and no one seemed to hear Paul passing overhead, so he stood back up and continued.

After walking the full length of the iron walkway, he came to the thick vault door that sealed the gold factory from the network of caverns on the other side. The vault door was securely locked from the other side.

Paul looked around and saw the fire extinguisher and glass covered fire alarm in the rock wall on either side of the vault. The glass over the fire alarm was intact. Hadn't it been broken before? Then he turned around and examined the bridge. He had an idea.

He headed out over the bridge again until he came to the gateway that Von Krod had told him they used to cast people to their deaths. He opened it and the gate swung out over the abyss below. He then removed his shirt and hung it on the railing. Heading back to the vault door, he broke the glass with his elbow and set off the fire alarm.

He heard the men in brown uniforms on the floor far below make a stir. "Fire! The alarm! There's a fire!"

Suddenly the vault door made a sound. Someone was coming through.

*   *   *

When Keith Landon swung his Tommy Gun over his shoulder and opened the door to the men's restroom in the lounge, he heard muffled sounds in one of the stalls.

He swung open the door and found a man in his

underwear, bound and gagged with torn pieces of a white lab coat.

He removed the gag and asked, "Who are you?"

"I'm one of the buglers! This lady from the lab followed me in here and hit me over the head. She stole my trumpet and uniform!"

Keith untied the man and then went over to the fire alarm, located behind a glass box by the mirror. He smashed the glass and sounded the alarm.

Suddenly, outside the vault door, officials were running around in the tunnel with fire extinguishers.

"Clear the tunnel. There's a fire!"

Wendy already had her disguise. She didn't need a distraction, but it didn't hurt that the fire alarm was sounding.

The guards spun a large circular wheel mounted in the center of the vault door, and Wendy lowered the cap on her head. She hoped her hair was not showing, or that they wouldn't discover she wasn't a bugler at all. All she knew was that Mary was supposedly on the other side of this door. She'd heard the lab technicians tell her, who were probably still tripping on LSD chained to a gurney back at the lab.

The circular wheel in the center of the vault door stopped spinning, and the guards pushed hard.

As the vault swung open, Wendy heard the sound of steam, and she whiffed an awful smell – something burning. It smelled like a construction site with hundreds of welders melting metal.

Carrying a trumpet, she and the other bugler stepped through just as the fire alarm stopped. She heard someone say, "There's been an intruder! Secure that vault door!"

But she was in. Once stepping onto the rock ledge on the other side of the vault door, she saw she was in a vast room the size of an airport hanger carved into the bedrock. A bridge with a blood-red walkway stretched before her, spanning great cauldrons of molten metal.

* * *

When the vault door swung open, Paul pressed himself

against the rock wall near the fire extinguisher. Two guards with Tommy Guns came dashing in through the open doorway. One of them noticed the open gate out on the bridge with Paul's shirt hanging from it. "The bridge! Someone has fallen!"

As the guards came through, Paul slipped out the vault door and pushed it closed from the other side. Then, as quickly as possible, he turned the giant wheel that locked it securely.

He never saw Wendy.

They were in exactly the same place, separated only by time.

Meanwhile, the vault door pulled shut behind Wendy. She picked up a large rock from the ground and hit the other bugler over the head. She tied him up with torn pieces of his own uniform and hid him out of sight behind some stalagmites.

CHAPTER 33

Paul faced the long tunnel ahead, back against the vault door. The tunnel was full of people, milling around, going from the pleasure rooms to the lounge, to the casino, to the slaughter rooms. The armed guards were gone. Paul had locked them inside the vault. The fire alarm shut off. No one had found a fire.

A man and woman emerged from the pleasure rooms. The woman, in her thirties, saw Paul's muscular frame, wearing no shirt. She approached, smiling seductively. Placing a soft hand on his war-torn chest, she said, "Need of a nurse, handsome?"

He brushed the woman aside and dashed past her bewildered partner. The man turned to face the woman and lustfully smiled, happy to get her back. The couple locked hands and reentered the pleasure rooms.

Moving quickly, chest heaving, Paul ran past the lounge and the casino on either side of the tunnel. He came upon the slaughterhouse on his right. Here, he stopped. There was a butcher hosing down the floor and washing away bloody animal parts strewn on the floor.

He stopped to catch his breath.

How was he going to get out of here? He wasn't even wearing a shirt, and he was bleeding. Obviously someone would see him running down the tunnel. Even if he made it all the way to the elevator, the military was up at ground level. It would be impossible to get around them.

He had an idea.

Time Gods

He ran back to the lounge and found a drunk who had passed out, lying over a table. Under his right arm, hand still loosely clutching a bottle of whiskey, Paul noticed a poster advertising a placed called "Milam Valley." He pulled the poster from under his arm and examined it. At the bottom was written, "The Ultimate Destination, July 31, 1966." There were pointed, snow-capped mountain peaks surrounding a beautiful valley with an aqua colored lake at the bottom.

Milam Valley. Paul had heard that name before. But where? And why advertise a tourist attraction in Kali's underground complex? The drunk obviously thought it was important. Paul folded it and stuck it in his back pocket.

The drunk was wearing a jacket. Paul removed it and put it on.

Snatching up the nearly empty whiskey bottle, he made his way down the tunnel again. He buttoned the jacket on his way.

Arriving back at the slaughter cavern, he entered and approached the butcher. His foot slid on a puddle of blood, but he regained his footing.

"Excuse me," McPherson said, cautiously looking around the room. The floor was sticky. The bottoms of his sneakers were red with blood, but they were alone. The hamburger and steak shops were closed for reasons unknown.

The man looked up and was surprised to see Paul, battered and bruised, shirtless under a buttoned jacket. "Whadaya want?" he blurted, peering through blood spattered, round spectacles. "We're closed. The entertainment sections are a little further down the tunnel."

"The bandage on your head," Paul observed. "I heard a guard tell Durukti you had been attacked, but I see you took off your head bandage already."

"Ain't had no bandage and ain't been attacked by nobody. You got me mistaken for someone else," the butcher said.

"No, I don't think so. Aren't you the guy that I saw killing a cow earlier?"

"Cow? Cows are tomorrow," the man declared. "Today it's pigs."

"I saw you kill a cow earlier today."

"Look, I told you. Today it's pigs. Haven't done a cow all day. We haven't even had a shipment of cows for a week."

"No, how can that be?" Paul asked. "I saw you..."

Or had he? Maybe he saw the man killing a cow *tomorrow*. Maybe punching that button in the little room really had worked, and Paul was now one day in the past.

If that was so, the man hadn't killed a cow today. He would kill a cow tomorrow. Paul looked at the man sternly. "Ever hear of the law of karma?"

"What?"

"Karma," Paul repeated. But before the man could understand the question, Paul swung the whiskey bottle and hit him on the head. The man was out cold before he hit the floor.

Checking that no one was watching, Paul bent over and checked the man's neck. Heart still beating. Wasn't dead. He removed the stun gun from the butcher's belt. "Trust me, buddy. I know how that feels."

According to the label on the side of the stun gun, it had been manufactured in 2010, forty-four years in the future. Kali's people must have brought it via time machine. The stun gun was powerful enough to produce a non-lethal but powerful discharge, and small enough to fit inside a pack of cigarettes. The rubberized shell made it easy to grip and it had a handy built-in LED flashlight, technology rarely seen in 1966. LED diodes were first used in 1962, but those early versions emitted only dim, red light, unlike the powerful versions of Paul's time capable of visible, ultraviolet and infrared light of high intensity.

There was a hose nearby. Paul sprayed the bottoms of his shoes and washed off pig blood. It didn't have to be good enough to fool a forensic scientist. It just had to be good enough not to leave bloody footprints.

Then an alarm went off again. The guards he had locked inside the vault were trying to get free. Time was running out.

He ran down the tunnel until his sides hurt and his lungs screamed, away from the vault door, passing several junctions of similar crisscrossing tunnels.

He passed a junction that said, "Elevator to Subway Access: 7 AM to 7:10 AM and 7 PM to 7:10 PM only." Two hundred feet down that cavern was a sealed vault door blocking the exit. A room branched off to the side.

Paul turned and went in that direction. He passed a lab and peered through the window in the door. He saw two lab technicians pouring coffee. Some people were locked in cages. One of them even looked like Wendy. Weird. But the woman was sleeping along with the other people in cages. Couldn't be Wendy, anyway. She was safely back in her apartment as far as he knew.

Further down the tunnel he came to another vault door. But alas, this one was sealed from the other side and had a small windowed porthole. He looked out and saw two uniformed men, carrying those damn Thompson submachine guns, standing with their backs to the vault.

He didn't know what time it was, but he thought about waiting until 7 PM and going out with everyone else that was down here. He didn't know if they would check every person leaving or not. However, the alarm had already been sounded, and he needed to get out fast. His own existence might be at stake if Kali were to kill his grandparents. Their lives and Mary's life were clearly in jeopardy. His only chance was to save them before they got kidnapped. That's why he had managed to jump one day into the past. Now time was running out. He couldn't wait until 7 PM.

Abandoning this route, he retraced his steps back to the main tunnel and ran until he saw the main elevator. He stopped, trying to catch his breath. There was a door to some kind of utility closet on his right. The sliding elevator doors ahead. He reached to press the up button.

He never made it.

A sharp *ding* and a light appeared above the elevator door.

Someone had arrived. The elevator door was about to open.

He slid into the only hiding place available, the utility closet to his right, and pulled the door shut. It was dark. Paul remained quiet and peered through ventilation slits near the bottom of the door.

Three men wearing army fatigues and carrying M14 assault rifles, accompanied by a man in black with dark sunglasses, poured out of the elevator and dashed down the tunnel. They were probably going after Paul. They didn't know they had already run right past him.

He looked around. The closet was dark. He turned on the LED light on the stun gun and looked around. This was no utility closet. This was where all those men in black hung their suits. There were dozens of black ties, black jackets, white shirts, and black pants hanging on hooks. Boring clothes. He stripped and put on a set of new clothes. He also found a dark baseball cap on the shelf. He fitted this over his short hair and *sikha*, and turned his LED light off.

He peeked out the door. The military guys were far down the tunnel. He could still see them, but they were running the other way, and they weren't likely to look back. He stepped into the light and punched the up button. The doors slid open immediately and the elevator was vacant.

The journey upward was long and tense. As his ears popped, Paul buttoned the white shirt and tried to fix his tie. He didn't know how he was going to escape, but escape was something he had to do. He shuffled his feet and something attracted his attention. Under the black pants he was still wearing white sneakers.

At last the elevator arrived at the surface. Paul slid open the metal gate, and cautiously slid open the outside door of the cube building. There, standing with his back to Paul, was another man dressed in black. The man turned, and seeing Paul, went pale. As the man reached for a microphone on his lapel, Paul lunged forward, pressing the stun gun to his forehead. The man fell unconscious as the voltage surged through his body. Dragging him inside by the ankles, Paul hid him inside the elevator. He removed the man's sunglasses, shoes and security card clipped to his suit. He put on the shoes, attached the card on his own suit and slid the sunglasses over his eyes.

Pressing the "down" button in the elevator, he stepped outside the cube building into the bright sunlight, tie in disarray.

The golden Rolls-Royce was not parked where they left it, probably because he was now one day in the past. However, army soldiers stood guarding the chain link gate. Paul approached the gate, flashed his ID card to the guards, and walked calmly outside the fence. They said nothing.

He walked down the street. Around him were brick buildings with boarded windows. A block ahead he saw a second checkpoint. Armed guards with M14 assault rifles flagged down an approaching army truck and Paul saw the guards carefully checked identification cards and the faces of everyone in the vehicle. He knew he would probably get caught if he tried getting past them.

He slipped into a narrow space between two derelict buildings, barely wide enough to squeeze his muscular body. Edging along the tight space, he emerged into a small lot enclosed by vacant buildings. Across from him he saw a wider space between buildings, Paul walked over and went into it. At the end of this passageway a metal gate blocked his way.

Damn he was sore, but he had to get over it.

He made a running jump and started to climb the gate when he heard the chopping of a helicopter. His muscles tensed and he looked back over his shoulder. A black Bell Huey circled above, not far behind. The sunglasses fell from his face and shattered on the ground.

Paul resumed climbing. Four-inch metal spikes spaced three inches apart protruded from the top of the gate. He placed his right hand against one of the buildings and swung his leg over the spikes to the other side, straddling the top of the gate. As he did so, his foot slipped and he almost impaled himself, but his hand caught a drainage pipe. His crotch perilously hovered an eighth of an inch above one of the spikes. He steadied himself, took a deep breath, regained his footing, and then swung his other foot over the top.

The roar of the helicopter was getting louder, and Paul saw it headed fast in his direction. Wide open, he ducked as the helicopter roared over the top of the building and disappeared behind another.

There was an alley to his right, littered with cardboard boxes, old factory parts and a dumpster. He ran into it just as the helicopter reappeared in the crack between the buildings behind him, hovering just above the height of the roof. The chopper machine gun fired into the alley. Paul dove behind a dumpster as bullets ricocheted off metal and brick. The helicopter passed over and circled for another strike.

A fence blocked the other end of the alley. Paul ran as fast as he could and started to climb. He heard the helicopter close behind. He swung his legs over the top and dropped to the pavement on the other side, baseball cap flying into the wind. A spray of bullets ricocheted along the walls and pavement behind. Paul ducked around the corner.

He found himself on a deserted street surrounded by a two block perimeter cordoned off by chain-linked fences crowned with coiled razor wire. He'd never get over that.

The Bell Huey reappeared above and began to descend, preparing to land. Nearby, six men donning military uniforms and brandishing assault rifles pointed in his direction filed out from an old building and ran toward him.

Paul was trapped.

CHAPTER 34

Chinatown, New York City. 1966

Anantamati Ku Shin stepped into the sweltering heat from the Tibetan Buddhist center near Manhattan's Canal Street and looked up at the cloudless sky. He wiped his sweating bald head with a clean cloth, stepped off the curb onto the street, and stuck out his arm. He was a middle-aged Buddhist. He wore orange-brown flowing robes so he was not difficult to spot.

Omar Rivero saw him from a block away and made a beeline straight to him. Pulling near the curb, he came to a gentle stop and the Buddhist opened the rear door. "Where you going, Amigo?"

"Mid-Manhattan Library. 455 Fifth Avenue. Do you know where that is?"

"Claro, Señor. Si. Very beautiful building. Get in."

Anantamati climbed into the cab, closed the rear door, and Omar turned on his meter. They started heading uptown.

"Very fine building, Señor. One of the finest buildings in New York."

"Yes it is," Anantamati agreed.

"Did you know the man who built it was killed in a traffic accident before the library was completed?"

"No I didn't know that," Anantamati admitted. "Is it true?"

"I wouldn't lie, Amigo. One of the top fifty favorite architectural structures in the United States."

Anantamati said nothing.

Omar took pride being a tour guide for his passengers, but this Buddhist guy didn't seem like he wanted to talk, so Omar continued to drive silently. After a minute or so he couldn't stand it anymore. He had to get his passenger to say something. Passengers were *supposed* to talk. It was the custom in New York.

"You a tourist, Amigo?"

"No."

This was going nowhere. Omar was annoyed.

"You from New York?"

"No."

"Where you from, Señor?"

Anantamati realized his driver was insistent. "I am from Nepal, but I was born in Tibet."

"Oh, I hear that is very beautiful country. Mount Everest! What do you do at library, Señor?"

"Research."

"Oh, very interesting, Amigo. What kind of research?"

"I'm a bit of an expert on ancient legends of lost civilizations."

"You research Atlantis?"

"Not Atlantis. Himalayan civilizations."

"Mountain people?"

"Places like Shambhala and Milam Valley," Anantamati explained.

"Oh, I have heard of Shambhala, Señor."

"Interesting," Anantamati admitted. "Then did you know that in both Shambhala and Milam Valley there were once civilizations older than my own Buddhism?"

"That is very strange, Señor. I do not know about that. I know only what I see on the TV."

"Don't believe everything you see on the TV," Anantamati warned.

"But I saw on the TV that world leaders are going to Milam Valley for summit."

"I highly doubt that," Anantamati said.

"¿Por qué?"

Anantamati had been in New York long enough to know

that his cab driver was asking him "why?"

"Because Milam Valley is completely inaccessible. There are no roads and it is surrounded by snow covered peaks."

Omar Rivero continued driving up the Avenue of Americas until he came to 44th Street. Here he turned right and drove a short distance to 5th Avenue. He turned south.

"We have arrived at your destination, Señor."

Anantamati looked from the rear window at one of the five most important libraries in the United States, the others being the Library of Congress, the Boston Public Library, and the libraries of Harvard and Yale Universities.

After paying the cab driver from money that had been appropriated to him for his research, Anantamati stepped onto 5th Avenue and walked up the stone steps. Two large stone lions nicknamed "Patience" and "Fortitude" guarded the entrance.

CHAPTER 35

Secret government facility, Queens, New York. 1966

A hobo poked his head through a doorway of an abandoned building across the street to see the goings on. The man was white-haired, with a short, grizzly beard and frowzy clothing. He carried a half-empty bottle of whiskey. "How are ya?" he called out. He made a few drunken whistles and gestured for Paul to come in his direction.

Paul recognized the man from the storefront at Second Avenue. The man had interrupted Prabhupada's lecture to bring toilet paper into the bathroom.

With the helicopter about to land and men with assault riffles closing in, Paul ran toward the hobo and in through the door of the abandoned building.

He found himself in a grim and dusty corridor with the disheveled man. "Got a way out of here?" Paul asked him as he wiped sweat from his brow.

The man eyed Paul carefully. "Hey, I've seen you guys. Manhattan, Lower East Side. I wanted to go there tonight. A church or somethin', right? Gonna bring some bathroom tissues."

"Yes," Paul said. "Look, can you help me?"

"You in some kinda trouble?"

"Big time," Paul replied. "How did you get past the fence around these buildings?"

"The basement," the man said. "Manhole with a ladder.

Leads to subway tracks." His speech was slurred but comprehensible.

"Got it, thanks. You saved my life!"

"Pleasure," the man replied sincerely. "Hare Krishna."

Paul ran along a hallway littered with beer cans, broken glass, and dirty blankets. A crowbar leaned against a wall. A possible weapon, he realized. He took it, and then came upon a flight of stairs leading up. Beyond that there was another flight going down into darkness. He went down the dark stairs until he couldn't see his own feet. At the bottom he found a door and fumbled for the handle.

He heard a door crash open and then boots on the floor above. The sound of excited voices. The old drunk misdirected, "He ran upstairs."

"Alright. Split up in twos. You men, search upstairs. You and I will search this floor. You two, find if there's a basement. Search that."

"I said he went upstairs," the derelict complained.

Paul pushed quietly through the basement door and closed it behind him. A sliver of light trickled through the window from metal grating in the sidewalk above. The air was musty. He saw no manhole here, so he ran ahead into the next room, closing the door behind him. This room was cluttered with furniture covered with white sheets. Still no manhole. Perhaps the drunkard had given bad directions.

He heard boots echoing on the stairs and the door of the basement behind him swing open. Two young soldiers entered the basement.

Paul slipped through the next door and closed it behind him. There was a manhole cover in the cement basement floor. He used the crowbar and lifted the heavy cover, exposing a dark hole with a ladder leading down.

* * *

The two soldiers cautiously moved through the outer room pointing their M14 rifles ahead of them, and came to a closed door. The door was stuck and they forced it open. One of them quickly checked behind the door while the other aimed his riffle around the room. Dust covered objects covered with musty sheets were everywhere. They ripped off the sheets one at a time, exposing pieces of upholstered furniture. Nothing.

There was another door. It opened easily. Raising their rifles so they pointed straight in the air, they slid inside. The room was dark. There was an open manhole cover.

"Down there!" one of them ordered.

"Too easy," said the other. He looked around the room suspiciously. The soldier cautiously opened a closet door with the muzzle of his gun, but found it full of boxes stuffed with dusty clothing. The man kicked the boxes and then pulled them out into the room. Nothing. He turned to face his companion, nodding his head toward the manhole cover. "Alright. He must've gone down there. Let's radio for help and then we'll..."

He did not finish his sentence. Paul McPherson swung his legs down from the upper closet shelf and kicked the man in the head. He spun around as Paul landed on his feet, crowbar swinging, and when it impacted his head, the man fell unconscious, rifle flying in the air. In one smooth and well coordinated movement, Paul caught the M14.

The other soldier reacted and scrambled to point his rifle, but before he could level aim Paul kicked him in the groin and zapped him with the stun gun. The man fell unconscious on top of his colleague.

Paul checked the pulse of the soldier that he had struck with the crowbar. The man was still alive.

He shouldn't leave the men with their rifles. Scooping up both M14s, he realized he had no experience how to use them. Did you just pull the trigger, or was there something more you had to do? He didn't know, but slung them over his shoulders anyway, and climbed down the ladder into the hole.

He was very sore now and the muscles ached in every limb of his body. His thirst screamed for him to drink water. He reached up and took hold of the heavy manhole cover and pulled but it did not move. He rested for a second, took another breath, and tried again. This time he was able to slowly drag the heavy lid and worked it back into place above his head. He continued to climb down in the darkness perhaps a hundred feet and finally landed in a few inches of stinky water. He held his nose. He was in a sewer.

He reached into his pocket, pulled out the stun gun and flicked on the LED light.

He guessed that the smelly gray water would flow away from the subway station, so he walked against it. Eventually he came to another ladder. Turning off the light just in case, he climbed up and emerged into a pitch-black space that smelled of filth and charcoal. A rat scurried by and brushed his arm, startling him.

Crawling out of the hole, belly first, he labored to stand, but a painful cramp in his leg caused him to buckle over again. He slowly stretched his leg and attempted to work out the tight muscle.

Turning the LED light back on, he saw a railway track.

This would lead to a way out, he realized, but he wouldn't be able to walk through a subway station or New York street carrying M14 rifles over his shoulder. He decided to ditch them in the darkness and he wondered if some homeless person might find them. He hoped not.

It was probably getting pretty late. He had to make his way over to Mary's apartment to save her.

CHAPTER 36

Mary's Apartment. The previous day

"Those were odd questions you asked," Paul said to Special Agent Sidney E. Dale. "Except about the money. I can understand that one."

"It's an odd world," Dale added, looking at Paul. "We follow all sorts of leads. Let me give you my card in case anything else comes up or if you happen to come across any more of that 'funny money'. Alright?"

Dale produced a small business card and handed it over.

Sidney E. Dale moved toward Mary's door. Unlatching the bolts, he pried the door open and waved before stepping into the hallway.

He shut the door behind him staring at the face of Paul McPherson number two. Confused, he glanced back at Mary's closed door, then again at Paul. He was sure that he had secured the door with both Paul and Mary inside, yet here was Paul in the hallway. He was dressed differently, though. This Paul wore a black suit, smudged white shirt and disheveled tie, and he appeared bruised and weary. It was if this were Paul McPherson's identical twin brother.

"Hello, Mr. Dale," Paul cautiously ventured. "We meet again."

Sidney Dale was at a loss for words. "I thought I just..."

"Yes, you did. You just finished talking with my other self inside Mary's apartment."

"Your other self?"

"Yes, that was me from yesterday and this is me from today."

"How is this possible?"

"Time travel, Agent Dale. I traveled one day into the past to prevent tomorrow from happening."

"Remarkable!"

"It must seem very confusing," Paul said.

"No," assured Dale. "Just remarkable, not confusing. But we mustn't stand here talking." He ushered Paul toward the stairway. "Someone might look out through the peephole in Mary's door. Let's go downstairs and we can talk."

Meanwhile, inside the apartment, Mary was with Paul's other self from the day before. She indeed was looking through the peephole, and what she saw made the blood run from her face.

"Oh my God!" she exclaimed.

"What's the matter? What did you see?" Paul's other self asked.

Mary swallowed deliberately and took a deep breath. "I saw *you*. Outside, talking to that FBI guy in the hallway."

"That's ridiculous. Let me see."

He looked through the peephole and saw Dale and someone dressed in black with a baseball cap, about his age, turning to go down the stairway.

"I see Mr. Dale with someone," he explained. "I admit that he looks like me. But it's not me." He turned to face Mary. "How could it be? I'm here!"

"You don't have a twin brother, do you?"

"No, of course not," he assured her.

Mary glared at him. She *knew* what she had seen. "Did you see his face? It was *your* face!"

* * *

Washington Square Park. July 13, 1966

Sidney E. Dale and Paul McPherson walked under night skies down MacDougal Street and into the northwest corner of Washington Square Park. Along the way, Dale remained conscious of the 45 semi-automatic loaded with hollow point bullets concealed under his trench coat.

When striking soft tissue, the metal around the inside edge of a hollow point bullet expanded outward on impact. This disrupted more tissue as the bullet traveled through the target and slowed the projectile, minimizing the chance of hurting bystanders.

Passing near the tall arch and circular fountain, they found a bench on the main walkway under an overhead lamp. Paul opened the discussion. "Mr. Dale, let's be perfectly frank. I came from the future, and you know it. Am I right?"

"Yes," replied Dale cautiously. "And you lied to me when you said you didn't have that small electronic device."

Paul raised his eyebrows. "No, I didn't. Why would I lie about that?"

Dale eased his grip on the pistol under his coat. "But you just said that you traveled from the future."

"Yes, that's right. I did."

"How you manage to do that if you didn't have the device?"

"You mean that device you were looking for with the weird dish antenna was a time machine?"

"Of course. And you must have one, otherwise how are you doing what you're doing?"

"I don't have any device like that. I found a different kind of time machine."

Agent Dale's grip on the pistol under his coat tightened. "And do you have it with you?"

"Have what with me?"

"The time machine."

"I don't know what you're talking about. The time machine I found is in this room in a cavern, deep under New York. It's not something you can pick up and carry around."

Dale let his grip on the concealed weapon loosen. "I see. So you've located the original prototype stolen by Professor Cali, then."

"First of all," Paul explained, "he's no professor. That guy is evil. Second of all, what's this about a prototype?"

"In the future a particle physicist at Princeton

hypothesized how a time machine could be built, but needed finances to test his theory. Professor Cali financed the construction – what they called a space-time dilator prototype. The people where I work nicknamed it a time machine."

"Who do you work for?"

"I'm with TDC," Dale explained. "The Time Displacement Commission, a division of the National Security Agency, or NSA, the cryptology branch of the Department of Defense. We've been looking for you. You're causing quite a disturbance, you know."

"I beg your pardon?"

"Time quakes – in the future. I've been sent here to get information and to neutralize the threat these quakes are causing."

"You mean kill me."

"We call it neutralization."

"Now you listen here," Paul shouted. "This has got *nothing* to do with me." He took a breath and lowered his voice. "I've risked my life to escape from Kali, who must be the most dangerous guy around. He has secret underground bases, soldiers, henchmen, everything. Got the United States Army on his side. He's the one with the stupid prototype you talk about. If there's any disturbance then you should be looking for him!"

Dale appeared surprised and studied Paul carefully. "I see," he said.

Suddenly Dale heard a noise behind them. Startled, he turned and peered into the dark shadows of the night. It had been faint, but it was unmistakable. "Did you hear that?"

"No," Paul replied, shaking his head, still looking at Dale intently.

Perhaps it was nothing. They were in a public park in a big city. He turned his attention back to the muscular and bruised monk. "I have to be cautious in my line of work, Mr. McPherson."

"Which is what exactly?"

"As I already explained, I work for the government of the year 2075."

"That's even in my future," Paul said. "I'll be 74 years old by 2075."

"You'll be a lot older than that if you stay here in 1966," Dale observed.

"Got a point there," Paul agreed.

Sidney E. Dale, continued. "You see, our time machine prototype was stolen and at the same time Professor Cali was kidnapped, but we've learned since there's another time machine device floating around as well, developed in the one hundred and forty-fifth century. We assumed that was how you got here."

"Say again?"

"Apparently, our technology for time travel is primitive. There are other time travelers from the far distant future with hand-held time machines. We didn't know about them until recently. Their devices leave a unique signature in the time-space continuum that we're unable to duplicate. Your presence here left the same unique signature that those time machines make."

"Woah," said Paul, holding up his hands. "Look, I don't know anything about the one hundred and forty-fifth century. I woke up in the hospital after an accident and it was sixty-one years in the past. I don't know how I got here."

"Could it be you are one of the time travelers yourself, suffering from amnesia due to your head injury, Paul?"

"Are you nuts? You actually think I'm a time traveler from thousands of years in the future with amnesia?"

"Is it possible?"

"People with amnesia don't remember their past. I remember my past. I'm Paul McPherson. I'm a Hare Krishna devotee from 305 Schermerhorn Street in Brooklyn, New York."

"We looked it up," Dale said. "We couldn't find any record of your birth."

"What?"

"The technology exists where we can alter your memory through the use of certain chemicals and electric shock. Professor Cali has those drugs in his possession."

"So you're thinking my mind was altered by Kali and that I'm really a time traveler from thousands of years in the future?"

"Well, as far as we can tell, you don't exist," Agent Dale said icily. "There is no Paul McPherson. Never has been."

"If that's true, then the future is already changing," Paul suggested. "Nobody altered my mind."

"You wouldn't know if someone did."

"No one did. Look, I've got a goddamn ID from 2027. Here, look at it!" Paul flipped open his wallet. "I didn't show this to you before in Mary's apartment because I didn't know what you'd think."

Agent Dale examined the ID. "My goodness. Haven't seen one of these old driver licenses for a long time."

"It's more than a license. It's our ID. We use it for driving, credit, you name it. Everyone's got to have one, and well back here in 1966 it really amazes people."

"You showed this to someone else?"

"Of course I did. To Mary."

"Do you think that was wise, Paul?"

"How would I know? I'm just an ordinary guy from 2027 who somehow got hurdled back in time sixty-one years. Since being here I've been kidnapped, beat up, and shot at. To tell you the truth, I'm totally freaked out by this Kali. I want out."

"Don't you think it's strange that you can remember everything except how you traveled back in time?"

"Yes, I do think it's odd," Paul agreed.

"They could have faked the license."

"Who could have faked my license?"

"The people who want you to think you're Paul McPherson from 2027."

"Do you really believe the crap you're saying?"

Dale shook his head. "Probably not." He reached into an inside pocket in his coat and handed a small envelope to Paul. "This is what happens if we don't succeed."

Paul opened the top of the envelope and removed a photograph. "What's this?" he asked, and then without waiting for a reply, examined it under the light from the overhead park lamp. It appeared to be a demolished city. "Where is this?"

"Los Angeles," Dale replied. "In the future."

"Oh God. What year was this picture taken?"

"2056," Dale replied. "Destroyed by nuclear, chemical

and biological weapons."

"Might explain why you couldn't find any record of me in the future."

"Possibly, but in my time there was no such disaster. This appears to be an alternative branch of the time line."

"Was the entire population of L.A. wiped out?"

"Not just Los Angeles," Dale sighed. "Every major city in the western world. Nuclear winter followed."

"Look. I don't know about nuclear holocaust in the next century. Tomorrow I will be kidnapped by Kali and his people – not only me, but Mary and my future grandparents. I have to stop this from happening by doing something about it tonight."

Dale sighed and said simply, "Not possible."

"Why not?"

"Because of the Granny Paradox."

"Kali mentioned that term. What's it mean?"

"The Granny Paradox means you can't travel back in time and kill your grandmother, because you would never be born to kill your grandmother, so your grandmother wouldn't be killed."

"I'm not trying to kill my grandmother. I'm trying to save her."

"I understand. For you the Granny Paradox means you can't travel back in time to prevent your kidnapping because that would mean you'd never be kidnapped and never escape to travel back in time to prevent the kidnapping in the first place."

"That's a mouthful."

"To say the least," Dale said. "Think of it as a law of physics which enables us to time travel in the first place."

"But if I can't stop my own kidnapping, what about preventing the kidnapping of Mary and my grandparents?"

"You can try. You won't be able to do it. From what I understand, they kidnap you too near the time they kidnap them."

"Shit, this is confusing. Can't we can do *anything* to stop this from happening?"

"Possibly. We've managed to trace anomalies in the time line right back here to 1966. Because of that I now believe that Professor Cali himself was not kidnapped as we originally thought, but personally stole the time machine from 2075 and traveled here to 1966 in order to change the outcome of the future."

"So you think you've got to somehow stop Kali from stealing the time machine prototype in the first place."

There was another noise, faint but distinct. Special TDC Agent Dale looked nervously over his shoulder.

"What's the matter?"

"Thought I heard something," Dale replied.

Paul strained his ears. He *had* heard something. Then again, there were other noises too. A car horn honked and some drunks on the other side of the fountain were talking.

"Do you think someone followed you after your escape today?" Dale asked.

"Impossible," Paul replied looking over both shoulders, "I had a narrow escape, but if they were still on to me they would have caught me by now."

Dale settled his fedora on the top of his broad forehead and turned back towards Paul. "Let's get going. We've only got one option to stop all this from happening."

They stood up from the bench and entered the dark, long shadows that were part of night, passing the fountain in the center of the park.

As they walked away, a three foot tall man watched them from underneath the arch. He removed a laser-like gun from under his belt and examined it in the dim light from the overhead lamps. It could emit lethal beams of concentrated nonnuclear charged protons traveling at the speed of light. Kali called it a particle beam gun. The barrel was about seven inches long with circular rings to modulate the electronic frequency of the emitters. He pressed one of the buttons on the side of the handle and the weapon beeped. Red and green lights flashed along the side of the cylinder, indicating that it was armed and ready to fire. "Now the action begins," he said roughly, in his own, distinct language.

He tucked the weapon away and proceeded to follow McPherson and Dale, wobbling slightly due to his physical stature.

CHAPTER 37

TDC Headquarters. New York Financial District

After walking a long distance, Sidney Dale and Paul McPherson entered a bookstore on Beekman Street and Theatre Alley in lower Manhattan, across the street from City Hall Park and two blocks from a 16 acre site where construction of the new World Trade Center towers had just begun. An engraved triangular insignia was etched into the glass door. A sign read, "Used Books." At this hour, the only person in the store was an elderly Hispanic gentleman who had a round face and short mustache. He sat behind the cash register. As the man looked up, Agent Dale gave a knowing nod and walked to the back of the store with Paul.

Dale glanced over his shoulder and then pushed a corner of one of the bookcases, which slowly revolved to reveal a large, metal door. The door had an electronic keypad, and Dale punched in a code. It swung open and they entered. Inside they met a security guard seated at a desk. "Sanjeev," Dale said, as the door and bookcase automatically closed behind them.

"Sidney," the man replied, looking suspiciously at Paul. He noted the short hair and *sikha*, which was not unfamiliar to him as a Hindu. He wondered if the monk had clearance.

Dale removed his fedora and held it in his hand. Looking at Sanjeev he nodded toward Paul. "He's okay. I've cleared him. Tell Grace it's going to be Plan B. I'm going to show this young man around and explain a few things. I'll need just under an hour."

Dale and Paul approached a sliding metal door. Mr. Dale, standing close, pushed a button and a beam of light flashed at his face. He kept his eyes wide open.

"Retina scan complete," stated a female computerized voice. The door automatically slid open.

"Security," he said apologetically. "Can't be too careful, you know."

"Didn't know they had this kind of technology in 1966," Paul mumbled.

"They don't," Dale admitted.

The two men descended a flight of stairs and followed a winding corridor, arriving at another steel door. Dale placed his hand on a small, dark-red piece of glass mounted on the wall. It instantly lit and scanned his palm.

"Scan complete. Welcome, Sidney E. Dale," announced the same computerized voice as the door slid open.

"Hungry?" Dale asked, as he led Paul into a room with a sink, refrigerator, and a few scattered tables and chairs.

"I'm ravaged and thirsty," Paul explained. "Been a hard day."

"Eat. There's food here. Like doughnuts and coffee?"

"Got anything without eggs in them?"

"You allergic to eggs?"

"Not exactly."

"Well take look. There's a ham, I think, some bread and lettuce. You could make yourself a ham sandwich. Whatever you like."

Paul nodded. Maybe he could make a lettuce and tomato sandwich or something. Maybe throw on a slice of cheese if they had any. Dale didn't know about the vegetarian thing and it didn't matter.

Paul found ample supplies to fix himself a veggie sandwich, which he gobbled quickly. He chugged down a bottle of apple juice while Dale waited patiently.

"Satisfied?" Dale asked.

"Yeah. Thanks. So where are we?"

"Refectory. Our break room."

"No, I mean this secret place."

"TDC Headquarters. Come with me and I'll explain everything."

Paul washed his hands and mouth in the sink and followed Sidney Dale out of the room. They walked down a brightly lit corridor and entered a viewing room. Large plate glass windows extended from floor to ceiling. Through the glass, Paul observed a large, circular room with fifteen widescreen LCD monitors. Technicians wearing white gowns sat at keyboards, occasionally glancing up at an enormous, back-lit mural-map of the world.

There was a long silence while Paul watched the technicians at work. "So you're tracking time disruptions?"

"Yes. We trace anomalies through time and space," Dale said simply.

Paul cleared his throat awkwardly. "Mr. Dale?"

"Yes?"

"I haven't been to the bathroom all day. I gotta go."

*   *   *

After Paul relieved himself, Mr. Dale sat him down at a table and they had a long talk.

"This man. Professor Cali," Dale said. "He's brilliant. A member of the Woodrow Wilson Fellowship and National Science Foundation Fellowship. Helped finance and invent time travel technology from findings at Geneva. Never was happy that scientists at Princeton made the prototype an LTTA."

"LTTA?"

"Limited Time Travel Apparatus. It was the limited part that the Professor didn't agree with."

"Limited in what way?" Paul asked.

"Turns out that when you travel back in time and change something, it causes what we call fluxes. These time fluxes are like big earthquakes in the time line. After the quakes subside, the future branches out. The more severe the disruptions, the more severe the quakes. Time layers are different branches of the future, like parallel universes, that branch out when the time line is disrupted by an unnatural event, like a time traveler changing the past. After a period of time, one of the parallel universes or time layers will wither and vanish, and everyone and everything that ever happened along that time line is lost forever. So you can change the past and have two futures temporarily, but eventually only one future can survive. That's why scientists built the time machine with a safety lock limiting time travel to no further than 150 years. It was a decision of Princeton University Investment Company, PRINCO."

"And the Professor didn't like that," Paul said.

"He said they had plundered and pillaged his mathematical suppositions on dimensional discrepancies, ruining thousands of years of planning. Never understood the thousands of years part."

"Why didn't he just remove the locking device?"

"He was the theorist, not a technician. Something to do with time resonance capacitance. I don't really understand that aspect of the project, Paul. I'm not a scientist."

"Two more questions," Paul said. "It seems when you use Kali's time machine, the time machine stays behind. If that's the case, how did he manage to bring his time machine here? For that matter, how did he bring that Rolls-Royce of his here?"

Dale nodded thoughtfully. "The time machine has a setting. You can either take the time machine with you when you go, or leave it behind. As for his Rolls Royce and other equipment, they simply drove it into the machine. That time machine isn't anchored to his underground facility. He can move it anywhere he likes."

McPherson nodded, thoughtfully. "You know, Mr. Dale, this Professor probably stole that machine himself."

"Well I get that now. A couple of technicians from his lab, Mr. Lobe and Mr. Von Krod, told us that terrorists broke in, stole the prototype, and kidnapped the Professor. Took us awhile to realize the Professor himself stole the LTTA."

"For what purpose?"

"Time travel is a powerful terrorist weapon. Surely he told you that already. He's gathering all the world leaders in some place called Milam Valley."

Paul pulled the folded poster from his back pocket and showed it Mr. Dale. "This the place?"

"Yes. Where did you get this?"

"Some drunk was sleeping on it down in Kali's tunnel."

"Well, that's the place. From what my people have been able to learn, this Milam Valley is somewhere in the Himalayas."

"That shouldn't be hard to find."

"Except that the Himalayas pass through a few countries including Bhutan, China, India, Nepal, Pakistan, and Afghanistan. They stretch 1,700 miles and are anywhere from 60 to 250 miles wide. It's a huge area, some of it completely unexplored."

"So how do you stop him from doing this?"

"Our scientists have built us a new prototype, without the limiter, so we can undo the whole problem. It's how we moved all this equipment from the future to here."

"So now you're going further back in time to stop Kali?"

"Yes. It's a bit complicated."

"The whole thing is a bit complicated. Try me."

"Well, Paul, it works like this. The National Counterterrorism Center from 2075 now labels time travel as a national security issue because of what the Professor is doing. We've been ordered, therefore, to change the time line and make time travel impossible."

"How do you plan to do that?"

"Oswin Köhler theorized that tachyon particles aimed at physical objects causes time travel, which became the basis for Professor Cali's theories and construction of the space-time dilator prototype, or the time machine. If we can travel in time and prevent Köhler's birth, we will eliminate time travel from ever being invented."

"That your best shot?" Paul asked incredulously.

"That's what our computer suggests," Dale affirmed.

"And how do you propose to keep this man from being born?"

"By making sure his parents don't meet up with each other. A simple redirection. No violence necessary."

"You're crazy, you know that Mr. Dale?"

"We've gone over this hundreds of times, Paul, using artificial intelligence technology from 2075."

"Well, I don't know about artificial intelligence, but this plan doesn't even make common sense."

"Why not?"

"Look, Mr. Dale, if you eliminate time travel, you'll also eliminate the TDC, won't you? Your whole operation here from the future won't exist. Won't that be a Granny thing?"

Dale smiled and nodded. "Not in this case. Our computer model suggests we have an eighty-nine percent chance Kali's mischief here in 1966 will be prevented and the future will be restored the way it was meant to be."

"But if time travel suddenly doesn't exist anymore, what will happen to you and me and all of your lab techs here in 1966?"

"We already ran some experiments. We think we'll all be hurled by the forces of nature back into our respective time zones. Call it an untested law of physics."

"Will any of us remember anything?"

"We don't know," Dale admitted.

"And when are you going to do this?"

"Right now," Dale said.

"Earlier you said something about Plan B. Is this Plan B?"

"Yes, that's right. Plan A was to kill you."

Agent Dale led Paul out of the room, down another hall, and through a series of stainless steel security doors, each requiring a different code before they could gain entry. Finally, they came to a large room. In the four corners of the ceiling Paul saw huge ceramic coils aiming at a black chair in the middle of a large circular metallic platform. Along the perimeter of the room were panels lined with lights and switches.

"This is the launch room. We'll sit an agent in those chairs and send him through time," Dale explained. "He has specific instructions to prevent the birth of Oswin Köhler by diverting his mother away from meeting his father."

Sidney Dale waved at a forty-two-year-old red-haired woman with freckles on a balcony, overlooking the room. "We're all set, Mr. Dale," the woman called down.

"Excellent. Let's proceed," Dale replied. "We'll see how accurate our computer model works."

Paul shook his head in disbelief. This was insanity, but no one seemed to realize it except him. Was stopping the invention of time travel really the best idea? Was that even possible?

"Mr. Dale, I'm not sure this is a good idea."

"Too late, Paul. The wheels are turning. It's a done deal," he said firmly.

A man in his mid-fifties, sporting a mustache, appeared from a door. He was naked. They directed him to sit down on the chair and technicians began to strap him down.

"Why is he naked, Mr. Dale?"

"It's always been like that, Paul. You just can't travel through time wearing clothes."

"I'm here to tell you," Paul explained, "that it works even if you're wearing clothes."

"Oh?"

CHAPTER 38

Out on Beekman Street the sky was dark but Maria Ortiz was sizzling hotdogs on the corner of Park Row, across from Theatre Alley. As an entrepreneur, Maria could never fathom a desk job, but there was a lot more in running a hotdog stand than she originally thought. Besides the permit and meeting health code requirements, there was the expense of the cart itself. Then there was the problem of spoilage which cut into profits, she discovered the hard way.

Maria looked at the sidewalk and saw the tiniest man she'd ever seen walk past her, cross the street, and stand outside a bookstore. Maria couldn't help but look at him. The midget was dressed in short, black slacks and a dark brown shirt that was too big for him. Binoculars dangled around his neck.

"Hey Miss. You selling Kosher hotdogs here tonight?"

Maria turned and saw John and Lisa Friedman, a husband wife team from Weinstein and Holtzman Hardware around the corner.

"Sure am. Guaranteed pure Kosher," Maria reassured them. "Can't sell hotdogs in this neighborhood otherwise!"

"Good, 'cause we've been working late. Give us two," John Friedman ordered.

Maria cast a quick glance back across the street. The lights were still on in the bookstore and the three foot tall man reached up, opened the door and walked in.

Wayne Boyd

* * *

The bookstore cashier heard the door jingle and noticed a surprisingly short man enter.

After wandering up and down rows of bookshelves, the little person came over to the cash register. "I'm looking for a couple of men." His accent was peculiar.

"What did they look like?"

"You must have seen them. A man with a brimmed hat and younger man with really short hair, dressed in a black suit."

"A lot of people come in and out," the cashier explained. "I can't remember everyone that walks in."

"Is that so? I've been outside on Beekman Street for awhile. Frankly, I can't see how you manage to stay in business. No one comes in here."

"I'm sorry. I haven't seen anyone matching your description. Maybe they went into G.S. Smokers next door. They sell cigars."

The little man looked around once more and saw no one. He was annoyed, and checked his watch. "Okay, thank you," he said with a sigh, and went back outside to wait.

There was a chili and hotdog vendor across the street. He walked over and looked up at Maria Ortiz. "Selling many hotdogs?"

"Hey little fella. Just sold two, but it's been slow."

"That's what I thought," the tiny man said. "In a few minutes none of this will be here. Good luck."

* * *

"The fate of the world is in your hands," Dale told the naked man strapped to the seat. "I don't say that lightly."

The man nodded. "I'm ready."

Technicians moved in and strapped various sensors to his wrists and forehead.

"What's all that for?" asked Paul

"We want to be able to monitor his movements," Dale explained.

"You mean you can actually track his movements in the

past?"

"To a degree."

Paul frowned. "But if he's successful and stops time travel from being invented, none of this will be here anymore and you won't be able to track him!"

"Only if we're successful," Dale explained.

As Paul and Dale looked on from their position, the technicians stepped back and quickly manned their stations along the outer perimeter wall.

"We should step back a little. Sometimes there's a good deal of energy that emits from the chair when we do this," Dale cautioned.

A red light began to flash above the door. "Ten seconds until launch time," announced a voice over the sound system. The countdown began. "Nine – Eight – Seven – Six..."

"Are you afraid?" Mr. Dale asked Paul.

"I'm scared out of my wits," the monk confessed.

"Three – Two – One."

"You absolutely sure about this?"

The lights dimmed and a loud, deep, hum filled the room. Paul held his hands over his ears and watched in amazement. The chair and its occupant started to glow brightly while the sound became louder and deeper.

Ribbons of blue electrical energy shot from the four corners of the room, enveloping the occupant of the chair.

*   *   *

From across Beekman street, the little man watched the lights in the bookstore flicker and nearby streetlights dim.

Maria Ortiz was alarmed. "What the hell?"

The little man looked up at her. "See you later." He drew a huge weapon from under his oversized shirt and checked that it was still activated. Maria had never before seen anything like it.

Next the man reached into his pocket and removed an electronic device which had a small parabolic antenna at the top. He punched in the year 2027 on the keypad and pressed the button. A four foot wide blue circle appeared in front of him and the little man jumped in and vanished in a flash of light.

Maria Ortiz fainted.

*   *   *

Paul watched the man on the platform vanish. Two seconds later the lights went out, the room went pitch dark, and all sound stopped instantly.

"Guess you blew a circuit," Paul laughed.

But Agent Sidney E. Dale, did not reply.

"Mr. Dale?"

His voice had a hollow quality to it. There was even an echo in the room. He reached out into blackness to touch Mr. Dale, but felt nothing.

"Hello?"

He shuffled his feet and kicked what sounded like a glass bottle, which rolled away.

"Where did everyone go?"

Paul realized he was completely alone. He stood stationary for a half a minute and tried to let his eyes adjust to the dark, but he still couldn't see.

He removed the stun gun from his pocket and turned on the LED flashlight. A bluish beam pierced the blackness. The floor was cement, he saw, and littered with broken glass, nails and bat guano. About twenty feet away he saw a doorless entryway.

He heard a fluttering sound above. Paul swung around, pointing the light upward at metal beams, large air ducting and PVC plumbing. He saw a florescent fixture with shattered tubes and eerie dark shadows. He lowered the beam, but heard the sound again. A bat flew across the light.

"Hello? Anyone here?"

He heard another sound. A peculiar raking noise. It began, then stopped. It came again. He walked ahead, hearing tiny bits of debris crunching under his feet. Passing through the doorway, he noted the raking sound come and go, come and go. The noise was louder here and Paul's light fell onto an old, torn mattress in the corner, upon which slept an old man in tattered clothes, bottle over his chest. The noise came from the drunk, and Paul realized he was snoring. He had never heard a snore like that before. It sounded thick, congested, and unhealthy.

Suddenly there was a prolonged surge of white light that shined in through a second doorway. The light was very bright, and flickered faintly, sustained a few seconds more, and went out. Paul ran toward this doorway and passed into an outer room. Here he found plate glass windows with an outside view and a glass door opening onto Beekman Street. There was a very tiny person standing on the other side of the glass door, peering in. He rapped the glass.

Paul unlocked the door and when he opened it saw a dark street outside. There were no street lights, and none of the windows in the towering buildings around him were lit.

He looked down at the little man, who had binoculars dangling from his neck and was wearing a dark brown shirt that was too large. Paul recognized him. This was the same man he'd seen at the hospital in 1966, and the same man from the photograph Kali had Von Krod give him. He'd been ordered to kill him. Damn. Paul realized he was still in 1966.

"Excuse me, Sir," Paul said. "Can you please tell me the date?"

The little one pulled out his weapon and aimed it straight up at Paul's nose. Red and green lights flashed up and down the side of the cylinder. A series of rings were mounted around the barrel of the gun. Paul had never seen a weapon like that, but he did not doubt it was dangerous.

"Don't ask questions," he warned abruptly in a strange accent Paul couldn't place. "Do what I say. Put your hands up, and step outside!"

CHAPTER 39

Beekman Street and Theatre Alley, New York, NY. 2027

At least he had grabbed a bite to eat and refreshed himself when he was back in Dale's TDC headquarters, but now he was very tired. He needed sleep, but first he needed to know what had just happened.

Paul tried to think. TDC sent someone through time to prevent two people from meeting, so they wouldn't marry and have a child who would later come up with theories that Kali could use to invent time travel. Sidney E. Dale also said that if they succeeded, Paul would be hurled back to his own time in 2027. Therefore he must be back in his own time.

The only problem with this theory was that sirens were sounding in the distance, the whole city was in the dark, and a three foot tall man from 1966 was pointing some kind of gun at his face.

With his hands in the air, Paul stepped from the building onto the sidewalk. Across the street he noted a row of butcher shops, closed for the evening, which he didn't remember seeing in 1966. CCTV cameras atop three tall, metal polls, pointed at the stores. He couldn't remember seeing them before, either.

The city looked vacant. The vehicles parked at the curbs all looked like they were from the 2020's, as they should, but Park Row was only 50 feet away and there was no traffic, and he saw no pedestrians on the normally busy sidewalk in the city that never sleeps.

"Now, you see that car? Squat down so that you're hidden behind it."

Paul hesitated. Perhaps the little man suffered from schizophrenia, believing a fancy toy was a real weapon. On the other hand, he'd seen enough in the last few days to consider that it might be some kind of real weapon.

"I've seen you before," Paul said. "In the hospital and in a photo given to me by Von Krod."

"I've been following you all over the place," the man replied. "You're pretty hard to catch up to. Why didn't you meet me in Central Park back in 1966 like I told you on the card I slipped in your wallet?"

"That was you that put that card there?"

"Yes. In your hospital room. Remember?"

He watched the little man closely, but the man kept sufficient distance to protect himself. The nozzle of the weapon remained pointed in Paul's general direction.

"Problem with that," Paul said, "is that I woke up in the hospital in 1966 and you were there, and now you're here."

"I followed you."

"Through time?"

"You got a problem with that? Now stay down!"

Paul put his hands down and stood up. "Look, I'm done with all this time travel stuff. If that's a real weapon then go ahead and shoot me. Otherwise, I'm exhausted and going back to Brooklyn to sleep."

"You won't be able to do that," the man said. "There still is no Hare Krishna temple in Brooklyn."

Paul was dumbfounded. "Where is the temple, then?"

"Sit down on that sidewalk and crouch behind the car like I told you. I will explain everything. I'm not here to hurt you. I'm here to protect you."

Paul slid down on the sidewalk, back to the vehicle.

"Then why the weapon?"

"Keep your voice down!" the little man snapped. "They're almost here!"

"Who *are* you?"

"My name is Odus," he said. "From the one hundred and forty fifth century. I'm trying to protect you from bounty hunters coming from my time period."

"Why would bounty hunters from the future be looking for me?"

"Because after you escaped, Kali went to the future and hired killers to hunt you down. He knew you'd go back to your own time period, and he knew you'd be outside the former TDC headquarters. So the bounty hunters are coming here, now."

"How did he know all that?"

"Because that's where the bounty hunters killed you a few minutes from now before I changed the time line again."

"I'm confused."

Suddenly, a red shaft of light streaked past Paul's face and smashed the side of a nearby building making a small explosion. Pieces of masonry fell, engulfing Paul and the little man in smoke. The shot had been fired from across nearby Park Row. Through the smoke, Paul noticed four little people near City Hall Park wearing polymer fiber suits and brandishing similar laser like weapons.

"We've got to run," Odus shouted. "Follow me!" He ran toward the corner of Beekman Street and Park Row and dove behind a gasoline-powered Toyota 4000 GLX, the latest design coming out of Chinese-controlled Japan. Paul followed, and ducked behind Odus. Multiple red streaks sliced into brick and glass in the buildings behind him as the bounty hunters fired and missed.

Odus returned fire, and another beam shot back, vaporizing the Toyota.

"Run!"

They ran further south on Park Row and hid behind a box truck.

"Where's all the traffic?" Paul asked him.

"Are you kidding?" Odus replied. "With gasoline over fifty dollars a gallon, there's a law against driving after curfew."

Paul peered under the truck and saw the little people in polymer suits spreading out, two to the left, two to the right, ducking behind vehicles on their side of the road.

Odus took a moment to explain to Paul. "This is a very different 2027 from where you're from. Because you left Kali back in 1966, he's been changing the future. Even religion is against the law here. That's why there's no Hare Krishna temple in Brooklyn!"

"Why is gasoline so expensive?"

"What did you expect? Kali bought all the oil companies and outlawed development of hybrid, electric and hydrogen fuel-cell vehicles. China now owns Japan. We've got to go back to 1966 and change all of this back!"

"Explain this," Paul insisted. "Sidney Dale sent someone back in time to prevent time travel from being invented. What happened?"

"They succeeded. That's why you were hurled back to this alternative 2027, even though you were originally transported to 1966 by my time device, not his. What Dale didn't know was the invention of time travel was inevitable. Someone at CERN in Geneva came up with the same theory and a time machine was developed anyway. Kali stole one of the new time machines."

A 2027 Police SUV from the First Precinct, light bar flashing red and blue on the roof, careened down Broadway and made a hard left onto Park Row, siren blaring. The cruiser skid sideways, burning rubber, and sped quickly north toward them.

Paul felt relieved. "About time the good guys showed up!"

A bounty hunter across the way aimed his weapon, fired, and a stream of energy struck the speeding patrol car. The vehicle flipped over, burst into flames, and slammed into a fire hydrant. Water spewed high into the night air, just a hundred feet from Paul and Odus.

"What are they doing?" Paul screamed. He stepped around the front of the box truck and shouted across the street. "You morons! Those were cops!"

A streak of light hit the truck an inch from his elbow, peeling off the hood and slamming it into the building behind Paul. Odus grabbed Paul by the leg and pulled him back behind the truck.

A second police vehicle skid around from Broadway and slammed on the breaks, coming to a full stop. The front doors flew open and two officers jumped out. They crouched behind their doors and drew their guns. "NYPD! Come out in the open and throw down your weapons!"

The First Precinct was on the corner of Ericsson Place and Varick Street. To get to Park Row from there, you could drive down Broadway, and head north, or drive via Chambers Street and head south. That route brought two more cruisers in from the other end of the street.

Coming to a full stop to the north, these police also climbed from their vehicles and hid behind their open doors.

"Now they think we're cop killers," Paul said.

"Never mind the stupid police," Odus said. "It's the guys with the particle beam guns we have to worry about."

A burning, red shaft of light shot straight toward the police to the north. One of the newly arrived squad vehicles exploded – two policemen killed instantly in a crimson blaze.

"That's it," the police shouted. "Open fire!"

Bullets began flying down the street. One of the police SUVs was hit in the headlight by friendly fire. Another bullet careened off the top of a vehicle not far from Paul and Odus and smashed the windshield.

A black helicopter flew around the Park Row Building and opened fire. Machine gun bullets ricocheted along the pavement.

Odus tucked his weapon under his belt and pulled out a calculator sized contraption with a small parabolic antenna. Punching in some keys on the face, it chirped twice. He keyed in another sequence, and the device began to hum. "I'm lucky I found you back in 2027. You'll have to learn how to use this thing one day."

"What is it?"

Light beams shrieked from across the street. Bullets fired. The air was dark with smoke and Paul started to choke.

Then he noticed a peculiar glowing portal hovering above the sidewalk only a few feet away. It was perfectly round with three glowing blue bands of light separated by empty space. Hovering above the ground and suspended from nothing at all, it was blue-black inside, while the perimeter glowed brightly.

"What the heck?"

More bullets showered down the street. More particle beam blasts from the opposite direction. One of the little people on the other side of the street shot up at the helicopter, vaporizing the tail rotor. The chopper started spinning out of control, rapidly spiraling downward. It crashed into the side of the Woolworth Building, bursting into flames.

Grabbing Paul by the arm, Odus jumped into the mysterious hole in the air, and Paul followed. There was a bright flash and both Paul and Odus vanished into thin air.

CHAPTER 40

Kali's Underground Kingdom, New York. July 14, 1966

After stepping off the red grating, Wendy followed a pathway on a high rock ledge. A minute later she arrived outside an enormous golden door. When she pushed the door open a crack, she heard people talking on the other side. She strained her ears to listen.

Inside, Kali did not notice the great golden door creak open an inch. He stood from his throne and glared angrily at Von Krod. "Fool!"

Mary and the two McPhersons sat wide-eyed in shock, looking in the direction where Paul had vanished. Since Mary wasn't gagged, her mouth was open in amazement.

Kali was infuriated with Von Krod. "You are supposed to be Anger Personified, but you let your rage get the better of you! Now look what you've done!"

He raised his left hand and a field of energy hit Von Krod, who winced in pain and held the sides of his head with both hands. He dropped to his knees.

Kali's beaded eyes narrowed and he sneered. "Does Paul McPherson think he can outwit *me?*" He turned to Durukti. "Find out where he went!"

She headed toward the time machine room and Kali called for Connie and Lobe to step forward and untie the hostages. "It's time to head for our private jet to Milam Valley."

Once unbound, the three hostages staggered to their feet, rubbing their wrists. "I want to know what the hell's going on!" Henry McPherson demanded. "Why did you bring us here, who *are* you, and who was that person called Paul?"

Kali stood up from his throne and removed his golden helmet. He placed it elegantly on his seat and stepped down the stairs to floor level.

"He's the son of your son," Kali said. "Your grandchild."

"But we're childless!" Helen McPherson said.

"For now, but not in the future."

"But how could you know that?" Helen asked.

"Time travel," Mary interrupted. "These people have all come from the future, just like Paul!"

"You catch on quickly, Mary," Kali said. "Paul has taught you well."

"That's absurd," Henry McPherson exclaimed.

Durukti returned and Kali spun around to face her. "What did you find out?"

"The panel indicates he jumped through time twice. The first jump was twenty minutes into the past, just before we arrived in this room. The second jump was exactly one day. That's where he is now."

"I knew it," Lobe said nervously. "He's behind us on the time line! That's extremely dangerous!"

Kali turned to look at him. "He can do nothing," Kali said. "He's a religious fool."

"Lobe is correct," Durukti warned. "Despite everything, even you are controlled by time. If McPherson changes the time line before any of this takes place he can erase the present events entirely."

"Then we'll go in the other direction. To the future!" exclaimed Kali.

"The future?" Lobe asked.

Durukti smiled. "Yes. Don't you understand? It's brilliant. We can send an army of little time travelers from the future to hunt him down!"

"Precisely," Kali said. "They have their own portable time machines. We won't need an army, however. Just a few of their private bounty hunters. They can kill Paul before he does anymore damage! We all know he's going to TDC headquarters in lower Manhattan."

Von Krod stepped forward. "You don't need to do that. You've got his grandparents here. Just kill them and be done with it."

Durukti nodded. "It's true. If he doesn't have any grandparents then he can never be born. McPherson will be wiped from existence!"

Kali glanced at them dangerously with his narrow, beady eyes as he contemplated his options. "Can't," he said at last. "These two relatives will give birth to a daughter, Paul's Aunt. She will marry the brother-in-law of Doctor Oswin Köhler. I need Doctor Köhler's help to invent time travel in the future. If we kill McPherson's grandparents, there is a chance that could be disrupted."

Connie looked at the hostages. "Another Granny Paradox. So we're taking these three to Milam Valley?"

"Yes," Kali explained. "All three of them must go because if Paul or Odus show up here again we still have a bargaining chip."

He turned to Durukti. "Go set the time machine for a journey to the future. Hire some bounty hunters to kill Paul McPherson and come back as soon as possible. We still have work to do here in the past. I'm planning to start purchasing oil stocks."

Durukti bowed to her Lord and returned to the adjoining room. A moment later blue streaks of electricity shot from the room and Durukti had vanished into the future.

"What happens now?" asked Mary nervously.

"We're going to Milam Valley to make preparations," Kali replied. "I have a meeting with world leaders coming up. I don't want you to miss it!"

Von Krod and Lobe handcuffed the three hostages and they all headed for the golden door.

They stepped out onto the ledge and crossed over the bridge with the blood red walkway.

*   *   *

When she realized they were about to come through the golden door, Wendy, climbed over the ledge and down the rock face to a foothold below. Her fingers clutched chucks of stone. Kali and his entourage walked right overhead without seeing her hiding on the rock cliff directly below them.

*   *   *

Paul and Odus stepped onto the stone ledge from the time-space vortex and the opening in the air vanished behind them with a flash of light. Odus activated his weapon and pointed it at the large, ornate golden door. He fired. There was an explosion and the entire door fell inward with a huge crash.

They climbed over rubble and entered Kali's cavernous throne room. A bugler dropped his trumpet and drew a pistol. Odus fired. The powerful particle beam swept him off his feet and his horn went flying. He died instantly.

Odus turned the weapon on the other bugler. He dropped his trumpet and raised his hands.

Unfortunately, except for these two, no other person was inside the room.

An alarm sounded. "Not good," Odus mumbled to Paul.

Paul looked toward the surviving bugler. "Tell us where they went or you're dead."

"They went to Milam Valley," he replied, but immediately went for his gun.

"He's got a gun!" Paul shouted.

Odus fired and a beam shrieked out and killed the man instantly.

A woman screamed. Paul and Odus spun around and saw a blonde woman standing in the entryway, hands to her mouth. Odus aimed his weapon, but Paul quickly pushed it downward.

"Who are you?" Paul asked.

"Wendy Murphy," she answered, "I'm a friend of Mary Pierce. I saw them kidnapping her, and then they kidnapped me as well. I escaped and came looking for her."

"You know this woman?" Odus asked.

"Well, we never actually met. She's Mary's best friend."

"Who are *you* two?"

"I'm Paul McPherson and this is Odus."

"I saw you jump out of a hole in space on the ledge outside. How did you do that?" Wendy asked.

"A long story. You know where Mary is?"

"She left here a few minutes ago with the others. They said they were taking the three hostages to some place called Milam Valley."

Odus went over and started searching the dead bugler's pockets. "Is that in the Appalachians?" Odus asked.

Paul looked at Odus with surprise. "I thought you were the one with all the answers."

Odus then admitted he had no idea about any place called Milam Valley.

"Mr. Dale told me it was somewhere in the Himalayas," Paul said.

Guards appeared in the doorway behind them. Odus spun around and fired his weapon, missing. Paul, Odus and Wendy ran behind Kali's deserted throne. The siren continued to sound.

The guards aimed their Thompson submachine guns and automatic weapon fire riddled the base of Kali's throne.

"Best we leave the same way we came," Odus said. He pushed a button on his portable device, and a time-space hole opened up in front of them.

Wendy looked on in amazement.

"Now, Wendy," Paul said. "You have to trust us on this. We need to jump through that thing all at the same time."

CHAPTER 41

New York Public Library, 5th Avenue. July 12, 1966

Paul, Wendy and Odus made an odd looking group. Paul and Wendy were over five feet ten inches tall, and Odus was only three feet tall. They were hard to figure, especially stepping out of a time-space vortex outside the door of the New York Public Library. The way Odus saw things, the world was going to fall apart if Kali couldn't be stopped, so why worry about discretion? Certainly the mode of arrival provided by Odus was more efficient than taking the subway and there was no time to lose.

Ken Zogi was an African American workman on his lunch hour sitting at a table near the library entrance. A bottle of water sat on the table. He was still wearing his hardhat. When he saw the three people step from a hole in space onto the library steps he had to put his sandwich down. "Now, that's something you don't see every day," he said to no one in particular as he watched the three strange people enter the building.

The main reading room of the library was 78 by 297 feet long and the ceiling was over fifty feet high. The room was lined with thousands of reference books on open shelves along the floor and open balcony. The entire room was lit by massive windows and grand chandeliers, furnished with tables carved from African Mahogany and Brazilian Cherry. Surrounding these sturdy tables were comfortable chairs and brass lamps. The building was a National Historic Landmark.

Readers studied books brought to them from the library's closed stacks. There were special rooms for notable authors and scholars, many of whom had done important research and writing at the library in the past.

Additionally, the library housed the largest circulating and general reference collection in the New York Public Library system. It seemed a good place to search for a place called Milam Valley.

The sprawling library had five floors, including books, periodicals and microfilms. Computers would be introduced in the future, but since Paul was back in 1966 again that option was out.

"The Himalayas cover a lot of ground," Paul said. "We don't know where Milam Valley is or what we're going to do if we find the place."

"First things first," Wendy said.

Paul learned how to use the viewfinder and busied himself searching dozens of microfilm sheets. Meanwhile, Wendy paced up and down rows of book shelves. When she returned empty handed, Odus was still standing nearby.

"I'm wasting time," Paul said to them. "This is going nowhere fast. I know that in my time they had computers in this library, but this microfilm stuff is impossible."

"Maybe a librarian will be more helpful," Wendy suggested.

"Worth a try," Odus said.

The odd trio made their way to an information desk where they encountered forty-five year-old Gloria Lopez. She was wearing her reading glasses examining the return dates stamped inside a book.

"Look at that," Paul muttered in amazement. "They actually still stamp the books. Where I come from they just do it by barcodes."

"Where I come from they do it exactly like the lady is doing it," Wendy added with a hint of sarcasm. She had already been briefed on the time travel adventures of Paul and had traveled through a time-space portal herself to get to the library. She was up for anything now.

"Excuse me," Paul said, noticing the lady's name tag and

a ring on her left hand. "Mrs. Lopez, can you help us? We're looking for a book on a place in the mountains called Milam Valley. Ever heard of it?"

"Why don't you try the atlas department one floor below?" She caught herself staring at Odus who was the smallest adult male she had ever laid eyes upon.

Half an hour later they were sitting around a table with a pile of the most comprehensive atlases they could find. Paul was searching the books.

Wendy looked at Odus. "Would you be offended if I told you that you were the shortest midget I've ever seen?"

"I'm not little. You're big."

Wendy laughed. "That's one way of looking at it!"

"What I'm saying is that people from my century are all my size," Odus explained. "Humanity has grown shorter over time."

Wendy looked at Paul. Paul said, "Don't ask me, but after what I've been through I'd believe anything."

He went back to the atlas books in front of him.

"It doesn't seem to exist on any map," Paul concluded as he thumbed through yet another index. "Maybe Milam Valley is a name that someone gave to some private resort or something. That would explain why we can't find any reference to it."

"Maybe," Wendy concurred. "But where do we go from here?"

"I'm not sure," Paul replied hesitantly. "What do you think, Odus?" He turned, but saw Odus was not there. They looked up just in time to find him wobbling away, turning down an aisle of book shelves.

"Where's *he* going?" Wendy asked.

They quickly followed behind him, turning down the same aisle of books, and saw little Odus talking to a very tall man dressed in orange robes with a shaved head and no *sikha*. The man had a book in his hand and was looking down kindly upon the little man.

The man turned to Paul and Wendy, and then down toward Odus again. "Are those your friends?"

Odus nodded. The man looked back up at Paul. "I hear you're looking for Milam Valley."

The man was clearly a Tibetan Buddhist. He had light

brown skin and his eyes slanted slightly, but not as much as a true Oriental. He could have been in his forties, but it was hard to tell. He introduced himself as Anantamati Ku Shin from Nepal, sponsored by the Buddhist Society of Kathmandu to give discourses in a number of American Buddhist communities.

"Why do you want to know about Milam Valley?" Anantamati asked.

"It's kind of hard to explain," Paul said evasively. "We just need find it."

"Well I have heard of this place. Come with me. We should talk privately."

The Buddhist led the three of them to the third floor, where there were private reading rooms only large enough for four or five people at a time. They sat down in one of these rooms.

"The hidden city," Anantamati began, "is thought to exist somewhere in the Himalayas, just west of Nepal inside of India. They say the only way to reach it is either climb over the mountaintops or go through the back door. It is said there is a ancient tunnel, a back door if you like, at Roop Kund, but no one has ever found any secret entrance there."

"Where is this back door at Roop Kund supposed to be?"

"Roop Kund is on the slopes of Mount Trisul in the Indian Himalayas. It is the first mountain over seven thousand meters to ever have been climbed."

"How do you get to it?" Odus inquired.

"Wendy, can you write this down?" Paul directed.

Wendy produced a pen and paper and Odus was surprised.

"Generally, hikers travel to Loharjung by road." He spelled it for Wendy. "From there, you can hike three or four days to Roop Kund. It is over 5,000 meters above sea level."

"How high is that?" Paul asked.

"That's between sixteen and seventeen thousand feet," Odus said. "Pretty high up there."

Anantamati agreed. "Yes. It is well above the tree line."

"This should be right up my alley," Wendy said. "I've got experience in rock climbing."

Anantamati continued. "On the way up the mountain

there's a grazing ground for mules, horses and sheep. From there you'll need to hike an additional eleven kilometers where the climate is hostile most of the year. Weather permitting, you might catch a glimpse of Trisul and other peaks, some of the highest mountains in the world. You must be careful of the many waterfalls and landslides on the extreme slopes you will hike across."

"That sounds like fun," Paul observed.

"Roop Kund is only a day's climb from there."

"Practically around the corner," Paul noted sarcastically.

"No, no," Anantamati said. "It is in India. I thought I was clear."

"You were clear enough," Paul said.

"I think I've got it all down," Wendy said. "So what's at this Roop Kund place?"

"Roop Kund is a frozen lake that should be thawed this time of year. If you go, bring sunscreen. You will get burned. The clouds will be below you, not above, and you will need to hike over a snow-covered slippery ridge along the way. If the weather is not stormy you might manage an unobstructed view of Trisul and Nand Ghungti."

"What's that?" Paul asked.

"They are famous mountains," Anantamati said.

Odus interjected. "You have given us very detailed directions how to climb up to this Roop Kund in the Indian Himalayas. Is there anything else we need to be aware of?"

"I'm a researcher," Anantamati explained. "It's my specialty to know about ancient, lost civilizations. Ancient Tibetan texts say that at Roop Kund there is a secret tunnel that goes all the way to Milam Valley. Unless one travels through that tunnel, one will never be able to see the real Milam. I understand from my studies Milam Valley is kind of a mythological place like Shambhala that can't be seen by the naked eye without passing through the Roop Kund tunnel."

"But didn't you say that no one has ever found a secret tunnel beginning at Roop Kund?" Paul asked.

"Yes, I did say that. Many have looked. None have found any evidence of any kind of tunnel or cave or anything of that nature. There is simply a giant mountain with a natural terrace, and on that terrace is a frozen lake surrounded by human skeletons which are hundreds or even thousands of years old."

"Well, surely we can search the area. People may have missed something."

"Roop Kund is not a big place," Anantamati explained. "We are talking about a small, uninhabited lake that is frozen most of the year. There are no people and no buildings at that place. Human skeletons lay on the ground around the lake, and there is nothing more. I suggest you bring some local porters to help with your journey. There is a Buddhist temple a little higher on Mount Trisul where you can spend the night before beginning your journey back down to Loharjung."

"Where did the human skeletons come from?" Odus asked.

"They are remains of a group that supposedly tried to reach Milam Valley through the secret tunnel, rumored to have been killed by the Yeti, though no one knows for sure."

"Who were the Yeti?" Wendy asked.

"I think in your country they are called the Abominable Snowmen."

"This is getting better all the time," Paul said.

CHAPTER 42

Time and space, the two interwoven threads in the fabric of the Einsteinium universe, enable a time traveler to journey not only through time, but through space as well. Unfortunately, a small, portable time machine couldn't safely transport the three of them across the Atlantic, Mediterranean and Indian Ocean, all the way to the Indian subcontinent. For that kind of distance, Odus explained, they needed something a little more conventional, like a commercial airliner. *That* required plane tickets, passports and visas.

As they left the library, Wendy told them that she already had a passport because she had visited London two years previously. Paul and Odus obviously didn't have the necessary documents.

They discussed the problem standing outside the library on Fifth Avenue.

"I have an idea," Wendy said. "Mary has an ex-boyfriend I'm sleeping with named Peter Wilson."

"I met him," Paul said. "You're sleeping with him? He acted like a jerk in Thompson Square Park."

"Mary calls him a jerk, too," Wendy agreed. "But he's got some connections. He told me once that for a hundred bucks he could get me a false ID."

"I wouldn't believe anything he said," Paul quipped.

"Let's hear what she has to say," Odus objected.

"He's a draft dodger. He knows how to make false identification. He can get us some fake passports."

"I have paper money," Odus said. "They give it to us for our trips into the past."

"Well, for an extra fifty Pete can supply a driver license, social security and a valid passport with a visa for any country in the world."

"Speed is not an issue," Odus said. "Even if it takes weeks, once we arrive in India we can jump back in time and it will become today again."

"And you're not thinking pragmatically," Paul said. "You must remember that Kali is having a meeting of world leaders. It wouldn't be wise to wait long, or else the world will change so much it might not be possible to go jump back in time."

"You've got a point there," Odus agreed. He handed five hundred dollars to Wendy to give to Peter Wilson.

* * *

Even though it took Pete a week to get the passports, visas and other identification, Odus was unconcerned. "The meeting isn't until the end of the month. We have time."

Paul, on the other hand, was in terrible anxiety about the fate of Mary during that time, and could hardly sleep. He slept on her couch, because he had no where to go, and Odus slept in her bed. Wendy slept in her own apartment, but visited them often.

"It doesn't matter how much time it takes," Odus kept reassuring Paul. "As long as we get there, then I can adjust the time. Furthermore, you still exist, so we know your grandparents are still alive."

One night in the apartment, Odus showed Paul his weapon, which he called a particle beam gun. "It isn't a laser," he told Paul. "It emits an ultra high energy beam of electron particles, therefore the name, particle beam gun. When the electrons strike a target, they disrupt the molecular structure. The discharge appears to be a beam of light because a laser mounted on the gun helps us see where we're shooting, but the damage that it causes has nothing to do with lasers."

Fortunately, before the terrorist attacks on the World Trade Center on September 11, 2001, airport security was not difficult. Odus convinced the authorities that the particle beam gun was a toy and his time machine was a calculator. He had no difficulty at all getting the two inside his carry-on luggage.

On the flight from New York to Amsterdam, Wendy, Paul and Odus went over her notes from the conversation with the Buddhist, studied maps of the Himalayas, and corrected Wendy's spelling of place names, villages and mountains.

They spent six hours in a hotel in Amsterdam, time only for a nap. Before heading back to the airport for the flight to Jordan and New Delhi via Royal Jordanian Airlines, they stopped at a nearby restaurant.

On the flight from Jordan to India, Odus talked with Paul and Wendy about his own time period. They learned that time travel had been quite regular for decades before Odus was born and regulated by the Unified Nations Company, or UNC.

Odus preferred not to call UNC a "government" per se. It was a company – the ultimate conglomerate. People spoke a common language which had distantly evolved from Chinese, English, Spanish, Hindi and Gaelic. The tallest person alive was only about three feet three inches, and the average lifespan was about forty-five.

Days were slightly longer in the future. The gradual slowing of the earth's rotation, a phenomena scientists monitored regularly, had been caused by massive atmospheric change from greenhouse gases, earthquakes and the movement of the oceans and air.

Polar ice caps had thawed and the land-based population of the world was only two million. Many people lived in underwater cities. People also inhabited Europa, the sixth moon of the planet Jupiter, and had established large cities under the frozen surface.

They didn't get into outer space with rockets anymore. Odus said they used "space elevators." Essentially, a space elevator used a very long carbon-nanotube cable. One end of the cable was attached to the equator and the other end stretched beyond geosynchronous orbit, at an altitude of 21,000 miles, attached to a space anchor. Centrifugal force kept the cables stretched outward from the earth's surface and climbing machines carried payloads from the equator up the cable into space. That facility proved invaluable to relocate the bulk of the population from the shrinking landmasses.

Two classes of people existed: the Employed and the Unemployed, or those who worked for the UNC and those that didn't. Those that were Employed had full benefits such as education, medicine and housing and could trade with each other. They lived thirty percent longer. Those that were Unemployed made a living by being bounty hunters, pirates and scavengers. A constant war raged between these two classes. Religion had long ago been outlawed.

"As for me," Odus explained, "I joined a group who are dedicated to preserving the cultural and spiritual heritage of the human race. They are the good guys, in my opinion – my supervisors."

Odus said his supervisors sent people back to do historical research with the stipulation that no history be changed by their presence unless it was to eliminate future outlaws. Unfortunately, since the invention of portable time traveling devices, the technology had fallen into the hands of criminal elements as well, like bounty hunters.

Time Gods

Wayne Boyd

PART FOUR

'Clearly,' the Time Traveler proceeded, 'any real body must have extension in four directions: it must have Length, Breadth, Thickness, and Duration. But through a natural infirmity of the flesh, which I will explain to you in a moment, we incline to overlook this fact. There are really four dimensions, three which we call the three planes of Space, and a fourth, Time. There is, however, a tendency to draw an unreal distinction between the former three dimensions and the latter, because it happens that our consciousness moves intermittently in one direction along the latter from the beginning to the end of our lives.'

H.G. Wells
The Time Machine

CHAPTER 43

International Airport, New Delhi

From the moment they stepped from the airport into the sweltering heat that was New Delhi, Paul, Wendy and Odus were confronted by dozens of "taxi-wallas" asking, in broken English, if they wanted to go to the Taj Mahal.

How Paul wanted to visit Vrindavan, the most holy place of pilgrimage! It was Vrindavan, on the way to the Taj Mahal in Agra, where Lord Krishna is said to have manifested His pastimes five-thousand years before. It seemed so close, so alluring. Paul felt inextricably drawn there, to see the Krishna Balaram temple started by Srila Prabhupada in that holy land.

But then Paul realized that the Krishna Balaram temple had not yet been built. It would be built nine years in the future.

Besides, there was no time to go. Vrindavan was at least a five hour taxi drive to the south (the Delhi-Agra Highway was not yet constructed and the roads were miserable). Paul, Odus and Wendy were heading in the opposite direction toward a mythological place supposedly in the Himalayas.

The monsoons usually started in mid-June and continued for about two months. But this year they had tapered off earlier, and the sun was shining when they climbed into their Ambassador taxicab, the only taxi model available. All three of them quickly discovered that the heat was unbearably hot and muggy. Furthermore, there was no such thing as air conditioning in an Indian taxi.

For the trip, Paul wore blue denim pants and a short-sleeve button shirt. Wendy wore shorts and a white cotton blouse. Odus wore children's clothing that they bought in Macy's before the trip. They each had a huge duffel bag with additional clothing, including rock climbing gear and snow shoes. Odus financed the expenses, and nobody questioned where he got the money.

The taxi ride to Haridwar was long and hard. Paul, Wendy and Odus got to see a great deal of the Indian countryside as the taxi bumped over the pothole filled road. Paul eagerly watched out the open taxi windows hoping to catch a glimpse of the great Himalayas, but he saw nothing of that. Rather, his eyes feasted on throngs of people, bicycles, rickshaws, Ambassador cars and fruit market stands that littered the roadside. Behind the fruit stands stood simple stores, each displaying a sign in Hindi and occasionally in English, too. There were cloth shops, brass stores, and medical supplies, someone cooking something in a large wok, someone fixing bicycles, someone selling coconuts. Each shop was no more than ten or twelve feet wide, and the entire storefront was open to the street – they had three walls and a street side, and were not much more than a shack with a tin roof and wares to sell.

A few cows and bulls lazily walked across the streets here and there and occasionally sat in the middle of the road chewing their cud as drivers carefully steered around them. Homeless, brown and black dogs chased each other down side streets. A group of monkeys raced along the shop tin roofs while shop owners shook sticks to chase them away. One monkey grabbed a bunch of bananas from a fruit vendor and quickly climbed a nearby tree while the vendor shouted angrily. A wagon carrying a load of bundled hay, recklessly swaying twelve feet high, blocked their way until the taxi sneaked by and they could see the two large, black water buffalo labored to pull it.

The taxi driver incessantly blew his horn, and so did every other driver. They drove on the left side of the road - the steering wheel was on the right side of the car - but Paul quickly understood that in India the painted line down the middle of the road was more a "general indication" rather than a set rule. All the cars, trucks and motor scooters seemed to wander all over the road, and only scuttled over to the left when there was an imminent head-on collision to avoid.

At length, the busy life of New Delhi and the suburbs faded into a more relaxed countryside, full of trees and farmland, and here Paul, Wendy and Odus saw the rural life of northern India. The road was miserable. It was too narrow, full of potholes and overcrowded. Most vehicles, including trucks, didn't have rear-view mirrors. If someone wanted to pass someone else, they would start honking their horn. The driver of the slower vehicle would respond by squeezing slightly over to the left so the car behind could pass on the right. Sometimes a passing car would narrowly escape a collision from another car passing a truck coming from the other direction. The whole driving experience was harrowing.

The land was flat for the most part, and the fields were full of lettuce, broccoli, cucumbers, wheat, watermelons, and just about everything else imaginable. Trees were few and far between, but in and around small towns there were an abundance of coconut, mango, banana, date, and sprawling banyan trees.

By the time they arrived in Haridwar, hours later, the scenery had changed. Here they were surrounded by rolling hills and trees on the outskirts of the busy city. But where were the Himalayas? Wasn't Haridwar supposed to be at the foothills? These hills reminded Paul of rolling hills in New Jersey, not jagged snow packed peaks he'd seen in photos.

From Haridwar they boarded a narrow-gauge train to the smaller town of Rishikesh where the trees were greener and more plentiful and the rolling hills larger.

They checked into a small hotel on the bank of the Ganges, and Paul spoke with the manager about ways to get to Loharjung, where the Buddhist had told them the trail starts.

"Ah, you are planning a hike into the Himalayas!"

"We're climbing to Roop Kund," Wendy explained.

"Roop Kund? Be careful, my American friends. They call that place Skeleton Lake. There are very bad rumors about that place."

"Yeah? Well, we don't believe in fairy tales," Paul snorted.

"It is not fairy tale. Explorers have found hundreds of human skeletons at Roop Kund. Some tall people like you, and some short people like him. Hundreds of years old. Something evil is up there." He leaned over the counter to draw nearer and spoke in a hushed voice. "Some say the Yeti live there."

"Yeah, the Abominable Snowmen," Paul said. "We've heard and we don't believe in that."

Wendy decided it was time to make a relevant inquiry. "What about porters?"

"There are porters at Loharjung," the manager said in a normal tone of voice, straightening himself up behind the counter. "For a price they will take you to Skeleton Lake." Then looking puzzled, he asked, "Why are you looking to climb to Skeleton Lake?"

"No reason in particular," Paul said. "We just wanted to go there."

The manager furled his eyebrows. "Well be very careful my friends. That is no climb for amateurs. You are talking about the Himalaya Mountains. So you don't believe in Yeti?"

"No," Paul said. "I don't."

"I can respect that, my friend. Many people say there is no Yeti. They say there is only King Ashvatam. He was cursed when he tried to kill King Pariksit before he was born. Lord Krishna banished him to live thousands of years in these mountains."

Paul shrugged. "Well, I'll let you know if we see any Abominable Snowmen or King Ashvatam."

The manager nodded. "There's a bus that leaves right outside the hotel at eight-thirty in the morning. It will get you in at Tharali around 3 PM as long as there are no mud slides. From there you will take a taxi to Loharjung." His thick accent was classic.

"You do have a second room, don't you?" Wendy thought to ask.

"A second room? Yes, Madam. I just assumed you were all together."

"We're not together in that sense."

The hotel manager nodded and soon two rooms had been arranged.

For a so-called three-star hotel, the facilities were primitive. There was only the ground level, and the hallway floor was cement. The doors to the rooms were made of thin wood, which would be easy to kick through. There were two lumpy beds that creaked and a tiny bathroom with a sink and a squat toilet which was not much more than a hole in the floor. The rooms did not have televisions. Each room cost only sixty rupees, which in 1966 prices amounted to about eight U.S. dollars.

That night the three of them sprawled out a map of the Himalayas on one of the beds and closely examined it.

"So, we're here, in Rishikesh," Paul said, pointing. "The bus must go along this winding road up into the mountains. We'll pass through a few towns and villages on the way to Tharali where we catch another taxi to Loharjung."

"Roop Kund shows on this map," Wendy pointed out. "Looks to be around 16,500 feet above sea level. That's serious mountain climbing, more than twice the height needed to get altitude sickness."

"What's altitude sickness?" Paul asked.

"It's when you can't get enough oxygen to your brain because the air is too thin on tall mountains. Makes you feel dizzy and nauseous. It can even kill you."

Paul looked up from the map. "That sounds lovely."

"That hotel manager was helpful," Wendy said. "I wonder if he knows anything about Milam Valley."

"Lets go ask him," Paul suggested.

Paul and Wendy marched back out to the lobby and found the manager again. They put to him their question.

"Oh, Milam Valley!" he said.

"You've heard of it?"

"Everyone has heard of Milam Valley lately," he replied. "Very remote place. No one has ever managed to scale the peaks that surround it. Near the border with Tibet."

"Why has everyone heard about it?"

"Because someone has built a huge tunnel right under the mountains, and there is a train that goes directly there. They say it is a very beautiful place. Very secure. Indira

Gandhi was there just recently!"

"Well, why didn't you say so before? How do we get to that train?"

"Oh, you cannot get to that train, my American friend. It is a special tunnel and special train. The entrance is guarded by the Indian Army. All of the world leaders are coming there in three days, so security is very, very tight. No, my friend, you cannot get to Milam Valley through the train tunnel."

"But where is the entrance?"

"It is in Tharali, of course. That is where you are catching the taxi to Loharjung."

CHAPTER 44

Rishikesh, India. Elevation 1,745 feet

Paul took a stroll in the early evening to the bank of the Ganges River, not far from the back of the hotel, across stubbly grass and rounded stones. He paused to watch the powerful, yet silent river gently caress the rocks.

He removed his sneakers and approached the river in bare feet. He dipped his toe into the holy river water, which he found icy cold, but after a hot, humid day, he welcomed the opportunity to take a quick dip. He began to remove his clothing.

Meanwhile, toward the center of the river, thousands of burning wicks individually placed in small clay cups began floating downstream. Though the sun had not yet set, this was now early evening. The candles had been lit upstream by devotees praying to the Goddess of the river to fulfill their spiritual desires.

What a river that Goddess ruled, formed by the confluence of six great Himalayan headwaters! After cascading over waterfalls and through vast canyons for 125 miles high in the Himalayas, the river then passed through narrow, inaccessible valleys. Here were dense jungles occupied by tigers, elephants, pygmy hogs, red pandas and the occasional one horn Indian rhinoceros. Emerging from the foothills at Rishikesh, the river crossed the northern plains of India toward what was, in 1966, East Pakistan.

Time Gods

There the river divided into hundreds of mouths as it flowed into the Bay of Bengal.

Stripping down to nothing, Paul donned the traditional *gumsha*, a small cloth for covering the waist, and waded in over slippery rocks into the freezing water. He felt the odd sensation of his feet numbing as the icy water swirled quickly past his legs.

Wading out to chest deep water, he squatted down and dipped his head under the surface, sapping his breath away. He shot back above the surface and let out a hoot. It was *cold*. The water felt like melted ice.

Here at Rishikesh, the Ganges water was crystal clear, yet dark with depth. Paul could see foot long fish swimming at the bottom. But it was too frigid to remain long, and after another dip he clamored to the shore. He felt the warm, humid air on his bare chest, water dripping from his muscular arms.

* * *

Wendy rubbed a dry washcloth over the glass of her window to get a better look. Paul McPherson was stark naked, gathering his clothing by the riverbank, not more than fifty feet away. He was a handsome man, she thought. Even though he seemed enthralled with Mary, she knew she could seduce him if she wanted. It wouldn't be the first time she'd slept with one of Mary's boyfriends. Besides, Mary hadn't slept with him herself, so Paul was still open territory.

* * *

Though it had cooled by early morning, the sun rose bright orange and shot straight up from the horizon, making for another hot day. Paul took an early morning shower over the squat toilet and began chanting on his beads. Odus busied himself setting up highly efficient solar collectors outside the window to recharge the particle beam handgun and time device. Within minutes of direct sunlight both the time device and the weapon were fully charged.

When Paul came from the shower with a towel around his waist, he looked at all of the electronic gadgetry that Odus had spread out.

"So tell me. That time machine of yours also transports people through space?"

"Time and space are connected," Odus explained. "Don't think all your unidentified flying objects are fantasy. They move by creating a distortion in space time ahead of their craft. This creates a 'gravity' space for them to 'fall into.' As they can control the distortion, they can choose where to move and at massive speeds. My time device works on a similar principle, but with much greater relative time distortion. It's infinitely more sophisticated than TDC's archaic design."

"So why don't you have that thing transport us directly into Milam Valley and forget all these other problems?"

"I can't do that. Without the exact coordinates we could wind up inside a mountain or under a glacier, or we might step out thousands of feet from the ground. The distance of only a few feet could be catastrophic. Let's say we wanted to be on a particular slope on a mountain, but we missed by a few feet and instead found ourselves standing in the air over a tall precipice. We'd only be inches from where we wanted to be, but we'd fall to our deaths."

"But you were able to get the two of us into Kali's underground hideout under New York."

"I had the precise coordinates," Odus explained. "You have to understand. I've been down there before. On your linear experience, this is the first time you've been here, but in my linear time line I've done all this before."

"Well, had to ask," Paul said.

"This is the same reason we needed to fly to India and take a taxi to Rishikesh. I can only step out of time and space if I'm sure of the precise four dimensional coordinates. Here, let me show you what all these buttons and dials on this time machine look like."

Paul sat down next to Odus and he began describing the controls on his portable time machine.

Meanwhile, Wendy took a shower in her own room. She then gathered her climbing gear, ropes, and canned foodstuffs for the trek ahead. Dispensing with a bra, she

Time Gods

chose to wear tight shorts and a light blue, blouse, deliberately unbuttoned from her neck to just below her cleavage. Though she knew she would raise eyebrows in conservative India, it was Paul's attention she hoped to grab. On her feet she wore soft, white socks and brown leather climbing shoes up to her ankles. The rest of her clothing and gear went into her duffel bag. Porters would carry that for her.

Paul wore new climbing boots, blue jeans and a white, sleeveless shirt. He had thermal underwear, a winter coat, mittens and extra socks packed away. Odus wore shorts and a short-sleeve, orange Hawaiian t-shirt that was too big and children's sneakers. The three met together and went over the maps one last time.

Before departing, Odus produced a small disk shaped object. "Put one of these in each of the duffel bags," he said.

"What is it?" Wendy asked.

"They're time-space hooks. Call it insurance. Just put it in your bag and don't lose it. They guarantee our luggage stays with us."

They did as Odus requested.

Outside they found the weather had taken a turn for the worse. It was drizzling, cold and miserable. Nearby mountains were cloaked in low hanging clouds. They waited outside the hotel.

When the bus eventually arrived, most seats were taken, though not everyone was headed for Tharali. In fact, most were either en route to Badrinath or some point in between. There were local stops along the way and most passengers would get off somewhere in the mountains.

The three of them squeezed onto the bus between people standing and were lucky to find seats vacated by a departing couple and crippled man. Some people stared at Odus. Some men stared at Wendy. Paul was ignored.

* * *

Prateep Tripathy from the year 2075, now in Rishikesh in 1966, eyed Paul, Wendy, and Odus getting on the bus. He was an Orissan man from South India with a black mustache and pockmarked face, his eyes were hidden behind dark sunglasses. He deeply inhaled smoke, then dropped his cigarette and crushed it with his foot. Damn cigarettes were illegal in 2075. It's one reason he kept volunteering for these trips into the past. The other reason was he just loved killing people.

Tripathy turned and entered the hotel. He picked up the telephone receiver that was dangling by a wire. The antiquated instrument was the only communication device available to him in this primitive century.

"Tripathy here. Still there? Good. The three of them just got on the bus. I'm in place for McPherson's assassination."

* * *

Paul, Odus, and Wendy waited patiently for the bus to pull away, but there was a delay. After a few minutes they noticed a man with a pockmarked face, black mustache and dark glasses emerge from the hotel. He approach the front window and spoke to the bus driver. As they were speaking, the driver turned around and stared directly at Paul and Odus. There was something about his eyes, but Paul didn't understand what his problem could be. The driver turned back and continued talking quietly to Prateep. A few seconds later he nodded and looked at Paul and Odus again, this time casting a decidedly poignant glance at Wendy, who instinctively reached up and pinched the top of her loosely buttoned blouse.

"Why do you think that man is staring at us?" Wendy asked from across the aisle.

"I get those stares from people all the time," admitted Odus.

"I'd say it was the way you're dressed," Paul said, glancing over at Wendy. "Button your shirt. People are conservative in India. Especially in a small town like this."

Wendy ignored the advice and after a few minutes allowed her blouse to fall partway open again.

Soon the man at the front window walked away, and the driver pulled the bus away from the hotel. The driver yanked a chain and a deafening horn sounded.

The third-world bus was shaped like a rectangular box and had a flat roof where people stacked their suitcases tied with ropes. The seats were made of metal and exceedingly uncomfortable for long trips. The driver had two assistants: a man who sat next to him who might have been a family member or friend and a man stationed at the side door in the middle of the bus. This third man's responsibility, it seemed, was to collect fares and to reach outside the door and loudly bang on the outside of the bus to warn people not to get too close as they moved ahead in tight traffic or with pedestrians nearby.

Within minutes the town of Rishikesh passed from view. The bus wound its way slowly uphill, surrounded by lush green trees and wild flowers that blossomed only during the rainy season. The sacred Ganges River, clear and blue, flowed across stony banks on their right side. There was no air conditioning, so when the rain stopped and the sun burned away the clouds, the bus was hot. People kept the windows open.

"Very pretty scenery," Paul noted.

"If we can preserve it," Odus remarked. "It may depend on how successful we are at our mission. The whole world is at stake. If Kali gets his way within the next fifteen years this river will become so polluted no one will be able to bathe in it or drink the water."

The road passed through lush, dense jungle sanctuaries, home to over two-hundred fifty varieties of birds. Gradually, as they gained altitude, they found themselves at the true beginning of the mighty mountain range that separated the north Indian plains from the almost inaccessible snowbound plateau of Tibet.

*   *   *

Elevation 2,936 feet

At last they reached a town perched perilously along the walls of a steep canyon. Here two churning, brown colored rivers met. The bus pulled to a stop and Wendy saw the houses were all built from river stones.

Along the route Wendy had made friends with a nice Indian man who spoke fluent English. He gathered his bags at this town and Wendy asked him where he was going.

"This is Rudraprayag," he replied. "Here is the confluence of the Alakananda and Mandakini Rivers. I get off here."

Sitting now on the other side of the isle, Paul examined the map again. "We're here," he pointed. Wendy glanced over and saw they were about half way to their destination. "Downstream from here this river joined with the Bhagirathi river to form the Ganges. Here we'll follow the Mandakini, a big tributary." He looked out the bus window and pointed at the confluence of two mighty rivers. "Look. That's the Alakananda River. Follow the road up that way and you'd eventually get to Badrinath. That's supposed to be a very important religious place to Hindus."

Viraj Jyoti, another passenger on the bus, overheard the conversation. "You are going to Tharali, no?"

"Yes," replied Wendy. "How much longer will it take?"

"Oh, I am afraid it is still a bit of a ride. You will next pass through many villages on the way, all considered Hindu holy places. But the scenery will be very interesting from now on. I must be going." He then exited the side door of the bus and was gone.

Odus stretched himself to look out the window as the man walked away, noting another man with a black mustache and pockmarked face that bumped him accidentally on the shoulder as he was leaving.

Seeing the vastness of his surroundings, Paul wondered how they would ever find Mary, if indeed she were even up in these mountains. It all seemed so hopeless, but he had to give it his best shot.

As Paul peered at the grandiose mountains and white water of the two merging rivers, he inadvertently leaned into the aisle, closer to Wendy. She reached out to place her hand on him when suddenly a man pushed rudely and violently between them as he made his way to the back of the bus.

Wendy saw the man had turned and was looking straight at her. It was the man with the pockmarked face from Rishikesh. She felt a shiver go up her spine as he coldly looked her over, undressing her in his mind. Then the man abruptly turned, and proceeded to the back. He sat in the middle of the last row of seats, and kept his eyes fixed on her.

Odus, still standing on his seat, tapped Paul on the shoulder. "We saw that man in Rishikesh. Remember? Talking to the bus driver."

"So?"

"I think he's following us."

"Don't be ridiculous. Lots of people in India look alike."

"No," Odus insisted. "It *is* the same man. Remember him?"

Wendy nodded in agreement. It *was* him. She saw it in his eyes.

Paul started to look, but Odus, settling back in his seat, grabbed his arm. "No! Don't look. It will be too obvious. Take my word for it."

"And you're *sure* it's the same guy?"

"It's him," Wendy whispered. "Must have followed the bus here."

After a minute or so, the driver's assistant reached out the open side door and started banging. He shouted to the driver up front, and the bus pulled out from the station and continued on an upward trek toward Tharali.

Five minutes later, Paul stood up in the aisle, stretched and yawned, and then meandered back toward the rear of the bus, bending occasionally to look at the scenery going by the windows.

Finally he approached the row of rear seats whereupon the man with the pockmarked face was seated. Paul looked at him briefly, smiled, then looked out the window again.

"Beautiful scenery," he said, glancing down at Prateep Tripathy. "I'm new to this country. This is all amazing to me." He shook his head as he looked out the window, then stood up straight, and stretched. "I'm tired," he continued. "Long trip. Hey, mind if I sit next to you for awhile?"

Prateep was alarmed and tried to look away, but Paul settled into the empty seat next to him.

"Paul," he said to the man. "Paul McPherson." He held out his hand but Prateep did not accept it. "I'm an American. First time to India, but always wanted to visit."

Prateep remained silent, eyes away.

"You speak English?" Paul asked.

No reply.

"Well, that's good," Paul continued, "because I think you're an ugly son of a bitch."

The man's face contorted with anger.

"Gotcha," Paul said. "So we've established that you *do* speak English. And we also happen to know that you're following us. Why?"

The man looked suddenly confused. "I... I..." He looked around desperately for the nearest exit door and suddenly pulled out a 44 Smith & Wesson Special. Paul lunged and grabbed the barrel of the gun, pushing up as it fired. A bullet put a hole in the roof of the bus.

People screamed and shouted and many scrambled toward the front of the bus. The bus driver slammed his foot on the brake. Paul struggled with the gun as a second shot rang out. A side window blew out next to an elderly Hindu man and his wife. They lunged to the floor.

Paul twisted the gun barrel violently, jerking the weapon out of the man's hand, simultaneously jabbing him on the side of his leg below the knee with his foot. The man's knee buckled and he went down on the floor. Paul pulled back, popped the cylinder release on the Smith & Wesson, and dropped four live rounds and two empty shells into his hand. He pocketed the ammunition and stuck the revolver under his belt.

The bus skidded to a halt and the standing passengers crammed near the front lurched and tumbled to the floor. Prateep Tripathy climbed to his feet, reached in his pocket, and flashed a New Delhi Police badge. "Stay where you are!" he commanded, putting his hand out, fingers outstretched. "You are under arrest!"

"Paul! Run!" shouted the voice of Odus from behind. Paul glanced back and saw Wendy carrying Odus and jumping out the side door of the stationary bus.

Prateep Tripathy suddenly reached for his boot, pulled out a six inch knife, and lunged at Paul, dropping his badge on the way. Paul stepped to the left, deflecting the attack and then slammed the man's head hard against the metal back of one of the seats. The man collapsed nearly unconscious, forehead bleeding, as Paul pulled the serrated knife from his limp hand.

He reached over and examined the badge the man had dropped on the floor. Prateep Tripathy was the man's name. The badge felt too light.

"This man is not a police officer!" Paul called out to the frightened passengers in the bus. "His badge is made of plastic!"

"Look out!" a Hindu lady called out in English.

Paul turned and saw the bus driver making his way through the crowd toward the middle of the bus, knife in hand. Paul ran toward the side exit and jumped right into a time hole. There was a flash and Odus, Wendy, and Paul were gone.

Since that time, people were of two minds regarding the foreign visitors. Sentimental religionists in the area worshiped them as three gods who had reappeared on earth to vanquish evil. Some people called them Time Gods. Police and politicians became convinced they were from the CIA and had sophisticated cloaking devices to escape their enemies.

There is a certain tea shop on the side of the road at Rudraprayag where believers of both versions debate over this endlessly. Even now they have a sign outside their shop that reads in English, "Rudraprayag – Home of the Time Gods."

CHAPTER 45

Paris, France. 1966

President Charles de Gaulle approached the government owned, black Mercedes-Benz 220b and nodded to the civil servant who was holding the door open for him. He slid into the back seat as the door closed and quickly glanced at himself in the specially mounted rear-seat mirror.

He could hardly believe that he had agreed to the shenanigans to be held in India. "*Ceci est la bêtise,*" his advisors had told him – complete foolishness. "*Ne pas aller,*" – do not go. Still he was obliged because of the Americans. LBJ had made a point of it. It had to be done.

He adjusted his brown silk tie, brushed his short mustache, and checked to see that his black hair was slicked down and parted properly on the left. His brown, probing eyes peered deeply in the mirror, noting his somewhat large ears and protrusive nose. He was an exceptionally tall man at over six feet five inches.

His wife, Yvonne, was generous, intelligent and dedicated to her husband and their three children. Charles frequently sought her opinion regarding his speeches, writings and the political climate of the world.

"You always wanted France to have the atomic bomb," she had told him. "Why shouldn't we also have the latest technology that the Professor is offering? Would you rather Britain have what we do not?"

Charles pondered this as he glanced at the streets zipping by his Mercedes window. It was cloudy, and now it began to drizzle. The driver turned the wipers on intermittent as they drove toward the airport.

He had spoken personally and in fluent French with the Professor. So many promises. Reassurances. Still he felt something wasn't quite right. He didn't care what LBJ said about the Professor. His gut told him something was amiss.

The Americans would be there, there was no doubt. The British would be there. The whole western world would be there. France *had* to go. *He* had to go. And yet, did he really trust the whole arrangement?

Even if the Professor's claims were correct, namely that he would reveal to them incredible advances in technology, should the world have these advances? After all, though France, the United States, Britain, the USSR and, as of last year, China, all had nuclear arsenals, was the world a safer place to live?

"*Nous sommes arrivés à l'aéroport*" his driver announced.

"*Merci*" de Gaulle replied. The journey was now beginning.

He was on his way to a heavenly valley nestled deep between jagged and as of yet unscaled Himalayan peaks near the Tibetan border. Milam was close to the disputed border between India and China, but not *in* the disputed area.

*   *   *

Washington, D.C.

Lyndon Baines Johnson took a moment to take it all in. Standing on the tarmac along side the Vice President, Hubert Horatio Humphrey, he looked up at Air Force One, the aircraft that was about to carry his American entourage across the Atlantic for the meeting in Milam Valley.

"Sir, we're ready to go," a secret service agent told him.

"Lets get her done," the President said. "Hubert, you ready for this?"

As LBJ and the Vice President climbed the steps to the

aircraft's doorway, they were surrounded by secret service agents and several men dressed in black, wearing dark sunglasses, carrying briefcases at their side.

* * *

Elsewhere, the Governor-General and Prime Minister of the Commonwealth of Australia, Richard Casey and Harold Holt, were boarding a jet bound for the Indian subcontinent. Meanwhile, Indira Gandhi, the Prime Minister of India and Lester Pearson, the Prime Minister of Canada were making their preparations. Also getting ready were Gustavo Ordaz, President of Mexico, and the Secretary General of NATO, Manlio Brosio, from Italy. Eisaku Satō, the Prime Minister of Japan, along with his cabinet were on their way. Even King Aziz Al Saud of Saudi Arabia was making himself ready. Then there was Charles Swart, the President of the Republic of South Africa, the Prime Minister of New Zealand, Keith Holyoake, and leaders of many countries in South America and Asia – all heading for private jets and commercial airlines.

All were to meet in a place called Tharali, a small village in the Chamoli District, Uttaranchal, India, situated near the state highway connecting Gwaldam and Nauli. Karnaprayag, Nanda Prayag and Chamoli were the nearest major cities, although many of the dignitaries were flying to New Delhi and taking the private helicopter service that the Indian Government was providing for transport to Tharali.

LBJ was going to be air lifted on a United States military helicopter from New Delhi directly to the heavily guarded tunnel entrance.

At Tharali they were to board a specially designed wide body train that would travel underneath the Himalayan mountains to a remote valley where fully secure residences and a large meeting hall would accommodate everyone.

CHAPTER 46

Elevation 4,053 feet

There was a flash and a four foot circle of light appeared just above the ground. Paul, Wendy, Odus, and their luggage tumbled out of it and then the hole in space disappeared.

Paul looked at Odus in amazement. "I thought you said..."

"The map has altitude, longitude and latitude. I took a chance they were accurate," he explained. "Better than what we faced back in the bus."

Paul pointed at the duffel bags. "How did you manage to get our luggage through with us? Weren't all the bags tied to the roof of the bus?"

Odus dug into his luggage and produced a disk shaped object. "Remember these? I told you to put one in each of our bags. They're time-space hooks."

Paul scratched his head. "You mean...?"

"Where are we?" Wendy asked as she looked around.

They were on a tree covered hill just above the southern bank of a raging river. Nearby, there was a bridge across to the other bank where there were a few dozen stone buildings.

Odus replied, "Tharali. Remember? That is the river Pindar. This is where that tunnel is supposed to be located. If we can't get into Milam Valley here we still have the option to continue on our mountain trek looking for the back door."

"You took a big chance," Paul complained. "If you had been even a few feet off, we could have materialized over the river and drowned."

"Wouldn't be the first time I landed in a river," Odus said.

"That's reassuring."

Wendy crossed her arms. "Will you two give it up? Odus, what date is this?"

"Six days before the meeting in Milam Valley," he explained. "I hope it's enough time."

Paul lifted two of the duffel bags. Wendy picked up the other one. The three of them headed for the bridge. Odus slipped the disk shaped time-space hook from his baggage into his pocket. He didn't know it, but later it would save his life.

The little town was bustling with uniformed Indian Army personnel. Paul stopped one of them. "Excuse me. What's going on here? How come all the military people?"

The man replied, "Classified information, sir."

In the distance they saw a wide body electric train with four huge train cars on wide tracks that led into a massive arched opening in the mountain. Guarding the train were hundreds of tanks and infantry armed with self loading automatic rifles with 20 round box magazines, general purpose belt fed machine guns known as Gimpies, Browning 9 millimeter pistols and Sterling submachine guns with 9 millimeter side loading magazines.

"Looks like pictures I've seen of NORAD in Colorado," Wendy observed.

"And about as much security as NORAD," Paul agreed.

"Well, what do you think?" Wendy asked the other two.

"You're asking us?" Paul smiled. "You're the one that broke into Kali's underground facility in New York."

"I didn't break in," Wendy complained. "I was already there. All I did was get through the vault door. I was a prisoner, remember?"

"She's right," Odus admitted. "This is a whole new ball game, as you people say."

They were silent while they watched the activity around

the tunnel entrance.

"I think we're not getting inside that tunnel," Paul said at last. "In my time we have a lot of 3D video games. I've seen this type of scenario before. You go in there and you get clobbered. You've got to find a way around it."

Wendy looked at Odus. "Now what about that time machine of yours? Can it transport us through there?"

"Not a chance," Odus sighed. "The tunnel must have many twists and turns, and we have no idea how long it is. I don't have the coordinates of whatever lies on the other side."

The three of them watched the movement of troops in and around the tunnel opening. This normally should have been a serene mountain village, hills lined with terraces where local farmers grew wheat and barley by the side of a beautiful river. Instead an entire platoon of the Indian Army guarded a gigantic hole in the mountain next to an exceptionally wide train on tracks that began at the edge of the river and went inside the mountain.

"There is still another way," Odus reminded them. "We can get to Loharjung according to our original plan. That secret back door tunnel the Buddhist told us about still awaits us in Roop Kund."

"Okay," Paul said. "Let's ask around. Maybe we can get some kind of transportation."

There were no taxis available, but despite the military presence in the village, they managed to find a local man who was willing to rent them a Jeep. Paul volunteered to be the driver.

With a full tank, they departed Tharali and drove along the river, passing a military check point. The army was stopping vehicles headed into the village, not out, so they just drove right by them.

The road was rough. In fact, *road* was not the correct word. This was a stone path along the edge of the river. Their wheels bounced over huge rocks. After some time Paul pulled to a stop.

"What's the matter?" Wendy asked.

He pointed at a huge ditch crossing their path. "We've got to throw some stones in there before we can get across."

Paul and Wendy climbed out and busied themselves

picking up heavy river stones and tossing them in the ditch. After a few minutes, Wendy stood off to the side while Paul navigated the wheels of their vehicle over the impasse. Once on the other side he stopped and she climbed back in.

She patted Paul on the knee. "Good job!"

Paul smiled and Wendy kept her hand right where it was.

He didn't know what to say or do about the hand on his knee, so he just left it. He glanced over at her as she watched the magnificent scenery, her blonde hair blowing in the wind. She was a very beautiful woman, he realized. She turned her head and their eyes met. Wendy smiled at him and Paul felt the pinch of attraction.

Odus, in the meantime, bounced around in the backseat. He leaned forward. "Don't forget our mission," he said.

Paul looked briefly back at him. "Of course not. Save the girl and my grandparents."

"As well as the world," Odus added.

Wendy slid her hand off Paul's knee.

Over the next several hours they bounced and wobbled their vehicle over rough terrain and large rocks. Occasionally they would pass a small village. The homes, if they were indeed homes, were built from piles of rocks. Every hamlet had a military check point watching for anyone headed in the direction of the tunnel. Since they were headed away from Tharali, they waved and the guards waved back, unconcerned.

An hour or two later the constant bumping up and down was too much for Odus. He started feeling sick to his stomach. He asked them to pull over and he got out to vomit.

"How's he going to make it at higher altitudes if he's sick down here?" Wendy asked.

Paul thought about it. "He's pretty small. Maybe we can rig a sling or something, so the porters can carry him on their backs."

"Yeah, with porters helping we should be able to work it out."

One of the villages had a hand painted sign advertising a restaurant for tourists and climbers. Paul pulled over and stopped. "Hungry?"

"This should be interesting," Wendy said.

Inside, the "restaurant" had just a single table, a Hindu lady with a wood stove, and large cooking woks. They sat down at the hand-made wooden table and ordered. Wendy and Odus tried eating some fried mountain fish – a local delicacy. Paul had paneer makhanti, which was made using fried squares of pressed, curdled cow milk, fresh cream, tomato puree, fenugreek leaves and red chili.

After their short break they climbed back into the Jeep and continued on their way.

Bouncing along the side of the river, Wendy watched Hindu ladies hanging clothes on a simple clothesline to dry in the sun. "You know," she commented, "this part of the world is filled with as many devout Hindus as the Middle East is filled with Muslims."

"No kidding!" Paul agreed. "Look how simply they live. It's like we traveled back in time."

Wendy looked at him and laughed.

"What's so funny?"

"Well, you *have* traveled back in time! You and Odus are both from the future!"

"Oh yeah," Paul smiled. "Got a point there."

Wendy looked up and her eyes got big. "Look!" She pointed.

The three of them captured their first glimpse of snow-capped mountaintops. "Wow," Paul mumbled.

"They look pretty tall," Odus said.

"They're the Himalayas," Wendy explained. "They're the tallest mountains in the world."

Soon the road became so rough that it was downright treacherous. By the time they pulled into Loharjung the sun was setting.

There were no military people here, thank goodness, and no streets other than the rock strewn excuse that they had driven along. That road ended here at Loharjung. They could drive no further. A hand painted sign pointed up the hill and read, "Guesthouse."

Gathering up their bags, they hiked up a path fifteen minutes until they came to a sizable log building.

When they entered, they were greeted by a Hindu

gentleman and his wife. He had a red smudge mark called *tilak* on his forehead indicating he was a religious Hindu. She had a large red dot on her forehead called *bindi*, indicating she was married.

The three visitors booked three rooms and ate a lovely vegetarian dinner with dessert. Later, they lounged on the steps outside trying to become acclimatized to the thin air. The night was clear and thousands of stars shone brightly above them. Paul pointed out the milky way.

"What do we do about porters?" Paul asked Wendy.

"You act like I've done this before."

"Well, you're supposed to be the one experienced at rock climbing."

"Climbing the Grand Tetons and climbing the Himalayas is not the same thing. I guess we'll just ask the guesthouse manager."

That night they were entertained with prerecorded songs from Indian movies while a young girl dressed in a beautiful sari and jewelry danced for them. Wendy enjoyed the traditional dance so much she stood up and tried to imitate the dance. Her awkwardness at this attempt made everyone laugh, including the hotel hosts.

After the fun and dance, Wendy approached the manager and asked about arranging for porters to assist in their hike. He explained to her it wasn't necessary to prearrange porters to act as guides. Tourism wasn't sufficient for the number of guides available. He promised he'd arrange to have some porters come for an interview in the morning.

When they finally went to bed, they slept very soundly. It would be the last regular night's sleep they would have for a long time.

CHAPTER 47

Elevation 8600 feet

At daybreak a group of ten young men, all in their early twenties, marched into the guesthouse and knocked on Paul's door.

Paul was half asleep as he looked at them and scratched the stubble on his chin, one of the men asked, "Do you need porters, mister?"

"Oh. Yes, hold on. Let me get everyone together. Just wait in the main sitting room. We'll all be out in a few minutes."

When Wendy came from her quarters, she looked over the young men and sat down. She talked with them one by one. "We don't need all of you," she explained. "We're just a small group."

During the selection process, Paul spoke with the guesthouse manager's wife about the problem of hauling a small person like Odus up the mountains. He wanted to know if someone could make a kind of harness that they could use to carry him when the going got tough. He said if it could be made quickly they would pay a fair price.

The woman gathered three of her local friends and spoke to them in Hindi about the project. A lady rushed over to Odus and began measuring him.

"What are they doing?" Odus asked.

"Making you a harness," Paul explained.

Within an hour Wendy hired four people. This group consisted of Sanjay, who was a professional trekking guide with an official Government of India license, and three strong porters, Swaroop, Vallabh and Naresh.

Sanjay, being the leader, charged ten dollars fifty cents per day, and the others charged six dollars per day. Beside their salary, the costs included insurance, food and accommodation.

"Seems pretty cheap," Paul noted.

"Here in India the American dollar goes a long way," Wendy explained. "Besides, in your time I'll bet the dollar isn't worth as much as it is here in 1966. Be happy we have some good helpers. We're going to need them."

Odus agreed the price was reasonable.

By mid-morning, Paul, Wendy, and Odus were ready to head out toward Roop Kund with their four hired helpers. Seeing Wendy's rope over her shoulder, Sanjay laughed. "You won't need any ropes," he told her. "We'll be crossing snow and ice, not rocks."

Wendy nodded and packed the rope in her duffel bag.

"Is this going to be a difficult climb?" Paul asked Sanjay.

"You never know what will happen," he explained. "We might encounter bad weather, or you all might get altitude sickness. We're not climbing with oxygen, but we'll eventually go as high as 17,000 feet where we'll stay at a Buddhist temple to rest. Many people experience illness after only 8,000 feet. They get symptoms like fatigue and headache, and concentration is difficult. At 14,000 feet, forgetfulness, incompetence and indifference can occur. At 17,000 feet, you might be seriously handicapped. You might lose consciousness, collapse and even die."

"That's encouraging," Paul said.

"Mind you, not everyone gets sick like that, but if anyone does the trip will have to be cut short for your own safety."

"I can hardly wait," Paul said sarcastically.

*　　*　　*

Time Gods

Elevation 9,800 feet

On day one they climbed up, down, and up again along a meandering trail through grassy slopes. It was warm, and during the trek Paul and Wendy started peeling off layers of clothing.

The group encountered water buffalo crossing their path, and rested on a large hollowed log. Soon more buffalo, cows, horses and mules sauntered down a slope and wandered past them. After resting, they hiked across a beautiful meadow with thousands of wildflowers.

By the end of the day they came across a blue lake with crystal clear water. Here they caught their first glimpse of the towering, snow covered Mount Trisul. They sat down to eat warm Pakodas wrapped in tin foil provided by their porters. As the sun set the temperature dropped and they put their warm clothes back on.

After pitching tents, Paul, Wendy, and Odus spent the night shivering in their sleeping bags as frost formed on the tent poles.

*   *   *

Elevation 11,500 feet

On day two the sun rose bright and early, but the trio was miserable, tired, and cold. Worse still, Odus emerged from his tent sick to his stomach with a headache.

Sanjay examined the little man and said it was altitude sickness. "He cannot continue. It will be dangerous."

Odus wouldn't hear it. "No, Sanjay. I must go on. If I don't, we can't succeed in our mission."

Sanjay turned to Paul and Wendy. "It's your call. I say send him back. One of us can escort him back down to Loharjung."

Paul shook his head. "Isn't there anything you can do to help him?"

"I know some breathing exercises," Vallabh chimed in. "Like yoga."

Naresh nodded his head. "Yes, Sanjay. We can teach him

how to breathe slowly and deeply."

Paul turned to Sanjay. "Give him a chance. He wants to go with us. This is more important than you can imagine."

Sanjay agreed and the two porters, Vallabh and Naresh, showed Odus some breathing exercises. A half hour later, Odus said he felt a little better, and they agreed to continue.

Picking up camp, they started their day's climb.

While on the first day they had done a lot of up and down climbing, gradually gaining altitude, today, it was slower and more vertical.

The weather was sunny. The sky was clear.

For awhile they found themselves closed in tightly by rock cliffs. At openings on either side of the ravine were fan shaped slopes. Here local farmers cultivated terraces filled with wheat and barley concealed behind dense growths of apricot, walnut and poplar trees. The huts that local people used were made from stone and clustered thickly on the hilly knolls. Towering near these huts rose gigantic walls of granite to peaks thousands of feet above, the steepest and smoothest precipice faces that Paul, Wendy, or Odus had ever seen.

"It's amazing to me that people live up here," Wendy said to Sanjay.

"These are seasonal hermitages," he explained. "People come here during the summer, and head down for the winter."

Engulfed by awe inspiring landscape, they walked toward the snow capped peak of Trisul on a winding path. At times they navigated sideways along steep slopes with long grasses and many jagged rocks. Sometimes they had to climb over large boulders, and other times they climbed along the top of ridges.

As they continued slowly, huffing and puffing uphill in sunny weather and warm temperatures, clouds gradually closed in around them. Within minutes it started to drizzle. They stopped for awhile, standing on an open slope to put on their rain ponchos.

"Let's hope this doesn't last," Sanjay said, and they began to trudge onward and upward.

Odus found it difficult to keep up and he started to lag, though he was doing remarkably well considering his diminutive stature. His poncho was too large for him, and he had to hoist it over his knees with his hands as he walked.

A few minutes later the rain turned into piercing ice pellets. Forced off the trail, they took shelter under slippery snow covered rocks near a growth of beautiful flowers and waited out the weather.

After an hour the hail pellets stopped, but the drizzle continued. Sanjay told them they had to move on, and so they came out from their rock shelter and navigated along the now slippery and wet trail.

* * *

Elevation 14,500 feet

By the end of the day they found a level area and made camp.

Once everything was set up, Paul, Wendy, and Odus crawled wet and soggy into their respective tents, fingers and toes feeling like icicles. Soon the rain turned to snow, but the experienced porters managed to provide a hot dinner anyway.

Sanjay, their guide, came to see Paul in his tent. "Tomorrow we might reach Roop Kund," he said.

"The air is already pretty thin," Paul complained. "I feel like I can't breath."

"The weather could get worse. Are you sure you want to go all the way?"

"I don't have a choice," Paul replied. "It's critical that we reach our destination as soon as possible."

"People have died on this trek. The mountains are very dangerous."

"All we can do, Sanjay, is the best we can do."

Sanjay nodded. "Alright, my friend. Your order is my command."

He left and Paul spent the rest of the night trying to stay warm and occasionally gasping a lung full of insufficient air.

On day three they had to dig their way out from the snow covering their tents. When they emerged, the sun was shining brightly. Though freezing cold, there wasn't a cloud in the sky.

The porters were not bothered by the snow cover and went about fixing breakfast. Because Paul did not drink caffeine, they made him a hot herbal drink while the others enjoyed Indian tea. They ate reheated potato samosas that Naresh had packed in his bag, and they found them delicious and filling.

After breakfast, Vallabh hooked Odus into his harness. Paul and Wendy hoisted him onto Sanjay's back. The three porters, Swaroop, Vallabh, and Naresh, each carried bags. Thus they set out on day three of their journey upward.

The path became steep and slippery and the snow was deep, making each step difficult.

As they climbed upward in the snow, Sanjay was ahead with Odus on his back. Paul and Wendy were next, and further down the slope followed Naresh, Vallabh, and Swaroop.

Vallabh dug his foot deep into the snow and felt the firmness of a rock. He pushed himself forward, but the rock rolled, his foot slipped and he fell backwards, tumbling over and over down the mountain. Swaroop tried to grab him as he slid past on the snow covered slope, but couldn't reach him in time.

"Man down!" Swaroop cried.

Sanjay and the others turned to look.

Vallabh rolled and slid out of control down the steep slope and over the edge of a ridge. Below he crashed into craggy rocks protruding from the snow and came to a violent stop. There he lay still.

Sanjay unhooked Odus and told him not to move. Then he, Swaroop, and Naresh headed down the mountain searching for Vallabh. When they finally found him, he was sitting against the rock, dazed, but not seriously hurt.

"Anything broken, brother?"

"I don't think so," he explained in Hindi. "But I've been beat up a little and pretty badly bruised."

"You're lucky to get away with your life," Naresh told him.

"Can you walk?" Sanjay asked him.

"I think so."

"Then go back to last night's camp. The tents are still set up. We'll continue without you. Do you think you can make it back there? Downhill is always easier than uphill."

"I think so. I'm sorry, Sanjay," he apologized. "I don't know how it happened."

"Go, brother. We will continue with these Americans and meet you in a few days."

An hour later they had reorganized themselves, Odus was lifted onto Sanjay's back, and the group continued more cautiously than ever up the mountain.

Now they climbed extremely steep snow covered slopes, always upward, one step at a time. With each step, breathing became more and more difficult. Their pace was slow and steady, and they stopped frequently to practice breathing exercises so blood would continue to flow to their brains.

The snow was more than three feet deep in places, and their feet sunk as far as they would go. Occasionally, Paul and Wendy could not feel the rocky ground under the snow, and they worried about slipping like Vallabh.

At this altitude, exhaustion came easily and rest was required frequently. Sanjay taught them to dig in their feet and hands in the snow to prevent from sliding off the mountain while they tried to catch their breath.

Fatigued and taking insufficient gulps of air, they sometimes resorted to crawling uphill. While climbing, snow would often break loose under their feet and tumble down on people below. No one talked much. The effort to climb took every ounce of energy, including from the porters.

* * *

Elevation 16,498 feet

When they finally arrived at the lake on the side of Trisul Mountain, they were all still alive. Here at last, their exhilaration superseded their exhaustion. The ground surrounding the lake was level and the lake itself was half frozen.

Sanjay sat down happily on the snow and said, "I give

you Roop Kund, the Skeleton Lake." He unhooked Odus from his harness and let the little man stand on his own feet.

"We can stay here for awhile. Tonight we'll rest in the Buddhist temple. It's a short hike uphill from here."

Swaroop and Naresh dropped the luggage and climbed up the side of the steep slope which continued to the peak of Mount Trisul. Here they enjoyed sliding down to the lake shore on a plastic bag, and later by throwing snowballs and making a Ganesh snowman. Paul, Wendy, and Odus looked around for the mysterious opening to a cave that no previous explorer had ever found.

They didn't find it either.

What they did find were two human skulls peering from under the water.

Paul showed them to Wendy.

"Guess Skeleton Lake lives up to its name," Wendy said.

CHAPTER 48

Elevation 17,320 feet

Wearing a thick, brown wool coat, Balji Kapoor rubbed his eyes with his snow covered mittens in disbelief. He was watching three foreigners and three porters struggling up the mountain. Amazingly, one of them was a midget being carried in a harness.

"Hello!" Balji called out, holding up his gloved hand and waving nonchalantly. These three must have passed through the Valley of Flowers and climbed the steep snow covered slopes. With the recent snow cover they must have encountered many dangers.

They looked fatigued as they slowly hiked up the remaining incline, aided by ski poles which they used as support. They arrived at the steps of the Temple of the Immortals and their guide, someone called Sanjay, began to speak.

"This is called the 'Temple of the Immortals.' Here the local Buddhist monks provide food and shelter for climbers attempting the summit of Mount Trisul."

They leaned heavily on their poles, looking intently at Balji. "Speak English?" Paul asked after catching his breath.

"Most definitely," Balji replied. Quite well, too, the climbers noted.

"We're Americans," Wendy explained, and Balji then

noted her blonde hair protruding from the edges of her wool head cover.

"Ah, Americans," Balji chuckled to himself. Even worse than the British. "Follow me."

Balji started across the snow and the expedition followed closely at his side. "What route did you take to get here?" he asked.

Sanjay explained how they climbed from Loharjung.

"It has taken you long?" Balji inquired to the sound of their feet compacting snow.

"About three days," answered Odus. "Because they had to carry me at times the journey has been tedious. We're cold and tired."

"My name is Paul McPherson."

"How do you do?" Balji inquired.

"And I'm Wendy. The little guy is Odus. These are our helpers, Sanjay, Swaroop and Naresh. We lost a man on the way up."

"Killed?" Balji asked.

"No, just injured. Had to return to camp."

"I'm Balji Kapoor. I'm originally from Chandigarh, in North India, but have been living in the mountains for several years. I am a converted Buddhist."

They came before an ornate Buddhist temple in the middle of nowhere, covered in snow, surrounded by a high wall. As they passed under the entryway, they saw a complex of buildings.

"This is just an elaborate labyrinth of temple buildings, but very few actually live here. The weather is severe. The monastery is located in that large complex there. The main temple of Buddhadev is in the center, where you see that tall structure."

"What's that building out there?" Paul asked, pointing to a smaller temple building outside the temple walls.

"That is where the golden Buddha stands."

"Lived here a long time?" Wendy asked.

The young Indian Buddhist did not reply, but rather continued to lead his strange guests toward the main building.

Balji proved an amicable host. He was a friendly face among the multitude of fairly expressionless Buddhist monks of Tibetan origin that inhabited the temple grounds. Although Paul, Wendy, Odus, and their porters stayed two days in three simple guest rooms, they found most monks unwilling or uninterested in conversing with them. Their supplied meals were *kichari*, *puris* and goat milk, something all found much to desire, but filling, nonetheless.

On the last night, Balji was sitting on Paul's sleeping bag, discussing Buddhist philosophy with his three guests. Although they were in an agreeable mood, when Balji stated there is only void after the completion of material life, Paul had a slightly different point of view.

"Being born in a Hindu family, surely you are familiar with the *Bhagavad-gita*. So you know that the *Gita* says that the material body is just a casing, and that the real life – the soul – exists independently of the body. Never was there a time when I did not exist, nor you, nor in the future shall any of us cease to be! That's what Lord Krishna says!"

Balji nodded and frowned before answering. "Buddhism is not concerned with the soul. We consider belief in God or the soul to be ludicrous. Buddhist philosophy teaches how to be relieved of the pains and pleasures of the flesh by dismantling the elements that make up the physical body. Nirvana, the goal of Buddhism, is the state attained when a person has finished with the material combinations." Balji smiled, and then concluded, "After all, pain and pleasure are due to having a material body in the first placc."

Paul objected. "No, no. Just as we change body from childhood to youth to old age, similarly we change bodies at the time of death, and thus we are spirit soul, not this body."

Paul explained that Lord Buddha was aware of the Absolute Truth even though he didn't teach it. "You must know that Nirvana liberation is unnatural for the living entity, and therefore it can't last. We are not meant to be void. We are meant to enjoy and be happy in our eternal relationship with God. Devotees of Krishna don't preach that any of the religions are better than the others. That's what the *Bhagavad-gita* teaches: non-sectarian love of God, and acknowledgment of our eternal existence as His loving, eternal servants."

Whether or not Balji Kapoor could ultimately be persuaded to change his faith was not discovered that evening, but Balji certainly was impressed with his philosophical counterpart, and at long last excused himself to retire for the evening. Quite to everyone's surprise, in parting, he turned and said, "I have heard from my colleagues that you are seeking the secret entrance to Milam Valley."

The three visitors turned their heads sharply. "You know where it can be found?" Wendy inquired. In the two days they had spent here, no one could give them the slightest clue where Milam Valley was.

"No," Balji replied, disappointing his guests. "I do not. I only know of a mysterious entrance to a place where I have dared not venture. I do not know if it leads to Milam Valley, but it is a most interesting discovery."

The three guests implored Balji to reveal this place to them, insisting this was the reason they had made their trek through the snow. Balji was fascinated by the prospect. "We must be careful. No one should know what I will show you tonight!"

Ten minutes later, in the dead of night, he and the three guests were outside under the sub-freezing star-filled sky. Cold gusts of wind blew drifting snow as they walked briskly toward the temple of the giant, golden statue of Buddha. Balji continuously looked around, but the snow covered, stone pathways around the temple grounds were devoid of people.

Entering through a large, thick, wooden door, they found the interior of the temple much warmer. Beyond a second archway they entered a large room lit by burning lamps. In the center of the room was a giant, golden statue of Buddha. The figure towered about twelve feet high and sat on the floor, cross legged. Buddha's eyes were fixed straight ahead with uplifted palms resting on his knees.

They were alone, for which Balji was relieved.

Balji went forward and grabbed the left knee of the giant deity and began pushing. Paul and Wendy came forward to assist him.

Gradually the giant deity began to rotate backwards,

revealing a small trap door in the floor. Paul lifted the door and peered down a seemingly endless stone staircase.

"One night I saw strange visitors descend from higher in the mountain and go down these stairs," Balji Kapoor explained. "Perhaps it was a month ago. I never saw them return, so I think it must lead to some other place. They seemed to know exactly what they were doing."

Paul and Wendy turned to Odus. He nodded. "Where do you think it goes?" asked Paul.

"I dared not follow those visitors," Balji explained, "because once descending down these stairs, the great statue rotated back to its original position, blocking the trap door. If I were to have followed, I would have no way to return. However, I've read in ancient books stored in our library basement that the Temple of the Immortals has an entrance to the mythical Milam Valley. Perhaps this is it!"

"We'll need torches – pitches and lamps," Odus suggested.

Wendy smiled, and produced three flashlights and a Coleman lantern. "I think we'll have plenty of light with these," she said.

"What about your sleeping bags and other things? What about your porters? Will you take them with you?" Balji inquired.

"Well, if the stairs merely go into some underground temple caverns, we'll be back tonight. Otherwise, we won't need them anymore," Paul replied as they began to descend the staircase. "Come back in two hours and see if we need your help to get us out. We'll knock loudly on the inside of the trap door. If you don't hear anything, check every night at this time. After two days, tell the porters to go home."

Balji agreed to the proposal. About twenty feet down the stairway they heard the trap door close and the statue of Buddha slide back into place, sealing them off from above. Paul produced the handgun he had taken from Prateep on the bus in Rudraprayag. "This will be our insurance policy," he said, as he continued down the stairs. He took the four bullets from his pocket and loaded them into the revolver's cylinder.

Odus struggled with the stairs which were steep for his little body. "Yes," he agreed. "I have my particle beam gun with me as well."

*   *   *

Meanwhile, at Skeleton Lake, a giant being over ten feet tall leaned down and sniffed the tracks left behind by the climbers. He was dressed in white, covered in snow, and his face disfigured with a large dent in his forehead.

He stood up and looked up the mountain, toward the Buddhist temple. "Intruders," he said in perfect Sanskrit. He'd killed hundreds of intruders. Some of them taller, like Paul and Wendy; some of them short, like Odus.

His name was King Ashvatam. Although not an Abominable Snowman, he was over five thousand years old and the leader of the Snowmen. Formerly he had attempted to kill King Pariksit before he was born, and had thus been cursed to wander the earth for thousands of years. Now days he killed intruders who sought the secret entryway to Kali's valley, Milam.

He would hide and wait. If any from the group came back down this way he would kill them all.

CHAPTER 49

Milam Valley. Elevation 8725 feet

Face up, strapped firmly to a gurney, legs together, arms against her side. That's how Mary Pierce found herself. She tried to move but could not. The room was unpleasantly cool. A ball gag was inserted in her mouth, and a leather strap wrapping around the back of her neck held her head firmly in place. The only independent movement she could manage was her hands and feet. Even her forehead was strapped down so she could not lift it. Her nose itched, but she was unable to scratch. Her jaws ached from the ball gag, and she felt a need to swallow, but that was difficult.

She was in a white room with two florescent light fixtures overhead. An doorway on her right side opened into some other room she could not twist her head to see. Just behind her, standing by the head of her gurney, she could see a stand looming overhead with some kind of monitor placed upon it. Just to her left, almost within reach, was a metal cabinet on wheels, full of drawers.

They had drugged her on the way to Kali's private jet then held her captive in a room somewhere. She had no idea how much time had elapsed or where she was.

She noticed, in taking a reckoning of her situation, her arms, both lower and upper, were securely fastened. Padded protrusions wedged against the side of her face on both sides prevented her from turning her head. Straps were also around her legs both above and below her knees. Her entire mid-section, however, was free.

She took a deep breath and thrust her chest and stomach upward. The gurney moved slightly on its wheels and then stopped. The motion attracted the attention of someone and she heard a man's voice in the next room. "She's awake!"

Two men and a woman, all dressed in white gowns, appeared in the doorway and moved toward Mary's gurney. "So she is," said the woman.

They surrounded the head of the gurney and looked down at Mary. "I see you're awake again," one of the technicians said. "Of course, in a few hours you'll be completely under our control. Your previous life was probably pointless anyway."

The woman reached behind Mary's head, unfastened the leather straps to the ball gag, and removed it from her mouth.

Mary swallowed hard and exercised her sore jaw. "You've held me captive in a room for two weeks. Now I wake up tied to this gurney! Where am I?"

"The Kingdom of Milam Valley," the male technician replied. "In the Himalayas. You've been here ever since we took you off the private jet."

"What are you going to do to me?"

"We're going to do the same thing to you that we're going to do to everyone else in a few hours. I've been instructed to tell you that within a few hours the President of the United States will arrive," said the technician. "He will be accompanied by the Prime Ministers of Britain, Canada and Australia and a host of other politicians."

"Now that we have our cocktail of medications perfected controlling them will be child's play," the woman in the white technician jacket sneered.

"Why are you doing this?" Mary asked.

"Lured by the promise of technological advances," came a familiar voice. Mary darted her eyes to the side, only to see Kali himself, adorned with his kingly dress, entering the room. He approached the gurney and the technicians politely stepped to the background.

"Leave the rest of the debriefing to me," Kali told them.

He turned to Mary. "I wanted you to witness the extraordinary events that will transpire today. After a few private demonstrations, I've managed to convince the world leaders that I will teach technological advances so great that they can completely wipe out their enemies. What I'm really offering, however, is our cocktail of psychopathic drugs and a spot of hypnotism. By this time tomorrow, all of the leaders of the so called free world will be completely under my control, changing the course of history forever. There will be no more free world."

Mary was stunned. "This is insanity!"

Kali turned to glance at the technicians, who nodded silently. Returning to face Mary, he continued, "Indeed, even as we speak, the leaders of the world are being transported by special train here to Milam Valley."

Kali smiled broadly. It was all coming together now, as planned. The ancient tunnel, built five thousand years previously and uncovered in the last six months, led straight through the base of the mountains, to the Valley of Milam on the other side. Originally intended by Kali as a secret entrance to his newly created oasis, it had proved the perfect headquarters for his nefarious deeds. He no longer needed the less efficient tunnel that led up to Roop Kund.

"My dear Mary Pierce. By tomorrow your mind will be my puppet and all of the leaders of the free world under my control. I will purchase all the oil companies, outlaw religion, and create my own future, freeing myself of the restrictions set by Emperor Pariksit thousands of years ago."

He looked down at her and placed his hand on the mound of her right breast, squeezing lightly. "You can do nothing to stop me, so just relax. The world as you have known it is about to end. I want you to watch."

CHAPTER 50

As the three of them continued down step after step, Odus showed amazing resilience for such a small man. They spiraled downward in a vast circular cavity twenty-five feet in diameter. It was dangerous. There was no railing and when they tested by tossing a rock down the space in the center they never heard it hit bottom.

Gradually they could feel pressure building on their ears, which indicated they had come a long way down from the thin atmosphere above. They were making good time, even though Odus repeatedly reminded them that wasn't an issue. It didn't matter how long it took to make the journey. As long as they arrived at the right place, they could then just travel back in time as if the entire trip had taken only minutes.

The stairway had taken them hundreds of feet into the center of the mountain, but soon they encountered a steep slope, which Odus found more conducive for his small legs.

After descending thousands of feet, they arrived at the definite bottom of the circular cavity, and a sizable lighted tunnel stretched out horizontally to their left. Bundles of electric cables ran along the tunnel wall, disappearing into the distance. Parked here were eight 1966 Harley Davidson 4-wheel Electric Golf Carts, each plugged into an electrical outlet.

Paul placed his hands on his hips. "Where have I seen a tunnel like this before?"

"This looks like New York," Wendy observed.

Odus agreed. "He's got tunnels like this under a lot of cities in the world, deep underground. This must belong to Kali."

Paul pointed at the golf-carts. "For someone with Kali's financial clout, I guess bringing vehicles and other luxuries like these to India isn't a problem."

Wendy walked over to one of them and noted it had two seats.

"These weren't brought here from the stairs we just came down. They must have been driven from that tunnel."

"And that must mean," Paul surmised, "that this tunnel leads to somewhere outside."

"Probably a long distance," Odus said. "Otherwise, why need the carts at all?"

Wendy sat behind the wheel and found the key was hanging from the starter. She turned it and the cart beeped, but made no other sound. When she tapped the accelerator the cart lurched forward.

"This one works. Paul, unplug this thing and let's see where this tunnel takes us."

"Okay. Odus, come on. You can sit on my lap."

When everyone had climbed in, Wendy steered the quiet vehicle down the tunnel and away they went full speed, traveling 19 miles per hour down the smooth, polished granite floor.

"No wonder Kali put golf carts down here," Paul exclaimed. "This tunnel goes on forever!"

They drove underneath the mountain peaks known as Trisul, Maiktoli, Nanda Devi and Trisuli One. At top speed the trip took well over an hour.

*   *   *

Lahore, Pakistan. July 31, 1966

General Charles de Gaulle's jet glided to a smooth landing at the four year old Lahore International Airport in Pakistan.

From the airport, his own security detail transferred the General and his military associates into a waiting helicopter.

The blades began to spin, and within a minute the President of France was airborne, headed straight over the Pakistan/India border heading toward a small village at the foothills of the Himalayas. The General arrived late at the entrance of the ancient tunnel into the mountains.

Setting down on the helicopter landing pad, an official from the Indian Government greeted them at the chopper's door. "We're sorry, sir. The train departed ten minutes ago with the leaders from all of the other countries."

"Well, order a car and we'll drive ourselves," ordered the French President.

"That's impossible, sir," the official objected. "The tunnel is not navigable by automobile. It has been equipped for rail travel only."

"I see," said the General. "And how long is the journey through the tunnel?"

"Our tunnel begins here at Tharali village, and traverses seventy-two kilometers under the mountains to Milam Valley. That's forty-five miles as the crow flies."

"When was this tunnel constructed?"

"No one knows the origin of the tunnel for sure. It was only discovered by the Government of India recently. The entrance was covered over and had to be excavated. The wealthy Professor Cali has been renovating the tunnel walls and reinforcing them where necessary. The tunnel is as straight as a ruler and is entirely safe to travel by Cali's special train system."

"When will the train return so that I may enter into the tunnel?"

"It won't return until after the meeting," replied the Indian official. "Professor Cali gave strict instructions that no further crossings would be attempted after 3 PM. I'm sorry, Sir. You've made such a long journey for nothing."

The General looked up at the tall mountains through which the tunnel passed, and then glanced back at his helicopter.

"Thank you. You have been very helpful."

The military man saluted and walked away. The French President then turned to his pilot. "Can you get a heading from what he just told us?"

"Yes, sir!"

"Pretty tall mountains. What's the maximum altitude that thing will fly?"

"We can reach around 25,000 feet moving forward, General, but the maximum height at which we hover is much lower."

General de Gaulle growled. "Well, I'll be damned if I came all this way for nothing."

* * *

The wide body train was smoothly traveling through the tunnel from Tharali. The President and Vice President of the United States were about to arrive. General Morgan was with them too, as was Harold Wilson, the Prime Minister from the UK, and leaders from every continent except Antarctica.

Kali and his assistants left Mary tied to the gurney and prepared to greet the incoming guests. She had no idea where Helen and Henry McPherson were. Before leaving, Kali ordered the ball gag reinserted in her mouth, and his assistants complied.

Bound and gagged, she could wiggle her fingers, hands, and feet. She could also lift her chest an inch off the gurney, but that was all she could manage.

Once she was sure she was alone, she lurched her chest up and down and heard the gurney wheels squeak.

She tried again, and the gurney moved ever so slightly.

Again she heaved her midsection upwards, and she noticed the gurney rolled very slightly closer to a metal cabinet just to her left. If she could just get a little closer, perhaps she could touch one of the drawers with her fingers. She had to try, anyway.

* * *

The tunnel was cool and damp, but remained well lit the entire journey. One hour after starting to drive, Wendy pulled the Electric Harley Davidson golf cart to a full stop and pointed at the cave wall. "Look at that," she said.

Painted onto the stone wall was a hovering disk-shaped object, and in the center a small being with huge, dark almond-shaped eyes.

"That's identical to the Lolladoff plate discovered in Nepal," Odus said. "Ten thousand years in your past. Our time traveling researchers studied it."

Paul looked at Odus with surprise. "Evidence of possible UFO tampering on earth?"

"Time and space are connected. Told you that already."

"Look over there," Wendy pointed. "More paintings on the wall."

"Some cave drawings in Europe date back as far as 32,000 years from your time period," Odus explained. "These paintings may be ancient Tibetan, judging from their appearance. If I ever get back to my future, we'll put these on a list of archaeological finds to research."

Wendy started up the golf cart and they continued along the tunnel. There were no curves, but they noticed a gradual decline as they went along. After traveling for an hour and a quarter, a distance of 24 miles, they saw natural light ahead.

Soon they emerged from the inside of the mountain and pulled to a stop on a gravel parking area under blue skies and green trees. A small group of electric vehicles were parked here, plugged in and recharging at posts mounted in the ground.

They saw they were in a lush, green, bowl-shaped valley encircled by shimmering, glacier laden Himalayan peaks towering on all sides. Between these peaks, the bowl of the valley stretched five miles across at the widest point. Waterfalls from melting snow and ice above formed cascading streams that flowed from four directions into an incredibly beautiful, glacial lake at the center. Dozens of pure white swans floated upon the pristine waters of that lake. Enormous, lotus flowers bloomed near the banks. Trees on the slopes of the mountains were laden with ripe, tropical fruits like oranges, mangoes, lychees, bananas, avocados, gold skinned passionfruit, papayas, plantains and guavas. There were also cashew, macadamia, cocoa, and coffee trees as well as other nut, fruit and flower trees which none of them could identify. Modern, rectangular and oval buildings of exceptional architectural design surrounded the lake, all painted beige with mirrored windows. The sky was bespeckled with varieties of exotic birds, such as quaker parrots, scarlet macaws, cockatiels, kiskadees and keel-billed toucans.

"Oh my God" Wendy exclaimed. "This place is beautiful!"

Sleek, hydrogen fuel-cell powered flying automobiles silently floated in the air above the surface of the lake. These flying vehicles stirred not so much as a ripple of water, and gently landed on docks extending from the buildings over the edge of the lake. They then drove away on wheels along roadways paved with golden bricks.

Paul pointed at the flying cars. "There's nothing aerodynamic about the design of those vehicles. What holds them above the ground?"

Odus looked up at him. "We have anti-gravity vehicles in my time. I'm sure the technology here is either from the future or extraterrestrial."

"Did we just travel through a time tunnel?" Wendy asked.

Odus looked down at his time device. "No. We're still in 1966."

Wendy looked at the other two. "Now, what date was that conference supposed to be?"

"July 31, 1966," answered Paul, recalling the poster he had taken from Kali's New York complex.

"That's today," Odus said.

"Look!" Wendy pointed. "Those flying vehicles are all landing and heading toward that long building over there!"

"Aren't those train tracks I see coming out of the tunnel and into that building?" Paul wondered.

"Looks like it to me!" Wendy confirmed.

"Let's go investigate. This thing still got power?"

"Says on the dash we're good for four hours. We have about two hours and forty five minutes of power."

"Then let's drive down there."

Soon they were driving their golf-cart down a well-graded dirt road on the slope of the mountain. They reached a golden road and Wendy stopped. "Is that..." She pointed at the road.

"Real gold?" Paul interjected. "Looks like it. Good sign

this place is owned by Kali."

Wendy started up again and steered toward a huge oval shaped building with no windows. Its golden hue glistened in the sunlight and in the center of the structure stood an obelisk, an upright, four-sided pillar, gradually tapering at the top like a pyramid.

Passing this building, they saw several well dressed, elegant citizens walking the streets. Some of them waved politely, and Paul waved back. They were friendly sorts, it seemed. None of them suspected that these strange, new visitors on the golf-cart, were here to disrupt the proceedings.

* * *

With one, final heave of her midsection, Mary's gurney rolled within three inches of the metal cabinet at her side. Bending her left hand at the wrist, she hooked her index finger into the aluminum handle of one of the drawers and pulled it open. She could not see what was in the drawer, but her hand was able to reach over the top and her fingers felt around. She felt a long, hard object and grasped it. Clumsily, she slid it from the drawer. Feeling the object with her fingers, Mary determined it was a wooden pencil and dropped it on the floor. Useless.

Reaching with her fingertips into the open drawer she probed around again. She came across what felt like pressure-sensitive adhesive tape used in first aid. Leaving that aside, she continued to probe until she felt a metallic object. Scissors? She pulled it closer with the tips of her fingers until she could wrap all of her fingers around it.

She felt this new item with her fingers and determined it was indeed a pair of scissors. If only she could hook them onto the strap holding her wrist she might be able to cut herself free.

She grabbed the handle of the scissors and pointed the blades toward the upper part of her body. She fiddled with this for some time, almost dropping the scissors twice, and finally managed to get the strap on her wrist between the two blades. By systematic squeezing and releasing, she successfully cut her way through the strap.

Now Mary's arm was free up to the elbow. She passed the scissors across her abdomen to her right hand, and eventually cut through that strap as well.

          *   *   *

The lavish interior of the double-wide, two-deck train was incomparable. Although the train ride through the Himalayan mountain tunnel was over 45 miles and had taken only forty minutes, it was a well-spent period of reflection and socialization in the various meeting rooms provided in every other car. Not all the meetings concerned the admittedly far-fetched promises of Professor Cali. The U.S. President discussed the Vietnam War in depth with the Prime Ministers of Great Britain and Australia. The new Prime Minister of India, Indira Gandhi, actually had amicable discussions with the Pakistani delegation concerning the future of Kashmir. Some leaders expressed concern that General de Gaulle and his government had apparently decided not to come, even though reports suggested he had left Paris on schedule.

Eventually, the train slowed and passed into Milam Valley. The incredible lush scenery, gold brick roads, and hovering vehicles bedazzled the leaders of the free world. It looked like Kali's promises would be fulfilled. Indeed, all other topics of conversation ceased and the world leaders discussed nothing but the beautiful hidden kingdom that surrounded them.

As the train slowed, the prestigious passengers noted they were entering an elongated building. The world leaders had arrived at Milam Valley, and noted with satisfaction the platform was already swarming with secret servicemen, military police, and a multi-national security force that had all arrived earlier.

"When you put all of your eggs in one basket, you can't be too cautious," the missing French President had once told the British Prime Minister, and Harold Wilson remembered those words now with concern. He hoped Charles de Gaulle's suspicions were ill founded and wondered why de Gaulle wasn't on the train. When he mentioned his concern to Lyndon Johnson, the President scoffed at the idea. Afraid that security would be compromised if all of the key world leaders were in one place at the same time? Hogwash! The security arrangements thus far had been impeccable.

CHAPTER 51

When Wendy turned the electric vehicle onto a main boulevard paved with golden bricks she pressed the brake and brought them to a standstill by the curb. The street was wide, with a center divider complete with fountains and palm trees. Spacious residential palaces, beautiful gardens, and flowering trees lined either side of the road. People were walking, engaged in casual socialization.

Wendy said, "Check out these people. We're calling too much attention to ourselves driving this thing."

Paul agreed. "Even though we've been doing a lot of walking lately, maybe you're right."

Paul lifted Odus onto the street and he and Wendy got out of the cart.

* * *

Mary freed both hands and afterward cut the other straps that bound her. Slipping the ball gag from her mouth, she discovered a catheter had been inserted into her urethra. She pulled it out and slid over the side of the gurney. Quietly standing, she realized her legs felt like Jell-O.

She steadied herself on the side of the gurney. Tip-toeing on rubber feet, she made her way to an adjoining corridor and peered into the adjacent room. There she saw Henry McPherson and his wife Helen strapped to gurneys as she had been. A female technician stood over them, back to Mary, attaching electrodes to their bodies.

Mary quietly picked up a chair from the corner, sneaked up behind the technician, and brought it down hard over her head. The tech fell to the ground, unconscious.

"Mary!" Helen McPherson called in glee.

"Hey!" Mary replied as she pulled the catheter from Helen and freed her.

Helen then freed her husband and removed his catheter, and he jumped to his feet and ran to a closet. He was pleased to find white technician gowns and other clothing. "Put these on!" he called to the others.

* * *

There were many entrances to the building serving as the Milam train station. They selected an obscure service door. Paul placed Odus on the ground and climbed the stairs. He approached a guard wearing dark glasses and a black suit, nodded, and attempted to walk past.

"Halt! Business?"

"Gotta fix the AC unit!" Paul lied.

"Not now," the man said. "The VIPs are here."

"No. Now. Orders from the Professor. I have a pass."

"What pass?" inquired the guard.

Paul moved quickly and stealthily. As if reaching in his back pocket for his pass, he pulled out the stun gun he had taken from the butcher in New York. Pressing it into the man's side, Paul pressed the button and the man crumpled. As he went down, Paul struck him across the head with both fists. The man was out cold.

Paul and Wendy dragged the guard inside the building, and Odus followed behind. They found themselves in a corridor and pulled the man inside a small room. They pulled off his pants, coat and shirt. Paul put on his clothes, including the sun-glasses, and tied the man's hands behind his back with his own t-shirt.

As they emerged from the room they met another guard dressed in a black suit, sunglasses, and black baseball cap. Mistaking Paul as a member of security, he said, "Hey, how come you're not at the door? Never leave your post unattended. Especially not today!"

"Had to go to the bathroom," Paul replied.

"There's no bathroom in there! Who are these people?" He nodded his head toward Wendy and Odus, a very odd couple indeed.

Paul smiled. "I was just checking them." Before the man could understand what was happening, he slumped to the ground unconscious, jolted by the stun gun.

"You do that pretty well," Wendy observed.

"I have experience."

The man started to wake up and Paul slugged him. "That will keep him asleep a little while," he said.

A few minutes later, Wendy wore a black suit, too. When she settled the sunglasses on the bridge of her nose and glanced at him, Paul thought she looked downright sexy. He handed her the black baseball cap, and she tucked her hair up inside and drew the brim low over her forehead.

Paul unloaded the gun he had acquired on the bus at Rudraprayag and pocketed the bullets. He left the weapon in a desk drawer and picked up one of two Walther PPK semi-automatic pistols they had found on the guards. Both had long silencers screwed onto the barrels and 15 round magazines. "Look at this thing, will you?" He tucked it under his belt in the front of his pants but the long barrel made a bulge.

Wendy laughed. "Looks like a hard-on!"

Paul blushed and pulled it back out. "Well, where do I hide the thing?"

Wendy picked up the second weapon and tucked it in the small of her back. "That's how it's done."

Paul nodded and did the same. "Odus, put your hands behind your back. Make it look like we put handcuffs on you and we'll escort you down the hall. Otherwise, people are going to start wondering who you are."

*   *   *

The three escapees Mary, Helen, and Henry McPherson entered a long hallway lined with doors. Behind each door they found a large hall with hundreds of gurneys. "Looks like a giant lab," Henry said.

"This is probably where they plan to bring the dignitaries after they intoxicate them," Mary explained. "Kali told me what he was planning to do."

"Which is?" inquired Henry nervously.

"He's brought leaders here from around the world under false pretenses. He doesn't plan to teach them anything. Rather, he plans to brainwash them and bring the world governments under his control."

Henry McPherson nodded. "Kali might slip them all something in their meal. Having a meal will be one of the first orders of business, I would suppose."

"We had better hurry!" Helen urged. "When we were strapped to the beds I overheard that the dignitaries will be arriving soon."

"This way!" Mary pointed as they negotiated a few bends. They slipped right by four unsuspecting technicians and walked through a swinging glass door to the great outdoors.

There they stood in the Valley of Milam – a picturesque city with streets made of golden bricks, lush greenery, and towering Himalayan peaks forming an insurmountable fortress on all sides. They noticed sleek vehicles drifting over the lake and gently landing, all driving off in the same direction.

"Are we on Mars?" Henry asked.

"Flying cars!" Helen gasped.

"A lot of things get mixed up when you start time traveling, I guess," Mary supposed.

A yellow van glided in to a landing and stopped outside the medical building. A window automatically rolled down and the driver peered out at them. "Need a lift?"

Time Gods

CHAPTER 52

When the world leaders stepped off the train they were greeted by a cheering crowd of Milam Valley citizens. There were red carpets, flower garlands, live music bands and friendly speeches, including a welcome address by "Professor Cali" himself. During that speech, much to the surprise of the world leaders, Professor Cali announced that it was he who was the King of Milam, and that his real name was spelled with a "K" rather than a "C."

Talk was in the air of recognizing the Kingdom of Milam as an independent country, much as Vatican City was established as an independent country by the Lateran Treaty of 1929 and Israel became an independent state when recognized by the United Nations in 1948.

That proposition caused a stir amongst the dignitaries. It could be done, they realized. Milam was close to but not actually *in* the disputed zone between India and China. If the Indian Parliament and United Nations agreed, Milam might successfully achieve independence.

Paul, Wendy, and Odus could only watch from a distance. Despite their disguises, there were just too many people to get anywhere near the leaders. Paul wanted to shoot Kali when he made his welcome address, but Odus advised against using any weapon. Security was tight, and any potential assassin would meet instant death.

As Paul scanned the crowds, he pointed to a small delegation near Kali. "Look!" he said to the others, excitedly. "Lobe, Von Krod, Connie, and Durukti!"

Odus tried to stand on his toes, but couldn't see over the crowd. Wendy picked him up to see.

The welcoming procedures lasted thirty minutes. During that time, Mary Pierce along with Henry and Helen McPherson arrived and stood in the back of the crowd. It was not until the leaders were ushered out into hovering buses and taken to the palaces along the Boulevard that the crowd began to disperse.

Somebody tapped Mary on the shoulder. She spun around, expecting the worst, and was elated to see Paul McPherson. There too, were Wendy and the shortest person she'd ever laid eyes on. Paul saw Helen and Henry were okay. They all excitedly greeted each other as discreetly as possible amongst the bustling crowd. Henry suggested they move to a remote garden that he had seen in passing. Once there, everyone exchanged warm hugs, tears of joy and shared their adventures.

United at last, Mary informed the others what Kali had told her. Now that the leaders of the free world were in one place, he would drug, hypnotize, and brainwash each one. He had absolutely no intention of sharing any so-called secrets of the future as he had promised. The flying vehicles were just to bedazzle them and further convince everyone of his good intentions. However, his goal was plain and simple. World domination.

"So that's what they were working on when I was trapped in that cage," Wendy realized. "They were trying to perfect their drug cocktail on live subjects for use here in Milam Valley." It all made sense to them now. They realized something had to be done, and fast.

* * *

Still in Tharali, General Charles de Gaulle and his military advisors conferred independently of the Indian Army. They pored over topographical maps, not surprised to discover that Milam Valley was not mentioned anywhere. The mountains that surrounded it, however, were. These mountains peaks formed a tight ring around the valley which resembled the crater of a huge volcano. Geologists theorized that the valley had been created millions of years ago when a meteorite struck the earth and sank deep within a Himalayan volcano, long thought to be extinct. The deep bowl-shaped valley was often shrouded in clouds – virtually invisible to satellites and aircraft.

The ridges of the mountains surrounding the valley ranged from twenty-three thousand to twenty five thousand feet above sea level. There was, however, one slit in the south-east side of the slopes which had an altitude of just over eighteen thousand feet – negotiable as long as the weather was good.

The general's decision was firm. He would fly with his helicopter pilot up the slopes of the mountain, through the pass, and descend into the valley of Milam. The President of France would not be left out of the greatest technological advances in history.

*   *   *

Within hours Kali would be the master of the world. Control of the general populous would be a mere formality once the leaders were under thumb. The world would be a corporation that he owned. Of course, not everyone would bow to his new world order, but as long as the vast majority were subordinate it would be enough. He would nuke the communists. He knew they wouldn't buy into his leadership. His FDA approved food additives in everything from soft drinks to meat would be adaptations of his mind control "medications." The people of the world would ingest these foods daily and forever be his compliant, mindless robots. Not only would the populous be drugged, but they would be further hypnotized by senseless media doublespeak. Networks would abandon impartial investigative journalism in favor of having opinionated colleagues sit in front of a live camera and bitch about politicians that have opposing political views. They would call this sham "fair and unbalanced," and "news" all in the same breath. Investigative journalism would die out and TV "newscasts" would spend hour upon hour talking about movie stars, cooking ideas and the weather. Kali would have his people invent an Internet, 3D video games, smart cell phones and interactive TV to mesmerize the public. He would outlaw religion world-wide and bombard people with so much information about meaningless topics that their eyes would glaze over and their minds shut down. With their minds preoccupied, no one would care when Kali would eventually outlaw books.

Before any of that could happen, however, he had to first accommodate the heads of states comfortably in Milam Valley. The leaders of various governments were thus put up in lavish palaces decorated with the finest carpets, crystal chandeliers and plush seating. Meanwhile, King Kali retired for a few hours to his private palace on the north shore of the lake. The timing was crucial. It would have to be after nightfall that the plan would take effect, for at nightfall the leaders would all be indoors. Temperatures dropped dramatically at night in Milam. All through the residential palaces, tiny vents were ready to start spewing halothane-fentanyl gas at a touch of Kali's finger. The sleeping leaders and their staff would then be quickly transported to the medical building for further processing.

*   *   *

They were now six: Paul, Mary, Wendy, Henry, Helen, and Odus. As the group surveyed the medical building from outside they observed it to be a large one-story structure built upon what appeared to be a huge mass of pumice stone from an ancient volcanic eruption. The building sat fifteen feet above the shore of Milam Valley Lake, with tall, mirrored windows overlooking the shimmering water. A dock made of steel extended about twenty feet over the lake, upon which was a paved roadway for the flying vehicles to land upon. The building appeared to be brown sandstone and glittered in the sun. At one end a white marble staircase led up the face of the pumice stone base to a columned entryway decorated with figures of sitting lions formed out of solid gold. The words "Milam Valley Medical" were written in large English lettering across the top of the doorway, and above that was a round plaque depicting the image of a deep, blue pyramid, a black circle with a halo and a naked eyeball.

"This is where Kali had us captive. There are hundreds

of gurneys in large labs inside. I suspect this is where they're going to bring the leaders once they've been drugged."

The setting of the building was breathtaking. Milam Valley Lake was clear with a tinge of aqua, the color of melted glacier water. Within those icy waters they could see foot long carp swimming restlessly. The sand on the shore was black. Obviously volcanic in origin. A large fountain sprayed mist into the air from the center of the lake, as did smaller fountains in front of impressive lakeside buildings. Extending a half-mile lengthwise, the lake appeared oval in shape. Almost directly across the lake from the medical building stood a grand palace that glittered gold – the residence of Kali himself. All around the shore between buildings were lush foliage such as Weeping Willow and Banyan Trees. Great golden arches spanned the mouths of four small rivers that emptied into the lake from the melting snow and glaciers of the Himalayan peaks above. Volcanic cracks in the lake's bottom sucked water into an underground river which eventually flowed under the mountains to the Pindar, one of the headwaters of the Ganges.

The six of them climbed the marble staircase and entered the medical building. Three of them still wore technician clothing. Odus still wore climbing clothes and boots. Paul and Wendy were dressed in black suits and dark sunglasses. They found themselves in a spacious lobby, about which several technicians were standing.

A thin, middle-aged man with white hair approached them with a curious expression painted on a face and too many wrinkles born of years of excessive anxiety. A puzzled look washed over his face as he tried to understand the identity of these six strange characters. He looked down at the little man and tilted his head as words escaped him. The little one held on to a weapon with flashing lights.

The man frowned, forming the wrinkles in his forehead into deep crevasses as he studied the group. Something wasn't right about this. Why would three technicians be accompanied by the Special Guard? Who was the little man? "Who are you people? I don't recognize any of you."

Paul quickly pulled out the stun gun, pressed it against

the man's stomach, and pushed the button. With a sharp crack, the man buckled over and fell to the floor. No sense in wasting time.

Seeing their coworker collapse, three other technicians in the lobby rushed forward. Odus held up his weapon and ordered everyone to stay back and they complied. A siren began to sound. With Odus waving his weapon at the technicians, the party of six started for the hallway through which Mary, Henry, and Helen had earlier escaped.

They didn't make it very far.

A stainless steel door rapidly slid shut across the hallway entrance, sealing off the remainder of the building.

"I hate it when they do that," Paul blurted.

Odus fired the particle gun and the beam melted a three foot hole in the steel. The six of them climbed through the smoldering gap and proceeded.

CHAPTER 53

Deep within his luxurious chambers, Kali received disturbing news on his intercom. There were intruders in the medical building. Help was needed immediately.

Summoning his hovering craft, Kali quickly left his residence and, accompanied by several top advisors, headed across the lake to the medical building on the south shore. By now a ring of Royal Guards surrounded the building, weapons drawn. He landed on the dock road and stepped out.

"What's going on?" he demanded from the Chief of Security who was taking shelter behind a vehicle and speaking on a radio.

"Intruders," he replied. "They've broken into the main hall!"

"And you're worried about that?"

"They have weapons, my Lord!"

"Idiot. Surround the place. All the doors and windows. Nobody exits."

While the Chief of Security busied himself following the instructions, Von Krod, Durukti, Convoitise, and Lobe arrived. "What's going on?" Von Krod asked.

"I'm not sure," Kali replied. "Some kind of security breach. Might be just a lab technician having a breakdown. The drugs don't work equally well on everyone."

"Maybe one of our hostages escaped."

Kali turned to Durukti. "This is too important with all of the dignitaries here. We already know that the five of us are more powerful than this entire security force. No sense in having these idiots charging in and damaging the equipment we'll need in a few hours."

Kali and his four associates marched up the marble stairs and stepped into the medical building. Inside they saw a technician lying on the ground, apparently stunned, while three others hunched over him, trying to revive him. The room was filled with smoke. An automatic sliding door had been blasted through. Four other technicians pointed toward the hole in the door. "They went that way my Lord!"

"Odus," Kali seethed. "This is not good. Not now."

They stepped over the rubble and through the hole in the door. Without trepidation, Kali and his people marched down the hallway to a second door, also blasted through.

Finally he entered one of the main halls where over two hundred gurneys were waiting for the world leaders. There, to his astonishment he saw Paul, Mary, Henry, Helen, Wendy, and Odus. Paul was wielding a particle beam gun blasting away, melting and shattering cabinets full of the dosages Kali needed for the world leaders.

Outraged, Kali boomed: "How dare you!"

Paul released the trigger and the beam from the particle gun shut down. He turned to face Kali. They had been expecting him to come. Now they had him right where they wanted, away from the world leaders and here in front of the particle beam gun.

"What's the matter?" Paul asked. "Somebody crash your party?"

The gurneys started to rattle and what glass remained in the medicine cabinets against the wall shattered. Kali was confused. So was Paul and everyone else. Suddenly the floor heaved, the whole building rocked, and Mary fell to one knee. Outside, a huge geyser erupted in the center of the lake and spewed hot water and steam hundreds of feet into the air.

"What was *that*?" wondered Henry McPherson aloud.

"A time quake," Odus explained. "The time line is changing again."

Paul pointed the weapon at Kali. "It's over! I escaped your bounty hunters in New York. Now we've managed to find your hideout in the Himalayas."

"Yes, that *is* surprising," Kali laughed sardonically. "I have to admit I'm puzzled to find you all here, but it's too late to stop me!"

"We've already stopped you!" proclaimed Paul proudly. "As you can see, all of your instruments and drugs have been destroyed."

"What? You mean this?" Kali gestured toward the cabinets as if they were insignificant. "You think that's my only supply? I have many such rooms in this building, and other buildings holding additional supplies all over the world. It's all been decentralized so no one attack can destroy everything. This is nothing more than a minor disturbance."

"I believe the time quake we just experienced indicates otherwise," Odus pointed out. Time quakes, he knew, were symptoms of the creation of a parallel universe – a time layer. The future now had more than one possible outcome.

"And now we will kill you!" Paul declared defiantly.

Kali laughed. How absurd. "If Emperor Pariksit couldn't kill me five thousand years ago, I certainly can't be killed by the likes of you. Furthermore, I have diplomatic immunity in every country of the world, as evidenced by the dignitaries gathered here tonight."

"Thousands of years ago, when Emperor Pariksit was about to kill you, you begged him for mercy," Paul said. "It's written in the Vedic scriptures. You may be powerful, but you're a mortal. You can be killed just like anyone else."

Kali laughed again. What was the use of discussion with this imbecile? "I've been empowered by arrangement of the Supreme Being, God. Otherwise, how could I even be here? We're all instruments in His hand. When you threaten me, you're interfering with the universal plan. Do you intend to interfere with the plan of the Supreme?"

"We just intend to put things back the way they were before you got hold of your time machine. As a Hare Krishna, I know about you."

"That was always a problem," Kali admitted. He turned to Odus. "Why did you have to select a Hare Krishna? Couldn't you have used a Muhaddith, Mullah, Mawlawi, Sikh, Rabbi, Bishop, or anyone other than these freaks?"

"Just trying to be a thorn in your side," Odus replied.

"I will admit it. You and your Hare Krishna friend have been more than thorns. I never expected you were capable of following me here to Milam Valley!"

"Well we're here. Deal with it," Paul said.

"Oh, I will deal with you alright," Kali warned. "After I kill you, I still have the world leaders and you can do nothing to stop me. Look at you. Just the six of you, and outside this building all of my security, what to speak of the security forces of the different nations. What plan do you have to escape?"

"It seems to me we are the ones with the weapons," interjected Wendy, who drew her Walther PPK with silencer from the small of her back. She never managed to point it at Kali.

With the speed of sound, Kali raised his arm, palm facing out, fingers up. From that palm a fireball six inches in diameter and bright as the sun appeared and shot forward like a bolt of lightning. It struck Wendy in her midriff, folding her at the waist and tossing her backward. The pistol she held arced into the air, hit the floor, and slid out of reach of everyone. Wendy crashed violently into the wall behind her, knocking the breath from her. Her head next flew back, banged the wall, and she slid to the floor unconscious.

The action had been so sudden, so unexpected, that Paul froze in astonishment. What kind of weapon did Kali have, and where was he hiding it? The fireball seemed to come from his hand!

As he had seen Connie previously transmogrify into a hideous being before vanishing into thin air, now Kali was himself demonstrating supernatural powers. He had much more than a time machine. He was an ancient being cursed to live here in this valley by an Emperor named Pariksit thousands of years ago. Christians called him by a variety of names such as Azazel, Beelzebub, Belial, Tempter, Prince of Darkness, Lucifer and Satan. In Hebrew he was called Heilel and in Islam he was Shaitan. In Zoroastrianism he was known as Angra Mainyu. Hindus called him Kroni, the spirit of Kali Yuga, omnipresent in this age. He was known in Buddhism as Mara and Ancient Egypt called him Set. In politics he was Professor Cali and in Malam Valley he was the King.

Kali raised his hand and snapped his fingers. There was a blinding flash of light and the King of Milam vanished and reappeared in another part of the room. "Do you still think you can kill me?"

Paul spun the particle gun around and aimed it again at Kali.

"Maybe I'm here," Kali said, snapping his fingers again. Another flash blinded them. Kali vanished and reappeared to the other side. "Or maybe I'm over here!" Paul spun again and aimed his weapon. "You see, you can't kill someone who is everywhere."

Henry and Helen looked at each other nervously. "Be careful, Paul!"

"You should listen to your grandparents," Lobe added.

Helen rushed over to Wendy who was starting to wake up. Mary and Henry stood near each other.

Meanwhile, Odus stood off to the side and watched intently. He knew he had his time machine in his pocket which could prove a useful escape device. He just wasn't sure what good it would do him at the moment. Sure, he could escape, but it would do no good to Paul or the others, and Kali would still carry out his plan. This had to end now.

Kali held up his hand, facing Paul. A second powerful ball of electrical energy streaked outward from his palm, striking Paul in the chest. It pushed Paul violently backward, reeling him onto the marble floor. His weapon slipped from his hand, landing near Mary and Henry's feet.

"Seize them!" Kali ordered, and immediately Von Krod moved in on Paul while Henry McPherson reached down and picked up the particle beam gun.

Durukti and Connie set their eyes on little Odus. Knowing him to be a trickster, they rushed toward him and Odus darted under their legs.

Lobe rushed forward and tried to grab the weapon from Henry's hands, and the two of them began to struggle. Mary reached out to help Henry, but Lobe pushed her away. She came at him again and he punched her on the jaw. Mary went down.

Again the floor heaved. Gurneys rolled across the floor and crashed into each other. Helen was already on her knees tending to Wendy and fell over. Connie fell to her knee and Durukti almost lost balance. Kali spun around looking at the ceiling. A large piece of sandstone broke away and crashed onto a gurney. Odus pulled his time machine from his pocket.

* * *

Outside the building, the entire lake began to drain as if a giant plug had been removed from the bottom. People ran to the receding shoreline and pointed in amazement.

* * *

Lobe punched Henry in the chest with one hand as he struggled to pull the particle weapon from his hand with the other. Henry kicked Lobe in the groin, and the particle gun fell to the floor.

Von Krod, grinding his teeth, reached Paul before he could pick himself up. Grabbing Paul by his shirt, he lifted him off the ground as if he were a doll. Holding him at eye level, he growled, "No more fooling around this time." He then raised Paul's body high above his head and threw him.

When Mary saw this, she picked herself up and ran toward Von Krod. "Paul!" she cried out. At that moment, a crimson ball of electricity shot from Kali's hand and struck Mary. She flew backward and crumpled to the ground.

The floor heaved a third time. More debris fell from the ceiling.

* * *

Valley residents and security forces stood at the lake shore. Soon all of the water of the lake had drained, and large fish flopped helplessly on wet rocks. The geyser that had spewed steaming hot water ceased. Another quake brought the spectators to their knees and the center of the former lake exploded. Huge boulders flew high into the sky and began to rain down on the golden streets. Black smoke spewed out at high pressure, and a reddish, glowing liquid shot up a hundred feet.

A man pointed. "The volcano is erupting!"

The crowds backed away. Some of the security guards abandoned their posts.

* * *

Hearing the commotion and feeling the earthquakes, Harold Wilson, the British Prime Minister, looked out the window from his palatial residence and saw lava spewing out from the dried lake bed. Lava, he knew, was molten rock that turned liquid at temperatures above 1,200°C or 2,200°F. Lava could flow great distances before cooling and solidifying because of what was called its shear thinning properties. If the eruption didn't stop, the valley was doomed and everyone in it would be killed, if not by molten lava, then by volcanic gases.

Other world leaders and their security personnel ran from their palaces. Seeing the lava spewing from the lake bottom caused panic.

* * *

"Mr. President!" the Secret Service Agent said urgently. LBJ turned to see a sweating and concerned officer. "We have to go! As you can see, the so-called extinct volcano just erupted!"

* * *

Henry McPherson struggled with Lobe's grip on the particle beam gun. He kicked Lobe in the groin and the weapon dropped to the floor. Lobe kicked it. Henry tried to pull away and reach down, but Lobe struck him in the stomach. Henry buckled and went to his knees. He saw the particle beam weapon nearby. He punched Lobe in the knee, sending him backward in pain, and he scooped up the weapon and pointed it at Kali.

Kali turned to him.

With Paul and Wendy still down, Lobe came up again on

Henry, who was now pointing the weapon at Kali. Henry saw him coming, spun the weapon, and was struck down by a fireball from Kali. Lobe reached down to pick up the particle beam gun.

Helen helped Wendy to her feet, and Helen turned to see her husband fly past. She charged Von Krod and kicked the particle weapon from his hand as he was lifting it from the floor. He slapped her and she went down. Wendy then charged him and he brushed her to the side, looking for the particle weapon.

The weapon, in the meantime, slid to Mary who was recovering from Kali's fireball. She picked it up.

Von Krod came at Paul again, and Paul, still dazed, struggled backward, kicking away with his feet.

Odus ran behind a gurney, Durukti and Connie chased after him. When Durukti went one way around and Connie went the other way, Odus ran out from under.

Kali, in the meantime, tried to understand the bigger picture. He heard screams coming from outside. He saw lab technicians in a panic run by the entrance to the room they were in. He felt the earth in a constant rumble. He had seen chunks of the roof cave in.

Ahead of him Von Krod closed in on Paul, Connie and Durukti were chasing little Odus, Lobe was fighting both Wendy and Helen, Henry was recovering from his fireball attack and Mary was pointing her particle beam gun at Kali.

Before Kali could bring his palm up to send her another fireball, she let the particle beam weapon fire and it struck him in the torso. Kali screamed in pain and disappeared.

Hearing the scream, Von Krod stopped advancing toward Paul and turned around, Lobe also turned and both saw that King Kali was gone.

Seeing Wendy and Helen both on the floor, having been struck by Lobe, Mary next redirected her aim toward Lobe. She was suddenly attacked from behind by Von Krod, who grabbed her around the waist and shook her up and down until the weapon dropped to the floor.

Paul stood up and tried to run to her aid, but Durukti saw the Walther PPK pistol on the floor and picked it up. She fired at Paul and the silencer made a pop sound. A bullet struck the floor near Paul, then another, then

Time Gods

another.

Connie saw the particle gun fall to the floor and ran toward it, while Odus saw Durukti firing a semi-automatic pistol at Paul. Odus ran at Durukti's legs and tackled her to the ground. A shot fired up at the ceiling.

Lobe ran to help Durukti who was struggling with Odus on top of her, as Henry and Wendy ran to help Mary, who was being squeezed by Von Krod.

Seeing the particle gun still on the floor and ignored, Connie moved in and grabbed it. Abruptly, a foot stepped on the weapon and pinned it securely to the ground. Looking up, she was surprised to see it was Helen McPherson. "Looking for this?" she asked, punching Convoitise in the face as hard as she could. Connie tumbled backward, howling and holding her hands to her face, more importantly for her, it had ruined her false eyelashes.

Paul saw Lobe running to pull Odus off Durukti, and he got up and ran in their direction. He tackled Lobe just as he was reaching for Odus.

Durukti tried to point the pistol at Odus, but he bit her hand and she screamed and threw him to the side. He slid under a gurney and she fired at him. The bullet struck the gurney wheel near his head.

Von Krod grabbed Mary with one arm and Henry with the other smashing them into each other. Wendy struck him on the back and he ignored her. Paul punched Lobe in the face and Connie charged at Helen McPherson in a rage. Odus ran and Durukti fired another shot, missing the little man by an inch and striking a medicine cabinet.

Paul had Lobe on the floor and punched him again. Seeing Durukti firing at Odus, he lunged at her and a struggle for possession of the Walther PPK pistol ensued. Flailing wildly, the silencer popped off another round which struck the floor between Mary and Henry just as Von Krod was picking them off the floor.

Free for a moment, Odus surveyed the situation and saw all eyes were off him. Slipping behind a host of gurneys and cabinets, he took his time travel device in hand and began pressing the keys.

The building began to shake violently, and a huge piece of stone fell, hitting Von Krod on the head. He went down.

Another smaller piece of the ceiling collapsed on top of Odus. He fell to the ground, time device sliding away.

Convoitise was still crouched on the floor, her lip cut and swollen from Helen's blow. Helen took her chance and seized the particle beam gun. Convoitise jumped up and attacked her and before Helen went down she deliberately slid the weapon across the floor toward Wendy, Mary, and Henry who stood over Von Krod.

Henry went to pick it up but Von Krod, still conscious, kicked the weapon away. Then Wendy, Mary, and Henry all jumped on him, hitting him with pieces of stone from the ceiling.

Meanwhile, Kali was invisible, but not gone. He started to laugh loudly, and this caused everyone to stop what they were doing and look around.

Convoitise ran forward and grabbed the particle beam gun, spinning around and pointing it directly at Helen McPherson.

Henry saw Convoitise aiming the weapon at his wife. Quickly, he looked around, grabbed a gurney, and ran it straight into Connie's side. Convoitise was swept off her feet and fell to the ground. The weapon fired and a beam went shooting between Paul and Durukti, missing each by inches. "Woah!" Paul gasped.

Helen took the opportunity and quickly grabbed the weapon.

Again came the haunted laughter from Kali. Kali's followers were confused, for their master was invisible! Lobe stood bewildered, blood dripping from his broken nose. Connie struggled from the debris that covered her, and Von Krod raised himself to his knees.

Paul, Mary, Wendy, Henry, and Helen regrouped. Odus was off somewhere, they didn't know where. There was a moment of relative silence. Outside they could hear screams, and the ground continuously shook.

Odus opened his eyes. He sat up and surveyed the situation. He knew it wasn't over yet. He looked for his time device, but found it missing.

They could hear Kali's frantic laughter, but he could not be seen. For a moment, it sounded like it was coming from behind them. The next moment it came from in front of them and then from above. Paul approached his young grandmother and took the weapon from her hands. She gave it willingly. He pointed it in the direction from where the sound seemed to be coming and fired. There was an explosion on the wall, but nothing else. There was more laughter.

Kali appeared with a blinding flash of light. He stood on a table top, still laughing. Paul fired, but Kali vanished again and reappeared elsewhere. Paul fired. Again, Kali vanished.

There was more laughter. Paul spun to his side, and there was Kali carrying a staff. Paul fired just as Kali vanished from sight.

Again he heard laughter. Paul spun around and saw Kali, still with the staff. He was very close, and raised the staff high to smash Paul over the head. Panicking, Paul dove and simultaneously fired the weapon. Kali vanished. The streak of light instead struck Von Krod in the shoulder. Clutching the wounded area, he roared and fell to his knees.

Meanwhile, Odus searched frantically for his time travel device. It must have fallen from his hand when he was knocked unconscious. He crawled to a metal cabinet on wheels and looked under it. No. It was not there, but he finally saw it a short distance away.

Then Kali suddenly appeared near the cabinet Odus was crawling towards. Small Odus stood up just behind Kali's legs. Paul saw Odus, but Kali did not. Odus waved his hand to grab Paul's attention, and Paul understood. They had a plan.

Paul thought carefully. He knew that as soon as he pointed his weapon, Kali would disappear again. He decided to surprise him by pushing a button on the side of the weapon. The lights along the cylinder went out and the gun was deactivated.

"It's no use," Paul declared. "I know I can't defeat you. It was foolish of me to try. I surrender to you. Here, you take the weapon."

Kali raised his eyebrows in surprise. Paul took the gun, held his arm wide, and then swooped down and slid it across the floor towards Kali. Kali glanced at the weapon inches from his feet, then at Paul. He laughed. "You want me to pick up that weapon, don't you? You fool," he snarled, and with that, held up his hand. An electrical fireball shot out from his palm. Paul was struck on the chest and thrown painfully into a gurney and then onto his back on the floor.

Kali laughed again. "Now you will die. I don't need your foolish weapon." Another jolt shot from his hand. Paul rolled quickly to the side and the electrical fireball missed him and dissolved into the floor with a cracking sound.

The ground heaved. A wide crack opened in the floor.

Henry made a dash for the weapon at Kali's feet, but Kali spotted him and shot another bolt, sending Henry straight to the floor. With Kali's attention on Henry, it was Paul's turn to move. He made it to his feet quickly and began running. With great momentum, he tackled Kali to the floor as they both slid right past Odus.

"Kill them all!" Kali shouted to his agents.

Meanwhile, Odus stepped back, still out of sight. When the time was right, he would make his move.

Von Krod moved in to assist his master. He dashed toward Kali and Paul as they struggled on the floor.

"Paul! Watch out!" cried Mary.

Odus could no longer remain passive. He jumped forward, grabbed the weapon, activated it, and fired at Von Krod, striking him on the leg. Anger Personified lit up like a light bulb and fell to the floor screaming.

Henry McPherson prevented Greed Personified from getting involved by wrestling him into a half-nelson headlock. Odus then made his move, pointing his lethal weapon straight at Kali. "Get up!" he demanded.

Kali sat up and laughed once more. "It's about time," he told Odus. "You're a determined little fellow, aren't you? How long will you keep trying to interfere with destiny? You know all I have to do is insert myself in the exact moment of time when you meet Paul and destroy both of you. My plans will be unimpeded. You're destined to lose. Why not just surrender now? I may even spare your life! You're one of my men, after all."

Kali stood and dusted himself off. "You can't kill me or my associates! We're immortal, fool!"

"I have no intention of killing you," Odus commanded. "I just want to discuss your travel plans."

"Travel plans?" Kali said. "What travel plans?"

"That's why we must discuss," the little man said. "It's only polite."

"Nonsense," Kali replied as a ball of light shot from his hand and knocked the weapon from Odus' grasp. "I've grown tired of this charade!"

Kali turned toward Paul and a rapid succession of fireballs leaped forward, enveloping Paul like a helpless animal in the grips of a python. Standing and watching, Connie and Durukti laughed and clapped. Paul was stiff like a board, yet his arms and legs began to shake violently and his head began to wobble. His body slanted towards the floor, yet he did not fall, being held by the grips of the electrical force. Seeing Paul helpless and about to die, Kali chuckled without releasing his doomed victim. This was the moment he had waited for and he wanted to cherish it.

Mary took the particle gun, made sure it was activated, and pointed it at Kali. Seeing her, Connie and Durukti both ran toward her, but they were stopped by Helen and Henry and another struggle ensued. Lobe remained near Kali.

"You ruthless, sinful wretch!" Mary cried out as she fired the weapon, striking Kali in the chest. As Kali fell to the ground, the fireballs ceased and Paul was released. He fell backward onto the heaving floor.

"Goodbye," Odus said to Kali, pointing his time device. "See you in the future!"

"What?" Kali questioned. Suddenly a time hole opened up all around him and he was sucked into it with a blinding flash of light.

Kali was gone.

CHAPTER 54

The ground shook violently and the ceiling collapsed all around them in big chunks. "We've got to get out of here quickly!" cried Odus.

Von Krod picked himself off the floor. Lobe, Durukti, and Connie joined him at his side. The four of them went to where Kali was last seen and stared. "Where did he go?"

Gradually recovering, Paul climbed to his feet and turned to Odus. "Where did you send Kali?"

"10,000 years into the future. Now we've got to get out of here quickly! The time quakes are upsetting the universal fabric!"

"Paul, watch out!" cried Mary. Turning, Paul saw Von Krod and Lobe approaching, but Mary fired the particle gun and they backed off.

The team of six bolted past the rubble that was once the door and left the room. Mary turned and fired the particle beam weapon at the entryway, collapsing huge chunks of stone on the floor, blocking the exit behind them. Hopefully that would hold off those demons for awhile.

They ran down the hall over huge piles of rubble, trying to find a way out.

*   *   *

Lava continued to spew out from what used to be the center of the lake, and the earth trembled violently. An avalanche came roaring down the west side of the valley. An entire forest uprooted and was buried under a wall of snow and ice. Buildings on that side of the valley were crushed and buried.

People ran here and there. Security and lab techs had long ago run from the scene. The lava had filled the former lake bed and now began to flow onto the street.

The world leaders, who were housed along the Boulevard panicked and scurried around in the streets. American secret servicemen urged everyone to head for the train station as quickly as possible. Men in black disappeared in a fleet of helicopters.

The station was already crowded, and not everyone there were politicians and government leaders. Panicking valley residents also ran in that direction. Finding the train doors open and officials urging people to take shelter inside, people flooded onto the train and took refuge everywhere they could find a place. "Hurry," a train conductor shouted at the leader of Peru as he approached the train. "We are leaving in five minutes!"

* * *

As Wendy, Mary, Helen, Henry, Odus, and Paul ran down the hallway, suddenly the building split open. A ten foot wide gap in the floor opened up, from which they could see molten lava flowing fifty feet down. Wendy and Helen were on the side of the gap that lead to the outside. Mary, Henry, Odus, and Paul were still on the other side. Unless they could cross this gap, they would die.

At the same time, a portion of the roof collapsed on top of Odus, crushing him and sending his time travel device reeling through the air.

Mary lunged for the miniature time machine and caught it just before it slid into the crevice and into the lava below, and in so doing, inadvertently dropped the particle gun on the floor which became instantly covered by falling rubble from the ceiling. Paul and Henry headed back to the pile of debris covering Odus. They began lifting stones and chunks of cement and found him underneath, badly hurt and barely conscious, still covered with wood and steel beams.

After pulling him out, Henry took him into his arms.

"Now what?" asked Henry.

"Look!" Paul shouted. "That steel beam over there! It's the only way!"

As Henry continued to hold the injured Odus, Paul and Mary grabbed the steel beam which had fallen from the ceiling and with difficulty slid it across the floor and over the gap, trying to make a bridge. Before the end could reach the other side of the gap, the heavy beam fell and instantly melted in the lava below.

"Too heavy!" Paul shouted as he ran back to grab a two by six board.

"That wood will catch fire from the heat over the magma!" Henry objected, wiping sweat from his forehead.

"It's our only chance!" Paul insisted. He leveled the board over the gap, making a narrow bridge. "You go first! Take Odus with you!" Already the bottom of the board began to blacken and smoke began to spew sideways.

Henry inched his way across the board, almost losing his balance twice, but finally reached the other side where Helen and Wendy received him.

Now it was Paul and Mary's turn. "Let's go together. You hold my hand. I'll go first."

"Take this!" Mary insisted, handing Paul the time travel device. Paul placed it in his pocket and the two started across the board, feeling the intense heat from the molten lava below.

Suddenly, a powerful time quake threw them off balance. The board swayed wildly and pieces of rock rained down from above. Paul and Mary lowered themselves to their knees.

"We must keep moving," insisted Paul. "The time quakes are tearing the place apart!"

Crawling on their hands and knees across the hot, smoldering board, Paul and Mary continued to inch forward.

Henry passed Odus to Wendy, and reached out to grab Paul's right hand. A pipe above them split and spewed steam.

Paul was just about to reach solid floor when another quake struck, widening the crevice and sending the board sailing into the lava below. Mary screamed while grabbing Paul's left hand tightly. The board disappeared from under them and flashed into flame. Paul's right hand caught Henry's right hand. Dangling in this way, Paul and Mary swung wildly and crashed into the sides of the crevice. Henry managed to keep his grip on Paul's wrist, but he was holding the weight of two people.

"Paul!" Mary cried. "I'm slipping!" Wet with sweat, her hand slowly and surely slid through Paul's fingers. Then, to Paul's horror, Mary's hand fell away from his and she was in free fall over the magma below.

"Mary!" Paul screamed in desperation. Then he felt a sudden powerful jerking on his body as Mary caught hold of his feet. The bottom of her shoes began to smolder.

Henry almost lost his grip because of the weight and the sweat on his fingers. He reached down and grabbed Paul's wrist with his other hand as Helen and Wendy grabbed onto Henry. Together they struggled and slowly hauled them up. Finally, Paul was out of the pit and Mary followed. She kicked off her shoes which were smoking and had fire on the soles.

Once they had their feet on solid ground, Paul embraced Mary tightly and kissed her head as she sagged into him, tears in her eyes, her body trembling.

A hallway door crashed open. There, standing and waiting in front of them, was Von Krod! Mary reached for the particle gun and realized it was missing. "The weapon! It's gone!"

Von Krod lunged at Paul but with his quick reflexes dodged sideways. Simultaneously, Henry barged him with all his weight. Wendy also gave a shove and that was enough to send Von Krod toppling over the edge and into the lava pit behind them. As he fell into the pit his hand reached up and caught hold of a piece of protruding marble from the floor. Dangling over the edge, holding on with one hand, his other hand shot upward. Like a cat catching a mouse, he caught hold of Helen's foot. She screamed and fell to the ground and Von Krod began dragging her over the edge with him.

Paul kicked him viciously in the face, bashing him again and again with his heel, but still Von Krod relentlessly dragged Helen into the pit. She helplessly clawed the ground with her fingernails as her legs were drug over the flowing lava below.

Henry grabbed for Helen as Paul gave one final blow to Von Krod, forcing him to let go and sending him roaring helplessly into the abyss.

The group momentarily stood, shivering with relief and breathing heavily from the exertion.

"Let's get out of here!" Paul yelled, and immediately they scrambled down the hallway and outside the building.

* * *

The train left with more passengers than had arrived. As it rushed full speed through the tunnel, a great avalanche crashed down the inside of the mountain slope, completely cutting off Milam Valley from the rest of India.

* * *

Climbing their way over the top of the rubble that blocked their way, Durukti, Lobe, and Convoitise arrived at the ten foot gap in the hallway.

"Where's Von Krod?" Convoitise cried out amidst the noise of the crashing stones and heaving ground.

Lobe pointed down into the chasm. "There!" he shouted.

The women looked. Von Krod was clinging to the edge of the rocks just above the lava on the far side. His pants were smoldering.

"Get him out of there!" Lobe commanded. "We must leave this place!"

Connie spotted the particle weapon, covered with chunks from the ceiling. "Well, well," she said, dusting it off. "Look what somebody dropped. I wonder if they're still alive?"

"That's handy," said Lobe, looking at the weapon with a crafty smile.

"Yes, indeed," replied Convoitise. "What are we waiting for? Let's help Von Krod."

* * *

Time Gods

When Paul and the others arrived outside, they could hardly believe their eyes. What had been a lake filled with pristine glacier-fed water was now filled with red hot molten lava overflowing into the street. Everywhere trees and buildings were on fire. The south and east end of the valley had been inundated by devastating avalanches, which now were quickly turning to steam and water, causing explosions when it came in contact with the lava. It was difficult to breath and Helen began to choke.

The main train entrance was covered by a giant avalanche. They could only hope the international dignitaries had escaped.

Finding an abandoned Hummer with the keys still in it, they climbed in front and back and with Paul driving, headed toward the mountain, hoping that the back entrance was still open. Winding their way up the slopes of the mountain, they finally came to what used to be the end of the cave that Paul, Wendy, and Odus had used to enter Milam Valley. Now, however, they found only rubble. The cave had collapsed and they were trapped in a valley that was really the cone of a giant volcano.

"Shit!" Wendy shouted from the back of the Hummer.

"Now what?" Paul asked, hopelessly. "Odus, are you okay?"

Henry sat in the back with the little man on his lap. "He's in pretty bad shape."

"Well, that's just great," Paul griped. "He might be able to help us get out with his time machine device, but I don't know how to use it!"

A giant explosion rocked the side of the mountain and lava shot hundreds of feet from the former lake bed.

"Look!" Mary pointed. Everyone turned their eyes upward and to their relief saw a circling helicopter, the pilot and passengers apparently confused at seeing the eruption in the valley.

They climbed out of the Hummer and began jumping up and down, waving and shouting above the sound of the helicopter blades. Fortunately, the helicopter pilot spotted them and moved in.

When the chopper landed on the dirt road near by, they were surprised to see a member of the Government of

France waving them to jump aboard. They gladly complied, and to their surprise found themselves sitting next to General Charles de Gaulle.

General de Gaulle told them, "I have just heard your President managed to get out on the train before an avalanche covered that side of the valley. I believe all of the world leaders have been saved. In any case, at least all of you are now safe. What happened to this little one?"

"He was injured when we were trying to get away. He requires immediately treatment," Paul informed the French President.

"Oui," the General replied. "All of you look like you could use some medical attention. I'll ask my assistants to get you to a hospital in Delhi as soon as possible."

The helicopter safely carried them out of the smoldering valley.

* * *

Deep within the cavernous bowl that was Milam Valley, the ground continued to rumble and erupt violently. The entire valley floor became filled with molten lava, covering the buildings and killing all of the vegetation. When the lava finally cooled, the floor of the valley had been raised by thousands of feet. Over the years the valley became covered with snow and glaciers. Due to a world wide government cover up, no one ever heard about the eruption, but anyone who looked at satellite images of the valley in the twenty-first century saw only a desolate, snowy place devoid of vegetation.

Due to embarrassment over the incident and trouble that Indira Gandhi had with her enemies, she had the entrance to Kali's tunnel in Tharali blasted shut and covered with dirt. Local farmers have since terraced the side of the mountain and grow crops on it. None of the local residents discuss the incident anymore.

The Delhi Times would later report that plate-tectonic forces had caused the earthquakes in the Himalayas. The paper explained that two large landmasses, India and Eurasia, collided, forming the jagged Himalayan peaks and occasional earthquakes. Everyone agreed there was no such thing as volcanoes in the Himalayas.

"Due to the unexpected earth tremors, the summit of world leaders scheduled to take place in the Himalayas was canceled," the newspapers reported.

In fact, a monumental cover up of spectacular proportions soon wormed its way to the media. World leaders denied ever having made the journey. President Johnson had "spent the weekend at his ranch near Austin." The British Prime Minister had been "relaxing in a mansion in Devon."

When the press asked General Morgan if LBJ had gone to India with him, he replied the accusation was "absurd." General Morgan told the New York Times that he and President Johnson had spent the entire time relaxing and fishing together at LBJ's retreat ranch in Stonewall, near Austin, Texas. The story was confirmed by the Vice President, Hubert Humphrey, as well as the secret service detail that had been with him at the time.

CHAPTER 55

New Delhi, India. August 1, 1966

Paul hopped onto the gurney. Mary sat on a chair in the corner of the cubicle. Wendy was being treated for lacerations in another room. Henry and Helen were in the waiting room, having already been treated for minor cuts and bruises. The nurse drew the curtain closed. She opened a cabinet near the bed and removed a bottle, some cotton swabs, bandages and scissors.

The nurse looked him over casually. "The doctor says your X-ray shows no broken bones. A lot of bruises. No deep lacerations. Does that hurt?" she asked, pressing on one of his ribs.

"A little."

"And that?"

"Yes. Ouch. I'm worried about my friend, Odus."

"I'll check with the doctor as soon as I'm finished. Can you take off your shirt, please?"

Paul unbuttoned a clean, fresh shirt. He felt a twinge of pain as he did so. He wore no t-shirt underneath and Mary, who was wearing a bandage over the bridge of her nose and sitting in the corner, scanned him with her eyes.

"Was your little friend in the same accident?" the nurse asked with a strong Indian accent.

"Yeah, he was."

"Nasty," she said. "Especially for such a tiny man." She

looked over at Mary. "You are all so lucky to get out of that avalanche alive."

Mary managed a smile. "Yes, we are very lucky."

There was a moment of silence as the nurse quietly dabbed a cut on Paul's left shoulder. He reached into his pocket with his right hand and pulled out the time device. He ran his thumb over the smooth metallic surface. He pressed a button and it lit up. Red and green lights blinked on the side of the color display. The nurse glanced curiously at it. "What's that?" she asked.

"Would you believe me if I told you it's a miniature time machine?"

"No," the nurse said truthfully.

"I didn't think you'd believe that. It's just some toy from America." He pressed the button again and the lights on the device went dark. He replaced it in his pocket.

"You Americans have so many electronic gadgets," the nurse observed.

"Yeah," Paul said half heartedly. He noticed Mary had tears in her eyes. She had a bruise on her jaw where she'd been struck. Maybe she was in pain.

"I have heard the avalanche was caused by an earthquake in the Himalayas."

"That's what they're saying," Paul replied.

She placed small bandages on some of his cuts and iodine on others. "That about does it," she said. "You can put your shirt back on, and meet your friends in the waiting lounge."

"Thank you."

She stepped outside the curtain and was gone. Paul buttoned his shirt again.

They were at the Indraprasta Apollo Hospital in New Delhi, one of the best equipped hospitals in India. The Government of France was picking up the tab. The French Government also provided them with new clothing and accommodation at the Oberoi hotel, one of the finest luxury hotels of New Delhi, overlooking the Delhi Golf Club.

"What's wrong, Mary?"

Mary shook her head hesitantly. "That electronic device I handed you back in Milam Valley."

"You mean this thing?"

"That's what Mr. Dale was looking for back in New York, isn't it."

"I believe it probably is," Paul agreed.

"I know I shouldn't say it, but sometimes I wish it had fallen into the lava in Milam Valley."

Paul felt troubled. "Why?"

"Because now that you have it, you'll go back to your time, and I'll stay here in my time."

Her words struck a chord in Paul's heart, enabling for the first time a brutally honest look at himself and the troubling emotions he was feeling. On one side, he was undeniably overcome by his obvious depth of feeling for Mary, intensified by the physical ordeal he had endured to save her in the Himalayas. On the other side, he was conflicted by a powerful physiological attraction toward Wendy that he had allowed himself to experience during their adventure together. In one uplifting moment, he realized his attraction for Wendy had been nothing but shallow infatuation, unworthy of a true emotional investment. It was, after all, no one but Mary Pierce who had captured his love and changed his life forever.

Yet, still there was an immense conflict within him, the very conflict that had afflicted him from the beginning. Mary Pierce lived in 1966. Paul McPherson belonged in 2027. How could a relationship like that work? Either he could remain here in the past with her forever, or perhaps she could travel with him to the future. If she came with Paul, she wouldn't be able to travel back through time to visit her parents or good friends like Wendy, because the time machine belonged to Odus. In 2027 all of her friends and family would be either old or dead. On the other hand, if Paul chose to remain in the past with Mary, he would lose his chance to return to the future forever once Odus left. Of course, he could make a lot of money making predictions on future sporting events and the like. Either way, there would be no chance of a long-distance family relationship like couples from different continents that married. An English woman might marry an Australian man and travel by air to visit family once a year, but a time traveler from the future could not marry a resident from the past and travel to the future or past once a year to visit family if neither retained a time machine. Therein was the problem. In effect they would just be hitching a ride with Odus – a one way trip.

Maybe, despite their mutual bond, neither would feel they could leave their life behind. In that case there could be nothing but a tearful and inevitable separation forever.

Finally, there was still the problem of the Granny Paradox. A time traveler living in the past might unalterably change the future, or even endanger his own existence. A time traveler living in the future might not complete the influence of their lives in the past, thus also unalterably changing the future.

Tragically, there seemed there could be no happy outcome, and therefore Paul could say nothing at all. His silence was painful for Mary, but what could he do?

"Don't you have anything to say?" she asked.

From the very beginning, Paul and Mary had seemed an unlikely couple. They were, after all, from different centuries. How could he have allowed himself to fall in love, or allow her to fall in love with him? Why had he not clearly seen the inevitable futility beforehand?

Futility aside, he admitted to himself that he loved her, and he wanted to be with her. No matter what. The love between two people can overcome the impossible. If he loved her, and she loved him, and their love was strong enough, nothing could keep them apart.

"Yes," he replied at last. "I will probably be able to return to the future soon. I am deeply torn however, because I need to tell you how I feel about you."

Mary held up her hand and turned her head away. "Don't. I already understand what that means, and that is why it pains me. In my heart I always believed you were who you said you were. It's selfish to think I could fall for a time traveler."

"Well, excuse me if I'm being too forward, but couldn't you travel to the future with me?"

"And do what? Never see my father again? Give up my life here so totally that I never see anyone here ever again, or if I do, only when they are suddenly very old to me?"

"What if I just stay here with you?" Paul suggested.

"You know you can't do that. This whole problem began when Kali came from the future and created havoc. You will create havoc for the people of your future simply by remaining here."

They left the small bed and cubicle behind and walked down a long hallway. Paul looked over at Mary as they walked. "There is another problem," he said.

She looked at him.

"Odus is seriously hurt. I have the device, but take a look at it." He removed it from his pocket and pointed at what seemed to be a keypad.

"Strange symbols," she observed.

"Not any script I've ever seen before. The layout of the keys is weird."

Mary looked at the device, and then up at Paul. "So if Odus can't explain how it works..."

"This discussion we're having is only relevant if Odus can take me back to the future. Otherwise, I'm stuck here."

"That's a nice way to put it. Stuck."

"Mary, I don't mean like that."

"Never mind," she said. "I know what you mean."

Paul gently placed his hand around her waist as they continued down the hallway. Helen and Henry McPherson were sitting in the waiting lounge. They still looked visibly shaken. "Any news?" Henry queried, standing up.

"I'm sure we'll hear something soon," Paul told them. "The nurse promised she'd get back to me as soon as possible."

"We're very worried about him," Helen added.

"You're not the only one," Paul said sincerely. "How's Wendy?"

"She's okay," Henry replied. "Some minor cuts and burns. She should be back here in a few minutes. How about you, Paul? You okay?"

"I'm fine," Paul reported. "A little sore. A bit shaky. Nothing broken."

"We're alright, too. I'll go inquire what's happening with Odus," Henry said. "Why don't you sit down, and I'll go get a nurse or something."

While he was gone, Wendy showed up with her upper right arm in a bandage. Henry returned a quarter of an hour later.

Helen was first to greet his return. "Well?"

"Doesn't look good," Henry explained. "Odus is still in surgery. Some broken bones, internal hemorrhaging and maybe some other damage."

"That doesn't sound very encouraging," Wendy said worriedly.

"Let's wait it out and see," Henry added.

So they all waited. Paul found a stack of magazines, mostly in Hindi. However, there was also an American magazine dated April 15th, 1966. The cover was white, and in the upper left-hand corner was a bright red rectangle with the word "LIFE" boldly printed on it. "Louis Armstrong – I never did want to be no big star," the caption read. There at the top of the stack of other assorted periodicals was another issue form February 1966. On this cover was a large black-and-white photograph of two soldiers in a ditch. In the upper right hand corner the words "The war goes on" stood out grimly.

War and suffering in Vietnam, Americans struggling to go to the moon, hippies looking for alternative lifestyles, and the Hare Krishna Movement just beginning in the Lower East Side of Manhattan. Personal computers did not exist. There was no wireless Internet, no cellular telephones, no holograph stations, no hydrogen fuel-cells and no flat-screen LED televisions. It was a technologically primitive world for Paul. Yet, it was haunting to know that Kali had had an advanced infrastructure with the entire world under his thumb. He hoped that had been stopped, at least for now.

Within half an hour, a doctor appeared.

"How is he doing?" asked Henry.

"Not so well," the doctor replied sadly. "He's out of surgery. You can visit him now, but only two at a time, please."

CHAPTER 56

Paul and Mary opened the door and peered in. The large bed swallowed Odus's small body. He had tubes in his nostrils and a heart-monitoring machine was bleeping nearby. He was wearing an oversized hospital gown. Paul was pleasantly surprised that the hospital was relatively well-equipped.

They approached the bed and pulled up two chairs.

"Odus," Paul said quietly. "Can you hear me?"

There was silence for a moment or two. At first Paul thought he was sleeping, but then his eyelids fluttered open.

"How are you, pal?"

Odus managed to work his lips into a small smile. He reached out and his hand touched Paul's.

"The equipment here is too primitive to do what's required," he said. "No regenerative technology in this century."

"Why don't we send you to the future?" Paul asked. "They could fix you up. I have your device right here, in my pocket."

"No," Odus said. "You can't move me. I will not survive the journey. You take it. It's not difficult to operate. I'll teach you."

"What about you? I can't leave you here."

"You can't take me," Odus said. "I will need time. If I survive, my friends from the future will come and rescue me."

"I can't abandon you," Paul said. "I'll wait until you get better, then I can take you with me."

Odus closed his eyes, squeezing Paul's hand in acknowledgment of his friendship. "I'm not going to get better," he said with difficulty.

"Don't speak like that. You're *going* to get better."

Odus grimaced. "Pain," he said. "So much pain."

Paul looked at Mary and she pointed at the time machine in his hand. He understood her meaning and turned again to the little man in the bed. "You said you would teach me."

Odus remained silent, his eyes closed as his hand continued squeezing Paul's. After a minute he nodded his head. "Yes," he finally answered.

"Do I need a password or something?"

The dwarf grimaced and moaned slightly.

"He's in pain," Mary said. "He can't answer."

"Give him a minute," Paul suggested.

Paul was right. Shortly Odus reopened his tired eyes.

"Show it to me." Paul held it up for him. He raised his hand and showed him the first button. Then he pointed out a sequence of keys.

"Paul," said Odus. "When and where do you want to go?"

"New York, June 15, 2027 – five days after I disappeared."

"If you can't read the script..." He paused and closed his eyes. Then he shook his head. "You have to be able to *read*. Unless..."

"Unless what?"

"Let me hold it." He held out a weak and trembling hand.

Slowly he keyed in important information. "Now it's set. Remember, you can't jump any more than a few miles at a time. You have to fly to New York. All you need to do then is turn it on, then push this button."

"Blue one?"

"No, this other one first."

"With this symbol?"

"That is the letter *qublet*. There are 42 letters in our alphabet. So you first turn it on, then you press *qublet*. You see it here?"

"Yes."

"It will beep twice, and then you press this one. It will make a sound. Then you point it away from you. Point it where you want the time-space hole to be. It will appear a few feet ahead of you. Then you push this button."

"That's all?"

He nodded, then looked at Mary with concern. "Are you going with him?"

Mary looked down and shook her head.

"Paul cannot stay here. He is like a bull in a china shop. He will screw up everything here in the past. But you..."

"What about her?"

"I investigated her. Did research," Odus said.

Mary looked up. "You researched me?"

Odus nodded again. "Because you were with my man, Paul."

"But what about her family? She would never be able to see them again!"

Odus looked sternly at Mary, then at Paul. "She dies."

"Don't tell me that!"

"No, if she stays. Three months from now. Mary, you will die. A man will rob you at gunpoint in Central Park and you will be killed."

They were both stunned. "Is that inevitable?" Paul asked.

"Not if she goes with you. Then she won't be here for it to happen. Her leaving with you will not disturb anything because she wouldn't be here anyway. So you see, she *must* go with you."

That put the entire situation in a new light. "But if I go with him, can we be together?"

"If you mean, can you be lovers, the answer is of course. If you just do exactly like I told you, it will work," Odus said. "I preprogrammed it for you. Leave from that park – what's it called?"

"Tompkins Square Park in Manhattan?" Paul asked.

"Yes. I put those coordinates in the machine. Leave from there, and you will arrive there as well, but the year will have changed. Don't touch anything else. Good luck."

He closed his eyes. The room became silent. After a minute he opened his eyes again and looked at Paul. "It will be a difficult life for you. They will know about you."

"Who will know about me?"

Time Gods

"Both of you," Odus explained. "You will be fugitives. They will come looking for you. Do you understand? NSA and CIA agents from the future are after you even as we speak. They will come for you. There were too many changes in the time line. They will blame you. You've got to run from them."

"You mean someone is going to hunt us?" Mary asked.

"They are already hunting you, like the bounty hunters that Paul met. Trust no one," Odus replied. "Stay together."

Paul and Mary glanced at each other. The situation was not what Paul expected, but he was euphoric that Mary could remain with him.

"Where are my pants?" Odus asked. "I have something that I need you to get for me."

Paul opened a drawer and found the little person's pants. "Here they are."

"In the pocket. Is that little electronic disk still there?"

"You mean one of those time-space hook things you had us put in our luggage on the way to Loharjung?"

"That would be it," Odus said. "Is it there?"

Paul dug around and felt the device. He pulled it out from the pants pocket. "Here it is."

"Let me hold it," Odus said.

Paul placed it in his hand and Odus squeezed his fingers around it. "Just something to remind me of my future," Odus explained, and he then closed his eyes and fell asleep.

They waited for some time at the bedside. Mary placed her head on Paul's shoulder while he held her protectively.

They stood quietly to leave. As Paul and Mary opened the door, they were shocked to discover a familiar, tall man with a brimmed hat waiting for them in the hall.

"Hello, Paul," he said. He politely nodded toward Mary as well.

"Mr. Dale!" Paul gasped.

"Good evening," greeted Sidnet E. Dale casually.

"Mr. Dale, I thought your man changed the time line and eliminated the TDC. What happened?"

"That was before, Paul," he explained. "The time line has changed again."

Paul's mouth fell open. "What?"

"There is no need to understand everything. It will be

difficult for you to grasp. I need some information. How much does she know?"

"Everything," Mary said.

Dale nodded. "Very well. Let's go someplace where we can talk privately."

Sidney Dale walked with a rather bemused Paul and Mary down the hallway until they came to an empty waiting room. They sat on upholstered chairs.

"So, where should I begin?" Dale asked.

"How about explaining what happened when you sent a man back in time and then the whole TDC just vanished out of existence."

"Apparently the two of you have changed the time line drastically in an effort to save the world. While you've succeeded, in the present layer, the time machine was developed at CERN in Geneva."

"I guess the development of the technology was inevitable," Paul suggested.

"Yes, we didn't realize that the first time around. Now we have time travel again and the future is not so bad," Dale said. "Still, I think if you could go back to 2027 you'd find some changes."

"What kind of changes?" Paul asked.

"Paper money will still be in use, for example. I think originally paper money was no longer in print in your time line, but now in the new time layer they still use paper money in 2027."

"No nuclear disaster like before?"

"Not like the pictures I showed you in Washington Square Park," Dale said. "Too bad you'll have to grow old to see 2027 again."

"What do you mean?" Paul asked.

Dale sighed and shook his head. "Paul, we regrct that we have no means to bring you back to your own time," Dale said.

"Why not?" Paul asked.

"Unfortunately, our present equipment only allows one person to travel at a time. I could come here to talk to you, but I can't take you back with me. Our technology is not like it was before."

It seemed Mr. Dale was unaware that Paul had acquired

his own time travel device. Paul thought it best not to tell him otherwise.

Paul looked at Mary. "That's okay, Mr. Dale. I'm happy here. I was planning to stay anyway."

"I'm sorry, Paul," Dale said. "Previously TDC could have helped you, but that was on a different time layer."

"I understand," Paul said. "What about Kali? Where is he?"

"We don't know. That's why I've come. We were hoping you could answer that question for us."

"Well," Paul said. "Odus is there in his room. He's sleeping now, but when he wakes, you can ask him."

After a few parting words, Sidney Dale went to see Odus. Meanwhile, Mary and Paul returned to the waiting room feeling content they had not revealed the existence of Odus's time device.

*   *   *

August 2, 1966

Odus never again regained consciousness after speaking to Paul and Mary. Dale had to leave without any clue where to find Kali. Even more unfortunate was that Odus didn't make it through the night. The doctor told them he passed peacefully in his sleep in the early morning hours before sunrise.

Shocked with the news, Mary, Wendy and the others asked if they could offer their final respects, but the doctor shook his head. "After I declared the time of death, I left the room. A few minutes later when I returned to retrieve my stethoscope which I had left by accident, I saw the little man had already been removed."

"Where did they take him?" Paul asked.

"For an autopsy," the Doctor explained. "It is the policy of the Indian government."

They all felt sad. Wendy cried. "He was such a cool guy," she said. "I really enjoyed his company up in the Himalayas."

CHAPTER 57

Manhattan, New York. August 5, 1966

Once they arrived back in New York, Paul organized a special memorial service for Odus, graciously sponsored by Henry and Helen McPherson. Wendy, Mary, Paul, Helen, Henry and a local Christian priest were the only persons in attendance.

Paul gave a small eulogy based on the teachings of the *Bhagavad-gita*, which the priest appreciated. Paul explained that the soul was different from the body. Death of the body, he said, was inevitable, but the soul inside the body was eternal. Odus would be transferred to a new body according to the consciousness at the time of death, he said, and the ultimate goal of life wasn't to reincarnate, but to go "back home, back to Godhead."

"I am sure that for his service to Srila Prabhupada's mission," Paul said, "Krishna will be very kind to him."

As he spoke, he internally struggled with unresolved philosophical issues. Now that Odus was gone, Paul wondered, would his soul remain here or in the future? *Perhaps*, he realized, *the soul is not bound by time and space.*

As they were leaving the church, the McPherson's bid farewell to Paul, Mary and Wendy. "It's been a real learning experience," Henry said. "I don't really understand where you're from, or if you really are our future grandson, but

Helen and I want to thank you for saving our lives in India."

Everyone said a few more parting words before Helen and Henry McPherson departed.

*   *   *

26 Second Avenue, New York. August 6, 1966

Paul decided to visit Srila Prabhupada at Second Avenue one last time before returning to the future. Swamiji wished him well, and Paul became encouraged.

Afterward, Paul looked back at the storefront and wondered if he was really doing the right thing by returning to the future. The question was compelling, if not unrealistic. Odus had said Mary was going to die soon if they remained in 1966. The only way he could save her was to take her away to 2027.

He passed a newsstand and noted the New York Observer headline: *President Johnson Again in Washington.* The story began: "President Johnson returned from his extended vacation in Austin, Texas last week, where he and other world leaders were said to have had secret discussions on the future of democracy."

Paul knew they hadn't been in Texas at all. Another cover up. Of course the democratic world leaders couldn't let voters know about their failed meeting at Milam Valley. With no knowledge of the fate of Kali or access to his technology, continuing the war on communism by conventional means seemed the only option. The general populous should not be informed about what happened in India.

Paul sighed and wondered how much the future had really changed since Milam Valley. Perhaps not so much.

*   *   *

Tompkins Square Park. August 7, 1966

Mary had her suitcase. Paul had nothing except the portable time device and some notes he had jotted down from talks with Srila Prabhupada. Unfortunately, his cloth bag containing his chanting beads had been lost somewhere along the way, but he would easily get another in the future.

As they crossed into the park, they saw a group of youths sitting on the grass, some distance away. "There's Pete, again," Mary said. "Sitting over there. See him? Seems like he lives in the park these days. Did I ever tell you he used to play baseball?"

"Yes, you mentioned that," Paul said. He stopped by a vacant park bench and pointed at it. "This is as good a place as anywhere."

"Right here?" Mary asked.

"Sure," Paul said. "Who cares? We'll be gone in a second and all this will be sixty-one years in the past."

She reached out and touched his hand. "I'm ready."

Paul turned on the time device and the tiny lights began to pulsate. He looked once again at the strange alphabet on the keypad and tried to recall what Odus had showed him. He found the *qublet* key and pressed it.

The device chirped twice. That was good.

Mary swallowed nervously.

He pressed the blue button. It began to hum.

"Seems to be working," Paul said, scared to death.

He extended and pointed the beam antenna at the top of the device away from him and pressed the button on the bottom. There was a blinding flash of light and a glowing time-space portal opened above the grass near them.

"Whoa," Mary exclaimed. "That's just like what Odus did to Kali in Milam Valley!"

"It's a hole in time and space," Paul explained. "2027 is just on the other side."

Unexpectedly, a second time-space hole opened up next to theirs, making two. "Wait a minute!" Paul complained. "Something's wrong. There's not supposed to be…"

From inside the second time-space hole, a red particle beam shrieked out and struck the time machine in Paul's hand. It immediately shattered into pieces on the ground, emitting fire and black smoke. Paul and Mary's time-space hole became distorted and vanished.

Paul and Mary were completely shocked. "What

happened?" Mary asked.

Three bounty hunters in polymer suits stepped from the remaining time-space portal, weapons pointing at Paul and Mary. Behind them appeared Von Krod, Lobe, Madness, Convoitise, and Durukti. The time-space hole through which they had come vanished behind them.

"Who are they?" Mary asked quietly, nodding toward the little men.

"Bounty hunters," Paul explained.

"Sorry about the destruction of your little time machine," Durukti said, straightening her orange hair, "and sorry it has to end this way."

The little men raised their weapons and aimed them directly at Paul and Mary.

"You wouldn't kill us in a public park, would you?" Mary asked.

"Why not?" Lobe asked. "Makes no difference to us."

Paul noticed the bounty hunter on his right had a time device tucked in a small sack on his belt. All three of them were not more than four feet away. Lobe, Von Krod, Connie and Durukti stood further behind.

"Maybe we can strike a deal," suggested Paul with urgency in his voice.

"The two of you have nothing left to bargain with," Durukti declared. "Your time's up." Then looking at the three bounty hunters she said, "Kill them both."

Acting on adrenaline, Paul spun around, lifting his foot off the ground. With one stroke of his heel, he kicked the weapons from the hands of the little men. Shifting, he next kicked the bounty hunter on the left and middle off to the side. When the final bounty hunter turned to run, Paul quickly grabbed him and snatched the time device from the sack on his belt.

Von Krod produced a third particle gun, already armed with lights flashing. "Remember this? I think one of you lost it somewhere in Milam Valley!"

Durukti looked sternly. "Hand over the time device nice and easy. No fancy stuff. Keep away from those weapons on the ground."

"No," Paul said. "I'll smash it on the walkway."

"You'll do no such thing," Durukti commanded.

"Otherwise we'll shoot you before it even leaves your hand."

"You'll shoot me anyway," Paul said. "So what have I got to lose?"

"Just kill him," Durukti said to Von Krod, losing her patience.

Paul hurled the time device high into the air.

"What are you doing, you fool!" screamed Durukti.

"Pete, Pete Wilson! Heads up! Look out!" shouted Paul.

* * *

Mary's ex-boyfriend, sitting with his friends, heard someone call out his name. "What the hell?"

"High ball to first base!" someone loudly shouted. Baseball!

Pete looked up and saw an object flying in the air.

"Catch it! Catch it, Pete!"

Instinctively, Pete sprang to his feet, reached up with his right hand, and caught the device like a true baseball player.

"Run!"

* * *

Von Krod turned around wildly, pointing his particle gun towards the crowd of young hippies. Seeing a young man holding the time device, he took aim.

Paul scooped one of the weapons from the ground. He fired three times towards Von Krod. The last shaft of burning energy struck the weapon in Von Krod's hand and black smoke began to billow from its tubes. It was ruined! Von Krod threw it hard on the concrete walkway in frustration and it shattered.

Paul ordered them all to step back and he scooped up the two remaining weapons on the grass.

* * *

Mary ran toward her ex-boyfriend as fast as she could. "Pete!" she shouted "It's important. Be careful with it!"

Time Gods

Pete examined the device curiously.

Mary quickly arrived. "Pete. Umm, hi... Can you give me that please?"

"Who are those people?" he asked. "Are they causing you trouble?"

"Don't get involved," she warned. "Just give me that thing and get out of here quickly."

Pete and his friends looked at each other and shrugged. Mary continued. "If you weren't such a jerk all the time things might have been different between us."

"Yeah, well, look whose talking, bitch," Pete retorted. "You've got the dullest life of any chick I've ever seen! Here, you can have it."

He handed the device to Mary with a smirk she had learned to despise.

Mary ran back toward Paul, time machine in hand.

*   *   *

Paul kept the particle gun pointed at Von Krod and the others. Von Krod edged forward and Paul stepped back. "Don't even try," warned Paul.

Mary arrived and held out the time device for him, but Paul didn't look at her. His eyes were glued on his hostages.

"Keep it with you," he ordered Mary. "Do as I say. Is it on?"

"I don't think so."

"Push the button on the side."

She did it. "The lights are flashing up and down the sides now. I think it's on."

"Good. Find a key that looks like Pi with a half moon above it. It's in the upper right corner. That's the *qublet* key."

"I think I found it."

"Press it."

The box chirped twice. "Yes," Paul said. "That's good. Now point it to my right and press the blue button."

The box began to hum.

"Now the button on the very bottom. See it?

"You mean the one that looks like a sideways ampersand?"

"No, below that one."

"Got it."

There was a loud buzz, a flash of light and then a time-space hole opened up, hovering above the grass beside them.

Paul sighed with relief, but Mary was trembling.

"Okay, Paul," Mary said. "It's ready."

Paul glanced at her. "You jump. I'll be right behind you."

"I won't go without you," Mary insisted. "We go together or not at all."

"Then we go together," he said. He suddenly tossed the weapons towards Anger, who was nearest and still edging toward them. "Here, catch!"

When Von Krod scrambled to catch one of the weapons, Paul grabbed Mary firmly by her arm and together they jumped into the time-space hole. There was a flash of light, and they were gone.

*   *   *

"Fools" Von Krod exclaimed.

"Good thing the bounty hunters still have another time device," Lobe told the others. "Otherwise we'd all be stuck in this pathetic, backward place."

"And we still have the weapons," Durukti reminded them.

CHAPTER 58

NSA/CSS Headquarters. 2075

"So if Mary and Paul went back to Paul's own time, what's the problem?" Caufield asked.

Sidney E. Dale looked at Caufield. "I wish it were so simple. The time machine Odus gave them was destroyed by the bounty hunters when they emerged from the time-space portal in the park."

Suddenly it hit Hilmore. "You mean to say, sir, that we have *no idea* where they went?"

"Precisely my point," Dale replied. "We presume that in their confusion neither of them realized the device they were using was not the one programmed by Odus. Now they're lost in time and space."

Hilmore glanced back at Prateep Tripathy behind him and felt angry looking at the Orissan man. Tripathy returned the same crooked smirk he had used the day before. This was all his fault. He had them on the bus in the Himalayas and they got away. Damn him. Hilmore silently mouthed an obscenity, then turned to face Mr. Dale again.

Dale continued. "The time device they are using is difficult to trace. Fortunately, they are not being as careful as they should be and are leaving clues behind by creating ripples and quakes which we have been experiencing. Those are traceable."

A woman raised her hand in the back.

"Yes?"

"Mr. Dale, why not ask them to voluntarily hand over the device?"

"Well, first of all, we don't know where they are, and second of all, they know too much anyway. Since they are continuing to use the device they have to be eliminated for national security. I don't care if he's a monk or not. Now get to it."

Everyone nodded and stood, taking their folders, briefcases and 3D holograph phones with them as they filed out of the room.

Special Agent Sidney E. Dale watched everyone as they left. A solemn mood washed over him as he reached for a pen and scribbled something down.

"Mission complete. Awaiting further instructions."

Folding the paper carefully, he tucked it into his shirt pocket. A man with two masters. A plan within a plan.

When he left the building and went back out on the street, he was approached by a disheveled man. Dale recognized Madness immediately and stopped near him. He reached into his shirt pocket and removed the folded paper. "This is for your people. Will you deliver it?"

Madness read the note. "Yes. I will deliver it."

"Who is in charge now that Kali is missing?" Dale asked.

"Durukti is in charge now," Madness replied.

"What are all of you going to do?"

"We're looking for a better time and place to accomplish our mission," he replied.

*   *   *

Tel Aviv, Israel. 2035

One autumn afternoon Fred and Joan Solomon, on vacation from Chicago, sat on a boardwalk bench overlooking the Mediterranean waterfront while feeding the seagulls. The sun glistened off the water and sparkled on their faces.

Earlier in the day they had visited the Yemenite Quarter and Carmel Market downtown and had spent time touring

Time Gods

the traditional Flea Market before settling in this relaxing location. They wanted to take in as much as they could during their vacation.

Fred and Joan noticed the appearance of a peculiar glowing oval shaped electrical field just above the boardwalk, not more than fifteen feet from where they sat.

"What the hell is *that*?" Fred asked his wife.

"Not something you see every day!" his wife replied.

Three small figures stepped from the time-space portal, each brandishing particle beam weapons. Looking around cautiously, they observed Fred and Joan on the boardwalk bench. "Harmless," one of them said in his native language.

"Agreed," said another.

"Looks clear. Let them come."

One of the little men looked back at the portal behind them and made a hand signal.

Von Krod, Connie, Lobe and Durukti stepped out and then the hole in time and space vanished behind them.

"We're here!" the blonde woman smiled as she took in her surroundings. "Nice waterfront."

"We'll tear the town apart!" the red-haired man exclaimed gleefully.

Lobe turned to the surprised couple on the boardwalk bench. "Excuse me. Speak English?"

The couple nodded nervously.

"I thought so," Lobe said. "I can speak any language though. What year is this?"

"Why, it's 2035," the man replied nervously.

"Excellent," Von Krod remarked.

"Who are you people?" asked Joan Solomon.

Connie looked at the couple. "We're agents of Kali. We plan to set up headquarters here."

"That's nice," said Fred Solomon. "We're tourists from Chicago. Welcome to Tel Aviv!"

Lobe gazed up and down at the row of expensive hotels lining the waterfront and greed filled his thoughts. "Place has changed in the last few thousand years."

Connie smiled. "Oh, I think we'll fit right in," she said.

"Why stop there?" commented Lobe. "We'll take the world all over again."

Connie laughed loudly. She could hardly wait to bring in

their latest recruit – imported from 1966 – a success of the psychopathic drugs and Connie's persuasive ways. He was a mean one, and all of them had high hopes for him. Yes, Pete Wilson would do nicely here in 2035 Tel Aviv.

Time Gods

EPILOGUE

"Mommy, why can't we stay in one place long enough to make friends?" Jamuna complained.

Mary placed her arm around her eight year old daughter's shoulder and drew her close. "Because there are bad people out to get us," Mary explained. "You know that."

Paul reached forward and poked the logs with a stick, stirring the glowing embers. A slumbering flame lapped upwards as he tossed on another piece of wood. "If only we could stay hidden forever." He looked around the dark night, and towards the two tents, and then exchanged a meaningful glance with Mary. "Well, kids, have you finished your homework tonight?"

"Yes, father," both the children replied.

Six year old Haridas reached in his pocket and pulled out an electronic toy. He switched it on and a three-dimensional holographic image of a virtual battlefield appeared on the ground, a few feet away. Haridas started moving his avatar around, shooting at an unknown enemy. It made annoying explosive and gunshot sounds.

"It was nice being guests of the Royal Family in England," Mary said.

"Well, pity Edward the Confessor couldn't protect us from TDC," reflected Paul. "When they showed up we had to leave in a hurry."

"How long till they find us again?" Mary asked.

"Don't know. Usually seems to take them a few weeks." Paul cast a glance back at the tents yet again, remembering they had purchased them from the sporting goods section of Wal-Mart.

Little Haridas looked up from his holographic game. "Are we really going to meet Lord Chaitanya, Daddy?"

"No promises," Paul said. "It just seems that 1495 AD here in West Bengal is as good a place to hide as any. Now, Haridas, after tomorrow, no holographic games during the day," Paul warned. "You understand? Only when we are completely alone!"

"I know, I know," little Haridas whined. He'd heard his father's lectures about the dangers of changing the time line before. What he didn't tell his father, however, was that he had been showing the game to every child he met from King Edward's court to Jerusalem at the time of Christ, and from the American Civil War to 2027 where he purchased it on Eighth Avenue in Manhattan. What Haridas didn't know was that by showing the game to so many friends, even without his father's knowledge, he was changing the time line, which in turn set off time quakes and alerted TDC to their present location in time and space.

"Okay. Everyone to bed," Mary insisted, and marched the complaining children off toward the tent.

Paul, however, lingered behind, and Mary noticed him looking into the darkness between the mango trees. Did he sense something wrong? Surely TDC could not find them here so soon. They had been there for only a day.

After tucking the children in their sleeping bags, she returned to his side. "Is everything alright?" she asked.

He pulled out the hand-held time machine and showed it to her. The buttons were glowing. "Someone is coming," he said.

"I'll get the particle beam gun we picked up from the future," Mary said. She turned toward the tent.

Suddenly there was a flash of bright light and a time-space hole opened up, not ten feet away. There was no time. Paul picked up a large rock from the ground and readied himself. How could they have found them so soon?

A little man emerged from the hole in time-space, followed immediately by a blonde woman. Paul prepared to hurl the rock when Mary grabbed his arm. "Don't!" she cried. "Look!"

Time Gods

Paul blinked, but could not comprehend what he was seeing. How was this possible? "Wendy? Odus?"

Odus nodded and looked up at Wendy who waved hello.

"Odus, I thought you died!"

Mary ran over to Wendy and the two girls embraced. "So good to see you!"

"You too," Wendy agreed. "Odus told me you have kids now!"

Odus held up a disk shaped object. "Remember this? You placed it my hand at the hospital, from our luggage on the bus!"

"Yes," Paul recalled. "You wanted for me to retrieve it from your pants pocket."

Odus chuckled. "When the doctor declared me dead when I wasn't supposed to be dead it created a ripple in the time-space continuum. This ripple activated the disk in my hand, hurling me back to the future. Fortunately, the doctors from my time were able to save me!"

Paul sat down hard. "Well, I have to admit I'm elated to see you both, but what are you and Wendy doing *here*?"

"I can't do all the research my supervisors have requested on my own. Remember those cave drawing up in the Himalayas? That was an important find. I need help! I thought Wendy and I could be one team, and your family could be another. We'll be given projects to research and I'll report our findings back for the betterment of mankind. In exchange, my colleagues will use all the technology at their disposal to protect us from TDC agents!"

Paul looked at Mary. She shrugged and then nodded her head. "Oh hell," Paul said. "Why not?"

Wayne Boyd

THE END

Completed on Sri Gaura-Purnima
– the birth of Chaitanya Mahaprabhu (c.1486–1533) –
February 28, 2010

ABOUT THE AUTHOR

WAYNE EDWARD BOYD was born in Morristown, New Jersey, in 1953. He studied physics and psychology at St. Mary's University in San Antonio, Texas then moved back to New York where he joined the Hare Krishna movement and became a vegetarian in 1973. Initiated by A.C. Bhaktivedanta Swami Prabhupada as Vipramukya Das, he spent the next 30 years travelling, studying and teaching the ancient texts of India.

He started writing *Time Gods* in 1995 while in Brooklyn, New York. During its gestation, he lived in New York, San Francisco, Seattle, Vancouver, and London, stood at the top of the Eiffel Tower, hiked in the Himalayas in India and Nepal, and got married in Texas. In fact, in the course of his 57 years, he has visited 37 countries, 49 states in America, 9 out of 13 Canadian provinces and territories and 3 Australian states.

Wayne completed Time Gods fifteen years later while living in the Texas Panhandle where he currently works as a correctional officer.

OTHER BOOKS FROM
ATMA COMMUNICATIONS

Now that you have enjoyed Time Gods, you may also like to read other books from **Atma Communications**. For more details, sample chapters and ordering information, see www.atma-communications.com.

ANGELS CHIC BY ARJUNA KRISHNA-DAS

Set in 1990s Liverpool, India, Tibet and Chandraloka, Angels Chic is the gripping tale of two unlikely partners attempting to cope with contrasting lives of love, chaos and career. The appearance of a teleport machine sets them off on a trip of external and internal discovery, poses questions of ethics, conspiracy, mental health and philosophy, and puts them at odds with the Bavarian Illuminati as they seek an ancient and transcendental treasure without equal.